THE ZARDUTH IMPERATIVE
DISCOVERY

by

Helen Claire Gould

Helen Claire Gould Books

First published in the UK in 2023 by
Helen Claire Gould Books,
Peterborough, Cambridgeshire.

THE ZARDUTH IMPERATIVE
DISCOVERY

ISBN: 978-0-9930812-6-2

British Library Cataloguing in Publication Data.
A catalogue record for this book is available from
the British Library.

Printed and bound in England in 2023 by
4Edge, Hockley, Essex.

To Mike and Jason for their support,
and to my father Alan George Goff,
for his moral support for my writing.

*

Also to Tim, Phoebe, Phil, Carolyn, Julie, Carol-Ann, Mark
(who suggested the name 'Ayar' in relation to one of my other
stories –
his suggestion was too good to pass by!)
Lene Lovich, Pete Cox, Ange,
and especially to Pat Maren, who listened to this aloud
several times over as I read various versions on Skype.

*

My thanks to all of them for their invaluable feedback
and encouragement.

CONTENTS

PART 1

PART 2

PART 1

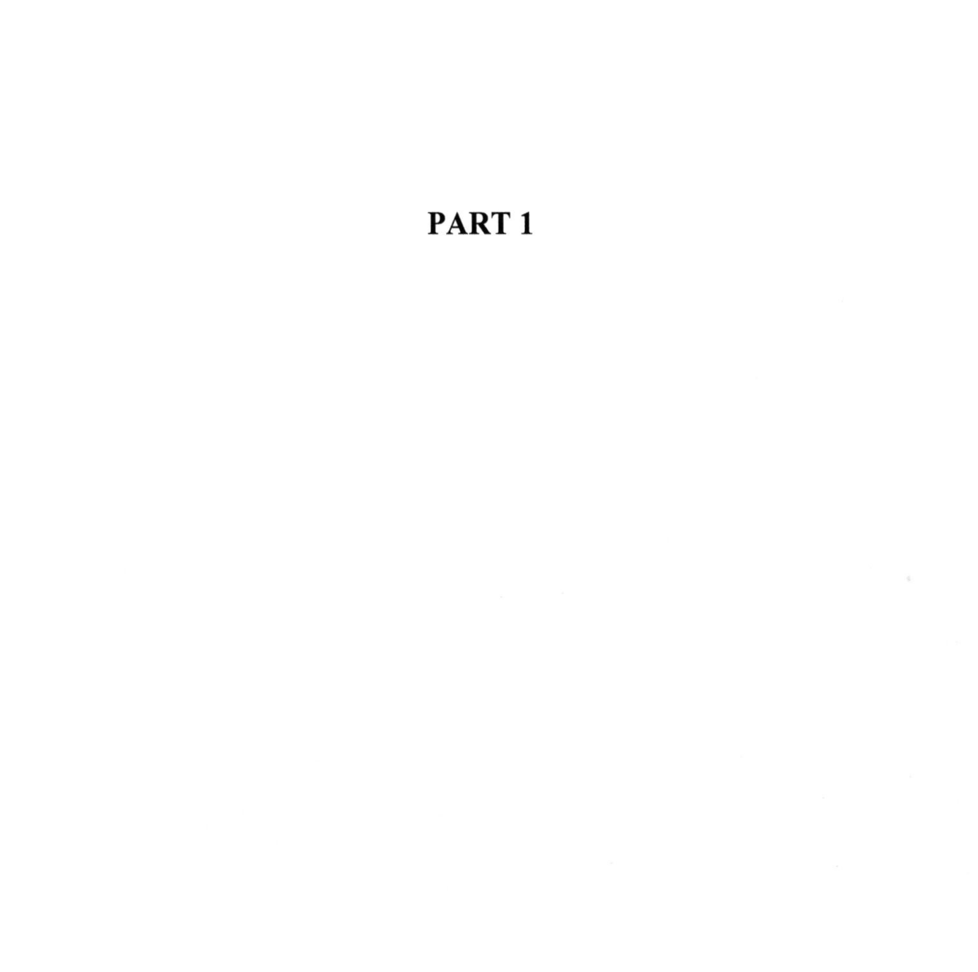

THE ZARDUTH IMPERATIVE: DISCOVERY
Helen Claire Gould

CHAPTER 1: A Question of Speed

The Bekel, *ship's time/date: 403.374.7.58.949 After Departure. Earth time: 19 Nov 2091.*

"KAYLAR, RAISE SHIELDS! And keep us hidden from Voth fleet scanners."

"Force shields raised, Rilla," Kaylar reported. "Scanner jamming already on.

Rilla Dekkutz acknowledged that with a palmraise and stared into the simtank projection between the forward sight-ports as she assessed the tactical situation.

"Nam – switch orbit *now*!" The *Bekel* would be vulnerable to visual detection during this manoeuvre, but the new orbit was the best defence this planetary configuration offered. A white hologrammatic dot marked the *Bekel*'s position between Declain's moons Bacar and Ammax, as they swung about their common centre of gravity. Bacar was nearest the planet as their orbit switched from it to Ammax.

On the far side of the planet the larger third moon circled further out. Below heavily-cratered Grus, the Voth space station lay in low Declain orbit. The eighteen red dots distributed along its four arms marked the Voth fleet.

"Missile incoming – the Voth must have visually spotted us!" Kaylar said.

"Computer, estimate time to approach and range of missile and nearest crawler."

[Missile approach in two hundredths and closing. Range, one thousand tondors. Crawler approach in three hundredths.]

"We may be faster," Rilla observed, "but their weapons would seem to have greater range. And computer, the further crawler?"

[Approach in five hundredths.]

"Raise force shields and begin a countdown." Closer combat conditions would have been more dangerous; but Voth vessels weren't nicknamed "crawlers" for nothing, though they could manoeuvre the craft by running an electric current through the diffractive material of their solar sails – as they'd learned during their alliance with the Kiai.

Rilla noticed the blue missile marker in the simtank as two "crawler"-class vessels – the Voth ships – crept towards the *Bekel*. External sensor data showed the missile followed a parabolic curve towards their position. The countdown sounded in the background. Rilla raised her arm to punch the siren panel by instinct, then stopped herself. *The only crew onboard are here in the control room.*

The nearest ship had broken docking formation from the space station, while the furthest approached from the Kiai system nearby, and paralleled the *Bekel*'s course. Either craft could have spotted them, but it was most likely the crawler from the Kiai system; it was in motion, and some distance out, so would have a different view.

"Evasive manoeuvre, Nam. Ready missiles, Kaylar – fire on my order and resume shielding immediately. We'll let their missile get close enough that they think it'll hit us, then fire and dive around the back of Ammax, so we disappear visually. Tambur, Nam – as we fire, take us between Bacar and Ammax again. Bacar will shield us from the Voth fleet, and Ammax from sensors on these crawlers."

Each woman signed their understanding with a palmraise.

The second crawler coasted without firing. *Out of range,* Rilla thought. *Neither's near enough for real damage.* Her gaze found icy Bacar and rocky, grey-brown Ammax in the simtank. "We'll proceed with caution."

She surveyed her skeleton crew. Nam Garangey sat at the nav/com column, head concealed by the navigator's headset, legs astride her chair to accommodate the child which had moved into the birth position only hours before. Vinta Pril monitored the environmental controls for the *Bekel*, plus the life signs from the secret sleep-chamber at its heart, and had also taken on the Science Op and Comms functions. Her pregnancy was less advanced than Nam's, but Rilla couldn't mistake the swell of her stomach, nor the careful embrace of the chair that enfolded her. Tambur Dar, the pilot, shared scanner ops with Kaylar. *Her baby won't be born for another half-year.* Kaylar Durana's fingers hovered over the weapons console as she awaited the instruction to fire. She was also responsible for scanner jamming and damage reports. Her pregnancy's duration had been confirmed just days ago, but all Zarduthi clothing had inbuilt dimensional instability, and would adapt to the coming changes.

Good job too! Rilla thought. Lastly, she laid her hands across her own abdomen. Her greenish leather tunic stretched over it, as did Nam's and Vinta's. Beneath her combat leathers, she felt the fine down rise on her skin as the child within her grew, just as when she'd carried her son, Ayar, fourteen years and more before. Her command console also had the engineering console switched through it. Resilient programming and back-up capacity ensured any functions could be switched through to any other console.

The countdown continued in the background. [Missile approach in one hundredth,] the computer informed her. [Nearest crawler will enter firing range in two hundredths, furthest in forty-seven thousandths.]

Rilla turned back to her weapons operative. "Ready to hit that missile, Kaylar?"

"I am." She allowed herself a grin as she tracked the approach of the missile in the simtank. "Hold...hold...Go!"

The amber panel flashed to tell Rilla the shields had

dropped to allow the release of their missile; the flash from the sight-port confirmed it. She tracked its lime green dot in the simtank. As the *Bekel* swept round Ammax a greater detonation told her their missile had destroyed the incoming one.

[Approach of nearest crawler in one hundredth. Entering firing range. Approach of furthest in forty-five thousandths.]

"Again, Kaylar. Target it!"

"I have." The flash of the release followed her words.

The *Bekel* slipped between the moons to follow the rocky outline. Ammax protected the ship from the force of the explosion. The amber panel went dark as their missile hit its target. But another lightburst brought Rilla's hand up to shield her eyes.

[Approach of nearest crawler estimated at twenty thousandths. Exiting firing range and passing around Ammax in opposite direction. Second crawler's approach in forty-four thousandths.]

"I missed." Kaylar locked gaze with Rilla, eyes wide with shock. "How could I have missed?"

"The other crawler took our missile out?" suggested Tambur.

"Then let's get out of here," Rilla said. "We should be able to hit it as we round the limb of Ammax." *The Zarduthi soul awaits the best chance,* she reminded herself.

Ammax slid into view.

[Crawler within firing range.]

"Hit it, Kaylar!" Rilla called.

Kaylar's fingers flickered over the weapons controls.

Light erupted against sightports. A greater detonation followed, silent in space.

Rilla leaned towards the simtank again. "You got it – well done!" The other crawler had disappeared too. "Hmm. I don't like that. Could you have got both of them?"

"*No* hope," Kaylar said. "Out of range."

"It must have gone round the far side of Bacar where the simtank can't pick it up."

"Playing us at our own game."

"They can't catch us. Take us out of the system, Tambur. Head for the yellow star system at 346 degrees." Rilla pointed into the simtank. "We'll lure it out after us – make it look as if we're escaping, then destroy it."

*

Omol Fadaifa's quarters, The Kazid.

Omol Fadaifa stretched, then folded his arms around Ghaneem Takaren again. "That was go-o-od."

"Mmm." Her hand was at his groin, and her mouth curved in mischief. "When can we do it again?"

"You're insatiable, woman!" But he grinned back. "What d'you want from me, a child?" He watched her eyes, as round and dark as his own. "You'll need a breeding token first!"

The smile faded from Ghaneem's face. "Too soon!" she snorted. "I've just settled in onboard the *Kazid*. I don't fancy being left behind to look after the children while you gallivant off to war. I want to fight beside you for a while before we do that."

"I'm glad," Omol smiled. "I'm not ready for parenthood, either. Not *just* yet." He glanced at the chronometer on the wall. "I'd better get a move on. I'm due back on-shift in fifteen thousandths." Omol threw back the bedcover, swung his legs over the side of the bunk, and headed for the steam shower.

Much less than a hundredth later, Omol settled into his com/chair and allowed it to contour itself around him. The chair moved with him so that his body was always supported, the instrument readouts legible. He checked them in the console simcube.

Everything was fine. He relaxed as the ship approached the Declaini system.

*

Nam looked sideways at Rilla. "That system's next in the Voth advance."

"Yes," Rilla agreed. "Eren says they've developed a form of spaceflight based on chemical fuel. He thought they might assist – if necessary."

"I'll lay in a course to get us into hyperdrive when we leave the Declaini system," Nam said, "and lock it in."

But as they emerged from between the two moons a percussion rocked the *Bekel*.

"Damage report, Kaylar?"

"Tank split – display damage. I'll share it to your console, Rilla."

Rilla craned forwards. The large-scale three-dimensional schematic of the *Bekel* showed no damage, thanks to the force-shields, but ahead lay the second crawler. She felt the blood drain from her face. *How did they get here so fast? They surely can't use a hyperdrive inside this system's gravity well – can they?*

Her hand strayed to her abdomen as a Voth commander replaced the simtank's hologrammatic representations. The image was two-dimensional video, and static punctuated the radio signal; but the creature's apparent lack of sensory organs of any kind sent a shock through her. "Identification immediately, Zarduthi ship."

"Answer them," Nam signalled across the control room. "I've nearly finished!"

The mushy metallic timbre that issued from the tank was a simulation, as Rilla knew from the clan's encounter with the Voth on Kiai. The *Bekel* had its own translator device; it could amplify the electronic signals but couldn't clean them up much.

"Voth ship, this is the *Bekel* on a routine patrol," Rilla replied. "Identify yourself."

"If Zarduthi ship is *Bekel* it must know that Voth ships lack individual designations," the Voth grated. "And if on routine patrol, why destroy one of our ships?"

"It attacked us first."

"By whose authority is *Bekel* on patrol?"

"A Zarduthi needs no authority to patrol!"

"Nor Voth." There was no trace of emotion in the synthesised voice, nor even a quiver of the coarse hairs that protruded between the creature's armour-plates. "Heave to and surrender, *Bekel*." The Voth paused only to add, "Immediately, or Voth will fire."

"We have complied," Rilla said. "We await instructions." And she cut the contact. *I'll message Omol. Voth ships don't have hyperspace technology, so they rely on radio and video comms, although we gave the Kiai leadership hyperspace communications. Hopefully they've kept it quiet.* "Nam, get me Omol."

Nam's fingers flew over the commgrid panel.

"Omol, this is Rilla Dekkutz of the *Bekel*."

Omol's holographic image filled one half of the simtank as he answered. "Shulai, Rilla, are you well?"

"We all are, but we've had an incident with a Voth crawler, and we aren't sure what happened." Rilla explained about the reappearance of the second Voth ship that had blocked their exit. "We need to enter hyperspace – how soon can you provide a diversion?"

*

Omol surveyed his control room. Bebb Jerda, Engineer, Faril Prazg on weapons, Tangar Derren, his navigator/pilot, and Jarane Hebor, comms op, were all intent on their consoles. The atmosphere of calm belied what Omol knew waited for them out in the void. His muscles tensed for battle.

Within a few thousandths, Jarane Hebor hurried over to him. "Omol, a formation of six Voth crawlers have left the Declain space station. They're headed this way, though nowhere near – yet."

"Thanks. Track them, will you? The *Bekel* too. Faril, keep your weapons console on standby." Omol glanced into the tank as he crossed to Bebb. "Computer, how soon to ETA at Declain?"

[Fifteen hundredths.]

"And to the *Bekel*'s current position?"

[Seven tenths.]

"Eren would have told them to get out at the first sign of trouble," Bebb said.

Omol stood and considered for a moment. "They need our help for that. Computer, zoom simtank in on the *Bekel.*" He leaned over the simtank. "Replay the battle with the crawlers."

The closer view allowed Omol to see what had happened. Scanner jamming hid their position on the commgrid, but a crawler's red telltale barred the *Bekel*'s way. "How could this have happened?" he asked. "Split tank, replay *Bekel* battle sequence."

As the replay started again in one half of the holotank Omol brought every scrap of concentration to bear on it. The battle between the crawler and the *Bekel* held no surprises until the Zarduthi ship passed between the Declaini moonlets, then the second crawler disappeared in a flash of light. Shortly after, it reappeared ahead of the *Bekel,* just as it emerged from its hiding place.

"That last shot should have destroyed the second crawler," Bebb observed, "but…if they have a version of the hyperdrive they could have avoided it –"

"It *can't* be the hyperdrive," Omol said. "Play it over, half-speed."

The sequence repeated in slow-mo in the simtank. The first crawler exploded with the same impressive lightshow. The second closed in. The *Bekel*'s missile sped towards it. The crawler disappeared in the burst of light that ballooned around it. The *Bekel* chased freedom between the two moonlets, and won – till the Voth reappeared to bar their way.

Faril spread his hands in puzzlement. "Somehow that second crawler deflected or destroyed every missile the *Bekel* fired, yet they should have been dead hits. I don't understand it."

"Nor me," Omol said. "They must have rigged a force shield on the solar sail to deflect the missiles. Jarane, message Rilla to warn her."

"On it. But how did they move so fast?"

"It's *not* the hyperdrive. There was no second flash," Omol insisted.

"True," Bebb said. "Let's help them, Omol. My sister Kaylar's –"

"I know. And they *haven't* got a hyperdrive. You know what would happen if *we* used our drive within a solar system."

Bebb shifted into the soft language to denote the subjunctive mood. "Maybe they've found a way to avoid tidal forces tearing them apart."

"There's no known way to do that." Omol turned the possibilities over in his mind. "But you know Kiai engineering…what if they've upgraded the crawlers to travel faster?"

Bebb shrugged. "It's possible…Look!" He pointed into the simtank.

A shuttle left the crawler, approached the *Bekel* and docked at one airlock.

"What are they doing?" asked Bebb.

*

"What are they doing?" Nam crossed the Control Room to stand beside Rilla.

Rilla peered into the simtank. Holographic cameras and sensors embedded in and around the hull fed a composite image of the *Bekel*, paced by the Voth crawler. "I'm not sure, Nam."

But as the shuttle backed away from their airlock it left a bubble-like construction that nestled like a Valdorian symbiote against the deadlocked hatch.

Our only experience of fighting the Voth was on Kiai. It wasn't pleasant. "Check hand weapons, everyone," Rilla said. "They'll board us."

The weapons check completed, Rilla turned back to the simtank. One of the clustered internal images showed the hole in the clanship's hull that gaped back at her where the airlock had been. "Our ship!" she exclaimed, and clutched Nam's wrist.

She zoomed the simtank view in. They used no cutting equipment. Instead, a group of Voth stood by the airlock. Plate armour displaced, feeding pseudopod extended, a Voth had already stripped part of the outer skin.

Shock jerked Rilla back in her chair. *Surely they can't eat metal?*

It moved to work on the next layer.

"Prepare for boarding," the Voth commander ground out.

Acknowledgement was unnecessary; Rilla cut the contact. "Voth khranen!" Rilla whispered. The Voth had been tagged as bloodsuckers ever since Kiai – with good reason. But none of them had realised the Voth could devour metal.

She squashed her anger and fear and played the column before her. The Zarduthi defeat on Kiai had been as hard to accept as it had been complete. She knew her duty. Her orders were to protect the ship, the children, herself and the other pregnant women and their babies. "Slow them down for as long as possible. Computer, close all internal doors." Her voice was as incisive as steel. “Prepare to fire on the crawler, Kaylar. Target the main body, not the solar sail.” It wouldn’t dislodge the bubble-craft but they couldn’t fire on that – the ships disruptors could only fire on external targets.

[All doors sealed.]

“Missiles targeted,” Kaylar confirmed. “Force shields in place.”

Nam’s talons clicked over the instrument panel. “I’ve set up the ship to auto-initiate hyperdrive at the entry point.”

We normally only use the auto-initiate function in case of potential destruction, or the loss of the crew. It was Rilla’s turn to give the palmraise to Kaylar, Nam and Tambur. She glanced at the simtank. The Voth had widened the hole in the door to start on the third skin. Beyond it stretched black space, studded with stars. They could see it through the bubblecraft. Rilla’s hand went to her belt holster. “I want that crawler destroyed this time,” she told Kaylar. “Fire!”

A flash came. Clouds of matter spread out in the simtank, echoed in real-time beyond the sightports.

“Nice shooting, Kaylar!”

In the simtank the *Bekel* swung out of its orbit. Chunks of debris from the crawler spun end over end towards them, swatted into further freespin as they impacted with the force-shields. Although the shields acted as shock absorbers, a major impact on them had the potential to do minor damage or force them off-course.

The ship rocked. But the Voth bubblecraft remained attached.

*

“Boarding them, then. But why?” Omol turned the possibilities over aloud. “Either they want prisoners, perhaps for ransom or exchange, or –”

“Or food, more likely, from what we saw on Kiai!” Bebb’s

tone was sharp.

Omol acknowledged that with a dip of his head. "Or…they're after something about the ship itself. The drive, perhaps."

"Why would they want the *Bekel* if they already have a version of the hyperdrive?" Bebb parried.

"That's the reason why I don't think they have one," Omol countered. "Computer, estimate speed of Voth ship during manoeuvres."

Although fast, the estimate wasn't even close to hyperdrive speed. It was a maximum obtainable speed within the confines of a solar system gravity well, limited by the short distance involved, the speed at which the operator could initiate the solar sail system, and proximity to planets and satellites.

"They're faster than we thought, though slower than our ion drive in a system," Omol commented.

"I hope not!"

"You saw how they shot round that satellite. Let's play that over."

Omol replayed the sequence again. This time, he saw it. A third crawler left the space station just before the *Bekel* fired on the second. It swooped towards the moons of Declain to confront the clanship. He could imagine Rilla's surprise.

"But could they always travel that fast, or have they been upgraded?" Bebb asked. "We only fought them on the ground on Kiai."

"Does that matter? We need to be aware of it in dealing with them now. Simtank, revert to one screen."

In the simtank, the squadron of crawlers continued their approach.

"The *Bekel* needs assistance," Omol said. "If we provide a distraction, they can leave and use their hyperdrive once out of the system. Computer, how long for Voth digestive fluids to dissolve the *Bekel*'s airlock door?" He raised his hands, palms outwards in the warding gesture.

[It dissolved the first skin in five thousandths. All three skins will take fifteen thousandths. Less if more Voth join in, but workspace is limited.]

"ETA with the ion drive at full?"

[Thirteen thousandths.]

"A slight time advantage to us. But it'll be tight for us to prevent the Voth boarding the *Bekel*." Omol glanced at the simtank and sighed, "View from above." He crossed to the tank. "Hell's seven demons!"

From that angle the distance between the two vessels was not foreshortened as in the previous view. Yet the Voth shuttle looked almost as close to the *Bekel* as they were. Omol made his decision. "We *must* help them. Take us to them, Tangar. We'll distract the Voth so the *Bekel* can get away. Is that course ready?"

"Yes." Tangar had his pilot's headset in place.

"Then let's move in."

[Ion drive initiated at top speed.] The *Kazid* responded to Tangar's new course.

In the simtank, the crawler squadron headed towards their exact position. "The Voth craft *has* seen us."

[Craft within weapons range.]

Omol locked gaze with his weapons operative. "Faril – ready missiles."

"Battle-ready, Omol," Faril reported.

Omol prepared to evade the crawlers. He assumed they'd force-rigged their solar sails; without that any such ship would be crippled. But he knew better than to interfere with his navigator's thought processes. He watched the simtank. The closest crawler now lay below the *Bekel,* its bows and solar sail facing away from them. *The perfect position.*

"Fire now!"

The missile flew. The crawler spun into oblivion.

"Duck and dive, Tangar!" The success of this fighting strategy depended on how fast Tangar could act on the co-ordinates for the crawlers' positions each time, and gave them just thousandths to reposition the *Kazid* while hidden by their jamming system from Voth scanners.

He checked the simtank. They approached a large planet with no obvious star, further from their next objective.

The second crawler fell into the trap.

"Fire *now*, Faril!"

Their missile sliced space, a lime green dot in the simtank. The crawler detonated.

Two down, four to go.

"They won't expect us to approach the *Bekel* again," Bebb muttered.

"Change tactics – fly behind and below them," Omol said.

The ion drive cut in, closer to the Declaini system. Another crawler lay above them.

"Fire, Faril!" Omol ordered. "They won't expect an attack from below."

Again the lightshow blazed as the crawler died.

Don't get over-confident. These moves won't work forever, Omol thought. "We should change tactics again – Bebb, Tangar, we'll use the Saridonai manoeuvre."

"Acknowledged."

Omol cut the lighting on the starboard side of the ship that faced the explosion.

Bebb allowed the starboard side of the *Kazid* to sink, as if shrapnel had damaged it.

In the simtank the crawlers' red tell-tales approached. "Take us out of here, Tangar!" Omol ordered. "Far enough away that they can't track us."

"Will do."

In the simtank their white tell-tale zoomed nearer the stellar system they'd seen before. Between solar systems they could use the hyperdrive. "Now take us back, use the previous manoeuvre," Omol said as the three red tell-tales clustered together and changed course.

"Zooch," Tangar acknowledged with a feral grin, as he zipped them back into the fight above a fourth crawler.

"Fire, Faril!"

The crawler burst apart like a squashed insect.

"Good one!" Omol couldn't exclude satisfaction from his voice. "Now we need to deal with the last two and get back to the *Bekel,* Tangar."

"Course laid in for that one-planet system at 280 degrees." The ship moved. "Have they followed?"

"Yep. Slowly. They may suspect a trap –"

"Keep going. We'll go behind the system and come out above them again."

"Good thinking, Omol." They moved towards the single-planet system.

"Omol," Faril interjected, "they've fired at us."

"Evade and intercept missile."

As before, Tangar manoeuvred them to come out above their prey.

"Arm ship's disruptors."

"Now, Faril!" Omol exclaimed.

Faril targeted the fifth crawler. Their missile still spun towards the crawler below. "Gotcha!" Faril punched the air. The crawler's solar sail and half the ship detonated.

But the explosion was louder than it should have been. Faril groaned. "We've been hit. Looks like they've played us at our own game this time. Their weapons op learned to anticipate where we'd strike next, Bebb."

"We lost the bet this time. Damage?" Omol was calm to the point of detachment.

"Starboard airlock hatch, the medical centre, education centre, hydroponics, some of the living quarters, the recreation area and gym, and the reactor – all areas sealed off against decompression," Faril reported. "But shields and power levels are way down. We don't have enough power to enter hyperdrive or evade further attack."

"Conceal ourselves behind the planet below."

Tangar dipped his head. "Good as done." The *Kazid* limped towards the dusty orange-brown globe below. "Computer, how long to make repairs?"

[Seventeen days minimum.]

"Too long to help the *Bekel*," Tangar murmured.

"Yes. Message Rilla," he told Jarane Hebor. "Tell them we're hit and have lost power generation. We can't help further."

Jarane did so. "And a third ship took the place of the second."

"We understand," Rilla said. "Jarane, your information was useful, and we're glad the crawlers *don't* have a hyperdrive. We'll pass a message to the other clanships about your repairs."

Jarane acknowledged and closed the message.

Omol saw the *Bekel*'s tell-tale approached the edge of the system. *At least we did some good.* "Put us into orbit around that planet, Tangar, Bebb." Omol saw that the last crawler had followed them. Apprehension shivered through his body, and he shook himself to release tension. "I suppose our luck couldn't hold forever."

The simtank image changed to a view of the Control Room of the Voth ship. The image had no depth; it flickered and deformed. Flashes of colour alternated with static bands.

"They're hailing us, Omol," Jarane murmured, "though there isn't exactly a seamless technological interface."

"No surprise there," Omol said. "Looks like they've not just stolen the Kiai fleet, but have also adapted bits and pieces from various incompatible technologies."

A Voth filled the screen; in the background several more stood on pseudopods before panels of instruments. Omol swallowed hard to clear the familiar twist of nausea, but the revulsion persisted. The Voth's armour-plates displaced to allow the extrusion of a gelatinous pseudopod. It hardened into a rod and extended towards the viewer controls.

In Omol's simtank view it reached for him; he ducked instinctively. There was a pause. He glanced at the others and saw disgust and fear on each face. *None of us have forgotten what we saw on Kiai.*

"Zarduthi warcraft!" a metallic voice grated. "You have destroyed five Voth craft but now you are damaged. Surrender, or Voth will fire."

Omol checked his throat translator was on and stepped forward. "I am the commander of this ship. We travel to a rendezvous. Let us pass and we'll do you no harm."

"Zarduthi is in no position to bargain. Surrender the ship or Voth fires!"

*

Ten thousandths later.

It's bluffing! Now Omol was sure it wanted the hyperdrive. *No! This is our home, as well as transport from one war zone to another.* He inhaled, breathed out, and said, "Then, Commander, you must give me time to consider –"

"Zarduthi has until the continent on the planet nearby disappears from view." The image in the simtank faded, replaced by one of the *Kazid*, paced by the crawler.

Omol strode to one sightport and stared out of it. He couldn't see the crawler, just the curve of the planet below. Its star hid behind the planet, and only a glow registered daybreak on the raised platform of the continent.

"Would they fire if they want the ship in one piece?" Bebb retorted.

"We can't take the risk – but they may only want the drive itself, not the ship."

"That'd make sense," Bebb acknowledged. "What will you do?"

Omol turned. "I haven't decided yet," he admitted, "but I don't want those bloodsuckers on our ship." He swung round. "Computer: how long before the continent on the planet below revolves completely out of view?" The edge of the continent had disappeared round the limb of the planet. Soon the rest would follow.

[Eight hundredths.]

"Not long then." Omol paced for a few thousandths as he considered the options. They could fight, but stood little chance of a win with a damaged power generation system. The clanship was both his pride and his responsibility. *And we need more time for repairs than we have. But I* won't *surrender the hyperdrive and let them devastate this sector of the galaxy! I don't believe they wouldn't harm us. They'll either enslave or kill us, as on Kiai.* He wouldn't allow the Voth to do either. *But there's one thing they may not expect.* He pressed his jaws together and felt muscles around his mouth bunch. "Determine presence of breathable atmosphere and temperature range on-planet."

[A breathable atmosphere is present, including oxygen and other gases. Most metals are in the core. The planet-wide magnetic field repels the solar wind and the interaction produces spectacular aurorae. High-velocity windstorms are common, with lightning discharges. Temperatures on-planet are generally below Zarduthi body temperature, especially at night. Low water availability and the rarity of surface metallic elements confirm the mass of the planet to be lower than expected for its size. Surface gravity is therefore also lower. However, polarimetry results suggest the biosignatures of limited plant life on-planet.]

That doesn't sound optimal, but it's better than nothing. Omol crossed to the intercom. "Abandon ship, clan-kin! To the shuttles, and bring whatever possessions you can carry with you!" His voice was rough with emotion. "Pilots will be myself, Ghaneem Takaren, Renn Khardar, Bebb Jerda, and Faril Prazg." He'd named the best pilots in the clan, a concession to his sense of failure and impotence. *So much for helping the* Bekel, he thought. "Report to me in the shuttle bay. We have strategy to discuss." His hands flew over his control column and locked in his orders. He cast a final glance around the Control Room of the only permanent home he'd ever known, then strode into the corridor to collect his few possessions from his quarters.

Forms as tall and slim as his slipped past him. He scanned the crowd of clanfolk for Ghaneem; she wasn't in sight. In their quarters, her most prized possessions were gone.

She's ahead of me. He hurried forwards between men, women and children, intent on reaching the shuttles. The clanfolk stood aside to let him pass since he'd named himself as a pilot. It was only when he looked back to see the ranks close behind him that he caught a glimpse of Ghaneem's face. Her hand lifted to him. Relief surged through him. He returned the palmraise and forged on.

The shuttle bay doors slid open ahead. A burst of energy carried him into the launch area. He headed for the first of five shuttles crouched flank to flank on their turnpads, halted before it and beckoned to his pilots. They clustered around him as he explained his plan. Behind them the clanfolk followed the permanent evacuation plans.

When he'd finished, he stepped towards the shuttle. The airlock door opened at his approach. He leapt up the steps, beckoned to the clanfolk, and slammed into the pilot's seat. It adjusted around him as his headset lowered into place. To his right he glimpsed heat traces through the tinted headset, as the clanfolk scrambled into their seats. His crew from the Control Room entered the shuttle's cockpit.

"Take-off imminent!" Omol snapped. His awareness of his passengers faded at the flash of a blue panel. The headset told him the airlock was secured. Other information flowed in: [Cabin air pressure: normal; air supplies: maximum; victualling: maximum; fuel supplies: maximum; engine condition sensors: functional; engine: fully operational; launch position: assumed.]

"What about the last crawler?" Tangar asked from the nav/com beside him.

Omol hadn't seen his navigator slide into the seat beside him. "Part of the plan. Plot us a course which will take us close above it. When we get within range, lock onto it and give it everything we've got. We should have enough speed to get away." Omol turned his attention back to his instruments, and adjusted the image mix of the simtank controls. "And I have something to do before we leave, so wait until I give the signal – I'll power up the shuttle." He flicked the switch on his translator back on. "Jarane, get me the Voth ship."

A Voth appeared in the simtank. Omol couldn't tell whether it was the same one as before.

"Well?" the creature's voice simulator barked. "Zarduthi is early. Decision?"

"As you said. We won't offer resistance if you come aboard." Omol had used a virtual background of the *Kazid*'s Control Room, and hoped the image mix wouldn't arouse the Voth's suspicions. *How well they can see? Can they can see at all?* He hoped it would think they were still in the Control Room. The cobbled-together Voth comms system might help there.

"Boarding party despatched," the Voth grated. The image

in the simtank dissolved and was replaced with a view of a bubblecraft sealed to the side of the *Kazid.*

"What are they up to?" Tangar whispered.

A handspread indicated Omol's puzzlement. "I suppose they'll eat their way in – the Voth exist to consume the universe! Anyway, the first compartment they come to will seal itself off. They'll be trapped till they can get through the door." He checked the time on his instruments, then powered up the shuttle. "It should give us time to get away."

There was a thousandth's hiatus as personnel sensors checked the launch bay was empty. Then the air pumped out. Omol waited, muscles tensed, for the launch bay hatch to open. "Course laid in?"

"Everything's ready," Tangar confirmed.

"Faril?"

"Disruptor powered up, missiles readied," Faril said.

The launch bay opened. Omol set the controls to flight and watched the ports. The shuttle lifted. Metal walls slid past as they thrust out through the gape of the hatch. Below lay the Voth crawler.

"Weapons locked," Faril said. "We're in range."

"Let 'em have it."

They swooped towards the crawler. Faril fired the disruptors. Missiles sped to their targets. The crawler exploded in a sheet of flame. Parts somersaulted towards the planet below.

The shuttle plunged after it. The other shuttles followed in formation.

"What about the ship, Omol?" Bebb asked.

"Set to self-destruct in fifteen thousandths. The Voth won't get hold of her." *Though it'll mean the end of the clan as such – if we're ever rescued.* He checked his control panel. "We'll make for that continent." He jabbed a finger at the simtank image. "This planet's habitable for a while. From there we'll launch a satellite and broadcast a distress call." Omol locked on the simtank view of the ship from the underside; the transparent dome of the bubblecraft clung to the side of the hull. He opened up the hyperspace commgrid to talk to all the shuttles at once, glad to see Ghaneem's face. "Let's get out of here. Top speed, keep formation."

"Yes, sir!"

Omol felt a flash of pride; Ghaneem was, above, all else, a good soldier. He checked the time. The *Kazid* completed its self-destruct sequence, as the shuttles streamed planetwards.

Omol dared look in the simtank. Behind them, the *Kazid* coughed debris and precious vapours into the universe.

CHAPTER 2: The Dark Planet

The Bekel, *a few thousandths later.*

"THE *KAZID* IS OFF THE COMMGRID," Nam announced.

A pang went through Rilla. "Are you sure?"

Nam pointed at the simtank. "Look – no marker! They've either been destroyed or gone out of range – either way, they can't help us now. Damn these khranen!"

"We're on our own, then," Kaylar said. "Did you notice? The Voth boarding party haven't tried to contact us at all. Not even to intimidate us."

"Don't expect a Voth to waste words!" Rilla murmured. She scanned her control console for inspiration. "They must expect victory."

"D'you think they know we destroyed their ship?" Kaylar asked.

"Must do." Rilla paced the control room. "The odd way they talk – like there's only one of them. Could they be telepathic? Or some kind of hive mind?"

"I wondered about that, too," Nam said.

"And we know projectile weapons don't work on them, from the encounter on Kiai." Rilla sighed and pushed the memory away. "I'll pull up a close-up from inside the ship in the simtank. It might give us some ideas."

At her voice command the simtank view changed to a view from inside the airlock. The feeder had enlarged the breach in the innermost skin of the inner door, and would soon enter the ship. Beyond the dribbles of sticky brown gel, the small Voth vessel ballooned around the wound in the hull, reminiscent of the protective translucent sac that enclosed every Zarduthi newborn.

THE ZARDUTH IMPERATIVE: DISCOVERY
Helen Claire Gould

Rilla's hand pressed against her abdomen. Although she'd seen Voth close up before, the impact had never lessened, and was intense now she was pregnant. Disgust, nausea and fear wriggled through her, but she couldn't look away.

The bubble held several Voth on a metal ramp, none suited against air or pressure loss. *Don't they need suits? Or can't they function with them? There might be an advantage there...*

"Suit up, everyone!" Rilla said. The other pregnant women obeyed. Rilla was last. She divided her attention between the main simtank and her control console. She devised and discarded plan after plan as she watched them come and go.

"Rilla? I'll do up your seals."

She looked up at Tambur. Under normal conditions the suits were easy for each crew member to manage, but pregnancy brought challenges. Supplies of the expanding pregnancy spacesuits onboard were limited; only twenty percent of a clanship's occupants could be under-fifteens at any one time. But pregnant women had a vital role during deployments, and buddying up to fasten each other's suit seals was an important safety routine.

"Thanks." She climbed out of her chair. A glance at the simtank showed her that even the large Voth had entered the corridor. She remembered their clumsy gait from Kiai; the memory convulsed her in a shudder.

"They're looking for us," Nam said. "They want the Control Room."

"D'you think they know about the children?" Vinta was focused on her assigned function.

"Would they care about them? Would they even understand?" Kaylar countered. "We could try to lure them into a trap –"

"I thought we might use the ship's defences, too." Rilla felt the pressure lift off her. "If we opened corridors to let them approach the centre of the ship, we could lead them to where we can deal with them. We shouldn't even have to leave the Control Room." She turned to the simtank. "We'd better keep watch on them, but I'll bring up a maximum-scale schematic," she said. The tank view split to display it.

Vinta jabbed a finger at three intersecting corridors. "These would lead them to the ship's defences. Let's open them before they get there so they don't realise it's a trap."

"Let's do it." Rilla gave the instructions and the doors slid open on the schematic. "Kaylar, check those defences are armed… I hope they're too stupid to smell a trap!"

In the simtank, the feeder passed into the next corridor, enlarged beyond the usual size of a mature Voth. Fluid oozed from between its plates, the usual coarse grey hairlike protrusions completely reabsorbed. The other Voth followed it on stumpy pseudolimbs, unaware of anything except their task.

Behind them a door slid open. Their whiskery protrusions twitched, then rippled.

"Perhaps that's how they communicate amongst themselves," Tambur suggested.

Two Voth stomped back along the corridor.

"Maybe." Rilla watched as, for a few thousandths, the Voth leaned towards the open doorway as if they peered into it. Their whiskers twitched, though no emotion was visible. But the rest of the Voth, except the largest, left the door they'd attached themselves to, and clustered beside the opened one. Blood thundered in Rilla's ears. *They've taken the bait.*

The lead Voth stomped through. The others followed, clumsy on jointless pseudolegs.

"Now what?" Kaylar asked. "Do we immediately shut the doors behind them, or wait till they turn the corridor?"

"We wait," Rilla said. "Keep them together." She swivelled in her seat to point to the feeder in the corridor.

"Machari! Look at that thing."

The feeder's side was enormous – and it still fed. As the hole in the next door grew, so did the feeder. Rilla checked the schematic of the ship. "The next section of corridor's sealed off," she said, "but I want this thing out of there, or it'll be in *here* with us before we know it!" The feeder devoured the door in a rough grid pattern.

"Look at its feed pattern!" Vinta said. "It's gobbling up as much of the door as it can."

"We *must* dislodge them before we enter hyperdrive," her high voice continued. "We don't *know* what will happen to it when we enter hyperspace – atmospheric decompression, most likely…" She hesitated. "And if they can dissolve a triple-skinned hull in thousandths there's no telling what else they might be able to do."

"Vinta's right," Rilla said. "Unless we can dispose of the bubblecraft – and them – before we enter hyperdrive we're no better off. And I don't fancy our chances with decompression in hyperspace –"

"*And* we'd just be taking the Voth with us to the yellow-star system." Kaylar said. "They're unlikely to help if we give a threat a ride straight there!"

Rilla acknowledged that and looked at each of them in turn. "Ideas?"

"If we could dislodge that bubble, the feeder would be sucked out by the vacuum as that sector depressurised."

"Good idea, Vinta," Rilla said, "but how do we dispose of the bubble?"

"Do we know what that craft is made of?" Tambur asked. "It might pierce with a projectile weapon. One of us could go down there –"

"And be sucked out with them?" Rilla raised both palms. "Too risky! I don't want to lose *any* of my crew."

"You may lose all of us – and the children – if somebody doesn't go." Vinta touched her suit. "I've got at least some protection, I can hang on to something in the corridor, and I'll have a line –"

"It might just work, you know," Kaylar said, "but it should be one of us who isn't *too* pregnant and can move quickly."

"Are you volunteering?"

"If you wish."

"All right. Computer, run a sensor sweep and find out what the bubble's made of." [Metalloplastoid mesh on flexible plastic. The floor is metal.]

"It might just work," Rilla said. "But we can't enter hyperspace yet. All we can do is put up the best fight we can."

"And hope Eren and the others are as well," added Nam. "It might be a while till we can come back for them."

"Got everything you need?" Rilla asked.

Kaylar patted her projectile pistol and the safety line anchored around her waist.

"Take the quickshift round to the other side of the ship," Rilla suggested. "It'll take you where you want to be and avoid the feeder-Voth." She transferred control of the weapons console to her column.

Kaylar raised a hand, then operated the switch that brought the leaves of her helmet together. Two flicks of her gloved fingers snapped the seals shut. She raised her hand again, then walked to the doorway. The two halves slid back into the bulkhead. She stepped through and was gone.

She arrived safely in the quickshift.

She might do it, Rilla thought, as she watched in the simtank. *Now – where are the Voth?*

They'd passed through the next open doorway. Rilla sealed the door into the outer corridor; necessary to prevent the rest of the ship from depressurisation when Kaylar fired. The

Voth feeder concentrated on its task. *Can they even pick up sounds? Yet they communicate with us.*

In the outer corridor, all that remained of the door was a triple-skinned strip at the top that the Voth couldn't reach, despite its height increase. The feeder was enormous now. Its side bulged. The plates had parted and occasional ropes of gel protruded, and were reabsorbed.

Of a sudden, the thing dropped to the floor, writhed, and pulled in its walking pseudopods. For a thousandth Rilla thought it was having a seizure. Then the plates on its side peeled back.

Rilla laid a trembling hand on her abdomen. She felt the movement as her baby turned and kicked in the nutrient-rich fluids of her womb. *I know why it fed like that,* she thought. *It's giving birth. But it's like nothing I've ever seen before.* Nausea choked her but she daren't look away.

The gel pseudopods snaked out with increased frequency, no longer reabsorbed. Soon there were four or five rope-like extensions from the creature. It made no sound, but continued to writhe. Its hunched shape made it appear to hug itself as the protrusions pooled at its side. Remembering her own birth pains, Rilla couldn't help a twinge of sympathy in spite of her revulsion. When the extensions separated from the creature's side, still attached to each other at one point it shocked her. She stared, fascinated and horrified, as tiny plates formed over its surface. When plates covered the form the five extensions separated from each other.

Five more Voth were now aboard the *Bekel*. Rilla watched as the immature feeders not only attached themselves to the door but also grew visibly in a few thousandths. Fear squeezed her lungs. She took a sharp indrawn breath.

The "parent" clambered upright as fast as it had fallen, its size reduced by half. Plates slid back into place over its breached side. It marched through the ruined doorway and followed the curve of the corridor to its fellows at the next door.

At least there's more than one compartment between us and that thing now, Rilla thought. *Although the "babies" are next door. I hope Kaylar can get the bubble off the side of the ship.* She split the tank view. Kaylar was almost in position. The rest of the Voth were near the centre of the ship.

"They shift, for sure!" Nam murmured.

"Yes." But Rilla had few fears for the slumbering children; surely, even a Voth's prodigious appetite couldn't take it past the line of nozzles that protected the sleep-room? A chill touched her spine. Without further comment she checked that the ship's log still recorded and fed signals through the simtank. She clamped her lips together in satisfaction and settled back in her seat, as she tried to relax and watch Kaylar's progress.

*

Kazid *Shuttle 4,* en route *for unnamed planet, ten thousandths later.*

"Omol." Berin Dateen's tone was urgent.

"What?"

"The planet below us looks dark."

"What do you mean, dark?"

"It looks like twilight, even on the side that faces its star – and I haven't yet spotted that."

Omol checked the simtank. "You're right – that's odd! I'll check on the starmaps." He gave a voice command, and the starmaps popped up. He was about to look at them, when Tangar spoke.

"What's that?" Tangar gestured towards a haze of subtle colours on the simtank image. It lay in a gap between two dark mountain ranges – or perhaps one was a continuation of the other.

"What d'you think it is?"

"A settlement, perhaps. Should I despatch an exploratory team?"

"No – scan for the usual things, especially water and minerals. We may be here some time, so we can explore it later." Omol turned back to his instruments and hailed the other pilots. "Status reports?"

Ghaneem was the only one to report any damage. "Just slight debris impact, nothing serious."

"You be careful, then," Omol said, watching her dear face.

"I will," she said.

"Tangar and I are looking for a suitable landing site. I'll speak to all of you again as soon as we have co-ordinates."

Ghaneem acknowledged that with a palmraise and her image flipped out of the simtank.

"Omol, what about Eren Gharm's ship?" Tangar asked. "I have kin on the *Bekel*. So does Bebb."

"Sorry, I can't pick them up *any*where. They must be out of commgrid range." Omol concentrated on the dataflows that streamed through his headset. "Planetary ETA five tenths," he murmured.

Dusty ochre punctuated this world's stretches of dark blue ocean, and grey clouds swirled above it. Polar ice caps topped and tailed it. *Clouds and a desert belt,* he surmised. *Oceans. What else?* "Zoom in forty percent."

The outlines of two continents, one above the equator and further round the limb of the planet, another below it, kept company with trails of islands. *Perhaps volcanic seamounts,* he thought. Occasional lightning flashes stabbed the planet's surface.

The world stretched and grew in the eye of the simtank. There was little to do but scan for further enemy activity in the region. There was none, yet Omol couldn't relax.

As they rounded the end of the continent Berin Dateen

finished her scans. "There are signs of trees at waterholes, and both lizard-like and insect-like life on this continent, fish and a slew of plant and animal aquatic life in the oceans."

"And the other continent?"

Berin studied her instruments for a thousandth. "Savannah. Life scans are negative at this distance. And at the tips of the continents, where there should have been temperate regions, the sea level has risen and drowned the land."

"Hmm. It's a weird world."

"Not as weird as its star."

That reminded Omol to check the star in the simtank. As he glanced into it, he saw a strange sight. The star was small and dim, with alternate bands of purplish-red and orange that gave it a lurid beauty. He zoomed in further. The star resolved into a dim magenta disk with bands of orange clouds. A dull glow escaped from beneath and between the bands. At the poles, blue, green and red aurorae danced like a troupe of Saytorian balleteers, in time with pulses of radio emissions.

Omol peered closer. "It's a brown dwarf. That's not good news."

"No. Most of its light emissions are in the infra-red range, though there are low levels of visible light – and very little heat. It fuses deuterium and hydrogen." Berin hesitated, then added, "And on the planet the water in the oceans is undrinkable – even for us."

"Are you sure?"

"I've run the check three times – the stuff's too full of chemicals even to distil water from it. We might be luckier inland – there must be access to fresh water somewhere. I'm scanning now. I haven't found any rivers, but there are rock formations that could form natural aquifers."

"Then we'll head for them," Omol said. "We don't have enough fuel to reach anywhere else." He hailed the other shuttles and fed in landing co-ordinates. As they sped over the landscape, the crescent shapes that marked a dunefield appeared on the plains below. *This is a dry, windy planet.* Lightning stabbed the dune-crests at irregular intervals.

Soon the desert rushed to meet them in the shuttle's simtank view.

Omol jabbed at a panel on the instrument array before him to activate the reverse thrusters. He felt the downwards motion slow as the shuttle hovered. A spray of sand spurted up from the desert floor; jets repelled it from sensitive areas. The shuttle sank down, and nearby, three others came to rest. They'd landed in the lee of the dunefield.

Omol's stomach curdled with shock. He turned to face Tangar. "Where's – Ghaneem's shuttle?"

"They're all down –"

The brow of a dune on the horizon exploded.

Ghaneem! Omol's mind reeled. He flicked simcube switches into life to hail the other shuttles. The simtank split to accommodate the images. Although the continent was on the day side, daylight on *this* planet was more like perpetual twilight.

There were only three shuttles.

Renn reported a safe landing. Then Bebb. Then Faril.

Still no image of Ghaneem.

Omol swallowed hard. His fists balled and the talons sliced into the softer skin on his palms. "I'll get search parties together," he said. His voice shook. With an effort he unclenched his fists. *It's just that Ghaneem's commgrid's out of action.* "Tangar, co-ordinates for Ghaneem's shuttle?"

"Just getting them." The nav headset still encased Tangar's face.

At the touch of a button Omol's pilot headset swung up to its storage pod, and the pilot's seat loosened its caress. He got to his feet, full of dread, and walked from the control area into the cabin.

Fifty faces looked to him for support. *They trust my leadership and judgement.* It was the children's expressions that tore at him most.

The food and water situation's very serious. A Zarduthi could adapt to most food sources in the field. The food stock onboard was of two types: pre-pack food they'd negotiated for and frozen, which could be used in its present form, and biomass, which would act as feedstuff for the synth machines. It could be made into whatever they needed, but started off as material even their zosas couldn't process. In feedstuff form it wouldn't be wasted and would last indefinitely. But neither would feed the clan forever without replenishment.

"Gerrad, one of the shuttles crashed and is out of contact. I want your unit to run a search – I'll come with you." He swung to face another of his lieutenants. "Davor, your unit will search for fresh water. Tangar will give you co-ordinates. We're near the edge of the desert but he thinks there are aquifers nearby, so you may find some by nightfall.

"Chutt, we can use onboard supplies for now, but I need you to organise two food search parties, and send them out in different directions. Check whether whatever you find is safe to eat in its present form, or whether we'll need to modify it to use as feedstuff." Though preferable to poisoning, that would use power they could ill afford. In this constant twilight the shuttle's solar panels must be switched to infra-red mode or they'd be useless.

How long will our power last? And how long must we survive here? He strode back to Tangar's seat and perched on the edge of the pilot's chair so it wouldn't mould around him. "Anything?"

"Still nothing from Ghaneem's shuttle. Sorry, Omol – she's off the commgrid. The damage must be bad. But I have co-ordinates for her shuttle."

Omol couldn't see his expression, but the compassion in the inflections and susurrations of the soft language were unmistakable. He acknowledged Tangar's sensitivity with a gesture. "Only to be expected from time to time, in our line of business," he said, voice steady now – which amazed him. "Co-ordinates for fresh water?" he asked Berin Dateen.

"I'll get on it. And I'll keep trying for mineral resources."

Her promise soothed Omol. "We'll need to locate the distress satellite to get a call for help out." Omol pushed himself upright and forced himself to walk back into the cabin, where Gerrad and his vudaki awaited him.

"Come, clan-kin," he said. "We'll take the shuttle when everyone's outside."

Disembarkation was soon completed. Omol saw that the work parties were already organised, and turned back to the controls.

Gerrad slipped into Tangar's place beside him. "Do you want someone else to pilot the shuttle?" he asked. "You've been in that seat ever since we left the *Kazid*."

"Pag, I'm fine." Omol needed something to occupy his mind. He still reeled from the loss of his ship, though he couldn't have made any other choice. *I* can't *lose Ghaneem as well,* he thought. *We've been together for exactly twenty-six days.*

The shuttle lifted. Omol watched the horizon. It took only thousandths to reach the wreckage. Small parts scattered a couple of nearby dunes. The main body of the shuttle perched on top of one of them. There could have been no survivors.

Omol rested his elbows on his knees and closed his eyes. "The nearest habitable planet just had to be one with nothing of any use at all!" He opened his eyes again. "But at least the drive won't fall into the wrong hands."

"Not ours, no," Gerrad murmured. "But – what happened

to the *Bekel*?"

In the distance, lightning spiked again.

*

Kaylar had anchored her safety line to one of the metal loops that protruded at intervals from the *Bekel*'s bulkheads, for use by repair crews. Its whiteness made it disappear against the bulkhead. She crept towards the breach in the hull. The bubble was now empty; she had no fear of discovery by the Voth. She clipped her line to the loop, grabbed it as well, took the projectile pistol from the holster slung at her hip, and fired.

The recoil sucked Kaylar out through the breach as the corridor decompressed, and freed a length of her safety line. The bubble split, then peeled away from the side of the *Bekel* and disappeared into the void in the ship's wake.

Five immature Voth forms followed a thousandth later. They soon disappeared into the void behind her. Kaylar's safety line twanged tight against the bulkhead hook.

"Kaylar!" Rilla yelled. Her voice sounded distant. "What happened?"

"She can't hear you," Vinta's voice was even fainter.

"I can – just. I'm fine." Kaylar grinned at them. *They'll be able to see me in the simtank.* "I did it! The bubblecraft's gone, and so are the 'babies'."

"We saw – now we just need you back onboard in one piece," Rilla growled. "Can you make it back inside?"

"Of course." Kaylar made to haul herself inside the ship. "I'm coming back to kill the khranen –" She reached for an external loop, but the usual pair either side of an airlock weren't there. *The Voth must have dissolved them along with the airlock hatch.*

Then she noticed that the line had lodged against some of the digestive gel. *If a metal door couldn't stand up to it,* Kaylar thought, *a lifeline, even metal-reinforced, won't be up to much.*

"Rilla!" she called, and told her what she'd seen.

"Stay there – keep as still as possible. Tambur and Vinta will come and get you."

In the background, Kaylar heard Rilla give them instructions.

"Keep calm, Kaylar. The slightest movement against that line could –"

"I know!" Kaylar hadn't realised that the spin of the *Bekel* would force the line against the gel. *How long can it last?*

Chung! Strands split apart. The shock reverberated up and down the line.

"Rilla!"

"I know. Keep still."

Where are the others? Kaylar took another deep breath, prepared for a gradual release. She forced herself to concentrate on the faint smell of the air from the tanks.

Chung!

Another breath. She began to count. *One, two, three...* Kaylar dared not even *speak* aloud lest the line rupture.

Chung!

Kaylar could see more strand-ends...*Seventeen, eighteen, nineteen, twenty...*

"Just keep calm and still."

Chung! More metal strand-ends showed grey against the white hull.

Where are they? Kaylar took a deep breath to release slowly.

Chung! The last few strands snapped.

Even using the ion drive, the ship became smaller and smaller within thousandths – a much shorter time than she'd expected.

Kaylar panicked when she realised she was utterly alone in the void. *"Rilla!"* she screamed. *"My baby!"*

*

Rilla heard Kaylar's anguished scream just before the commgrid went silent. *She's out of range –*

Her fingers punched the simtank controls to magnify the view. *A voice command can't convey urgency to the computer. It only works at one speed.*

There was no trace of Kaylar.

She sat forward on her seat, hand against her abdomen. "I should have known this would happen," she whispered. "I should never have let her go."

"It's not your fault, Rilla!" Nam said, from her console. "We had to lose the Voth bubblecraft, and she succeeded with that and the "baby" Voth."

Rilla felt guilt like a physical pain. *I have to recall Tambur and Vinta. I can't lose them as well.* She spoke with urgency into the intercom, restricting it to the nearest compartment.

There was no reply. Rilla became agitated as she tried again. Still, nothing happened. *Where are they?* She flipped along the compartments with the simtank to try to locate them, then tried the quickshift.

They were there. "What's happened, Rilla?" Tambur called.

"Come back," she sobbed. "It's too late – we've lost Kaylar!"

*

Fifty dead, Omol thought, *and Ghaneem one of them. I won't be the only clan member to lie sleepless and grieving that night.* He landed the shuttle near the wreckage. "We'll bring – the bodies – out for vaporisation," he said, the tremor back in his voice.

Close up, the wreckage held an even more final story. Nothing moved, except for the airlock door. It hung off its runners and creaked at every gust of wind. Gerrad pulled it off for safe entry and laid it on the sand. “Wait here, Omol,” he said, and entered the shuttle.

Omol stood in the deeper shade of the wreckage, paralysed by dread and shock. The low light level triggered his infrared vision. A blur moved in the wind and caught his attention. *Was that part of a plant that just whistled by?* The breeze moved light objects with ease in the lighter gravity of this world.

Thousandths passed before Gerrad re-emerged. They felt like a lifetime. Gerrad walked round the back of the shuttle, disappeared from sight, and came back into view at the front. “It’s easy to see the cause of the crash,” he said as he walked back over to Omol. “The rear stabilizers are badly damaged.”

“She said some debris hit the shuttle,” Omol murmured. *That must have happened when the ship exploded. It’s my fault.* Guilt assaulted his traumatised emotions.

Another plant fragment whizzed past as the breeze strengthened.

They entered in silence. Possessions, bodies and blood spilled everywhere. Faces were unrecognisable. A void opened up inside Omol.

Ghaneem lay in the cockpit. The pilot’s chair still embraced her, and her beauty was untouched by the chaos of the main cabin. Her head was tilted as if to listen…but Omol knew she would never hear again. “Take her out first,” he whispered. He wouldn’t allow himself to touch her.

The shuttle had no power, so Gerrad and his men had to unbolt her chair to remove her. But the lighter gravity aided this operation, and with careful reverence they carried the chair out into the dim day and laid it against the swell of a dune.

Omol stared at her body and tried to impress every detail of Ghaneem onto his memory forever. His thermal vision showed she’d barely cooled down. *She might still have been alive*... But he knew that was just a daydream.

"She is yours to take," Gerrad whispered in the soft language.

Omol raised his disruptor, aimed it, shut his eyes, and fired. When he opened them again Ghaneem's body had disappeared. A slight depression in the dune glowed white in thermal vision mode, and faded to yellow as he watched. It marked her presence – for mere thousandths – on this world. Numbness cloaked the void inside him.

"We'll bring out the others to give their closest kin the honour of vaporising them," Gerrad said. "He hesitated, then added, "Omol – you did the only thing you could. You couldn't let the Voth take the drive. We're all behind you." He still used the soft language.

"Thank you, Gerrad," Omol said. "I appreciate your kinship."

CHAPTER 3: The Ship In The Void

Kazid *clan settlement, unnamed planet. Zarduthi ship-time: 405.385.2.43.046 AD.*

"HAVE YOU SEEN THE SHOOTS?"

Omol turned to face Tangar. "What shoots?"

"Beside the spring. I noticed them yesterday. It must be a positive sign if plants colonise the area."

"I suppose so," he agreed. "Show me." He followed Tangar across the dunefield. The chill of day was barely warmer than the nights, which matched the frozen wound that had replaced his heart. Omol pulled the collar of his fur jacket up around his neck.

"Good job it's not far," Tangar said, as he did the same.

A large chunk of windweed flew by and almost hit Omol in the face. He caught it. It looked to be a type of moss.

"Have you seen this stuff before?" he asked Tangar.

"A few times, yes. Wind dispersal could be how this plant spreads."

Omol nodded. "That's what I thought, too." He dropped the plant and the wind blew it away. They walked on. Wind raised dust eddies up to their knees as they crossed the sand. Omol fell behind as he watched them. The air never rested, and although the planet was larger than some he'd visited, the gravity was lower than he was used to. Omol glanced at the distant column structures, where lightning danced at times, then quickened his pace and caught up with Tangar near the spring. Tangar had his forefinger extended to point.

Omol hunkered down for a closer view. "You're right, Tangar." There were shoots beside the spring. Even in the dim light they looked green and contrasted against the murky buff, lilac, ochre and red shades of the sand and rocks. "I suppose they might offer fruits, or something we can eat," Omol said.

"Anything to liven up our diet," Tangar replied.

*

Galatea Space Station, Earth orbit, 27th November, 2093.

Vimal Ashraf waited for Malek Sindram to rise.

"Anything?" he asked.

"The usual views from the main telescope," Malek said, "but you remember the dip in Titan's reflected light that Kepler III found yesterday?"

"Yes?"

"It disappeared about an hour after we picked it up, but came back overnight. This morning there's a distinct shadow on Titan's cloud tops. Whatever it is must have passed behind Titan as the moon passed behind Saturn. I fed all our data into the computer and ran an analysis. There could be something in orbit around Titan."

Vimal stared at her. "What sort of something?"

"Well...it appeared suddenly...perhaps a transiently captured moonlet or a spacecraft..."

Vimal didn't want to jump to conclusions. He waited for her reply.

"I was thinking," Malek added, "there's a mining survey vessel in that area. Could it take a closer look?"

"May I see your analysis first?"

"Of course." Malek turned to the computer.

"By the way, how did you and your husband get on with that specialist the other day?"

Malek regarded him with eyes that had become moist and shiny. "Jitindra's infertile."

"But you can have treatment. What about artificial insemination?"

Malek shook her head. "Jitindra's sperm wouldn't work, and the Neoluddites forbid the use of sperm from another man. I wish Jitindra hadn't got involved with them." She sighed. "No, I must resign myself to the fact that I will never have a child. Our only hope is adoption, but surplus babies are rare. The authorities can pick and choose who they go to." She put up a hand to wipe her eyes. "They don't usually choose Neoluddite families."

"I'm so sorry," Vimal said. "I didn't mean to upset you."

"I know." Malek attempted a smile. It didn't quite work. "I'm glad you asked. I wouldn't have mentioned it if you hadn't, and it's probably better that you know." She indicated the screen. "Here's the analysis."

Vimal leaned closer and rested his hands on the back of her chair as he scanned the data. He called up video footage of the object, and was shocked to see it appear at the edge of the Solar System as if out of nowhere. It drifted into its present position. After a few moments he said, "You're right, Malek. That's causing a small but definite dip in reflected light, and it appeared too suddenly to be a natural phenomenon." He stood up and paced about the room. "I think you're right." He looked across at Malek. "Your idea about the mining survey vessel's a good one. I'll mention it to Mission Control – well done!"

*

Kazid *shuttle 4, unnamed planet, ship's time/date: 405.015.6.79.732 AD.*

"Tangar, is there a condensation-gathering film kit on this shuttle?"

In answer to Omol's question, Tangar popped his head out of the airlock. "I think so, but I'm not sure where. We'll look out for them." His team had brought out everything they could use from Ghaneem's derelict shuttle, prior to dismantlement, so that they could cannibalise useable sections of its outer hull for shelter.

"Thanks. We could set them up near the shelter and collect the water from them each morning – to augment the stream supply.

Some thousandths later Tangar and Faril carried a slim tray over to him. Its length was at least the height of a Zarduthi adult. "Here. Where do you want it?"

Omol excused himself from his call and looked up from his personal communicator. "We'll take them back to the shelter with the other stuff – we don't want to have to walk too far for our water ration! The other teams will bring theirs back as well. If we deploy them all they'd provide us with some more drinking water, as it's so cold at night." The water would freeze, but the tray could be heated to melt the ice.

The contraption joined the pile of equipment and materials on the sand. Omol turned back to his conversation. "Yes, Tarvin, bring it back to the shelter with you. Out." He switched the communicator off and turned back to Tangar. "I'll need a few of your team to load the stuff into our shuttle. Make sure I can reach the controls!"

Just thousandths later, Faril stumbled out of Ghaneem's shuttle under the weight of a familiar shape: the distress satellite. "This what you're looking for, Omol?" he asked with a sly grin.

Omol felt a leap of hope inside him, and permitted himself a smile of pure relief. "That's it! Can you look for the matter conversion unit as well?"

"Will do."

The shuttle loaded, he sent his helpers back to Tangar, picked his way past the piles of food supplies, equipment and clothing, squeezed into the pilot's seat, and played the controls. The shuttle lifted off the ground.

He returned to the shelter the home crew had constructed

near the spring, opened the airlock and jumped down onto the sand. "Dolvan, Kandas, can you set up the condenser units in a group together, as the other kits arrive?" he asked the team that swarmed around the craft to unload it. "I'll help you when I've got the next load back here."

Dolvan and Kandas nodded and climbed into the craft, and soon reappeared with the condensation film kit. "Where d'you want them, Omol?"

Omol pointed. "We'll keep the kits together, but spaced apart." Omol watched as Dolvan and Kandas carried the kits to the place he'd pointed to. Kandas pressed a button on the side of the first tray and a frame unrolled itself. Another press of the button and a glistening film slid up from the tray to fill the frame. Thousandths later, condensation gleamed on the film. And just thousandths after that, with every buffet of the wind, droplets trickled down into the tray.

*

Joint Space Exploration Program Mining Survey vessel Athina, *7th December 2093.*

"What the hell...?"

Lenny Cowan swivelled the outside cameras on their mounts, increased magnification, and leaned closer to the screen.

"You *know* what it is." Phil Dalton turned away from the resource map his scanner had prepared, and both astronauts peered at the screen. The object drifted ahead of them. "More to the point, how did it get here?"

Lenny shrugged. "Well, it's definitely not one of ours," he grunted. "Never seen anything like it. I'll get some shots." He activated the cameras and concentrated on the derelict hulk again. It was so close that it dwarfed Titan. The ship resembled nothing so much as a nut or seed, plump in the middle and tapered towards either elongated end. The image modified as Lenny zoomed in further. The hull was mirror-silver against Titan's hazy orange clouds.

Aliens? We've had space travel for over a hundred years now, with no evidence yet that aliens exist. But I *hope they do.*

Lenny was engrossed in his examination when the mission commander, Bill Linford, manoeuvred himself through the hatch, across the cockpit, and into the pilot's seat beside him.

"I've told Mission Control we've started the camera run," Bill said. "Any sign of life?"

"None. See for yourself – I'm feeding the images through to the main scanner." Space stretched, bleak and unrelenting, on the screen. Against it Titan filled the sky like a gigantic apricot, the seed-like craft's shadow superimposed on the moon's cloud tops.

"I'll take the module round the other side," Bill murmured. "We'll do a complete circuit of the ship, then pass longitudinally. Our fuel won't allow more, but that should give them what they need to decide what to do about it."

The module crept above the surface of the craft. It took fourteen minutes just to reach the opposite side. Now the module's bulkhead concealed Titan. Its hazy orange clouds swirled on the reflective surface.

"Hey, Bill! Look at this!"

"What?"

Lenny pointed. "There's a hole in the side of it."

"Are you sure?"

For answer Lenny zoomed further in, and played the cameras over every inch of the craft. "There," he said, and pointed.

A man-sized, jagged tear in the hull revealed a dark interior.

CHAPTER 4: The Secret Chamber

JSEP vessel Tsiolkovsky, *9th March, 2094.*

ALEXEI PETRUSHENKO LEANED BACK IN HIS SEAT and studied the onscreen images. When his latest assignment had come through, he'd been about to take his ship back on the regular Moon–Mars supply run. He'd never done salvage work before. The ship had required a refit.

He'd never been out this far before, either. World President Langrishe had authorised the salvage mission once it became apparent that the alien ship was probably empty. Where its operators were wasn't Alexei's concern. The salvage teams were all experienced; they'd assembled laser communications satellites in orbit around Mars and the Moon, and had helped build the most recent Moon settlements. *Just as well,* Alexei thought. Although salvage was new to some of them, the teams were used to working in weightless and microgravity conditions. *At least I only had to pilot the ship.*

The JSEP authorities had sent specialists to rendezvous with the *Tsiolkovsky* on Mars in short order, and the trip had been smooth. Simi Felton's salvage team were about to return to the *Tsiolkovsky.* The left-hand screen split on Alexei's scanner showed the mosaic of shots of the alien ship the *Athina* had returned to Mission Control. Alexei turned his attention from that to the larger real-time image beside it.

He was relieved to have delivered them safely here; now he just had to get them back to Earth. He had little to do; the *Tsiolkovsky* paced the alien vessel on autopilot. He'd watched the salvage crew weld rocket-shapes to its mirrored surface. It had taken all day, even with three welders on each retro-tug. The remote-controlled craft would guide the ship to Galatea Station.

THE ZARDUTH IMPERATIVE: DISCOVERY
Helen Claire Gould

"We're back!" The videocom from the corridor to the living quarters showed Simi wipe the sweat from her face. "Any messages?"

Alexei shook his head. "Not yet. I've told them we're ready to move." He usually worked with just his co-pilot, Dmitri. Simi's seat had been rigged in place between them. A third person in his cockpit to remote-control the retro-tugs was the worst part of the mission for him.

"I'll go clean up, then," she said. The videocom flicked out.

The message came through from Mission Control soon after Simi had rejoined Alexei in the cabin: "Activate retro-tugs."

Alexei saw Simi's hand hover over the switch for an instant, as if she contemplated failure.

She threw the switch. Seconds later, the retro-tugs fired.

The alien ship left Titan's orbit behind it.

*

Nameless planet, same day, (ship's time/date: 406.51.7.79.564 AD).

The sky at dusk was a murky purple-blue that awaited streaks of magenta cloud. They brought night dews and strong winds that dried sweat on Omol's face during physical activity.

The trees beside the spring stirred. Their branches wept over the spring, and their leaves drooped in tubular clusters to the water's surface. Their growth was swift.

Omol shivered under the chill breeze as he turned towards the grove. I *brought my people here,* he acknowledged. I *am the cause of this clan's demise. When we are rescued we'll all be taken into other clans, and may never see each other again. The only mercy is that juveniles will stay with their parents.*

But – I couldn't *let the Voth get the drive.*

THE ZARDUTH IMPERATIVE: DISCOVERY

Helen Claire Gould

The time he'd spent with Ghaneem was a distant memory he kept locked away in a corner of his mind. But the image of her face – the second before he'd fired the disruptor – often overlay his vision. Her serenity in death mocked the clan's struggle for survival.

He ignored the flight of a clod of windweed past him and strode towards one bank of the spring. At the water's edge, he squatted and reached a hand into the water. The sensation of cold travelled up his arm and terminated in a nerve in his armpit; shivers invaded his body. He had to lean forwards this time to check what he thought he'd noticed the day before.

Surely the water level's gone down? This was the only stream in the area, though they now knew water existed in an aquifer below.

As light fled the sky, the shimmering reds, greens and blues of the aurorae skated across it. They marked the interaction of particles from the planet with the intense magnetic fields of the brown dwarf. Now Omol registered the trees' heat traces. Some things in this vision mode were easier to see, some harder. Lightning sometimes struck the ground and knocked out his heat vision mode momentarily. But the level was down in the stream. He looked across at the trees. *Strange*. The clusters of leaf-tubes were still in contact with the water. He moved closer. The trees, now as tall as he was, stirred in the breeze. He caught a branch in one hand and lifted the leaf-tubes out of the water.

It was true. *Yesterday that branch was shorter.* More immature tubelets had formed on the branch's end. He let it go, and it swished back into position, the leaves level with the stream. As he watched, the water level dipped.

"As if it were *thirsty*," he said.

The branches reached deeper into the water in response.

Machari! These things will suck up all the water. We won't even manage to send out a distress signal before we die of thirst!

And to think we welcomed them!

Omol stood up and pulled out his disruptor. He fired at the nearest tree, the one he'd touched. It disappeared in a burst of vapour and dust. A ragged stump that glowed with the heat of the blast remained. The tinted sands around it had melted to form a glassy surface. He allowed himself a moment's satisfaction, then fired again, and again, until all the trees were gone.

Then he turned and floundered across the tinted sand, back towards the shuttles the clan used for living quarters.

*

The Bekel, *Galatea Station, low Earth orbit, 20th June 2094.*

Chas Lawton surveyed with misgivings the hole that yawned at the end of the walkway. He peered closer. Brown gel had congealed – in the chill of space – on the jagged edges of what might once have been an airlock hatch. He wrinkled his nose. *What could have left a trace like that?* "We should avoid touching this stuff till we know what it is," he said. The others nodded.

The craft had arrived at the space station for further investigation the previous week. But with no attempt by any occupants to make contact with them, Chas' unit of JSEP marines were going in with an engineering team.

This is it! Chas realised. *I will be one of the first humans to step aboard an alien spaceship.* Tremors of apprehension rippled through his stomach and replaced the excitement of the choice of his unit for the contact team. Sweat wicked into the layers of his spacesuit. A pulse thudded in the heel of his hand. He closed his eyes for a moment to steel himself for whatever lay ahead.

"Move, Chas! I'll cover you."

Chas opened his eyes. Olga Varishkova, his unit leader. *Never patient at the best of times, nor one to confide in, or get close to.* His toes felt clammy inside boots that bore clip-on Magnetix sandals. He avoided the edge of the hole as he entered the airlock, glanced at each of his companions, then took a step forwards. Dials and gauges told him this had indeed once been an airlock; but a similar irregular hole marred the bulkhead opposite. *So, whatever got in destroyed the airlock.* "We should avoid touching this stuff till we know what it is," he said. The others nodded.

The airlock was empty. Behind them, on the walkway from space station to alien ship, the engineering crew waited.

"...Triple metal skin, composition an iron-based alloy..." Eddie Harkness stood back from the airlock, recording verbal notes on his in-suit recorder.

The hole ahead led into a corridor with a silvery metal floor. Varishkova and the other four crowded up behind him at the airlock entrance. As promised, her stun gun was charged and raised.

Chas breathed a sigh of relief and moved to give them room to enter, using the bulkhead for cover. The bulkheads were a dull white, coated with enamel with a hammered texture. He rubbed his fingers over the surface. His hand bounced over it, but he couldn't feel anything through the rigid, jointed glove.

"Sensors?" Varishkova asked.

Luis Accaro lifted his handheld analyser. "I'll tell you more inside the ship. It was repressurised when the walkway was attached, so the air in here's pure Earthside." He looked up and grinned. "Though at this stage I really *wouldn't* recommend you open your helmet."

"Not just yet," Varishkova agreed, with no hint of a smile. "We don't know what we'll find." She looked at each of her team in turn. "We stay together – understood?"

The unit chorused their affirmatives.

"Chas and I will cover each other as we advance. The rest

of you – work in your usual pairs, and cover each other. If we make contact, keep your weapons handy, but don't act with overt aggression. We don't *know* what to expect, but we don't want to antagonise anything that makes friendly overtures." She stepped forwards. Her hand hovered close above the butt of the stun gun that lay in its hip holster. "Luis? Anything?"

Accaro gave a thumbs-up. "Gravity: nil, radiation: nil. Any radioactive power sources onboard are well-shielded. I've screened for hazardous chemicals, leakages and so on, and this ship's as clean as a whistle, though I can't rule out biological hazards yet. But we should be fine as long as we keep our suits on."

"Good, let's go." Varishkova beckoned to the engineering team, then moved ahead of them all.

Chas glanced back just in time to see the engineering team climb into the airlock. The first suited figure to emerge into the corridor bore "HARKNESS" emblazoned on its chest in bold blue letters.

"Don't dawdle!" Varishkova barked.

Chas hurried abreast of her. Behind him he heard Eddie speak into his recorder again.

They approached a bend in the corridor that followed the curve of the ship's hull. On the door ahead a central line had once demarcated sliding doors; now it only split the top and bottom strips. Congealed gel smeared the edges. Beyond, the corridor curved.

Varishkova stopped at the door, hand raised. "Chas?"

He peered along the corridor. The size and shape of the doors argued the possibility the ship had been built and used by humanoids. But there was no sign of life.

"Nothing ahead. I'm going through." Stun gun drawn, he stepped over the ruined door.

Varishkova followed, then overtook him, stun gun held

two-handed before her. A fierce grin parted her lips.

Chas knew that grin. *She's enjoying herself.* He passed her only when she'd settled against the bulkhead.

They encountered two more doors, one breached like the last. The other was intact, set in the corridor itself, and led off at a right angle.

"Nobody's challenged us, and I don't think there's anyone onboard," Chas said. "But something must have happened here, from the state of the doors."

"It looks like something came aboard without permission," Accaro agreed. "Shall we move on?"

Varishkova nodded and stood back, stun gun poised, and waited for the door to open. It didn't. They bypassed it. "We'll get the cutting crew in here," she murmured.

They followed the curve of the corridor. There was another doorway ahead, sealed shut.

Chas felt the pulse thud in the heel of his hand again.

*

Eddie Harkness switched his recorder off as they approached the end of the corridor.

"Hear about Jouvin?" Brad Wilkerson asked.

"No. Don't even know him." Eddie exchanged a glance with Gaia Zwanji. They knew what to expect. *Brad's an incurable gossip.*

"You *do* know him," Brad persisted, "you've been here longer than me. He's in the station maintenance crew, though his wife is Jim Martin's deputy." He allowed himself a smug smile. "He was disciplined for drinking on duty yesterday…"

Eddie shrugged. "Again?"

Brad's smile gave way to petulance. "He should have been on the cutting crew today," he muttered.

Eddie tapped him on the shoulder. "C'mon, Brad, we have a job to do!" He jerked a thumb towards the chamber.

Beyond the smoke-hazed doorway, the cutting crew worked on the last door in the corridor. They moved the smoking panels aside with suction pads. Stun guns drawn, Varishkova's marines checked out the room. "No-one in there," Chas confirmed.

Eddie led his team into the room. *This must be the bridge*. The chamber was peopled only by several tall white columns with attached seating. At one end a white box-like structure mushroomed out of the floor, next to a line on the floor beyond which nothing occupied the space before the bulkhead. At eye level two large ports looked out on the hangar-like dock, one either side of the craft's nose.

Eddie switched his recorder back on. "The room we're in now looks like it could be the bridge." He walked over to one of the columns. It bore a series of instruments, labelled in black characters. Eddie studied them for a moment. *Ideograms.* He checked the other columns. Only one bore a panel with glowing purplish tell-tales. Some cells on the panel were dark.

"The life support system?" Gaia suggested.

It seemed a reasonable guess. Eddie swung himself into one of the seats. "Mmm! Comfortable padding!" As he leaned forward, the seat moved under him.

"It's adjusting itself," Brad exclaimed, "moving you nearer the console!"

The chair was too long and narrow for Eddie's fit, well-muscled six-foot-plus. "Strange…"

"What?" Brad's forehead furrowed.

He's a good engineer, Eddie thought, *but he lacks imagination. Not to mention discretion.* "The doors are intended for creatures taller than us –"

"That's right," Gaia broke in, "and these seats are narrow, but you'd expect the owners of the ship to be humanoid if they used chairs and doors."

Eddie leaned towards the console. "Which of these controls the drive, d'you think?"

Brad and Gaia meandered between the columns; neither answered him. He saw Brad's lips move as he counted under his breath. "Seven crew."

"It seems too large for that. They probably work shifts. There are seven posts in *here*, but we can't be sure of anything." Gaia stopped.

"We won't know till the marines have checked it out." Eddie glanced round the room. Its advanced instrumentation and streamlined décor broadcast an unmistakable purpose. "This *must* be the bridge, but it seems dead. Perhaps the whole ship's dead! But why would they just leave the ship unmanned?"

"Perhaps they didn't expect to leave it?" suggested Gaia. "Or not for long. Maybe something happened after they left."

"All of which leaves it for us." Brad grinned. "Finders, keepers!"

Eddie frowned. "It's *apparently* derelict," he said, "and found in *our* Solar System, so we've salvaged it. But the owners may not see it like that, if we find them, or they find us..."

"Well, we haven't found *them* yet!" Gaia smiled. She turned to the nearest column again. "O'course, you know who's going to have to find out how all this works, don't you?"

"Sure do!" Eddie tried to relate the symbols to his experience of engineering, but soon had to admit that nothing matched up. He sighed. *We'll need the cutting crews to get anywhere in* this *ship.* He climbed out of the seat and watched as it returned to its previous position.

"The answers are here," he said, "but unless we can decipher the language, we can't find them."

*

Chas sprinted past Varishkova, then stepped back against the bulkhead to check for signs of life. He held his gun ready, on stun. Seconds later, Varishkova overtook him.

Accaro gestured ahead to an opening in the bulkhead.

Varishkova said, "Cover me, Chas!" and strode into the breach.

The corridor curved sharply; Chas couldn't see her – and out of the line of sight, the radio was useless inside the ship; its structure acted as a Faraday cage. The pulse hammered in his hand again. He breathed shallowly. Blood thundered in his ears. He stepped forwards, mouth dry, weapon raised.

As he rounded the bend, he saw Varishkova at another sealed doorway. He felt the pulse subside, and breathed in deeply. The others followed in pairs.

"Frantisek, Suzanne, get the cutting crew!" They nodded and left. Within minutes, they returned with the technicians.

"These doors are bastards to get through," the crew chief groaned. "Wherever this ship comes from, the metal's bloody hard there!" But they set to work on the first layer. Chas flattened himself against the bulkhead as they manhandled discarded door skins to one side. Smoke drifted from the hole. There was little room; the corridor wasn't designed to accommodate such activities.

"Whatever breached the hull didn't get this far," Varishkova murmured.

The process of cutting through the door took about fifteen minutes. Chas relaxed and tucked his gun back into its holster. With a *clang,* the final skin came free. Varishkova beckoned to Chas to follow and stepped through.

He followed, gun in hand.

Varishkova's cry of shock and disgust carried over her suit radio.

Chas couldn't stop in time, and cannoned into an outstretched, stick-like limb. As it touched his spacesuit he glimpsed what floated in the microgravity. "Shit, what is it?"

Chas backed into Suzanne, startled. Hands steadied him, but his heart thundered again.

The body was naked, but for a metallic band partway down the trunk, and featureless except for plates of shrunken black armour. Coarse grey hairs protruded between the plates. It had no arms or feet. One leg had broken off. The limbs were more like tendrils than legs.

"It's not even humanoid –"

"Whatever it is, it's been dead for some time," Luis said.

"It's –" Chas didn't want to look again, but it was too close to avoid. The creature floated, frozen in time, appendages spread as if it reached for them. It was half his height. In one place a hole had been burned out of the creature's trunk, and strings of internal matter floated in the microgravity, still attached to the body. The wound edges were sealed and shrunken.

It took Chas a moment to realise that there were no recognisable sensory organs. It was like looking at a body without a face. He shuddered.

"Sensors report no decay," Luis said, "consistent with a low-oxygen environment." He wrinkled his nose.

Chas saw his expression through the helmet faceplate.

"Could this creature have built and used this ship?" Varishkova asked.

Luis shook his head. "Unlikely," he said. "It's not tall enough or the right shape for the doors." He consulted his analyser again. "According to this, it's where that brown gel stuff came from."

"One thing," Chas muttered, hands raised as if to protect himself from the creature. "I don't care if this *is* our first contact with an alien life-form. I don't want to be *near* this thing!"

Nobody disagreed.

Varishkova sent Suzanne and Frantisek for medics. The marines waited while they arrived and sealed the creature into a body bag that was too large, and covered it with an isolation shield too, then moved away down the corridor with it.

The passage soon curved in a semi-circle that told of a large complex nearby, hidden in the ship's depths. They moved on. They hadn't gone far before Varishkova said, "I think we're at the centre of the ship."

"Perhaps the drive's housed here." Chas quickened his pace. "What's that?" He pointed.

Just metres ahead, the otherwise featureless curve of the bulkheads showed rows of nozzles at the ceiling and floor levels. The black and silver hardware shocked the eye against the white background.

"Hmm. Hard to say." Varishkova stepped up to the nozzles and examined them.

"The sprinkler system?" Luis suggested.

Chas wanted to laugh, but contented himself with a grin in Luis's direction.

Halil eased forwards. The boot of his toe came in line with the nozzles. Nothing happened.

Luis too stepped nearer, analyser held out.

"It's a –"

A flash of pale blue flame stole Chas' sight. "Shiiiiit!" he gasped and jumped back by reflex. The analyser fell on the corridor floor with a clatter. When he could see again, Halil and Luis had vanished.

Varishkova had flattened herself against the bulkhead. "Christ, Halil, where are you?" she demanded. "Luis?"

Chas swallowed hard.

Varishkova looked weary. She sank to the floor, head in her hands. Suzanne squatted beside her and put a hand on her shoulder.

It was minutes before Varishkova spoke. "Suzanne, Frantisek," she said. "Tell Eddie Harkness what's happened and bring him here."

Suzanne made a thumbs-up sign and clapped Frantisek on the shoulder. "Come on."

When they'd gone, Chas went forward and retrieved the analyser. He handed it to Varishkova.

She hesitated, then took it. "Luis – was my lover," she said as her hand closed around the grip.

"I didn't know." Chas put his hand on her wrist. He didn't know what else to do. "I'm so sorry, Olga."

Silence stretched between Chas and Varishkova. After several minutes she hauled herself upright, so Chas followed suit, but kept his hand on her arm. She was badly shaken. Chas felt the same, but Varishkova's silence and his awkwardness prevented him from speaking.

At last Eddie arrived with the other two marines. "Suzanne told me what happened," he said. "I'm *so* sorry about your two men! The cutting crew are on their way."

Varishkova acknowledged that with a nod.

"I'm not sure what set this off, but it may be a defence system. We must assume they want to protect something here – probably the engines." Eddie scanned the corridor, back and forth, as he spoke. Then he exclaimed, "Aah!" and crouched on hands and knees beside a section of the wall near the nozzles. He inserted the tip of a screwdriver under a panel set flush with the wall and nearly invisible. Beneath lay another panel.

"What have you found?" Varishkova asked. She squatted beside him. Her voice was stronger.

"Just what I was looking for." Eddie pointed to several small symbols on the casing. "Looks like these people use ideograms to represent ideas, like some terrestrial languages," he said, and jabbed a short, thick finger at one of the symbols.

"Maybe it turns off the force-field or whatever it was," Chas suggested.

"My thought exactly," Eddie said. He lifted the second panel. Underneath was a single black plate set into the wall. "Stand back, everyone."

They obeyed.

Eddie isolated the power sources and touched the plate with his screwdriver. He avoided bridging the power source. The space between the two rows of nozzles glistened, then faded. Beyond it lay another unbreached door set into the bulkhead. As they approached, its two halves peeled back into the bulkhead.

Chas took the analyser from Varishkova's hands, and he and Eddie peered through the opening. It was dark in the chamber beyond, but as Eddie stepped inside and Chas followed him, the light that dawned was softer than the dull white glare in the corridors. Its source was concealed on the ceiling, and partway down the walls.

Chas checked the analyser; the atmosphere was breathable with no biohazards. He pressed the switch on his suit shoulder that folded back the visor and the curved panels of the helmet. They retracted back to reveal his face. Eddie likewise stripped back his helmet and visor.

The chamber was circular, and the same matt white as everywhere else in the ship, other than the hazy silver of the floor. The planes of the room faded into one another, which reinforced the impression of spaciousness, as in the corridors. But this room wasn't empty.

It held perhaps fifty horizontal transparent cases in rows. Each backed onto a boxy black console which supported the case that extended from it. On the consoles, coloured tell-tales – amber, lime green, orange-red and cobalt blue – shone or winked. There were illuminated readouts and graphs set into the black material.

Chas saw clearly into the two nearest cases. One contained a purplish-brown humanoid form that half-filled the case.

Needles that extended from tubes which opened into either side of the case punctured the insides of each arm. A wide band of stretchy fabric prevented it from floating in the microgravity, and concealed the body from its lower abdomen to its thighs. He peered forwards. "Look," he said. "Look, Eddie!" He pointed and put his hand on Eddie's shoulder.

"I know."

The figure in the case didn't move. It looked to be asleep.

In the next case lay another, similar, humanoid, which filled the case. Chas mentally compared the monstrosity in the corridor to the two forms in their cases. He felt no instinctive revulsion, as he had on sight of the armoured being. Then he realised what he saw.

"Bloody *hell!*" His voice was soft with surprise. "They're kids!" He turned to stare at Eddie. "They're alien *children*!"

PART 2

CHAPTER 1 – The Man with Ginger Hair

Space elevator to Galatea Station, 17th September 2094.

BARBARA BERESKOVA SLUNG HER BAG over her shoulder, flipped her case onto its wheels to pull it along, and stepped into the public space elevator. The only person there before her was a stocky man in a faded khaki jacket. He nodded his shiny, shaved head and smiled at her, then sat in one of the seats and buckled himself in.

She allowed the ghost of a smile to hover around her lips and crease her cheek into its dimple. Then she disconnected her gaze from the man's, found a seat in a corner, and rocked the case back onto its stand. She listened for further instructions as she fastened the seat restraints.

Next on board were a couple with a little girl who chattered incessantly, then a businesswoman with a document wallet tucked under her arm, and a sallow-faced man in a flat cap, with the sourest expression she'd ever seen. A trio of two men and a woman manhandled a holocam rig between them. Barbara's gaze was drawn to the woman: immaculately dressed, made-up and coiffed, Barbara recognised her as Bonnie Smith, a well-known HV journalist. Her expensive navy blue tailored lapel bore a press badge; a glance told Barbara the two men with her were her cameraman and his assistant.

[Departing Kennedy Spaceport for Galatea Station. Inner and Outer airlock doors will close in two minutes,] came the PA announcement. [Lift-off in five minutes. Please stow luggage items in the bay adjoining the passenger car.]

As more people entered, the cameramen manoeuvred the holocam rig into the luggage bay at one side of the car and locked the brakes, then strapped it in place. Barbara pulled her suitcase after her and put it into a locker at the side of the luggage bay. The car had filled up when she returned; her original seat had gone. One seat remained, next to the grumpy-looking man, who'd placed his flat cap on the seat. With reluctance she asked him if he could move it. He lifted the cap with equal reluctance. She sat down and strapped herself in.

[Airlock doors closing now,] the PA announcement continued. [No further admittances. All passengers, please fasten your safety belts.]

Barbara saw that the grumpy man beside her hadn't fastened his seat restraint. "Excuse me," she said, "you should fasten your safety belt."

His eyes focused on her mouth.

He's lip-reading, she thought, and smiled at him and mimed fastening a seat belt.

The man turned a quizzical look on her. "Ah," he said, "thank you." His voice had normal intonation. He strapped himself in, then. As she leant towards him she noticed the scars behind his ears.

"My pleasure," she said, and smiled again. *But have his implants gone wrong or something?*

[Lift-off in one minute.]

Barbara had been to Galatea Station on the space elevator once before. The turnaround was fast. Six passenger cars rode up and down the outside of the hexagonal structure, and kept up the flow of visitors into and out of the space station. The inner and outer doors functioned as an airlock, although commercial passengers and visitors weren't required to wear spacesuits in the elevator or onboard the station. For JSEP staff, it was different; their jobs might require them to space-walk for maintenance or other purposes. She spotted one or two spacesuited passengers aboard. *I'll need to attach magnetic soles to my footwear to move around the space station.* They were prohibited in the cars because they moved up and down the tether structure by maglev propulsion. *I'll get them out when I leave the passenger car.*

[Lift-off in five seconds. Five…four…three…two…one.]

Lift-off was smooth and quiet. Barbara watched the Earthscape slide away into the distance and wondered about the man who sat beside her. He wheezed as he read his electronic copy of the *Daily Despatch*, which she could see well enough to read over his shoulder.

Then she looked around at the fifty or so other passengers. The journey to Galatea Station would take about an hour, so some read, worked, or watched movies on their devices, while others, like Barbara, glanced around the room, or out of the viewports to either side of the craft.

One man she glimpsed out of the corner of her eye, though she tried not to make eye contact with him. Yet she felt his eyes on her several times, as if he were as curious about his fellow passengers as she was; and her gaze came back to rest on him several times. His ginger hair escaped from under the tilted brim of his bowler hat. *It must be clipped on,* Barbara realised. Bluish shades concealed his eyes; his dark suit was immaculate. *Perhaps it's that material you never need to press,* she thought, as her gaze passed over him again.

When the sky outside the sightports had turned from blue to navy and approached black, the man next to her touched her arm to get her attention. "Beware of that ginger man," he murmured. "He's watching you."

"Thank you," she said, and cupped her hand to draw in it the sign of the circled hatchet with her finger. She held her breath, because someone not involved in the movement wouldn't recognise the secret symbol; but if he did recognise it, he could be security.

He made the symbol back, and because she knew he was

deaf, it looked natural, as if they signed to each other. She let out a sigh of relief.

"I'm returning the compliment," he said in a low voice. "Paul Morgan. I'm your handler on Galatea Station. Careful – he's looking this way again." He passed her a card.

She looked at the card. It was an address in the German quarter on Galatea Station.

"It's a safe house, in case you need to leave quickly or disappear for a few days, for whatever reason."

She nodded. "Thank you." She tucked the card into her purse.

"Per appreciates your help," he said.

"I'll do what I can."

Paul didn't speak to her again during the journey, but said goodbye when the passenger car halted at the space station. She acknowledged him and went to collect her suitcase. She had to haul herself over to the luggage section in free fall. Her case floated, which should have made it easier to move, but prompted occasional collisions, one with the ginger man.

A reminder came from the passenger car PA to attach her Magnetix soles to her footwear for walking. Once out of the car she retrieved them and attached them to her black leather boots. At Immigration, she produced her travel documents, which were duly stamped. Then she caught the autonomous tram to her hotel.

*

Zero, Ship's date: 407.73.6.28.483 AD. 17th September 2094.

Omol brought up a starmap in the shuttle's simtank and studied it for some thousandths. He and Tangar had tracked the *Bekel* to its last co-ordinates, before the hyperspace jump. But they hadn't had time to follow up this work, thanks to the chronic lack of resources on this planet. He'd decided to name the planet

"Zero", as there wasn't much of use there.

"Computer, show positions of the *Kemeen* and the *Velakta* on the main starmap."

Two white dots appeared, neither near the Declaini system or their current position.

"Computer, show commgrid range from our position."

A pale green sphere appeared in the tank, showing a small range. *No chance of sending out a distress signal using the shuttles' commgrid.* The short-run craft didn't normally need more powerful communications equipment.

Omol sagged in his seat. He knew they were trapped here; he didn't need a reminder. "Show the last recorded position of the *Bekel* in the Declaini system."

A third white dot appeared beside the Declaini system.

He checked the ship's time and date entries. *Almost three years ago.* With an effort, he sat up straighter. "Computer, calculate a hyperspace jump from the last recorded position of the *Bekel*. What's the maximum range they could have travelled?"

A large pink sphere spread out through the simtank, the white dot of the *Bekel* at its centre.

Now where would *they have gone?* He peered into the tank. "Show me any star systems with even the beginnings of spaceflight."

Another seven systems sprang into being, marked by purple dots. Close to the edge of the pink sphere lay a system with several planets. One had a large moon that caused tidal bulges around the planet as it orbited.

"Computer, now show the last recorded hyperspace destination –"

"Sorry to disturb you, Omol," Tangar said, and peered into the shuttle from the airlock. "We've just heard from the satellite launch team in the other functional shuttle."

Omol's heart jumped with hope. Even should the Voth pick the message up, they wouldn't be able to decrypt it. Voth ships lacked hyperspace technology – though they'd given the Kiai leadership holocomms, for battle co-ordination.

"What did they say?" As soon as he heard his voice, Omol realised how impatient it sounded.

"The satellite blew up a few thousandths after launch. It didn't even make it into orbit. I'm so sorry."

Omol flopped back in his chair with a sigh. *Everything on this planet is shit,* he thought. *Our only chance of being rescued just let us down, and I've just wasted a few thousandths trying to track the* Bekel. *Why did I even bother?*

"It's not your fault, Tangar," he muttered. "Thanks for letting me know."

*

As the autonomous tram forged into the tunnel Barbara realised the ginger-haired man in the bowler hat was ahead of her. *Perhaps Paul was being a bit paranoid?* But he came level with her at the door, then passed her. She switched on the magnet in the base of her case so as to tow the suitcase behind her.

She entered the foyer of the hotel. And again, the man in the bowler hat waited ahead of her in the queue at reception.

It could just be coincidence that he's chosen this hotel, she thought, *but I'll know for sure if he follows me where I'm going.*

After he'd registered, he strode to the lift. He didn't make eye contact with her. Barbara tried to put him out of her mind as she registered, went to her room, and rested for half an hour, then sought a meal.

As she left the restaurant, she caught a glimpse of the bowler hat in the distance, and remembered Paul's warning. She stopped in the walkway that sandwiched the tram routes to consult the map on her tablet. Her sources had told her the alien spacecraft was docked away from the general berths, and was guarded. She could take the tram to a nearby stop but must walk the rest of the way. Her legs were already tired from unaccustomed use of the Magnetix, but the job must be done. She'd promised her cousin.

A tram pulled up. She stepped onboard. A glance around the car assured her that there were no bowler-hatted ginger men in it, and she sat down. At her stop, she got off, but checked the walkway to the docking area again. It was clear.

In the docking area, she entered the public viewing gallery, and marvelled at the vessels waiting for despatch there. The Mars run supply ship *Tsiolkovsky* lay next to a huge JSEP Explorer-class vessel. Workers refuelled and restocked ships with supplies for their next voyage. She risked a sideways glance to where the alien ship should be docked. A steady stream of silver-suited workers in that direction suggested a shift changeover might be imminent.

On the door from the viewing gallery she saw a notice:

NO ADMITTANCE
BEYOND THIS POINT
WITHOUT A SPACESUIT

That gave her an idea. She explored the area behind the viewing gallery and found a suit rental agency. "We can store your personal effects here, for a small extra fee," the proprietor told Barbara. "We get a lot of passing trade from all the workers they've brought in to explore that alien ship."

A few minutes later, a silver-suited figure locked her effects away and slipped out of the viewing gallery to follow the workers. And a five-minute walk to follow the workers led Barbara Bereskova to the dock she sought.

She stared up at the alien ship. It filled the dock, its hull a great mirror-dome of metal engineered so perfectly as to appear seamless. A lightweight metallo-plastic walkway led to the damaged airlock. The walkway's upper section billowed above Barbara, deforming in response to the pressure of the solar wind and the Coriolis force as the space station orbited Earth. The segmented flooring wasn't as flexible, but walkers' footsteps nevertheless produced a series of metallic clangs and a rolling motion similar to waves in a tide on it.

Barbara shivered as she joined the queue of workers waiting to enter the ship via the walkway. She craned forwards to see, as a stream of workers returned across the walkway to Galatea Station, pushing one…two…three gurneys. *Something important's happening.*

The workers raised their hands, though their applause was silent in the space station. Barbara joined in belatedly.

She looked around and several would-be workers were as curious as she was about the occupant of that first gurney. It was the size of a human seven-year-old, and was hooked up to various life-support systems. Then the next gurney passed and the form on it was longer than an adult human male, but more slender in build.

What Barbara saw amazed her. And the third gurney confirmed her suspicions. That form was in between the sizes of the previous two. *These are children and adults.*

No time for further speculation. A man delivered empty gurneys, similarly equipped with life support facilities, and gathered groups of four workers at a time to push the gurneys onto the walkway to take them onboard the alien ship.

She felt a sensation of butterflies in her stomach when she saw him gesture to her and another three space-suited figures. He pushed a gurney towards them. They clustered around it and pushed it towards the walkway.

Once on it she was glad of her Magnetix. They crossed the walkway and entered the airlock. Magnets in the gurney prevented it from floating away. She hoped none of the others would flick back their helmets, or the game could be up for her.

When the airlock gauges registered the correct air pressure the other side of the airlock slid open. They walked out, concentrating on wheeling the gurney between them – a hard task in microgravity. The white of the corridors soothed her sight, and the floors were a haze of silvery metal. Barbara tried to remember the route, in case she needed to escape. The problem was, all the corridors looked alike. *How would I remember which way I came?*

Eventually they arrived at a large chamber with softer lighting than the corridors. Barbara glimpsed rows of equipment with tubes and other fitments that disappeared below the transparent cases. Some were empty. But over half contained an occupant; some small, others full-grown.

The team wheeled their gurney into the chamber and waited in line until directed towards a bay. The medical crews worked with their helmets open. They opened and swung up the transparent case, disconnected various tubes from the naked figure, and gently removed cannulas from its arms, then lifted the small figure and laid it on the gurney. It took just moments to insert new cannulas and connect in-transit life-support tubes and needles. Then they covered the child with a thermal blanket. On a shelf under the gurney they stowed a container that resembled a backpack, and secured it with clips.

"What's that?" Barbara asked her nearest co-worker, pointing at the backpack.

"They each have one of those. We assume the symbols have their names on as they're all different." The man stared into her faceplate. "Are you one of the new people they've drafted in to help with all of this?"

"Yes."

"Cool. Glad to have your help."

"Thank you. Glad to be here." She pointed at the backpack. "Has anyone tried to open one of these?"

"Nobody's yet succeeded – they're probably morphometric locks. If they hadn't shorted out the lock to this room they wouldn't have found the children." The man beckoned them on. "Let's get this one to the medical facility."

The crew set to, though their charge barely changed the weight of the gurney. As Barbara tucked the thermal blanket under the child's shoulder, she realised how thin it was. *They probably weren't meant to sleep for a long time,* she reasoned, *since the ship was derelict when they found it.*

As Barbara concentrated on pushing the gurney, she noticed that the blanket had slipped off the sleeping alien child. She reached down and tucked the edge under its leg.

And then she saw that a space-suited figure that watched nearby sported a ginger moustache and matching eyebrows. The stolid build was familiar despite the lack of a bowler hat.

The team pushed the gurney across the walkway, and on to a field hospital facility set up to check the children's vital signs. No attempt was made to wake them. *It's probably easier to keep them sedated for the Earthwards trip,* Barbara reasoned. Several gurneys already awaited processing. Another team prepped them for shuttle embarkation, the only way to get them to Earth and maintain their sedation.

Several more trips, back and forth, and the shift ended. On those trips there was some desultory conversation between the workers in the team.

"My nephew, Denny, is in the Presidential security team," one of the men said. "According to him, the World President asked for suggestions of how to sabotage their revival so it would look accidental."

"Can they do that?" Barbara asked. "What if these children's parents show up?"

"Just what I said," a woman replied.

"You wouldn't think so, would you?" Denny's uncle regarded Barbara. "But Denny said that was discussed when they found them."

There's a story with an interesting twist here, Barbara realised.

*

Continental Hotel restaurant, Galatea Station, Several hours later.

I'll come back tomorrow and try to get into another part of the ship for a look around. But for now, Barbara thought, *I'm going back to the hotel for a meal and bed. I'll send Paul my report, though.* As she left the locker room, the rental spacesuit back in its place and her clothes back where they belonged, she glanced around for the ginger man.

He was nowhere to be seen. Barbara let go of the breath she'd held and stepped out into the corridor. She hoped she didn't look suspicious as she walked back to the tram stop. The tram soon arrived. She was back at the hotel within the half-hour. An hour later, she entered the hotel restaurant and requested a table for one.

A robot waiter led her to a table laid for two off the main walkway. She seated herself facing the door, to see who entered. But she could also be seen. She drew a deep breath and ordered from the menu.

Astronaut food had hardly changed from the days of the first explorations, and her starter of mushroom pâté arrived in a sealed bag, with crisp crackers in another, on a tray, no plates in sight. Everything was held down with clips, magnets or Velcro. She squeezed the pâté tube onto a cracker. She'd just popped it into her mouth and lifted the bev-pouch of rosé when a familiar face appeared.

The ginger man held his bowler in his hand. His moustache and eyebrows matched his hair, and the grey eyes scanned the room, but didn't linger on anyone in particular.

She chewed her pâté cracker and sipped rosé through the bev-pouch's straw. She hoped that would obscure her face. Her heart thundered.

He ignored her, strode past, and made for a table at the back. He sat down and clipped his bowler into place. Some conversation ensued between him and the robot waiter. Eventually it trundled away.

Barbara watched him covertly over the bev-pouch. He didn't seem interested in her; he looked often at his phone instead. She relaxed, determined to enjoy her meal. The pâté was delicious, and the chilled wine helped her relax. Her chicken dish and vegetables were well-prepared, and she enjoyed them, despite the feeling that she sparred with the ginger man.

*

Barbara's room, next day (18th September 2094), 08.20 am.

Barbara had sent her report to the Neoluddites the previous night, as arranged, but had yet to report her findings to her work – which had footed the bill for her trip in the expectation of a scoop. It was now urgent that she do so.

She sent the amended copy of the report (with references to Langrishe's original plan for the children removed) from her room at the Continental, and cast a glance around it as she did so. Her case had never been unpacked, apart from the basics. It might be best to leave it somewhere to collect later. There were luggage lockers at the Space Elevator terminus. *The safe house could be my route back to Earth.* She gathered up her belongings and slipped them into the case.

Now that she knew about the children it seemed logical that there would be security forces to protect them and even keep their existence secret for whatever reason. *I'm sure JSEP's like most other large organisations,* she reminded herself. *They all have their secrets...*

*

Don Harris sipped his coffee and scanned his newsreader. He glanced around the room from time to time, and once, at the clock on the wall. 08.37 EDT. Barbara Bereskova, his main suspect, hadn't yet made it to breakfast.

She was one of several potential Neoluddite spies. He'd delegated some of the work to keep tabs on them; one person couldn't do it all. He'd been there for over an hour; in another they'd stop serving. He sighed and raked his hands through his mop of ginger hair. *Perhaps she'll get breakfast somewhere else. Maybe she's already left –*

He broke off mid-thought as Bereskova entered the restaurant. She chose a seat at a table on the other side of the room, clipped her jacket to the back of the chair, and sauntered off to select breakfast from the buffet.

Don raised the newsreader and congratulated himself – he'd found a table screened from view by the biggest Swiss cheese plant he'd ever seen, from where he could see the room and anyone who entered. Plants were dotted about the room to clean the atmosphere and improve the environment.

He thought of Hardy and *his* mission. Knowing his attention to detail, he'd find out as much about the alien ship from Eddie Harkness and Dr Chapaire (or 'the old bird', as Hardy called her) as he could before he debriefed the children.

Now that some equipment functions have been identified, the children can be revived. Just as well they'll go to Earth for that. They should be kept away from the likes of the Neoluddites. Don sipped his coffee. *And the World President.*

He got himself another coffee, returned to his seat, and allowed his gaze to linger on the journalist for a moment. Her brown hair was tied back into a tight ponytail this morning, and her grey eyes scanned the room as if she expected something to happen. *Well, she's a reporter,* he reasoned. *She'll always be on the look-out for anything she can work up into a story –*

She turned to face him as if she sensed his gaze on her.

He dropped his newsreader on the floor, and bent to retrieve it. *With any luck, she'll miss my presence when she looks over here, and I won't be compromised. And my reader will still work.*

*

Barbara turned Paul Morgan's card over in her hand and wondered what to do. Her discovery the previous day was important, but she wasn't sure whether or not to try to find out more. But she judged it urgent to contact Paul and check that the Neoluddites had her information *before* it became public knowledge. *I'm sure Per Lakshar will be interested, especially in the dirt on World President Langrishe.*

She lifted the bev-pouch of coffee to her lips and took a sip. She glanced around the restaurant. The ginger man sat at the back of the room; he divided his concentration between his drink, his phone and his news reader. She took her phone from her bag, routed the message through a VPN, and selected the number Paul had given her. She sent him a text to the effect that the ginger man popped up wherever she went.

A text soon came back: Exit. Take the tour.

Take the tour? What does that mean? In case of disaster, she erased the text, and checked the interactive map of the space station she'd downloaded to her phone. There were tours of Galatea Station that included a trip to the original International Space Station, around which Galatea Station was built. They ran all day, and the stop-off point was near Paul's safe house. She booked on her phone. And as soon as she'd finished her coffee, croissant and fruit, she got up, put on her jacket, and headed for the door.

*

Impatience thundered in Don's veins, but he followed her progress on his phone. For some reason she'd returned to her room. He selected Hardy's number.

Hardy's holo sprang up over the tank of his phone. "How's it going, Don?"

"OK. I've had visual contact with several suspects for the last two days, but one checked out: Barbara Bereskova, a journalist of Russian extraction. She was on the space elevator – I made background checks. She works for an Earth-based internet news agency, *The Daily Update*. There was another suspect on the space elevator as well – a Paul Morgan. I made enquiries...he's profoundly deaf, but has links to the Neoluddites. They spoke together a little."

"I know of Paul Morgan. He used to be a handler in JSEP security, but a few years ago he became disillusioned. I guess the Neoluddites radicalised him. Then he disappeared from observation, and I didn't know he'd relocated to Galatea Station. And your journalist – Bereskova – I take it you're keeping a keen eye on her?"

"I am. Hardy, she knows what they found on the spaceship. She even helped bring some of the children out of the ship."

"*What?* How did she do that? She'd need a spacesuit."

Don shrugged. "There are commercial rental premises here. That's what she did – I confirmed it with them. She sneaked in before I got there – while I made sure she didn't realise I was on her tail. Anyway, I saw her help push one of the gurneys to the field checks station. Er – where are you now?"

Hardy sighed. "Waiting for my appointment with WP Langrishe. The President has to authorise the children's revival once I've briefed him on any threat they might represent. Once they've been revived, I debrief the kids. Then *he* debriefs *me*!"

Don chuckled.

"Where are *you*?"

"Back at the hotel. I've traced Bereskova's messages, though. I had some trouble acquiring the details from the telecoms company – breach of confidentiality and so on – but they co-operated when I mentioned the CEO's personal indiscretion. Bereskova's contacted Morgan, but not her newspaper – yet. I hope to stop the story from getting out."

"It's up to you to ensure it doesn't. Sorry I can't be there, though you are much better- suited than I am to working in space."

"No worries, I'll keep you posted." Don closed the call and strode back to his room.

Don opened the door. Although the hotel had attempted to make the room as attractive and homely as possible, furniture had to be bolted to the floor and equipment couldn't be left loose in microgravity conditions. Global warming and the need for sustainability had led to a return to remote-less appliances. He tramped over to the entertainment centre and put the HV on, then extricated his feet from his shoes. Within seconds he floated. He sighed a gusty sigh of relief and wiggled his toes.

The voice of the newsreader faded in. "…and from Galatea Station comes a report on *The Daily Update* that an alien ship has been found in the Solar System. Here's our science reporter, Bonnie Smith, with the full story." The face of a woman filled the small holotank: blonde hair, cute button nose, and lips the colour of ripe strawberries.

Don remembered Bonnie and her HV crew from the space elevator. *Perhaps they were there to cover the same story as Bereskova.*

"Hello, and welcome to another science bulletin. A report that appeared in this morning's *Daily Update* states that an alien spaceship found in orbit around Titan, Saturn's moon, was brought back to Earth and docked at Galatea Station for examination. This will take a while, but in the meantime, alien children have been found aboard the ship, in suspended animation. They are on their way to Earth to be revived. More as we find out what happens to them. Follow this story on our website, *Space News*, as it develops. This has been Bonnie Smith, reporting from Kennedy Spaceport."

Don groaned. He checked *The Daily Update*, then the Neoluddites' official website. The headlines were all over both of them.

Hardy won't be pleased – and President Langrishe definitely won't.

CHAPTER 2 – An Unexpected Phone Call

Galatea Station, 18th September 2094, 09.04 EDT.

DON HARRIS DIALLED Hardy's number. *He's due to meet with Langrishe this morning.*

"Don!" Hardy said, "I didn't expect to hear from you till this afternoon."

"Can you speak, Hardy?"

"I'm about to go into the meeting, but yes, if it's quick."

"I think you should know – the President will be in a mood."

"Langrishe? Why? What's happened?"

"Haven't you seen?"

"Seen what?"

"It's all over the internet. *The Daily Update* broke the story about the children. The Neoluddites' site has it as well." Don lowered his voice. "That Bereskova woman must have contacted *The Daily Update* and our terrorist friends – something like this would be a huge feather in their collective cap!" He sighed. "*Space News* has it too, though it looks like they got it from *The Daily Update.* I'm very sorry, Hardy. I must have missed something. Shall I move in and arrest her now?"

"That's a good idea. Make it swift, before she can do more damage or get away. Despatch a JSEP squad from Galatea Base to arrest Paul Morgan and his cell – I've had men on stand-by. Call this number to make arrangements with them." Hardy quoted the number. "And text me a holo of your mother when you've arrested Bereskova." They sent bizarre pre-arranged images to each other to signify mission objectives achieved or missed.

With that, Hardy rang off.

*

The White House, Washington.

Hardy Brencher knocked on the door of the Oval Office. *I wonder whether I'll still have a job after this meeting,* he thought. He'd read the reports Don had highlighted to him, and intended to ask his own questions.

Don Harris was Hardy's best agent; his report had come as a shock. Hardy had thought everything was under control up on Galatea Station. *I should have gone,* he thought, *but space and I don't mix.* And an unavoidable drawback of his new job as head of security on JSEP's Project First Contact was that World President Langrishe wanted his direct input, especially where the threat the children might represent was concerned.

"Come in!"

Hardy entered the Oval Office.

"Brencher! Why has *The Daily Update* blabbed about the children? I thought you said you'd sent your best man?"

"I did, and he's watched Bereskova like a hawk. But an ex-JSEP employee who's now a Neoluddite has also surfaced on Galatea Station, and Harris and a team based there have gone to arrest them both."

"You should have sent more agents." Langrishe had worked himself up into a rage. The bloated face, normally smooth, was creased.

"Several thousand people live and work on Galatea Station, Sir. A security squad would have aroused suspicions and public panic." Hardy drew in a deep breath, then coughed in the fug. Tobacco of all types was now contraband. Despite this, the air in the room was stale with cigar smoke, and the ashtray full of cigar stubs.

"I guess – but those reports could damage me – and I've an election in two years' time!"

"Mr President, Sir?" Hardy Brencher cleared his throat. "I've read the reports. The Neoluddites' site mentions a plan to do away with the children instead of reviving them. Who…suggested *that*?"

"It was…something I toyed with."

"You *must* avoid that and revive the children. Their parents could turn up at any moment. Show them you acted in their best interests, and you'll avoid an interplanetary war."

"This is your advice, Brencher?"

"It is. Think how angry they'd be if they came here and found their children dead. And think how you might feel if a society that salvaged *your* ship for *their* purposes had *killed* your child!" He slowed his speech and lowered his voice. "Then think how you'd feel if they'd been educated, accepted into our society, and raised in the human way, while their parents were absent, whereabouts unknown."

"I hadn't looked at it that way," Langrishe said, and thought for a minute or two. "That would wrong-foot the Neoluddites, and we might gain public approval if we can be seen to do right by the children."

"If you think you'll impress the Neoluddites, I'm not sure they're that easily influenced." Hardy snapped his fingers. "That's it – *that's* what we have to do!"

"What?"

"Hold a press conference about the existence of the children. Don't mention that information's got out, or about the drive or the dead alien. Release the information yourself, worldwide, now – or as soon as possible. Squash the rumours about putting the children down by taking positive action: show you can extend humanitarianism to these children. Take the initiative and seize the moment! You have to wrong-foot these terrorists."

Langrishe calmed down as he thought about the idea. "You

know, that could just work." He puffed on his latest cigar. Then he reached for the phone.

*

Fifteen minutes later.

Hardy returned to the Oval Office after a visit to the rest room, during which he'd also gone outside for fresh air.

"OK, I admit it! You're right about the press conference, Hardy," President Langrishe said, as Hardy opened the door. "I've set it up for four p.m. today." He drew smoke in, then exhaled. "I've given it further thought. We might make new friends with these aliens, with their fancy tech, if we do right by their kids."

"Exactly!"

"I have several problems – I'm concerned that the children might breed if they're kept together. And if religious organisations around the world heard I'd allowed them to breed together, there'd be trouble. People think it's their human right to breed like rabbits, and I want to avoid a repetition of the Population Law riots. Or, the kids might plot against us – but I've had an idea that'll get round *all* those eventualities."

That's it, focus attention away from your more inappropriate ideas! Hardy thought. He composed his face into an expression of polite inquiry.

The President explained.

"I follow your drift," Hardy said. "Maybe they know of something that can tell us *how* the drive works?"

The President raised his brows. "A manual, you mean? Perhaps they do. And think of the benefits this drive could bring us. The ship has come from another star system. If we can find out how it works, we can go there, or to any system. Our population explosion would no longer be such a problem – we might not even *need* the Population Laws any more. That would make voters happy."

Which might just keep you in power, Hardy thought. He'd followed President Langrishe's logic, but didn't like the sound of it. *Still,* his inner voice told him, *you don't have to like it. You only have to do your job.* "*If* we can find uninhabited planets to colonise," he pointed out. "But perhaps they'll know of those as well."

*

Continental Hotel, Galatea Station.

Barbara checked out on the terminal in her room, stepped outside it and locked the door, walked to the lift, and towed her case behind her. When the lift arrived she got in and went to the ground floor.

There was a commotion at Reception. Half a dozen station police were in an argument with the receptionist and one of the guests. It didn't look important, and might provide a distraction while she left the hotel.

Barbara pushed between families, couples, single people, and groups of tourists led by tour guides, pulling her case after her. She detoured only to post her room key into a self-seal receptacle as she left.

*

Don consulted his phone map of the space station and considered his options as he watched Bereskova board the tram on his phone tracker monitor. He'd seen in real-time Paul Morgan's message that told her to go on the tour, which would route her to the safe house he'd despatched the JSEP security squad to. In that direction, the nearest stop-off on the tour was the ISS. He could meet the security squad and wait for her at the safe house with them.

He sipped his tea through the pouch's integral straw. He checked the tram timetable on his phone. Tour trams ran every

15 minutes. The tram that carried Bereskova left the hotel frontage as he watched.

Don finished his tea and texted the security squad leader. Then he got up and sauntered to the exit. The tram stop was outside the foyer. When the next one came, Don got on.

*

The tram rumbled over its guide rails. The itinerary took in several popular tourist spots, but Barbara could stop off at any of them and rejoin the tour later. *That's handy*. She dropped her luggage off at the space elevator terminus, and got on the next tram.

At the ISS stop she got off. She'd purchased a code from Reception for entry; a credit chip was traceable. She showed the code on her phone and joined the other tourists and the guide as they trotted down the corridor to the old space station. Another door, and there it was. It floated in a glass bubble, enclosed by the space station built around it.

The bubble was enormous. Barbara was impressed in spite of herself. As a journalist she'd seen extraordinary sights, buildings and events. Although she'd seen this on HV, close up it was the most imposing sight she'd ever seen.

"It was incorporated in the new space station as a symbol of the worldwide co-operation that helped to build Galatea Station," the guide explained, "as it was also built with world-wide co-operation."

"Great symbol," a woman tourist said.

The guide pointed out various parts of the ISS: the solar panels, fully extended within the bubble; the science areas, exercise suite, and living quarters. Pictures on the walls of the huge bay showed conditions inside it. *It looks cluttered compared to the alien spaceship,* Barbara thought.

After three-quarters of an hour or so visitors drifted away, one by one. Barbara didn't want to be the first to leave, but felt the pressure of her mission. *It'll be fine to move on now,* she thought.

She left the building, passed the tram tunnel and headed for the safe house.

*

At each stop Don checked on his phone for Bereskova's position. He arrived at the ISS stop and saw she'd alighted. So did he. But he wasted no time visiting the ISS. Instead, he made for the safe house as soon as he'd texted the security squad leader again.

*

At the door to the address on the card Barbara hesitated and glanced around. She felt uneasy, but there was no sign of the ginger man. She rang the bell.

The intercom squawked, "Who's calling?"

Barbara turned the card over. On the back was scrawled, 'Initials.'

"BB."

"Your voiceprint matches. Come in."

Barbara stepped inside with relief.

Paul met her in the hall. "Are you in trouble?"

"I'm not sure. That man from the space elevator…he was at my hotel."

"Was he now?" Paul showed no trace of the deafness he'd exhibited in the space elevator.

"He was at the place where they're bringing the children out –"

"The children are one hell of a scoop for you," Paul said. "I read your report on our website –"

Barbara nodded. "But it worries me that they could be under threat of extermination by the World President. What *he* does could have a massive impact on everyone on Earth."

"He didn't think it through properly," Paul agreed. "Let's

talk to Per about it."

"I've been worried about talking to anyone through the usual channels, in case it comes back to me."

"We have quantum communications equipment in the basement. Come with me."

Barbara followed Paul down a flight of metal steps into the basement. He led her to a desk in the corner of the room and gestured for her to sit in the chair there. A quantum computer took up much of the room.

They spoke to Per Lakshar, who assured them not to worry, he would deal with it. "You've done enough," he said, and thanked her. Paul assured her it would be safe to leave now, so they went upstairs together. "Uh-oh!" Paul said, and indicated a shadow on the frosted glass of the front door.

"What is it?" Barbara whispered.

The sound of splintering plastic and glass curtailed Paul's answer.

"JSEP Security. Open up and surrender!" someone boomed through a megaphone. "JSEP Security. Open up and surrender!"

Someone put a hand through the hole in the front door to open it. Several burly men entered and made a beeline for them. They handcuffed and arrested Paul.

Someone stepped in front of her. It forced her to stop.

"Good morning, Ms Bereskova," said the man with ginger hair.

*

Hardy Brencher's phone vibrated as a message arrived. He checked it and found a holo of a middle-aged woman with ginger hair. He smiled to himself.

"What are *you* smiling about?" Langrishe demanded.

"My agent has arrested Bereskova –"

"Damned journalists!" Langrishe grumbled.

"– And the security squad have arrested Paul Morgan."

Langrishe looked relieved. One of his phones rang. He picked it up. "Hi, Hayley, yes, put him through." His hand shut off the image as he covered the receiver and leant forwards to tell Hardy, "It's Jim Martin."

"For me?"

"Both of us." He put the sound on speaker and the holo of the CEO of JSEP sprang up above the phone.

Martin greeted them. "I'm told the alien ship is powered by a suspected FTL drive. If that's the case, JSEP will want to reverse-engineer that technology for a new spacefleet."

Hardy listened without comment and memorised the information.

"I thought you might," Langrishe said. "Hardy here has just updated me on the situation up on Galatea Station."

"Most of the children are on Earth now," Martin said. "I take it you'll keep them together once revived?"

"It makes sense from a security point of view, for them and for JSEP, if you're asking my opinion," Hardy interjected.

"Can you authorise revival now, Mr President, Sir?" Martin asked.

"I – yes," Langrishe replied, with only a momentary hesitation and a glance in Hardy's direction.

"I'll expect you to debrief the children thoroughly once we've revived them, Hardy," Martin said.

"I anticipated that," Hardy murmured.

"Any information from them about the ship, the whereabouts of their parents, and their society in general will be useful."

"I'll bear that in mind, sir," Hardy said, "and perhaps we should add to that anything we can find out about the interplanetary situation, bearing in mind the presence of the dead alien."

"It's vital to discover that, now that *someone's* allowed the information about the children to be pasted all over the internet," Langrishe muttered.

Hardy ignored the pointed comment.

"But the dead alien is the last thing that should get out, if you want to avoid panic," Martin said.

"If I were in the President's position, I'd *really* want to find out how the dead alien came to be onboard, and what its relationship to the children and their parents is." Hardy crossed his legs.

"It'd be very useful to know that," Langrishe added. "But don't mention it unless the children do."

"I'll send you my report later today, Jim, but I can summarise it now." Hardy updated him on the events on Galatea Station.

"I'm none too pleased with the way it's been handled," Langrishe commented.

"Of course, Sir." Martin's tone was soothing. "But you can take comfort – not all the information posted on the Neoluddites' website was sourced from Bereskova. Some came from other agents on Galatea Station."

"That so?" The president's tone was sceptical.

"We have several goals, then," Martin said. "I'll get my people on them. Thank you for the authorisation, and goodbye."

Langrishe picked up and drained a cup of coffee that had long gone cold. The holophone rang again. He picked it up. He listened for a moment, then roared, "Well, damn well put him *THROUGH*, then!"

*

Neoluddite safe house, Moscow.

Per Lakshar was surprised to hear the World President's voice and see his image spring up above his phone. He hadn't expected to get through the layers of security. *Grigori was right,* he thought, and felt even greater respect for his Head of Operations.

"I hear Per Lakshar wants to speak with me," Langrishe said. "Are you he?"

"You know perfectly well who I am," Per Lakshar said. "And yes, I did ask to speak with you."

"How *dare* you make such a demand?"

"I dare a lot of things. You should know that by now, President Langrishe –"

The president continued as if he hadn't spoken. "Especially during a very important meeting –"

Per Lakshar gave a burst of laughter. "Oh, yes," he chuckled, as his mirth subsided. "I can just picture you, meeting your generals and commodores to decide if the children are a threat or not." There was a snort of incredulity at the other end of the line. "Can I suggest that *my* movement is more of a threat to you at this moment?" He saw the president exchange a glance with an unseen person nearby. *That means there's a witness. That puts things in a different perspective.*

*

Hardy caught Langrishe's eye. "Keep him talking," he mouthed. Langrishe sent him an imperceptible nod, and he got to work with an app on his notebook. *How long I can do that controls Brencher's ability to trace the call,* he thought, *but it's worth a try anyhow.*

"Our agents report firstly that there were more than thirty alien children onboard the ship, and secondly that there's a plan to kill them off and take the FTL drive that ship contains for Earth. So we want a slice of that: once the CRC have allocated colonists to Mars and the Moon, they can use the drive to find us a planet where humans haven't already wrecked the environment and we can start afresh with a low-tech settlement."

"And why would we do this for a group of terrorists?" inquired President Langrishe.

"Because I shall reveal your plans for the children, which my agents assure me have been in place ever since the discovery of the ship and its inhabitants –"

"I don't have *any* plans in place that I wouldn't want to share publicly," Langrishe interrupted.

Per Lakshar ignored him. "– to the wider world *if* we don't get access to a new planet for resettlement, once you've copied the drive."

"I'll consider it when our new space fleet is ready."

"I need more commitment than that. You may not be president then."

President Langrishe sighed. "I don't think you understand the situation. I may be World President, but I can't just make a decision like that. There are many factors to consider. Do you have any idea how much it will cost to find, research and allocate a suitable new planet?"

"I *have* looked into this. I'm not asking for it tomorrow morning, I realise it will take time to put everything in place –"

"Great, I'm glad you do!" President Langrishe toyed with the new cigar he took out of the box on his desk. "There are more deserving groups of potential colonists in the world than just the Neoluddites, sir! There are all those people affected by the megafamines, climate change, since we lost agricultural land –"

"And whose fault was that? Who was responsible for the lack of political will to put in motion unpalatable remedies for climate change caused by Capitalist greed and the energy demands of the high-tech lifestyle? Ordinary people may have created *some* of the problems we've faced this century, but many do their bit for the environment and try to mitigate climate change. But there are growing numbers of people who think like I do – that we need a place to start over, without heavy industry to fuck up the atmosphere, the environment and our chance to avoid extinction. Many of those affected by megafamines, rising sea level and climate change are with me on this. We have two billion members worldwide. Not all of them would go so far as to blow up iconic buildings in the name of our movement, and we don't ask that. Most just want that chance of survival for their families elsewhere."

"I don't doubt your sincerity, Per. But the more people you have who want to leave Earth, the less likely *we* are to be able to meet your demands."

"So what's with this policy of prevention of our members from joining the colonies on Mars and the Moon, then?"

"We have to think about the security implications of each person that joins a base. Anyway, considering you dislike the idea of yet more tech, why would you send people to live in conditions where they have to depend on life support systems?"

"Good question!" Per Lakshar riposted. "We'd rather have a planet with a breathable atmosphere to start with." He smiled in a knowing way. "We *are* something of a thorn in your side. Wouldn't you prefer us gone from Earth?"

President Langrishe gripped the cigar with his teeth. "Good question! Look, I'll take it that you've put in an application. But don't forget – the drive has yet to be reverse-engineered."

*

"Ah yes, the drive. Well, whatever kind of drive it is, I'm sure you don't want us to follow up the announcement about the existence of these children on our website with another that reveals what you're going to do to them to *get* the drive –"

"You wouldn't dare!"

"I'm here now, speaking to you. You know I dare." Per leaned closer to the phone. "Think of the scandal that would cause."

"There is no scandal to be caused," the president said.

"I think there is – in the future. Listen. I want *serious* consideration of this – in the form of a feasibility study, announced tomorrow, and set in motion within three months." Per Lakshar allowed a smile to crease his face before he continued, "We have evidence of the children's existence, and will release the information as to their fate on our website tomorrow if you don't comply with our – request. On the other hand, we can take that part of the report down if you do comply."

"OK, the feasibility study. I'll get someone on it."

"Oh, and – we'd like our agents back."

"You can whistle for *that!*" Langrishe growled.

CHAPTER 3 – Awakening

PRESIDENT LANGRISHE SLAMMED DOWN THE PHONE and caught Hardy's eye as he played the keyboard on his palmtop. "Any luck?"

Hardy shook his head. "Nothing. I'm pretty sure he was using a VPN. There was always a chance he would be, but it was worth a try. Sorry."

"Well, I've set up the press conference," Langrishe said. "As JSEP are reviving the children, I want you to keep in touch via teleconferencing from now on."

"I can do that," Hardy said. "How often should I call?"

"Whenever you have something to report, once the children are all revived and you've begun the debrief process."

Hardy nodded and got up. "I'll get back to Texas, then…Mr President."

*

Hardy caught the three p.m. flight back to Texas. He strapped himself into his aisle seat and pulled down the in-flight entertainment centre to discover how much news he'd missed. The pop-up holotank filled up with a newsreader's image. Hardy listened as he turned to the coffee and sandwich the steward brought him.

At four pm sharp, President Langrishe's news conference began. His announcement was smooth, slick, and to the point.

"Citizens of the world, an alien ship that drifted into our solar system has been salvaged by JSEP staff, who have checked it over. They rescued a number of alien children from the derelict vessel. We have begun to revive them from a sleep-like state. We wish to do right by them, but only when they are functional can we formulate a coherent policy. However, the situation is under control, and we will not allow any threat to terrorise our planet or its inhabitants.

"We do not know where these children came from, or where their parents are, but we intend to treat them as we would our own children. There will be further announcements as we learn more about them, and our policy towards them evolves." He turned and nodded at the reporters. "That's all. No questions. There will be further announcements when we have something to tell you."

The news channel switched to other topics. *Not so much a news conference as a press statement,* Hardy thought. *Good old Langrishe, keep a tight rein on the information you give out. It gives* you *the illusion of being in control – though other people don't always see it that way.*

*

Eisenhower Reception Centre, Texas, 19th September, 2094.

The first thing Ayar noticed as he opened his eyes was the blur of brilliant colours around him. The shock made him shut them at once.

He lay still for several thousandths as his heart thumped with fear. He reasoned that something must have happened during the Long Sleep. *And I haven't woken up properly yet.* He'd expected to see the white background of the Sleep Room with its machines and black fittings, and his father bent over him.

He opened his eyes again. The colours were still there. Still blinding.

And his father still wasn't there.

He panicked then, because something was very wrong. But being the latest child to approach adulthood on the *Bekel,* pride silenced him. So he pushed himself up on his elbow. But before he could roll onto his side and sit up, his blurred vision showed him the impression of someone nearby.

His vision crystallised into clarity, and the "someone"

resolved into two figures that hurried closer. His eyes focused normally now, though the daylight in the room had knocked out his heat vision. For a thousandth he thought they were Declainians, from their pale skins and features; but when one took his arm and pressed him back against the pillow, he saw that wasn't so. He allowed the one who had touched him to cover him again, and listened to its speech. Its voice soothed him.

Questions beat in his brain. Where am I? *Who are these aliens? And where are my parents?* But until he could communicate with them he'd get no answers. He raised his hand to his throat and activated his translator. It would assimilate the new language in a few thousandths, and then he'd be able to understand this person's speech, and reply.

While he waited, Ayar scrutinized the aliens. One was a head taller than the other, but both were shorter than the average for his kind. Their skins were light, and hair covered their whole scalps. That's *why I thought they might be Declainians.*

Ayar thought the one who had spoken to him was female, from voice and body size. Her hair was pale brown, with deep yellow streaks on the upper layers, her eyes a warm golden brown. Her skin was flecked with little golden speckles.

He assumed the other person was a man because their body shape and size, and voice pitch, differed from the female's. His hair was silver-yellow, his eyes so pale a blue as to appear colourless. Ayar noticed that the eyes of both woman and man were narrow and elongated, unlike those of his people.

He was in a bed, and efforts had been made to keep him comfortable. He was almost naked under the cover, but he felt something on each arm, and brought them out to examine. A neat medical dressing adorned each. The skin was sore under the dressings, and his arms were bruised. And Ayar had never had stiff limbs after the Long Sleep before. "Zechmad kaparr-kad?" he asked in surprise.

The translator unit at his throat followed with, "Are my arms injured?"

The woman looked as surprised as he felt. "The cannulas –" she began, and the translator formed words that made sense. Like many tongues he'd encountered, the translation mixed hard and soft phonemes. *It sounds so wrong!*

But then she spoke again. "You must have been unconscious a long time for the punctures to become so ulcerated."

Ayar stared at her. "They're ulcerated?"

She nodded, indicated herself with one hand, and added, "I am Doctor Edith Chapaire. We have given you an antibiotic that should be safe for you – it should help."

The translator gave "Doctor" the meaning in Zarduthi of Kadak. *A healer, then.*

Kadak Chapaire ushered forwards the man, who hovered behind her. Ayar noticed a semi-circular scar under his left eye. "This is Hardy Brencher. He wants to talk to you – if you feel ready. Do you have a name?"

Ayar stared, blinked, then relaxed. "I'm Ayar Dekkutz, the eldest child." His throat felt dry. "Can I have a drink?"

"Can you drink water?"

"Yes."

Edith Chapaire brought him a glassful. "Take it slowly," she warned. "We will try you with some food soon, if you are hungry. Can you talk to Monsieur Brencher first?"

The translator informed him that *Monsieur* was equivalent to Zarz in Zarduthi. *An honorific, then.* "Yes," Ayar said between sips. "What about?"

Zarz Brencher spoke as Dr Chapaire slipped away. "The ship," he said. He waved a hand at the rest of the room. "The other children."

"What do you want to know about us?"

Miril was asleep in the bed next to his, as they had been in the Sleep Room. He listened to their speech. Words tumbled out of their mouths, though each used different inflections. He noticed Zarz Brencher's accent differed from Kadak Chapaire's. Hers was nasal; his had a drawl, similar to the Mergahdi.

Zarz Brencher hesitated for a moment as he pulled up a chair and seated himself beside the bed. "What do your kind call yourselves?"

"We're Zarduthi. From Zarduth." Ayar felt a surge of pride as he spoke. "And you?"

"We're *humans*. From Earth." Zarz Brencher pointed at Ayar's throat translator. "This device. How does it work?"

"It's connected to my larynx to synthesise my voice when it translates what I say, and to my ears so I hear the translation as you speak. No, don't touch." Ayar leant back in alarm as the man leant forwards, hand extended. "It's sealed to my skin. If you pull on it you could damage my voice."

"Sorry," Zarz Brencher said, and let his hand fall. "I'm curious – damage wasn't my intention."

Ayar watched him. He seemed uncomfortable, or perhaps unused to children.

Zars Brencher hesitated. "You said you were a child, but are Zarduthi adults bigger than you? You're taller than most human adults."

Ayar grinned. "Height's usually an advantage for a fighter."

"You're a fighter?"

"All our adults are."

"You aren't adult yet?"

"I –" Confused, Ayar stared down the bed at the hump his feet made under the cover. It seemed further away, as if he'd grown taller. "I don't know. Maybe. It feels like we slept much longer this time." He sighed. "I've answered your questions as best I can, and now I think I deserve some information back. Where are my parents?"

"We very much hoped you could tell us that," Karak Chapaire said.

Ayar stared at her, stricken, for what must have been five thousandths.

"I am so sorry, Ayar," the woman said at last. "This must be a terrible shock to you."

And Zarz Brencher regarded him with his near-colourless eyes. "We don't know where your parents are, Ayar," he said. "We searched the whole ship. We only found yourself and thirty-two other children onboard."

*

Hardy Brencher's office, Eisenhower Reception Centre, Texas, 20th September 2094.

"President Langrishe will talk to you now," the holoimage of the receptionist simpered over the video-conference software.

It was a moment before the president came on. "Good afternoon, Brencher," he said. "What do you have to report?"

Hardy spread his hands. "Nothing more than you already know, Sir," he said. "The eldest child is Ayar Dekkutz. He has co-operated. I've talked to each of them now they've all come round, but most have even less idea of where their parents are than Ayar does."

"But there *are* parents?" the President asked. "Somewhere?"

"Oh yes. I gather that these people are space mercenaries. The parents are away fighting someone else's war. But the children don't know where, other than that they call the people there 'Declainians'."

"Hmm." The President stared into space for a few

moments. He roused himself to ask, "So, what's your assessment of the threat that these children represent?"

"I don't know that *they* represent any threat, Sir," Hardy said. "They're just bewildered kids. At the moment, the *dead* alien's species may be more dangerous to us."

"Have you seen it?"

"I saw the holo." Hardy grimaced.

"You didn't mention it to the children?"

"Of *course* not!" Hardy watched the President's holoimage through narrowed eyes. "Besides, they're still in shock about their parents."

"Good. Don't." The President reached for another cigar, his expression contemplative. He unwrapped the cigar and lit it before he answered. "Don't let anything come out about it anywhere. If the public find out, the children will, too. Just bury the whole thing. JSEP will continue to investigate it, of course."

"Yes, sir." *Which means,* Hardy thought, *the children will never know what happened on their ship.*

*

It was rare that Edith sat and watched HV, though it was always on in her office. But the White House had just announced a second press conference that morning, and she thought it might have relevance to her responsibility for the revival and care of the children.

JSEP had slapped a news ban on anything to do with the salvaged spaceship. Her orders were that the secret issue was not to be discussed with anyone not directly connected to the children. *But they called the press conference in a hurry; perhaps new information has come to light, or* le president *has changed his mind – again...*

Edith settled down to watch, a coffee beside her. The camera zoomed in on the podium outside the White House. President Langrishe stepped up to it to speak. "Citizens of the

World, humanity has recently passed its most stringent test: we have learned we are far from alone in the universe." He paused.

"I note there have been riots since my initial announcement of the existence of a number of alien children rescued from the derelict vessel. This is not acceptable behaviour by human beings in the enlightened age we live in, and we will not tolerate it. Nor will we tolerate any threat against the Earth or its population.

"The children will grow up in human families, as a valued and welcome part of our society. We will treat them as part of the extended family of humankind – similar to a student exchange visit, but via formal fostering.

"We don't know where they came from, but we want them to understand our society. They will be educated alongside human children. In their parents' absence, it's the best we can do for them." He turned and nodded at the reporters nearby. "That's all. No questions. Further announcements as appropriate." And President Langrishe turned and left the podium.

Edith checked her e-mails, shaken. She found new orders, opened and read them. *I should call a meeting,* she thought. She scanned the orders again. There was a list of placements with the names of the children included. At the bottom was a section about the children's care once they left the Reception Centre. It requested recommendations for the post of Social Worker.

A picture flashed into her mind: a young social worker she'd met on assignment in Paris five years before.

She typed a reply.

*

An hour later.

"Play back answerphone messages." The Reception Centre number was ex-directory, so any calls must be from a member of staff.

Hardy Brencher's voicemail confirmed that. "Dr Chapaire, I'm here at the White House again today to deal with a security nightmare. I may be back tomorrow." He rang off.

But what Edith had heard from the White House had disquieted her. She would have to explain it to her team. A frown connected her brows as she scrawled on her message board, "Meeting, 11 a.m., my office – Edith." She checked the time by the wall clock. Ten minutes to go.

She went to the dormitory and surveyed the room from the door. She matched faces to names on the print-out of the list she held in her hand. She watched as Ben, Zanaida and Yin Leng padded from bed to bed, checked monitoring equipment, arranged physio sessions, and administered or adjusted medications. Sometimes they'd smooth a hand across a forehead, or stop to talk. They all had their favourites; that was natural. Edith's eyes lingered on Miril Gharm, the youngest. He was asleep again.

She walked over to his bedside and looked down at him for a moment. In the past two weeks he'd woken only for food and the toilet. All the younger children slept a lot; she was sure the huge doses of anaesthetic all of them had received were the cause of their sleepiness; the older children, with their greater body weight, were more alert.

Edith saw Ayar Dekkutz regard her from the bed next to Miril's. On his other side, Miril's sister Davan watched her too. Edith smiled. "Do you need anything?"

"Thank you, no," Ayar said. "Is Zarz Brencher talking to us today?"

"You can relax today! He can not come in."

"What do you suppose this is about?" Edith heard Ben ask Lin Yeng. She could only hear the thread of sound that was Yin Leng's voice, not her reply.

She pursed her lips and turned away. *At least Monsieur Brencher will not be in today. Even the children know something is up.* She pushed open the door to her office.

What it lacked in size it made up for in comfort and facilities. Sofas lined two of the walls. She filled up and set the coffee machine to work, checked that the alarm to the reception ward worked, and sat down to prepare for the meeting.

Minutes later, Yin Leng, one of the nurses, and Ben, the physiotherapist, entered.

"Zanaida's just coming," Ben said. "She answered a call from Halka."

"There is coffee in the pot," Edith told them, with a wave of the hand to indicate that they should help themselves. "Make one for Zanaida too." Her mug was already empty. She perched against the desk on one leg, notes in hand. "So," she began. "I have just received an e-mail from Monsieur Langrishe, *le Président*. We have had the most important team assignment ever, to look after these children; and how well we do our job now may make all the difference to how our two species interact in the future." She gestured with the printout and sighed. "But I am not sure that Monsieur Langrishe has his head attached right."

"Why, what has the president decided?" asked Ben.

Just then Zanaida joined them. She carried the call monitor in case the children needed anything. She smiled at everyone as she sat down and accepted the mug Ben passed her.

Edith noted his frown and matched it with one of her own. She sighed. "The children will be split up."

"What?" This time it was Yin Leng who spoke. "But that would be cruel. They've grown up together."

"I know. Blast President Langrishe! Paranoia has turned his head." *But it would be even worse if we were still a conglomeration of states and not a world republic. We would never get a decision out of anyone at all –*

"Has President Langrishe said why he wants to separate them?" Ben asked.

"Or where they'll go?" Yin Leng asked.

"Or when?" Zanaida sipped her coffee. "Seems like I've just found one job and I'll need to look for another!"

"This is since M'sieur Brencher discovered the Zarduthi are space mercenaries." Edith had worked hard to win her team's trust, and they had all worked hard to win the children's. The team and the children were her responsibility, and she felt the new orders would let the children down, not to mention her team. *But it is something I have no control over. Miril and Davan will be devastated if they can never see each other again,* she thought. *And they are not the only siblings in the group.*

She inhaled and released the air in a gust. "The president is afraid, I think," she told her staff. "Monsieur Brencher mentioned a threat assessment meeting, and because the children are an unknown quantity, the decision of the president seems to be a prophylactic one. They do not know what the effect of keeping the children here as a group will be, yet they will not take the risk. President Langrishe wants each child fostered with a human family in a different country. He said *they* have selected families of JSEP staff, for security reasons. I have a list here." She shrugged. "I am so sorry. I was under the impression we would care for the children as they grew up. But these are my orders, and I have to follow them."

"But how will *you* know whether or not the children are all right, if they're scattered around the world?" Zanaida asked.

"JSEP will employ an experienced social worker to liaise with the children, the families and me, who will join us before the children are placed," Edith replied.

Ben got up and refilled his mug. "Of course," he said, "if the kids go to the homes of JSEP staff, Langrishe can keep an eye on them by proxy."

"That occurred to me too," Edith agreed. "There is also this: their DNA is too different from ours for them to breed, except with their own kind. To keep them apart is a way to control *their* population."

"Is it even ethical to subject them to our laws?" Yin Leng asked. "In my country we imposed strict birth control rules long before the Worldwide Declaration, but it was difficult to enforce, led to social problems, and eventually the government revoked the policy. That made the megafamine worse in China, since some people had larger families again."

"I guess it depends on whether they'll live on Earth or not," Ben said. "If they will, you can see some of the logic behind the decision, but..." He shook his head. "They may not want to stay here."

"Well, where would they go? And how? They are just children. Even Ayar is a child in many ways, despite his height," Zanaida said. "Surely they're no threat to anyone?"

"We're getting to know them now," Ben murmured, "and I don't think they'll like being split up."

"It is worse than that." Edith sighed. "Monsieur Langrishe says he does not want them to meet or communicate at all."

There was silence for several seconds as Ben, Zanaida and Yin Leng looked at her and each other.

"But that'll destroy them," Ben said at last. "We don't know how much of their natural development they've missed out on – or how quickly Zarduthi children develop compared to human kids – and we *won't* know unless the investigators on the ship find that out. But we know from our observations of them that they learn as a unit, so unless they can catch up with what they've lost – *as a unit* – they may never make it up."

"I told the President that," Edith nodded. "But he told me he had made the decision in the best interests of humanity." She shrugged. "I told him it was not in the best interests of the children, but who am I to argue with *Monsieur le Président*? I am *only* the paediatrician employed by JSEP to look after the children."

CHAPTER 4 – Data Thief

Reception Centre, Texas, 23rd September 2094.

ZANAIDA ALAM PUSHED HER MEMORY DRIVE into the port, and opened up the Recent files. *Good job Edith's at that conference today,* she thought, *though I suppose it doesn't matter, now that I'm leaving at the end of the week.* She brushed the dust on the desk away with a latex-gloved finger. *Edith's a sloppy housekeeper.* She shrugged.

She repositioned the monitor to read better, and scanned the files that appeared in the monitor's projection tank. Some were e-mails, but there were other communications. A new folder opened up with the scan and examination results of the children. One very recent e-mail bore the JSEP watermark.

That'll be it, she thought. She closed the others and concentrated on it. She flexed her hands within the gloves, and a sense of invincibility coursed through her veins.

The header line above the address list read 'Foster placements'. A list of addresses in a table followed, with names beside it – the names of the children and their placement families. *I've struck gold!*

She read the instructions that came with it: the children were not to meet or communicate, and as they became adults, breeding between them would be unacceptable, since this would cause anger amongst the religions forced to submit to the Population Laws. Girls in countries where marriages were still arranged would be wed to local people. No child could travel to a country where another child from the alien ship lived, or serve in JSEP or the armed forces of any country.

That's so unfair! Zanaida felt anger on the children's behalf. She supposed Hardy Brencher would say that President

Langrishe had made these rules to protect the people of Earth. *But they're just a bunch of bewildered kids. They won't cause trouble.*

She copied the relevant table to her memory drive, closed the files down, and turned off the computer. Then she left the room, and returned the master key to it to its usual place.

*

24th September 2094.

Edith Chapaire breezed into her office, poured herself coffee, then pulled her chair out and seated herself. *I'd better update Ayar's file.* But as she leant forwards to speak into her monitor's microphone, she noticed the monitor was set further back and at an angle that made it hard for her to read the screen. *That is very strange,* she told herself. *The monitor was closer, and not tilted like that.*

Edith pushed herself away from the desk for a moment and stared at it. *Perhaps Phyllis has been in here again,* she thought, "*tidying" my desk.* She'd had to ask her cleaner not to clean this office, once she'd understood how secret her latest JSEP assignment was. *But no, there is a layer of dust – apart from here at the front – that I meant to clean up, and it looks as if someone has run their finger over it.*

She drank her coffee, regarded the desk, and mulled over her options. *Well, that is how our dear Monsieur Brencher can earn his keep. I am certain he keeps watch on me and my team members, so now he can make himself useful when he returns this afternoon.*

Coffee downed, Edith got up and went in search of him.

*

Moscow, safe house, same day.

Per Lakshar leaned over the plans on the table in front of

him. "Are you sure this is where they'll have taken her, Grigori?"

"Definitely." Grigori's voice was the most memorable thing about him – more of a growl than a voice – and it didn't suit his mild and insignificant appearance. "I wasn't in their security forces for fourteen years for nothing!" His lopsided smile faded as quickly as it had arrived.

Per shrugged. "I stand corrected!" He permitted himself an ironic smile as he sat back in his chair and studied his second-in-command. Thin, hair the colour of mouse fur, with grey eyes and indeterminate features, he wore a grey suit. It fitted well enough not to draw attention to him in the street. His bootlace tie was darker grey, his shirt snow-white. He looked for all the world like a businessman.

Per Lakshar compared his appearance to Grigori's. His dark, monkish robes drew attention wherever he went. *But that's the difference between us – and how we function. I need to draw people to my cause, but for Grigori a high public profile would mean he couldn't do what he does best.* And function extremely efficiently he had; without him there wouldn't be the network of safe houses or the growing stores of munitions... *Yes, an asset to the group.*

"And what about our other agents on Galatea Station? Several were captured the other week – would they be with Barbara?"

"Possibly for a while. They'll most likely be transferred back here for interrogation. We can deal with them when they return to Earth."

"Well, then," Per said. "We'd better rescue Barbara."

"And not take too long about it," Grigori agreed. "She has more important secrets to spill than the others."

*

2.30 p.m.

Hardy Brencher strode down the corridor from his office to Dr Chapaire's, and rapped on the door. Through the vision panel he saw her get up to open the door.

"Ah, Monsieur Brencher," she said, "thank you for coming. Coffee?"

Hardy was about to shake his head until he noticed the trendy-looking coffee machine that looked as if it could deliver any type of coffee. "Please," he said. "Does this make cappuccino?"

"It does indeed." Dr Chapaire pressed a button on the machine and turned back to Hardy. "It will take a minute or two."

Hardy gestured with her note, which he held in his hand. He lowered his voice. "I gather you're concerned about a potential spy in our fold."

"Yes." Edith explained about her monitor's different position, and the fact that she'd already stopped Phyllis from cleaning her office. "I don't know who it could be."

"Do you keep your office locked?"

"Yes, of course. But there's a Master key, which I leave here when I go home, for the night staff. Ben and Yin Leng take turns. I have worked with them before."

That's not good security, Hardy thought, *though if the children go out on their placements there won't* be *any night staff here to worry about.* "Who else uses the master key?"

"I have my own key – but Josie Carter will share the office with me, and will have her own key." Dr Chapaire retrieved a china mug of coffee, complete with chocolate sprinkles on top of the milk froth, and handed it to Hardy.

"Impressive," he said. "Thank you very much!"

"Thank you, enjoy," Dr Chapaire said. "This is my computer, just as I found it. I do not change the position, because I can see well where I have it. See the dust?" She showed him the outline of the dust where she usually kept the computer positioned, and the finger-wipe mark.

Hardy took a photo of it.

"I haven't had much time to clean up since we revived the children. And when I went into the files, I discovered that someone has looked at the placement list for the children."

"How did you work that out?"

"You know how the modification date changes when you open a file?" Dr Chapaire asked. "I received the e-mail two days ago. I was not here yesterday – the date it now shows. I was at a JSEP conference in Washington."

"OK, of course – I have an office there too – I was there yesterday. That does seem odd," Hardy said. *I wonder if the Neoluddites have a mole in the department to target the children.* "Does it show a time as well as the date?"

"Yes, 10.36 a.m."

"OK – that's helpful. You mentioned a new member of staff –"

"Josie Carter, yes, but I worked with her in Paris five years ago, and besides, she's due to arrive this morning." Dr Chapaire turned, a hand rubbing her pointed chin. "There is also Zanaida Alam, another nurse, but she does not work nights. I have not worked with her before."

"There are a couple of things I can do," Hardy said. "Leave it with me." He turned as there was a knock on the door. "Oh, and don't clean or touch the desk or the computer until *after* I've come back with fingerprint powder. I won't be long."

Dr Chapaire nodded and looked over at the door. "That will be Mademoiselle Carter," she said. "Excuse me."

Hardy stood back so she could open the door.

A woman in her late twenties stood there.

"Ah, Josie, it is so good to see you!"

"It's great to see you, Edith. Many thanks for your

recommendation." The two women embraced.

Ms Carter's arrival rules her out, Hardy thought.

"Forgive me, Josie, this is Monsieur Brencher, our security chief on this project." She indicated Hardy with her hand.

Hardy took Josie's hand and shook it. It gave him a moment to appraise Josie. She was of average height, with fair hair and an 'English rose' colouring. She even smelled of roses. He drew in a lungful of the scent. Her skin was flawless and her blue eyes smiled like the sky on a sunny day. She wore a royal blue skirt suit with a lavender blouse, ruffled at the neck. "Delighted to meet you," he murmured. "What will *your* role be?"

"I'm the new social worker," Josie said. "I'll visit placements to ensure the children settle into their foster homes well, and deal with any problems that arise."

"Fantastic!" Hardy said. "Well, I look forwards to working with you, and assisting with any security problems. I'd better get on, but it's great to meet you." He raised a hand towards Dr Chapaire in a half-serious salute, reminded her not to use the computer or touch anything for the moment, and left.

He hurried back to his office, collected some equipment, and returned to Dr Chapaire's office. When she let him back in, he laid out the equipment beside the computer.

The women were intrigued to see what he was doing.

"Standard procedures," he shrugged. He put on latex gloves to dust the area in front of the computer with dark powder that would show up on the blond wood. He wasn't sure if he could get a viable imprint from the workstation, but he cut a strip of sticky tape, laid it on top of the mark, lifted it off, and placed the tape in a sample bag for further tests.

"What about the master key, Monsieur Brencher?"

"If several people use it on a regular basis it will be difficult to get any information from it," Hardy replied. "Smooth surfaces provide more information. Though I can try, if you wish. I'll take it with me."

Dr Chapaire nodded.

Now for the computer. He dusted the keys with talc and repeated the procedure. Finally he turned to Dr Chapaire. "I'm so sorry, but I need your fingerprints to eliminate you from the inquiry."

"Of course you do – I am the only user of this computer," Dr Chapaire agreed.

"Do you mind if I check the fingerprint mark against yours on file?" He'd expected protest, but she co-operated.

When he was finished, she asked, "Am I able to use my computer now?"

"If you have a spare keyboard, I could take this one with me and run some more tests on it. Otherwise, yes."

"I have something I could use," Dr Chapaire said. "It is just…I am concerned that the children's placements could be unsafe."

"Me too," Hardy pointed out. "The president's idea to separate them is a major security headache for me – that's what I meant about a security nightmare! But you did the right thing to keep them safe. I promise I'll let you have the keyboard back ASAP, though it may be a while. But you'll be good to go once the powder's wiped up – it would stain that nice light blouse –"

"I will do some housekeeping, Monsieur Brencher."

He nodded. "I'll take the key with me, but I can't promise anything." Hardy Brencher strode back to his office, deep in thought. *The old bird has great taste in coffee machines, at any rate! Might have to get one of those…and her friends aren't bad either!*

*

As he'd thought, any fingerprints on the key were partial and degraded. Hardy wrapped the computer keyboard for analysis by JSEP Security forensic analysts, despatched it and the samples, then turned to his computer monitor for CCTV footage of Dr Chapaire's office from the previous day. It was helpful that Edith had noted the time of modification. It narrowed down the time he'd need to spend looking through the footage.

He was keen to prove himself useful. The president's choice comments about him and his team had stung, he admitted to himself, and praise from a fellow worker – especially one who didn't approve of him – would be balm to his injured pride. From the social worker, whom he barely knew, it would be even better… He thought he'd detected a flicker of interest in her eyes when they met – and a glimmer of disapproval from Dr Chapaire.

He made himself more coffee and settled down to watch the material. He'd peppered the Reception Centre with CCTV cameras on his arrival at the start of this project, so he could keep tabs on what went on here even from Washington, where JSEP had inherited the offices of its predecessor NASA.

He ran the footage forwards at speed until he reached 10.15 a.m. From that point on, he watched it normally, and with full attention.

Soon he saw a woman enter the room and sit at the computer. He'd seen her around the Reception Centre. Hardy checked the time on the footage. It was exactly 10.36 a.m. She inserted a memory drive into the slot, adjusted the position of the computer, wiped a finger over the dust on the desk, pulled up a file, and copied it. Then she closed down the computer and left with the memory drive in her pocket.

Hardy isolated the footage and saved it on a memory drive, then checked the JSEP personnel files to identify her. When Zanaida Alam's face popped up in his monitor's projection tank, he recognised her as the woman in the footage. She worked for

Dr Chapaire.

He was about to leave for Dr Chapaire's office when an MMS from Don Harris arrived. He quickly checked it. The code between them changed each day; today's success message was a holovid of Gordon's dog. It even barked at him. *Code for a fantastic mission!*

He put his phone away and strode back down the corridor to Dr Chapaire's office and knocked at the door. When she opened it, he said, "You did mention a female nurse called Zanaida Alam, didn't you?"

"I did," Dr Chapaire said, "and the funny thing is, she has not come in this morning." She invited Hardy in. "That was quick, identifying her fingerprints –"

Hardy shook his head. "I found her on the security footage, at the time you mentioned, and identified her from JSEP files. But I've sent the prints and your keyboard off to Forensic Analysis. We won't hear back yet, though I got a partial print from your desk. Sometimes the print can bleed through the latex if the suspect has a lot of grease on their hands. She may have worn hand cream or something. Gloves don't always do what people think they will. It seems Zanaida is our Neoluddite mole, from the print on the desk. It's also suspicious that she hasn't come in today. I need to apprehend Ms Alam. Did she leave you a message?"

"No, no message," Dr Chapaire said. "But I have her address." She handed it to Hardy.

"Thank you." He pocketed the sticky note. "In the meantime, can you put your head together with Josie about these placements, because if Zanaida passes on the list of them, anyone could target the children at their foster homes or at school, sports clubs, activity clubs – anywhere. I'll get back to you when I've found her, but I'll need to report this to President Langrishe. Oh, and by the way, here's your master key back – I couldn't get anything off it."

*

Hardy's office, later that day.

"We should change *all* of these placements," Hardy said. "Zanaida's actions have put *all* the children at risk."

"I take it she's in custody now?" President Langrishe asked, as he lit another cigar.

"Of course. That's why I'm teleconferencing with you – she was a flight risk. But we can't know in advance – without inside intel – where the Neoluddites might strike."

"If that's even what they're up to. We might be able to change some placements," Langrishe said, "but some aren't negotiable."

"Well, why?"

"Because those placements are with essential JSEP personnel and their families, such as the engineer copying the drive –"

"Oh, so this is what all this security nightmare is *really* about!" Hardy observed. "Is it *really* necessary to spy on the kids? Couldn't you just ask them what you want to know straight out?"

President Langrishe frowned. "Coming from *you*, Brencher, that's a bit rich, isn't it?"

*

Zero, same day, ship's time/date: 406.81.4.82.549 AD (same day).

Omol looked around the shelter, but his mind registered nothing he saw. He planned to explore the sandstone towers they'd spotted on the way down. A preliminary trip had confirmed their potential value as a permanent place of shelter; they'd weathered sandstorms and stood for millenia. Some contained cave-like cavities, probably created by the action of the constant winds.

Tangar spoke in the soft language. "You look like you could do with a breather, Omol. Why not go for a walk? I can despatch the exploration crew."

Omol considered for thousandths. "I could…but I feel *guilty* if I stop work –"

"*Don't* feel guilty!" Tangar smiled and laid his hand on Omol's shoulder. "Everyone needs a break now and then. A commander who's worn out, depressed, and won't make time for his own needs isn't fit to be in charge. Take a break."

Omol met his gaze. "Thank you, Tangar," he said. "For *all* your understanding and support."

He stepped out into the twilight of day. His pace quickened now that he'd decided to take that break. *Where to go?* He spotted the spring in the distance. The cold beat at his skin and eyes as he trudged towards the topographical low where water bubbled to the surface.

A sandcreeper scuttled past, startled at his approach. The movement brought him out of his reverie. Another chance might not come for some time. He reached for his pistol, aimed and fired by reflex. The projectile hit true. One of its legs flew up and somersaulted in the air. He dashed after the creature, and realised he felt better. *Action's always good for me.*

As he arrived the sandcreeper tried to raise itself on legs that no longer functioned. He clonked it on the part that contained its brain with his projectile pistol. It ceased to move, and he picked it up and tucked it under his arm. The *chirrup* of a sandhopper distracted him, and he captured that in his hand. *A snack for one of the children,* he thought, and tucked it into his pocket. He turned to continue his walk when he noticed a green flash against the sand ahead.

Omol hurried towards the spring. Its underlying geology

had tinted the sand with lilac, deep red, buff, pale yellow, ochre, blue and deep pink, but the colours were altered by the dim light. They reflected the colours of the sandstone towers, another exposure of the same geology.

But there beside the tinted dunes, a familiar and ominous shoot had risen from the sand as if he'd never blasted the Thirsty trees with his disruptor. The skies might as well have filled with stormclouds wracked by thunder and lightning. Omol's mood evaporated, replaced by a sense of despair and impotence. *What's left of my clan will survive – I will make sure of that. I brought them here, and it's my responsibility*. He knelt down, laid the sandcreeper on the ground beside him, and holstered the pistol.

His talons sliced the sand easily. When he found what he sought his fingers were dry and gritty. *There! The root's exposed.* What he saw gave him no hope. The roots snaked across the hole, and from them green shoots erupted in many places.

It spreads by runners. By trying to destroy the Thirsty trees I made even more of them.

*

The Lawtons' apartment, Richmond, England, 26th September 2094.

Chas Lawton leaned back in his chair and smiled into the holocam. "Hi Steph!"

Steph smiled him a welcome. "Good to talk to you, Chas. It's Tuesday you come home, isn't it?"

"Yes. I'm looking forwards to it. And I've got a special surprise for you."

"A surprise?"

"Yes." Chas hesitated. Although the selection hadn't been his doing, he'd seen its advantages at once. "You remember how you said you wished we could have a child together?"

Steph sighed. "That's impossible, Chas, and you know it."

"Not necessarily…did you see the press release about the alien space vessel? The one the mining survey mission found in orbit around Titan."

"Yes," she said, "It was on *Newsround* the other day. I wondered if you knew anything about it. Something about some children found on board. But what's that got to do with –"

"We've been selected," Chas told her. "They want us to foster one of the children."

"What?" The colour had drained from Steph's face. "But why us?"

"Because I was one of the contact team." Chas felt the smile evaporate from his lips. "I actually found them." He waited as she gathered her thoughts, then added, "I thought you'd be *pleased*."

Steph stared at him. "You're making this up!" she exclaimed. "You've got some woman up there –"

"I'd never do that to you, Steph. I'd never lie to you. I know how *that* hurts." Chas' mouth tightened as he remembered how his previous marriage had ended. "Anyway," he added, "I was the first to see them, and there's no way these children are human. Humanoid, yes, but when you see him, you'll realise it's the truth."

"Him?"

"Yes. We don't know his exact age, but he's young." Steph didn't respond, so Chas thought she expected him to say something else. "He's weak from sleeping for a long time in microgravity, so he needs physio. That's another reason why we were chosen – because of your training and experience. I knew you wanted another child," he added, "so I thought this was a way..." He let his voice trail off.

"It's all rather sudden!"

Chas thought back to the night his ex-wife had told him that Flora was on the way. "It always is – and even more so with JSEP, it seems!"

"Well – do we have a choice? Because I wonder what Ronnie will have to say about it," Steph said.

"No. It was a last-minute decision – they had some security issue with the original placement."

"Hmm. Well, I need to think about this seriously till you get back here, 'cos it's rather a shock!"

*

Next day.

Steph sipped her coffee and checked her watch again. *Chas said the jet would be here by now,* she thought. She wondered whether she should believe him about the child; he couldn't even show her a holo of him – for security reasons, he'd said.

I can't help being suspicious. She tried to squash the feelings the call had revived in her. *Darryl was such a pig to me – I hope Ronnie hasn't inherited any of his characteristics!* That he might have caused her occasional worry.

The old-fashioned brass knocker echoed through the apartment. Steph uncoiled her legs from the armchair and went to answer it. A uniformed stranger stood there. It took her a moment to realise his jacket bore the JSEP insignia, though she'd seen Chas in his uniform often enough.

"Has something happened to Chas?" she asked.

The man smiled. "No, no, Ma'am. He's here. I'm just the escort. You're a lucky lady."

"Am I?" Steph saw Chas emerge from the lift opposite, and smiled with relief.

As he approached he beamed his pleasure at the sight of her. "Hi, Steph!" he called, hurried to her side, and flung his free arm around her.

Steph saw the figure in his arms, swathed in a blanket.

"I'll go, if you don't mind," the escort said. "I have to get back to the States, and the jet won't wait forever."

"Of course," Steph said.

"Ma'am, Chas." The man nodded to her and headed for the lift.

"Is this the new addition to the family?" She looked up at him and tried to harden her heart against the child, but couldn't squash down her curiosity. All she could see of him was a brown-purple blur.

Chas nodded. "We've got Miril on a trial during my leave." Because Chas worked a job share, like many JSEP employees, he got plenty of leave; he was now in Britain for three months. "They promised they'll try to find him another placement if it doesn't work out."

"I'm just not sure how Ronnie will react," Steph said. "He's been king pin, and although he *seemed* excited when I told him, he –" She bit her lip. "Let me see him."

Chas pulled the blankets back.

Steph's first impression was not favourable. For a child, the creature looked a lot like an old man; he reminded her of famine victim pictures on HV, on the most overcrowded continents worst-affected by climate change. "He doesn't look too well," she observed.

"No. Some younger children have taken a while to adapt back to solid food after intravenous feeding for however long, but that's now stabilised. Er – how long do you plan to keep us standing here?" Chas grinned and sought her wrist and moved his thumb over her skin. It was his way of wheedling.

Steph stood back for him to enter.

The child stirred in his arms, perhaps disturbed by their voices, perhaps by Chas walking, or perhaps by their voices. He opened round, dark eyes and stared around for a moment, then drifted back into sleep.

"Well?" asked Chas. His eyes were on her. "Shall we give him a try?"

Steph watched his face as she considered. *He's my best friend, as well as my lover and husband. I should have known better than to doubt him.* She smiled. "Yes. We'll give him a try," she answered.

Chas laid the child on the sofa in the lounge. His red shorts and yellow t-shirt did nothing to disguise the stick-thin limbs. His flesh hung on his bones like wrinkled clothing. Just then he stirred, sighed, yawned, and blinked twice, then fixed a stare on both of them.

"Hello, Miril," Steph said, and smiled at him. He lay on the couch and watched her. *Poor kid, he's too weak to move,* she thought.

"Miril," he said. He pronounced it with a hard r. More guttural sounds followed, then a sentence in English: "My name is Miril." The translation was in his childish voice.

Steph looked at Chas in surprise.

"They have these translator-things wired in," he said with a shrug. "But I assume he'll eventually learn to speak English anyway."

Then she caught sight of the flat disc of silvery-grey metal embedded in the skin of his throat. There was a stud on the side of it. She leant closer.

Chas caught her arm and pulled her back. "He gets worried if he thinks someone's going to touch it," he said.

Steph nodded and turned back to the child. "Miril." She couldn't say it as he did. *Just one sound's difference, yet it didn't sound the same at all!* "Miril." It still wasn't right. She smiled at him again and pointed to her husband. "Chas." Then she indicated herself. "Steph." She elongated the syllables for him, and when he repeated the names correctly she beamed at him. "Would you like a drink? Some fruit juice, maybe?"

Miril jerked his head upwards and murmured, "Zooch." After a pause, the translator echoed in English, "Yes."

Steph watched him and tried to assess his age. His limbs seemed long for a human child of any age below seven. *But he isn't human,* she reminded herself, *and perhaps we can't compare him to a human child.* She decided to play safe and use Ronnie's old trainer cup.

"Here you are," she said, kneeling beside him. She had to help him sit up; his body felt cooler than hers and fitted awkwardly against her, all long bones and angles.

He looked at the trainer cup, then put out a hand to touch it, but pulled back.

He doesn't know how to use it, Steph realised. She took the lid off to show him the juice inside, and mimed sucking through the lid.

He soon got the idea. After a couple of tries he gulped the juice.

"Take it more slowly," she said.

He ignored her.

Perhaps he doesn't understand. "Okay, good boy. Have the rest in a minute." She pulled the cup out of his grasp.

Miril tried to reach for it again, but then his eyelids wavered and closed.

"They said he sleeps a lot," Chas murmured. "Even during the day."

Steph laid Miril back on the sofa and studied him. Everything about him was in the right place, but his features didn't look human. His long narrow fingers – other than the thumb – had an extra joint, and the tips tapered into claws. She'd noticed them as he fingered the translator disc. His oval ears protruded from his hairless scalp. The skin was flaky, and along the slight raised crest which ran from his forehead to the base of his skull the hair had fallen out in patches. His eyes were round, and the lids sank back into the sockets when he opened them.

She pulled the blankets up around Miril and sighed. "Just what are we being asked to take on here?" she asked, and turned to face Chas. "You said he needs physio, but what about food? Does he need a special diet?"

Chas shook his head. "Apparently they can eat anything."

"I can't understand why they fostered him in this state."

"President's orders," Chas explained.

"So we *don't* have any choice?" Steph raised her eyes heavenwards. "I *must* be mad!"

"Not mad. Just compassionate," Chas said and hugged her. "And Miril has even less choice than us. Oh, and – he has a sister, but they aren't allowed to communicate with each other."

"*What?* Whose idea was *that*?" Steph was indignant on Miril's behalf.

"President's orders – to do with settling in and security. Allegedly."

*

"Everything's ready." Chas strode into the lounge. "I'll fetch Ronnie from school, shall I?"

"Sure." Steph was seated in a chair opposite Miril, so she could watch him as she sipped her coffee.

She can't take her eyes off him, Chas thought as he watched her, and hugged himself. *I think she likes him!*

"I *must* be mad," Steph repeated. "I don't know whether to be furious or flattered!"

Chas spared a glance across at Miril. He'd curled himself into a heat-conserving position on his side, arms clasped around his middle, the blanket up about his ears.

"The thing is," Chas said, "when you're in the JSEP Marines and the President says 'Jump!' you jump!" He wondered at the effect this intruder would have on Ronnie. *Still,* he told himself, *lots of other kids – especially in one-parent families – have to adapt to difficult changes in family life. It's the way society is these days…though they don't usually have* alien *brothers or sisters!*

Chas dismissed the thought with a shrug, and went to collect Ronnie. The school was ten minutes' walk away via the short cut over the stream which meandered between a housing estate and agricultural land. It was an oasis of less-developed countryside, and Chas enjoyed the chance to walk without the restriction of a spacesuit or magnetic-soled boots. He whistled to himself as he crossed the bridge over the stream. In the glasshouses nearby, a robot harvester cut early crops and ignored human activity and presence. Chas saw the school through the trees, and hurried towards it.

When Ronnie saw Chas, he grinned, rushed to him, and flung his arms around his waist.

"We can talk as we walk home," Chas said.

But they were almost there before Ronnie stopped chattering enough for him to ask what Steph had told him about his new brother.

"Oh. Yes." Ronnie's lip quivered; then his features twisted with rage. "I told Mum, I don't want a brother!" he shrieked.

"Quiet, Ronnie! It's rude to make a noise in the street. Anyway, you'll like this brother," Chas answered. "He's not quite like other brothers. You'll still be special, but so is he."

"How can *he* be special, if *I* am?" Ronnie asked, intrigued. "I wouldn't have minded a sister," he added.

Chas ignored this barb. His daughter Flora had chosen to live with his ex-wife, and he hadn't seen either of them for five years. He didn't enjoy reminders of that void in his life. Perhaps Ronnie didn't understand the subtle cruelty of his remarks about his desire for a sister; he'd never even met Flora.

Chas lifted Ronnie over the gate to the apartment block. It was a game they played. Chas always walked in, but his father had played similar games with him, so he never deprived Ronnie of this method of entry. "Everybody's special in their own way," he answered. "You, me, your mother – and Miril."

"Mirl – Mil?" Ronnie glared up at Chas. "What kind of a name is that?"

"Miril's different from you and me and your mum," Chas replied. "He comes from another world – we're not sure where yet. Somewhere up there." He waved at the sky. "I've been asked to look after him for a while. It's –" He hesitated. Then inspiration struck. "It's part of my job," he added.

"You mean – you get paid for it?"

For a seven-year-old, Ronnie's shrewd, Chas thought. "Something like that," he agreed. That was one thing he'd reassured Steph about. The years of being careful with money as a single parent had spilled over into her life with him, though a JSEP Marine's salary was more than adequate for the three of them. He'd never quibbled over the acceptance of Ronnie as his own son, but the trust fund meant Steph need have no financial worries about the foster placement.

"Oh well, I suppose I could meet him!" Ronnie sighed. "If we're getting *paid* to have him!" He bounded up the path towards the apartments.

Shit! I'm not used to this parenting thing. I spend too much time away from home. I always did. Chas passed a hand across his forehead as he wiggled his shoulders. The hours spent with Miril in his arms in the plane had stiffened his muscles. He placed his palm against the scanner, and the door to the communal area of the apartment block opened.

Ronnie leapt ahead of him into the lift. Chas followed and selected the third level. Ronnie hopped from one foot to the other and overbalanced as the lift moved.

"Ronnie!" Chas said, as they reached their floor.

Ronnie turned.

"When you go in, keep quiet – Miril's asleep."

"I don't want him to sleep!" Ronnie snapped. His voice echoed around the landing. "I want him to play with me –"

Chas clamped a hand over Ronnie's mouth and let them into the apartment. But before he could hold him back, Ronnie had escaped his grasp and skipped into the lounge.

Chas followed him, and saw Miril turn those almost lidless, round, dark eyes to stare at them.

"MUMMEEEEE!" Ronnie screamed.

CHAPTER 5 – Mystery in Nice

Nice, France. 29th September 2094.

"COME ON, HALKA!"

Halka Mozada looked up as she climbed out of the car, and adjusted her sunglasses. Papa Jouvin caught her wrist in one of his huge hands to steady her.

I'm not sure why, but I don't like him touching me, she thought. But she didn't protest as he steered her around the car and across the road. She'd need support to climb the flight of steps ahead. Her legs still felt wobbly when she had to walk, though Ben's physio exercises had helped.

The driver locked the car doors, but hurried to her other side when she stumbled. "Take it steady!" he said. His voice and eyes were kind, although Halka still wasn't used to the features of these humans.

One day I'll think I'm a *human, and get a shock when I look in the mirror,* she thought.

"I've a daughter of my own," the man added, "about your age."

"I don't know how old I am any more," Halka objected.

But the man just laughed. "Well, then, about your height."

Through the elaborate metal gate at the top of the steps, Halka glimpsed the garden that extended up the mountainside in terraces.

The driver hovered uncertainly. "Madame Jouvin," he began, "is she about?"

"She's in a chair," Papa Jouvin interrupted.

"I'm supposed to deliver Halka to *her*," the driver continued.

"This way." Papa Jouvin gestured for the driver and Halka

to follow him. They went through the gate into the garden. Halka had to watch where she put her feet. *I'm not sure I want to be here,* Halka thought; but even if she could have run, there was nowhere else to go.

They skirted the outside of the building on neat pink and white paving slabs. The villa was all on one level. Trees unlike any Halka had seen before flanked the path parallel to the communal entrance. Their leaves were pleated dark green splays; through the gaps between them she saw the car parked in the layby opposite.

Then she looked up, and what she saw made her halt. Ahead was an expanse of water, blue-green under the smiling sky. Halka remembered the sea on Mergahdi. As part of her education she'd accompanied the adults as they shuttled down to one of the islands there. She'd been allowed to watch them conduct negotiations when the contract was struck between clan Bekel and the sea-folk.

"Not far now," the driver said.

Halka saw that the terrace overlooked the sea. A canopied structure ahead had a wide seat suspended from it. On it a boy swung, lost in thought as he looked out to sea. He turned to face them as Halka and her escorts crossed the terrace, and rose in slow motion.

"Hello, Papa," he said. His voice was cool and quiet, his face pale as paper and just as expressionless. "I'll get Maman." Halka saw his pupils dilate as he looked at his father, and followed his gaze: the heavy-set body, craggy face and drooping black moustache; the heavy leather belt with its ornate brass buckle.

"She's working?" asked Papa Jouvin. He took a couple of steps nearer the boy, who nodded and entered the building through the sliding glass door.

Halka was surprised. She knew that JSEP employees

mostly worked away from their families for extended periods; Dr Chapaire had explained it to them. So she'd expected Papa Jouvin's son to rush to hug his father, as Zarduthi children did when they hadn't seen their parents for some time. *Perhaps human children don't do that,* she reflected.

"We'll get you onto the porch swing," the driver said. Halka knew he'd leave, and wished he didn't have to. But she held her head up high as he helped her onto the swing seat while Papa Jouvin held it steady. The breeze off the sea brought a shiver to her shoulders.

In a moment, the boy reappeared, accompanied by a woman in a chair on wheels which she controlled by a joystick on the armrest. She glided across the terrace towards Halka.

"Hello, *ma chérie*," said the woman. "I am Madame Jouvin, and this is my son, Robert. You must be Halka."

"Yes. Shulai. Ah – hello." Halka felt nervous and didn't know what else to say. It took her a thousandth to realise that Madame Jouvin had spoken in English; she knew she was in France and the people spoke French there. "It's all right," she said after a pause, "you can speak to me in French if it's easier for you. Dr Chapaire did, when she knew I was coming here, so I could use my translator straight away." She made a gesture towards her throat.

"Ah. *Très bien.* I shall do so. But Robert has little English, so it will be good for him to practice. It will be *fantastique* for him to have a companion, too." Madame Jouvin turned to her son. "Robert, have you said hello to Halka?"

"No, *Maman.*" Robert's eyes slid past his mother to Halka. He compressed his lips together for a moment, then murmured, "Hello, Halka."

Halka gave him the short bow of her people, as a Zarduthi adult would to an equal, and studied him. Shorter than her, he was almost as slender. His hair was black, and his eyes were a clear green, with greyish rims to the irises. Pale brown dots sprinkled his nose and cheeks. His lips were deep red against the pallor of his skin. *He looks like someone to trust,* Halka thought; but she wondered what his frown meant.

"Bring us some drinks, Robert," Madame Jouvin commanded. "I'm sure Halka is thirsty!"

Robert disappeared into the building without a word. *His mother treats him like a servant,* Halka thought. *Will they do that with me? And he doesn't seem keen for me to be here.*

The American escort seemed embarrassed, and excused himself with a salute for Madame Jouvin and a crisp nod towards Papa Jouvin. He gave Halka a cheery grin and a wave, then strode across the terrace. The last she saw of him was his cap through the strange trees as he walked back to the car. As it left the layby on the clifftop road that separated the house from the sea cliffs and beach, Halka regretted that she couldn't have gone to live with him and his daughter instead.

*

Richmond, ten minutes later.

"Miril! Miril!"

He lay with his knees against his chest, but Steph knew he could hear her. Her hand stroked his bare scalp. He didn't cry, or even whimper, but he'd covered his ears and face with his hands.

"Ronnie's calmed down now," Steph soothed. "He just wasn't sure about you." She touched his shoulder, and he made a small sound. "Come on. Ronnie's in my physio room. He won't hurt you, he's –"

"He *scared* me," Miril muttered.

"He was scared, too. You look different, and you're poorly just now. Sometimes people are afraid of other people who are ill, or different." Steph stroked his scalp once more, and tried not to dislodge flakes of dry skin. "Shall we try again later?"

Miril didn't answer; he just pressed as close to her as possible, then slumped back against the cushions and made a sound which she interpreted as a moan.

She guessed he had little strength left. "Do your ears hurt?"

"No."

"Good. We'll have food soon. Are you hungry?"

Miril's head moved. Steph couldn't be sure if the gesture meant anything or not. "Yes." She still heard occasional wails from the next room.

"What sort of things do you like?" she asked.

Miril thought for a moment. "I like sharp things, not sweet things."

"What about bread?"

"I can eat that."

"What did you have on the space ship?"

"I can't remember. It's…a long time ago." His eyes closed again. His eyelids retracted almost fully when his eyes were open.

Steph covered him with the blanket again and went into the other room. Chas held Ronnie against him.

"Ronnie, are you okay?" she asked.

"Mummy, he looks – ugh!"

Chas locked gaze with her over Ronnie's head.

"We probably look strange to him too!" Steph said. "You'll soon get used to him. And he's lost a lot of weight because he was asleep for a long time."

"Oh, but Chas told me he's getting paid for Mirl – Mil to stay with us, so he *will* have enough to eat!" Ronnie said.

Steph couldn't help a grin as she met Chas' gaze again. "I don't think that's the problem," she said. "We'll need to take things slowly and find out what things Miril likes to eat." She could see that he was interested now, in spite of himself.

"Why's Mil – Mirl – why's he different from us?" Ronnie asked.

"You know how birds, and fish, and horses, and spiders are all different life forms? Different from each other *and* us?" Chas said. "Well, Miril's a different life form, too."

Ronnie was silent as he thought about this.

Steph took advantage of the moment. "Why don't you come and help me get some food for both of you?"

Ronnie nodded and followed her into the kitchen to watch as she worked.

Steph gave him his favourite bread shapes, toasted with cheese melted onto them, a Pizza Face, and an apple, cored and cut into quarters. Then, as Ronnie tucked into his tea, she heated up soup and cut more bread shapes with the fancy cookie cutters she used for Ronnie.

By the time she'd finished, Ronnie had eaten his food, and followed her into the lounge. Miril still lay on the sofa. He was asleep; she touched his shoulder to waken him.

Miril's eyes opened. As soon as he saw Ronnie he put his hands over his ears again and curled himself up into a human-looking foetal position.

Steph put a hand on his shoulder again. "Don't be scared," she said. "Ronnie won't hurt you." She turned to Ronnie and made her expression as serious as possible. "He's sorry he hurt your ears before, and won't do it again, will you Ronnie? Here's some soup, Miril."

Miril watched both of them with his huge round eyes.

Ronnie stayed very still.

Miril lowered his hands and his expression relaxed.

Steph helped him sit up and spooned soup into his mouth, blowing on it to cool it.

Ronnie watched in silence while he supped the red liquid,

then got up and left the room.

Steph carried on feeding Miril until the last drop of soup was gone, then coaxed him to eat some bread shapes.

He put them into his mouth and chewed slowly. He'd just swallowed the last when Ronnie came back into the room, an old-fashioned wooden toy train clutched under his arm. "Look, Mil," he said, and held it out. "This was my favourite toy when I was little."

Miril took the train in his long-fingered hands but couldn't hold it up. He rested it on his chest and turned it over, looking hard at it. At last he said, "What is it?"

"It's a train, silly!"

Steph put her free hand on Ronnie's. "Miril's never seen a train before."

Miril looked back at both of them, and then pushed the train away from him, down his stomach. When he saw the wheels going round and round against him, he looked up at Steph.

"Feels funny!" he said, and laughed. The laughter sounded like great sobs.

Steph laughed too, and took the train and ran it up and down his front. "Does it tickle?" she asked.

"It's not meant for tickling!" Ronnie grabbed it. He banged it on the floor and ran it over the carpet. "This is what a train does." He made *chuff-chuff* noises.

Steph saw the alien child's eyes close, then open again. "Okay, Ronnie, that's enough. Miril's tired. He had a long journey here." She turned back to him. "D'you want to lie down again now?" She helped him lie flat.

Miril drifted away into sleep again.

*

Nice, half an hour later.

"I'll show you the garden, if you like."

"I'd like that. I could see the one at the Big Place through the window," Halka said. "But I'll need help."

"It's OK," Robert said, "I help *Maman* because she can't walk."

The rest of the day passed in a blur, as Robert showed Halka the garden. Three narrow terraced "rooms" climbed the mountainside, the lowest paved with pink and white flagstones and filled with pots in different shapes, sizes and colours. The next was gravelled, the highest grassed. Plants were everywhere.

Halka had never seen so many different kinds before. They climbed to the top terrace to look down on them – the view was spectacular. She was hot and tired, but Robert was right – it was easier to walk down.

Robert also showed her all the rooms in the villa, including her bedroom. He was quiet, and only told her things he thought she needed to know. He didn't ask any questions, but listened to any she asked him and replied in as few words as possible. She sensed a watchfulness about him, like that of an adult Zarduthi entering battle. Halka had seen that wariness as her parents fought the Voth, and wondered why he reacted like this to his father. *Perhaps he's shy,* she thought; and at once she knew it wasn't that.

Back on the terrace afterwards, Madame Jouvin chatted with her. She asked a lot of questions, mainly about the ship and her life on it, the other children, and where her parents were. Halka did her best to answer, but she didn't know all the answers. Papa Jouvin was silent. At the evening meal soon after he consumed several glasses of sour-smelling wine. It stained his lips a dull crimson.

After the meal, he and Madame disappeared into the room Robert had named as her study, and Halka heard raised voices. They were out of her translator's range, so she didn't know what they said; but Robert exchanged a glance with her. "Would you like to learn a card game?"

Halka nodded, and Robert brought out some flat cards, and first taught her how to shuffle them. Papa Jouvin came out of the study soon after and marched across to the table, poured himself another glass of wine, and went out on the terrace without a word to either of them. Robert cast a glance after him, caught Halka's eye, and turned back to the game.

Eventually, Halka went to her bedroom. It was strange to sleep alone, though her room was beautifully decorated in pastel shades of yellow. She wondered why human children didn't all sleep in the same room, as the children of her people did. But she dismissed the thought, because it reminded her that she was alone in a strange place. She was very tired, but sleep remained elusive.

After shifting position several times, Halka slipped out of the bed and crossed to the window. It was stuffy in the room, and she was used to a more controlled environment aboard the ship and in the Big Place.

And she missed Kaj, and Chaneg and the other children of her age group. Since the Awakening she'd already had to face the fact that she might never see her parents again, because the humans didn't know where they were either. It was natural for all the children to be together, and she still hadn't got over the shock of the day before, when she'd learned she must live with a human family in a different country.

She pushed the window open with difficulty. It was awkward to hold onto the sill, but her legs were still wobbly. Her room overlooked the palm trees, as Robert called them. They stirred in the breeze from the sea. She saw everything clearly. Even the plants had heat traces.

Halka wondered if Papa Jouvin had gone to bed yet. He was still out on the terrace when she came to bed. She'd seen the heat trace of the wine bottle on the stone flags beside him as he swung to and fro on the metal-framed hammock.

A sound came from upslope. *Perhaps it's an animal,* she thought. The noise repeated a few thousandths later, and again a few thousandths after that. Halka stood poised at the window. Her hands sought the fastenings.

The noise continued at intervals. Halka got back into bed and pulled the cover over her. But the heat in the room was so intense that she had to get out again.

After a while, she thought she heard a cry. There were words then, but her translator couldn't pick them up because they were spoken – snarled, surely? – out of range; but their tone was unmistakable. Contempt.

The noise ceased. Gradually the temperature in the room dropped. Halka fell asleep.

*

Next day.

Robert tapped on Halka's bedroom door. "Breakfast, Halka. You can come out in your dressing gown." He waited for a reply.

None came, but after a moment Halka opened the door, wearing a pink satin dressing gown. The colour gave her dark complexion a rosy tinge. She yawned; she looked tired. Robert supposed it was from travelling so far, and the heat. But she did look steadier on her feet.

He'd dressed already. "Maman enjoys breakfast on the terrace," he told her, "so I thought you might like to as well." He helped her out onto it.

When they reached it, she turned to him. "I thought you said your mother has breakfast here?"

"She gets up early. Papa's still asleep, and I thought I'd let *you* sleep some more."

"Thank you, that's kind…" Halka's eyes looked rounder than ever. "I thought you didn't like me."

Robert looked surprised. "What gave you that idea?"

"I don't know, really." She looked directly at him. "Your mother and the man at the Big Place kept asking me questions, but you don't. I thought perhaps you didn't want me to be here."

Robert stared back at her. "Who is this man that asks you questions?"

"I don't know, Hardy something." Halka spread her hands. "A big man – for a human – with whitish-yellow hair. He scares me a bit."

Robert held eye contact with her to show his attention.

"I don't think Dr Chapaire liked him much," Halka said, "She told him off for asking too many questions."

Robert smiled at that. "You know something, Halka? It's *because* I like you that I don't ask you any questions. I thought you might be fed up with them. Let's go to the beach this morning, before it gets too hot. We can swim in the sea. *Maman* is working, and we'll keep out of Papa's way." He hesitated. "He gets a bit...impatient with me at times." He sat down at the table and reached for a croissant. "Do you like spread on bread?"

"Yes. We Zarduthi have to be able to digest most things, so we have a special organ, called a *zosa,* to help us digest most things."

"Oh, that's interesting." He broke the croissant in half and smeared spread on it with a knife, just as she'd been shown at the Big Place, then passed it across on a plate. "Try some jam?" Robert pushed the pot in her direction. "It's not allowed on the ration cards, but you can get it in the market if you know where to ask. Or you can make your own." He watched her lift the spoon out of the pot, stare at it, move her head closer to sniff it, look to see if he had any, and finally replace the spoon. "Coffee?"

"Thank you." Halka looked troubled for a moment. "Robert, did you hear a noise last night?"

Robert looked up from his croissant. "What – what kind of a noise?"

"I don't know – I heard it in the night. I was a bit scared."

Robert's hands trembled as he put a spoonful of jam on the croissant. He took a deep breath. "I didn't hear anything," he said. "Perhaps you imagined it... You had a tiring day yesterday."

*

Reception Centre, an hour later.

"*Why* must I leave here?" Ayar demanded. "Why can't I stay *here* with my friends? Why couldn't we *all* have stayed here?"

Karak Chapaire looked embarrassed. "I know, Ayar," she said. "It will be difficult for you. Believe me, I would rather have all of you here together –"

"So that you can carry on *studying* us, as you put it?" he interrupted.

Karak Chapaire ignored the anger in his tone, and spread her hands. "But Ayar, how can I help all of you get strong and fit again, and how can I help if you become ill, if I don't know how your body works? And besides, I have not hurt you in any way, have I?"

Ayar slumped onto the side of the bed. He rested his chin on one hand and felt shame at his outburst – and its failure.

"No-o," he said. "You haven't hurt any of us." The scanners hadn't hurt at all, and there had been no physical cruelty. He supposed the needles used to sample his blood had only hurt as much as those for the Long Sleep, or a kraz-yal at clan-claiming.

Nine of his friends were still here. They had scans today,

and physio, but families would soon claim all of them, too. They used the teaching computers in the centre to pick up background information about this world and its ways.

"Let *me* stay here and you can study me, and the others can go back to the ship –"

"Not possible, I am afraid, Anyway," Karak Chapaire said, "And the Petrushenkos will be here any minute, so if you could get your things together –" A tone played from the office. "Excuse me. That is probably them now." She hurried to answer the summons.

For several thousandths Ayar stared at the door after she left the room. His stomach churned. Then he leant down with great reluctance to pull his clean clothes from the locker beside his bed.

"Hello, Ayar," a man's voice said.

He straightened when he realised someone watched him nearby, and glanced round. The man was tall, for a human – not as tall as him, but the woman with him was shorter than Karak Chapaire. They watched him as if their life depended on him. A girl stood beside them.

Ayar's gaze lingered on her. She was tiny, with a pert little nose, and she regarded him with what he read as curiosity. Her eyes were a deep silver-grey, but her hair was almost the same shade as Hardy Brencher's. *She's prettier than Yin Leng or Karak Chapaire,* Ayar thought. "Hello," he said with great reluctance. His translator turned the word into Russian.

"This is Commander Alexei Petrushenko, his wife Irina, and their daughter, Natalya," Karak Chapaire said.

Ayar's heart gave a leap, and started to pound. *Commander? Perhaps he has a military background –*

His gaze moved from Natalya to her father, alighted on Irina, then returned to Natalya. He listened and hoped to learn something useful as Karak Chapaire spoke, but the information was mundane.

"Commander Petrushenko will take you to live at his home. You will go to school with Natalya, though it is unlikely you will be in the same class." Karak Chapaire pushed his clothes into his backpack from the ship as she spoke. She didn't mention the weapons in it. "Talk to Natalya while I explain some things to her parents." She turned and led them into the office, and the lock clicked to behind her.

Ayar gave Natalya another once-over. "I don't want to go to your home," he said, though this time he managed to keep his tone polite. "I know it's not your fault, and that your father's following orders, but I don't think I should leave the other children. Some of them are quite young."

Natalya's eyes opened wide. "Ayar, my *father* may just be following orders, but *I've* always wanted a brother and I'm glad to have one at last." She sat on the bed beside him. "I *want* you to come and live with us."

Ayar looked sideways at her. *Does she mean this?*

"Please." Her brows lifted again and her eyes opened wide again. "You'll like our new apartment. When Dad was chosen to foster you he told JSEP we'd need to move so you could have your own room, and the new apartment is lovely. It overlooks Yeltsin Park. We moved in three days ago –"

"I don't want to go to school, though," Ayar interrupted. "I'm too old for that."

"How old *are* you, Ayar?"

"Old enough to fight for the clan. At least, I was fourteen when our parents left the ship, and I've reached full height since then, so I must be an adult now." He thrust out his lower lip and added, "I wish I could have gone with them."

Natalya watched him for a moment, then smiled in a way that made her silvery eyes glimmer. "Perhaps there's a reason why you were meant to stay behind," she suggested. "How old is adult for you?"

"Fifteen."

"That's young! We're considered adult at eighteen."

"We Zarduthi have refined ourselves so as to perform our primary functions to the optimum efficiency."

"Genetic engineering, you mean?"

"Of course."

Natalya looked thoughtful. "And perhaps a year for your people is longer than one of ours."

"Maybe."

"Don't you know?"

"Well, I..." Ayar squirmed into a new position on the side of the bed, but it didn't alter his inner discomfort. Natalya was tiny, but he felt at a distinct disadvantage beside her.

"See, that's why you need to go to school!" she laughed, though her tone wasn't unkind.

"I meant – I don't *know* how one of your years compares to one of ours. And going to school won't tell me that."

"It might, in time. Anyway, I thought Dad said they don't know how long you were asleep. You might have missed *lots* of schooling. And where else would you find out the difference between our years and yours?"

"The ship," Ayar said. "But they won't let me go back to it. Mr Brencher said I couldn't go." Behind him there came the sudden click of a lock. Ayar turned.

"Are you ready, Ayar, Natalya?" Karak Chapaire bustled through from her office. Behind her Ayar glimpsed the shadowy figures of the adult Petrushenkos.

"I'm not going," he said.

Karak Chapaire put her hands on her hips. "You must, Ayar. I will get into trouble if you do not go, and men like our dear Monsieur Brencher will come here and make you. It would be better to walk out of here than be carried, *n'est-ce pas*?" She paused. "I do not understand why you do not want to go where you can be with someone of your age group –"

"But not of my clan. The younger ones should have someone to speak for them," Ayar interrupted.

"Have no fear, Ayar. I will do that."

He gazed at her. "You…will?"

"Josie and I – and even Monsieur Brencher – we will not let harm come to any of you. We are all on your side, Ayar, even though it may not always seem that way. We will help however we can."

He felt a hand on his arm to propel him towards the office. He turned.

Natalya had picked up his backpack from the ship. "This is heavy!"

"It is time, Ayar. I am sorry." Karak Chapaire did look as if she regretted the need to send him with the Petrushenkos. But almost before Ayar knew it, he was through the door and out of the office, escorted by Commander Petrushenko on one side and Natalya and Irina on the other. They went past the small garden under the windows and across ground baked and dusty under the relentless glare of the afternoon sun. He blinked and narrowed his eyelids to reduce the incoming light.

The air was like syrup, still and laden with dust and unfamiliar smells. The horizon stretched into a haze, and it struck Ayar how large a planet was by comparison to the clanship. He thrust his hands into his pockets and set his shoulders back in an effort to banish his disquiet. *There was no time to say anything,* he thought, *and no chance...*

They approached the car. Ayar had seen this type of vehicle through the wide windows of the dormitory on one wall each time one of the children had been taken away. Inside sat a man in a uniform similar to Commander Petrushenko's, but black instead of dark blue.

"The car will take us to the airport, and we'll fly to Russia," Alexei told him. Ayar hesitated, then got in when he saw the Commander climb into the front passenger seat. Natalya and Irina got in, one on either side of him. Natalya's leg was warm against his.

He turned back to look at the building behind them, where a light-haired figure stood outside and waved. Then the growl of the vehicle increased, he felt movement, and the figure became smaller. Soon distance made Karak Chapaire's figure seem shadowy and unreal. Ayar felt alone.

Natalya put her hand over his. "So – don't you have to go to school on the ship?" she asked.

"No."

"How do you learn, then?"

"Using computers, of course – like you do."

Irina asked, "But don't you have to learn to share things, and how to get on with other people?"

Ayar listened to her voice. It sounded much deeper than Natalya's. "We all live together all the time, so we pick that up naturally."

"Ah." Irina settled back against the seat.

"Is it far to the...airport?" Ayar asked her.

"An hour's drive. Relax."

Ayar leaned back and tried to do just that, though there wasn't enough leg room, and after a few hundredths his shins ached. He watched the scrubby vegetation speed by and compared this method of travel to the clanship, when star positions would change only slowly until the ship entered hyperspace. Then there would be a soft double percussion, after which, if they'd travelled far enough, the simtank would show a different view of space.

It only occurred to him that he'd dozed when a touch on his shoulder brought him awake again. "Where are we?" he asked.

"The jet's over there." Alexei gestured.

The car approached a grey metal construction. The whine of its engines penetrated the car as they drew closer. Ayar pressed fingers over his ears in an effort to screen out the sounds, aware that he still needed to hear instructions.

"Too loud?" asked Irina.

"My hearing's very acute."

"It'll be quieter onboard. And if not, I'm sure the staff could find you some earplugs."

The car stopped and they got out, Ayar with his knuckles pressed into his ears in a vain attempt to keep the noise out. He felt a hand under his elbow as Alexei hurried him up the steps into the jet. Irina and Natalya followed.

Inside, the noise reduced to a distant whisper. It was cool. There were several rows of seats upholstered in black fabric, with red straps, probably a safety harness. Ayar relaxed as the pressure faded from his tympanic membranes, more so when he saw the windows. He could see the ground through them. He didn't resist when Alexei pushed him into a seat beside one of the windows. Natalya sat beside him and showed him how to fasten the seatbelts.

"Who are the spare seats for?" Ayar asked.

"This is a military jet," Alexei said. "We're waiting for our driver, so some seats will be empty." He leaned back in his seat across the gangway and smiled. "I don't usually have such a luxurious trip home on leave – I mostly have to catch a public airbus."

"You work for an army?" Ayar asked. "I thought you must work for JSEP."

"I do. I command a colony supply ship. We make regular trips to settlements on the Moon and Mars. I did military service for seven years, then transferred to the space section and got my space pilot's licence when the Committee for Colonisation and Resettlement was set up. I've been there ever since."

"You're a pilot?"

Alexei dipped his head.

"That's what I wanted to train to be," Ayar confided, "though I suppose your ships must be different from ours."

Alexei nodded again. "Yes," he said. "I salvaged your ship and brought it back to Earth."

Ayar was surprised. "Can we talk about that later?" he said.

Alexei nodded. "Sure."

At that moment the driver entered the cabin and sat down near Alexei and Irina.

"Screen on," Alexei murmured. "Latest news." The small screen set into the back of the seat before him lit up. "We might as well make the most of this." Irina looked out of the window on his other side.

A burst of noise came from the screen. Ayar laid fingers across each ear again, but Alexei pulled wires from an aperture at the side of the screen. They were connected to plugs which he pushed into his ears. The noise ceased.

But the noise from the engines increased. Ayar felt the jet's movement. He looked out of the window and watched the airport buildings race by. A sudden shaft of fear pierced him. *I'm going to live far away from the Big Place and the other children.*

He took a deep breath and turned to Natalya. "Tell me about your – country?" he said. There was more room between the seats in the aircraft, so he stretched his legs out in relief. The extra room gave him no excuse to sit as close to Natalya as in the car.

"What do you want to know? It's just where I live, so it's hard to describe."

"Is there ever fighting there?"

"Not usually, though in the south some people are trying to create a breakaway state – they have been for years."

"Why?"

Natalya considered this for a couple of thousandths. "They don't like the population laws and want to set up a country without them," she said.

"Population laws?"

"Yes."

Ayar listened while Natalya explained that it was illegal to have more than one child, an offence punishable in every country on Earth by extra taxation. "The world population became huge, and a lot of low-lying agricultural land was lost to climate change. There were famines in Africa, Asia, Russia and China. Our country was poor for its size, with industrial areas unusable from pollution. We couldn't produce enough food. Survival required population reduction."

"So to avoid these laws they have to set up their own country?" he asked.

"The World Constitution says that while all countries should retain their national identities, they're all subject to the population and pollution laws, the trade treaties and the leadership of the World Senate. All these agreements were set up so that no one country had benefits over and above any other."

"So is a breakaway state illegal?"

Natalia nodded. "Especially the way they do it. A bomb at the Trade Conference in St Petersburg last week killed or injured several people. They postponed the conference." She pointed with a tiny, white finger at her father. "I think that's what Dad's watching the news for."

"Why did they bomb it?"

"They're opposed to technology. They blame it for climate change."

"Climate change?"

"It's caused weather and many other problems on Earth. It goes back to the use of fossil fuels to build our technology, a century or more ago."

"But all civilisations have those limits imposed on them. If you can't get past the carbon ceiling, you can't make progress in technology. If you can't make progress in technology, you can't find a way to do without the carbon."

"Neatly summed up!" Natalya cast a glance at her father, who was still engrossed in the news, then turned back to Ayar. "So…you might be in sympathy with the Neoluddites, then?"

"I don't know enough about them for that."

"They're opposed to the Population Laws, IVF, stem cell research, organ transplants and limb regrowth research, most modern health advances –"

"That's – how does Mr Brencher say it? Cutting off your nose to spite your face. How can it be bad to make people healthier? If they live longer they can contribute more to their community."

"Oh. I hadn't thought of it that way." She paused. "I suppose the idea of countries sounds weird to you?"

"Some of the planets we visited had similar ideas."

"Oh. Is it only Zarduthi men that fight?" Natalya asked.

"We all do. You know, it'll take me a while to learn the ways of your world." Ayar sighed and looked out of the window. The ground was far below them.

*

Upper Richmond Road Primary School, half an hour later.

Ronnie felt important. The other children watched him as he told them how the alien boy had come to their house. It felt good to get so much attention.

"Huh! I don't believe you," Annie Vereker spat. "The

others can if they want." She turned and skipped away. "Just because your dad works for JSEP, you think you can tell a load of lies!"

Ronnie watched her from beneath half-closed lids. Sunlight made a brown blur of his lashes. He'd never liked Annie.

"Yeah, but he's not even your *real* dad," someone else called out. "My mum said so."

The others in his class never let him forget he didn't have a "proper" dad. He wasn't the only one, of course. Half the class were from single-parent families. But where other kids didn't let it bother them, it hurt him every time they mentioned it, because he wished Chas *really* was his dad. He could never think of that without a tug at his heart.

"Never mind that, when will he come to our school?" Billy Kindell's voice was a shrill note above the babble.

"I don't know. He can't speak English on his own yet. He has this thing –" Ronnie raised a hand to his throat.

But Billy interrupted again. "Well, when can we see him?"

"When he's better."

"What's his name?" Boris seemed genuinely interested.

Ronnie stared at the tall black boy in front of him and made a mental comparison. *Miril's almost as dark as Boris, but Boris's skin's smoother, less wrinkled, more like me.* He wasn't ready to reply yet. "Mil," he said at last.

"Mil. That's a funny name."

"Well, he *is* an alien!"

It was strange to think his new brother had arrived only yesterday. Ronnie remembered what Steph had said that morning, that it would be a while before Mil could go to school. *Good,* he thought. *None of the others have a brother from another planet.* He felt a warm glow inside at the understanding of his new-found power.

At the back of his mind he remembered that, the previous night, Mil had had all the attention at home. But here at school, he was king.

He felt better.

CHAPTER 6 – Moving On

Zero, ship's time/date: 406.95.8.74.738 AD, next evening.

THE DESERT STRETCHED IN EVERY DIRECTION as far as the eye could see. But it was the strangest, coldest and darkest desert Omol had ever visited. The night winds ruffled his fur jerkin, plucked at his cropped hair-crest, and scoured his face with sand particles. Lightning seared the darkness from time to time.

He looked back at the straggle of shelters built out of bulkheads and shuttle components. Behind them, the stream flowed from its spring, once more overhung by trees whose foliage drooped into the water, lambent with absorbed heat. Omol wandered over to the streamside.

Underwater, a forest of watergrass waved languid purple leaves in the current, their red stripes invisible in thermal vision mode. Water snails in shades of magenta and purple clung to the leaves. Water snakes that glowed fluorescent red and violet wove grazing paths in and out of the foliage fountains as they followed their prey. *We can eat the water snakes and the water snails, but they give us few nutrients for their biomass,* he mused. *Our pre-packed supplies are low, and although some of these animals are edible, the clan could easily starve.*

He reviewed the other edible animals they'd discovered on this planet. Tinglefish and salbut provided good nutrients, but were rare – and tinglefish came equipped with stinging "drapes" that must be removed before cooking. The other animals the game team had discovered so far were the six-legged vilnossi – a burrowing land reptile which was delicious roasted – and sandstars. These last were seven-armed, and undulated across the dunescape using suckers. Everyone enjoyed their delicate flavour.

We must get a message off-planet, he thought. *We can't survive here much longer, especially if the grove spreads. But for that, the shuttle must be functional.*

Ahead, the hump of a dune half-exposed the last remaining shuttle – his own. There was no guarantee that its engines would work at all; the sand had probably damaged them. It worked its way into everything, between layers of clothing, into eyes, mouths, ears – and any fold of skin.

The desert surface shimmered back at him, as if it questioned his very existence. He was aware of his insignificance against the dome of the sky. High in the atmosphere, the brown dwarf's aurorae danced and writhed in the sky, in blue, red and green, as magnetic fields from the failed star interacted with particles from the planet. Stars, denizens of the galaxy, glittered like short-circuiting sparks.

The lurid beauty of the night spoke to him. *We're all going to die here, and there's nothing I can do about it.* In truth, Ghaneem's death, and that of the people on her shuttle with her, had sucked the heart out of him. Omol felt a sudden gust of anger. He kicked the sand of planet Zero, saw it lift in the breeze, then fall back on the surface, as much a prisoner of this world as he was.

Ghaneem's had been the first shuttle they'd used to build shelters, once they'd found a suitable location. As they'd taken it apart, piece by piece, so they'd found another cause of the crash: damage to the fuel feed as they left the *Kazid.*

At least I know it wasn't her fault, Omol thought, as he had on numerous occasions. *I am proud of her, and honour her memory –*

But that vindication made him miss her all the more bitterly. He tucked the thought and its slender comfort back into a corner of his mind, and concentrated on the reason he'd braved the sting of the night winds. He watched the patterns they made in the sand. The desert glared back at him, enigmatic and ever-changing. *I'd better hurry,* he thought. *A storm's brewing.*

His boots parted the sand more quickly. In just thousandths he reached the lee of the dune that partly covered the shuttle, opened the only exposed door – whose mirror surface reflected the brilliant colours of the aurorae – and stepped inside.

It was darker than ever in the cabin; even his thermal vision could detect no shred of warmth. Omol felt his way to the pilot's console and his fingers sought the lighting controls. The reactor was intact; the cabin and cockpit lights came up at his touch on the button.

Individual sand grains piled against the cockpit ports. But a touch here and there on the instrument panel brought one system up after another. Omol squashed down his excitement and hoped it would serve them again, if they cleared the sand carefully.

The airlock door slid open again as Tangar trod sand inside in Omol's wake. "Thought you might need some company."

"Maybe," he admitted with a smile. "We should try to find another water source before we die of thirst. Didn't you run some scans of the surface for water when we came here?"

"Yes, as we came in. I collated the information from the other shuttles, though we didn't cover the whole planet –"

"Let's review everything we have."

Tangar settled himself into the nav position. He ran fingers over the controls and booted up the computer. "Here." He skipped to the relevant file.

The results were disappointing. The images showed a few streams, mountain areas, occasional outcrops of bedrock, groves of Thirsty trees, and the oceans, but little else. When they'd looked through them, he asked Tangar to check them again. "There must be *some* water and metallic resources," he muttered.

"This planet orbits a brown dwarf," Tangar pointed out. "Water scarcity and low metallicity are a feature of such planets."

"True, but…" Omol faced Tangar. "Night-time surveys might give us a better chance of finding something useful. Infrared images would give us more information, and we might find somewhere without the trees. We might even find minerals."

"It's worth a try," Tangar said.

"In the meantime, bearing in mind the lack of resources, I should call a meeting and ask everyone to avoid pregnancies until we leave here. And it might be a long time before we can leave."

"In the circumstances that seems the best course of action," Tangar agreed.

*

The Lawtons' apartment, Richmond, next day (1st October, 2094).

Miril was in the aircraft again. He looked out of the window at the fluffy white things they flew through. This wasn't like anything he'd ever seen before. It didn't relate to his life at the Big Place, or to the fog of memories from before the Sleep Room.

Where are my parents now? What happened to them? Why weren't they there when we all woke up at the Big Place? Who took them away?

He stared into the white stuff and played a game. He imagined the faces of his friends Kaj, Chaneg, and Halka, and his sister Davan. Images replaced the other children's faces. Himself as a baby. As a toddler. As an older boy – as he imagined he might look.

But when he looked closer, none of the images had his

face.

Every face in the clouds was the face of one of these "humans".

He stirred and cried out in panic. "Thughs marzh-hee?"

Who am I?

He reached a sweat-soaked hand out above the cover. His fingers touched silky fabric instead of a transparent sleepcase. The fabric had little ridges on it, raised threads that ran up and across. He opened his eyes. Sweat cooled on his face.

Miril watched the room come back into focus and forgot his nightmare. *I'm safe in this warm place,* he told himself. *Nothing will hurt me.* His eyelids closed. He turned on his side, slowly and with difficulty, sighed and drifted back into sleep.

*

3.30 pm.

"Mum, I'm home!"

"I'm in here, Ronnie."

Ronnie entered the physio room cautiously. Mil was propped up on Steph's physio couch, wearing long black trousers and a bright blue sweatshirt. His smile revealed gaps between his oval teeth.

Ronnie looked back at him uncertainly. Steph sat on the carpet to read him a story. She stopped after each sentence for Mil's translator to catch up. She looked up and smiled at Ronnie. "I'll make you something to eat when I've finished the story. Go and get changed."

Ronnie felt as if she was telling him off, but he went to his room anyway and did as he was told. As soon as he'd walked into the apartment, that good feeling he'd had all day had gone away. The place smelled strange.

I don't like it.

When he came back, Steph had finished reading to Mil.

The alien boy's eyes were closed and he breathed evenly, so Ronnie thought he was asleep. *He sleeps a lot...* "Mum! Where's my tea?" he asked loudly.

Mil didn't stir.

"Shush! Come in the lounge." Steph's grip on his shoulder was firm, her mouth a straight line. "Listen to me! I told you yesterday that Mil needs to sleep a lot. You must be quieter so he can sleep."

"But I want him to *play* with me!"

"He's not well enough yet. Give him time. Otherwise he won't like it here, and he'll have to go to another family."

"What, leave us?"

"Yes. Maybe go back to America." Steph put out a hand and stroked Ronnie's fair hair back from his face. "Give him time and he'll be able to play with you."

Chas put his head round the door. "I'll take Ronnie to the green till the food's ready. Game of football, Ronnie?"

"Yeh!" Ronnie was so eager he forgot to be quiet again.

"Come on." Chas stood in the doorway. He threw the football up in the air and caught it again.

Ronnie hugged Steph's waist for a moment, then followed Chas.

*

After tea.

Miril dreamed again. Everything was as jumbled up as usual. Memory mingled with dream like embracing twins.

Kaj was bigger than him. He towered over Miril and leant down to grab his hand and pull him upright. "Come on – let's practice fighting!"

The fierce invitation awoke an urge in Miril. He stumbled upright and tried to reach for the older boy's face. His fingers uncurled and he slashed. But the older boy was tall, and steadier on his feet than Miril was. He felt himself fall.

He tumbled through time itself. But the motion was always in tune with the thrum of the ship's drive. *Grrrum! Grrrum! Grrrum...*

That engine was surely his own heartbeat...

*

The Bekel, *Galatea Station, 2nd October, 2094.*

"*What?*" Eddie Harkness felt his face grow hot.

"Is it that much to ask? Some families give up the equivalent of several years' pay to have an extra child, and you won't even have to do that. You'll get an extra allowance for taking him." Terry Mellows gazed back at Eddie. "This project's too important to fail. You know as well as I do that we're onto something really new here. But we had to reorganise the placements due to that Neoluddite mole at the Reception Centre."

"I know." Eddie leant back in his chair and sighed. "But you've got to remember, Juli's about to have our own baby. It's not reasonable to ask her to take on another child at the same time, *and* an alien at that. I don't think she'll be happy about it." Eddie wasn't happy about it either. "There won't be much spare time once the baby arrives."

Mellows waved a hand towards the videophone. "Call her. Ask her what she thinks. You're due for paternity leave in the next few days, so we'll bring your jobshare in on a temporary basis as planned. Then you can have extra time with your wife when the baby's born, and time with the boy as well."

"That's more of a working vacation than paternity leave, isn't it?"

"You...could look at it that way."

"I was under the impression that paternity leave gave new parents time to bond with their baby, but you want me to find out about Kaj's ship during that time. No chance to bond with either the baby *or* Kaj." Eddie was angry that his boss had commandeered the only chance he had to have a baby.

"Eddie, we *need* that information about the ship. You've been working on the drive control circuit, but you can't get there fast enough. This seemed like a good way to get around that."

"It's true that trying to find the drive control circuit is a slow process," Eddie said. "If we rush it we could make stupid mistakes that cause further problems. Everything's got built-in redundancy, so it takes forever to take anything apart. The Zarduthi certainly know how to build things to last." He paused. "I suppose if the boy could help it would be useful, though I'm not sure how ethical –"

Mellows waved his hands in a gesture of dismissal. "You misunderstand my meaning," he said. "Kaj Kalinga is an older child who intends to become an engineer. Ethics needn't come into it – he'll probably be glad to help. Ethics may mean little to these people. They probably have no idea of them at all – certainly not human ones." He smiled like a shark.

Eddie paid attention as Mellows spoke again. "Kaj needs a home as much any of them, and *we* need to know about the ship. You could help us to kill two birds with one stone. Get him to trust you. When you come back from leave you'll probably know what you need to know to complete the job." He shook his head and leaned forwards. The smile vanished. The points of cold light in his eyes glinted back at Eddie. "We need that information. And *you* need a job."

"Is this a threat?"

"You...could look at it that way," Mellows agreed, a chill edge to his voice.

Eddie suppressed the urge to shiver. *I've worked with this guy for seven years. And all that time I never realised what a scheming, manipulative bastard he is!*

Nevertheless, he took the holophone Mellows pushed across the desk to him.

*

Neoluddite safe house, Moscow, same day.

Per Lakshar sipped his mug of tea as he checked his e-mails. One caught his eye. He opened it and scanned it. His gaze went first to the attached news bulletin transcript.

'NURSE ARRESTED FOR ESPIONAGE', the *Daily Citizen* headline ran. 'A woman has been arrested for crimes against the Joint Space Exploration Program (JSEP) whilst in their employment,' he read, 'and is expected to stand trial for leaking classified information about the provisions JSEP made for the socialisation and education of alien children to the Neoluddites, of which she was a member.'

The bulletin contained material posted on a site well-known for leaked material of an embarrassing or classified nature. But a Neoluddite analyst had found this article. The leak had had consequences. 'The arrest has led JSEP to switch the children's placements,' he read.

That means we need to find out where they've gone, Per thought. *I need to despatch someone else to find that out.*

And he had just the person in mind. "Grigori? Get me Exio Calendra. I have a job for him. Oh, and tell him I need him to follow up that feasibility study, too."

*

3rd October, 2094.

Hardy walked into Edith Chapaire's office, a grin on his face.

"Oh. It is *you!*" Edith heard the lack of enthusiasm in her voice quite clearly. She couldn't help it. "I suppose you have come for the report?"

"Yes. President Langrishe asked me to collect it in person."

Edith clenched one hand inside her jacket pocket. She'd guessed at the start of Project Revive that he knew she disliked him, and it amused him. "Have a seat while I get it," she said. She turned, walked through the door into the corridor, and approached her storage facility. Once she looked behind her to see if he'd followed, but it looked as if he'd taken her invitation to stay in the office to heart.

When she reached the metal door she looked around again. Hardy hadn't followed her. She was slightly concerned as she'd seen him look at things on her desk in the past. A*nd he did not even have the grace to blush!*

She pressed her handprint against the scanplate, the door opened and she entered. Blood thundered against her temples. The room was just a cupboard, about 3 metres in length, lined with shelves from floor to ceiling. The shelves contained refrigerated tissue and blood sample storage along its length on both sides. Opposite the door a series of file-cases hugged the wall. She wiped sweating palms down her jacket and stepped towards the file-cases.

She logged the memory drive's removal and slipped it into her pocket. She dared not think of Langrishe's reaction were he to discover that she had duplicated the information it contained onto all the report drives. *But if the children become ill, how will the foster parents know if it's serious?* She clamped down on that thought, returned to the corridor, let the door swing to behind her, and re-engaged the alarm. Then she returned to the office.

Hardy was seated where she'd left him, but she noticed his thoughtful expression. She laid the drive on the table.

"That it?" He jerked a thumb at it.

"Yes. I will need a receipt," she said, and brandished the

scanner.

"Fine. Where do I sign?"

He's unusually co-operative today, Edith thought. She passed him the scanner. "I have already filled in the details, as I knew you were coming," she said. "As you say, all you have to do is sign."

"This the only copy?"

"Of course," she replied, "other than mine. My work will continue." She marvelled at the steadiness of her voice.

"Naturally." Hardy squiggled a signature on the tablet and handed it back to Edith. "Now, the memory drive."

She handed it to him.

"Thanks." He pocketed it, but made no move to leave.

Edith wondered why he hadn't left. *He probably hopes to speak to Josie,* she thought. It hadn't escaped her notice that Hardy liked her. "I'm so sorry, Monsieur Brencher, you will have to excuse me now – I expect Eddie Harkness to arrive at any minute."

"Fine. Let's hope his foster-family can get more information out of Kaj than I could." Hardy stood up. "See you around...Edith."

Edith's lips tightened. "Good day, Monsieur Brencher," she said. Ice crystals made her voice sound brittle.

Hardy just grinned again.

*

Later that morning.

Edith watched the door close after Hardy, then sighed. She was about to go into the dormitory when the external door alarm sounded. She hurried to answer it.

A tall man, heavy-set, with brown hair stood on the threshold, accompanied by a JSEP marine. "Dr Edith Chapaire? Eddie Harkness," he said, and held out his hand. "I've been sent to –"

Edith shook his hand. "To collect Kaj," she finished for him. "I have been expecting you. Please come in." She stood aside for them to enter.

"Do you need identification?" Eddie asked.

"A handscan," she murmured, with a nod. "Please...come this way."

Eddie followed her along the corridor and back into her office with its two couches.

"Edwin Harkness, Mr," She told the office computer, then turned to Eddie. "Please place your hand on the scanplate."

Eddie did as she asked.

[Identity confirmed,] said the computer.

Edith repeated the identification procedure with the marine, then ushered them along another corridor into the dormitory. "Kaj is working on the computeach right now," she said. "I am pleased he will have a home at last –"

"Don't get me wrong, lady," Eddie interrupted. "It wasn't my idea. My wife's baby is due tomorrow –"

She halted by the door to the dormitory. "Ah! How delightful."

"What I mean is, I'm following orders."

"As were all the others."

"You mean – all the kids' are being exploited like this? Then there's no need for me –"

"I do not know what you mean about exploitation," Edith told him. "I hope the children will not be exploited. They have so much to contend with as it is."

"Of course." Eddie's voice was a low murmur.

"Monsieur Harkness, I understand you are an engineer. Kaj will be interested to hear this."

Eddie nodded and shifted his weight from one foot to the other. He looked uncomfortable. "He will?" he asked.

"Oh, but *certainement.*" Edith inclined her head. "Let us go in." She placed her hand on the scanplate set into the door before them. It opened and Eddie followed her in.

Rows of single beds stripped of their bedding lined the room. Only two were made up. They walked through the dormitory. Ahead, another door stood open. Edith gestured towards it. "Kaj is through here."

The next room was empty of everything but a few workstations, and a couch with a coffee table in front of it. A figure sat on the couch and read a book with such concentration, it didn't even look up.

And before one workstation another figure sat, absorbed in the screen before it. Edith wondered if this was the last time she would see him.

"Kaj?"

The boy looked up.

Eddie looked back at him.

Eyes as round as a lemur's pooled black in the shadows at this side of the room. Kaj's skin was purplish-brown. His nose was short, and nearly bridgeless; his mouth thin-lipped, the colour of purple wine-grapes. A luxuriant mat of glossy black hair sprang from the centre of his forehead and smoothed itself back over his hair-crest. From the bare scalp protruded lobeless, oval ears. Kaj had no eyebrows, but fine down covered his face, the arms exposed by his T-shirt, and the backs of his hands. The scars on his bare arms were only visible now in the glow from the computer monitor that reflected off the pale, shiny marks, where the down was absent. "Kaj, this is Eddie Harkness, whose family you will live with."

Kaj stared from Edith to Eddie, nodded and turned back to the computer.

Edith Chapaire watched Kaj and tried to gauge his reactions. "Kaj is very good at using computers."

Eddie turned to look at her. "Does he speak English?" he asked.

"Why don't you ask *me*?" Kaj said. He didn't look round from the screen.

"I see you do," Eddie murmured.

"Do I *have* to leave?" Kaj asked, turning to Edith.

"I am afraid so, Kaj."

"Davan will be alone, then."

"Davan will only be here till tomorrow," she said. "JSEP will close the Reception Centre, though Josie and I will be based here, and Monsieur Brencher will be here some of the time. Your foster-parents can still contact us here for advice."

Kaj sucked his lower lip inside his mouth and clamped his upper lip firmly over it.

Edith had realised some time ago that this was a sign of concentration. "Eddie is an engineer. His wife is having a baby tomorrow," she told him. "I am sure you will enjoy living with them."

"Engineer?" Kaj looked directly at Eddie for the first time, eyes opened wider than a human's. Edith noticed again the fine black eyelashes that protruded from his partly-retracted lids. *So similar to us, yet so different. Convergent evolution. Similar organisms evolve to occupy similar ecological niches, and develop similar features for similar purposes.* Her attention returned to the conversation.

"I – build spaceships."

"I think perhaps I'd like to do that."

"Your English is *very* good," Eddie remarked. "Can you read and write too?"

"Of course. Edith and Yin Leng taught me." Kaj turned to Edith. "Must we leave now?"

Edith nodded. "We will send the software on so you can continue using the computeach as well as attending school. Pack up your things, now, while Monsieur Harkness and I have another word together. We will collect you in a few minutes' time." She turned back to Eddie. "I will take you to meet Josie Carter."

Eddie followed her back through the dormitory. She closed the door after her with a distinct click.

"Kaj and the other child are the last two?" Eddie asked.

"Yes."

"The children are kept locked up all the time?"

"JSEP's orders." Edith sighed. "For their safety."

"And so they can't escape? Look, Dr Chapaire, I wanted to ask you something about these children," he said. "Is there any chance that they could be aggressive? And what about the dead creature we found on the ship?"

"You know about that?"

"I was one of the original boarding party. Chas and I found the children." Eddie sighed. "I guess that was why they asked me to foster Kaj."

"I see. Keep everything within the family." Edith met his gaze. "I understand your concern about possible aggressive behaviour because of your new baby, but you need not worry. The lab report and DNA profile on the creature shows it is not related to these children. There are similarities between humans and Zarduthi, but none between Zarduthi and the creature." She paused. "If you like, we have not just made contact with one alien species, but two – but the creature was dead. Now come with me." She led him into the adjoining office.

In this room Josie Carter sat at a workstation, and fed information from a notebook to her terminal. She turned as the door opened.

Edith introduced Eddie. "This is Josie Carter, who will visit you every six months to check on the health and general well-being of Kaj." They shook hands.

"Pleased to meet you, Mr. Harkness."

"Eddie, please. You too – Ms Carter? Josie?"

"Yes, please call me by my first name. I'll visit every six months or so. But you can contact me between visits as well, if need be."

"Eddie was concerned about aggression from the children," Edith murmured.

"Oh, I don't think you need worry about that," Josie said. "I'm pleased to say the children are have all settled down well in their new families. They seem more mature than human children would be – though we can't assign exact ages to them. But none of the families have mentioned aggression. And all the children have had social training – body language and so on. I'm sure Kaj will fit in well." She looked at Edith. "Does Eddie know about the monthly reports?"

"Yes," Eddie said, before Edith could reply. "I was told I'd have to do reports each month." He paused. "So you're sure there's no threat to the baby?"

"Certain. And Kaj will enjoy being with a younger child later on – he misses the others. They all grew up together."

"I can understand that."

"Then you'll also understand that he'll need some time to adjust. But I'll come to see all of you in a month's time."

Eddie nodded. "I'll look forwards to our next meeting, then, Josie. Goodbye."

Edith escorted him back to her office. "Wait here, I will bring Kaj to you." She bustled out of the room.

Kaj was ready, his backpack beside him. He'd switched off the computer and gone to sit beside the girl on the couch. His face was expressionless. When he stood up, Edith remembered how tall he was. His movements were graceful where she always felt awkward. "Come, Kaj," she said. "Have you said goodbye to Davan?"

"Yes." He picked up his holdall and followed her. "*Shulai*, Davan." He raised his hand, showing the palm.

"*Shulai*, Kaj." Davan acknowledged him with a palmraise.

When they reached the office she handed the holdall to Eddie. "His belongings are in here," she said, "and also in the backpack. On this memory drive you will find a link to connect you directly with our internet address, as well as the correct file layout." She handed him a USB stick. "You must keep a copy of your reports. They are due on the first of each month. Your wife can complete them while you are on a tour of duty – they will go through an ordinary household computer."

"What if Kaj is ill?"

"Now that they are over their initial difficulties, the children are all incredibly healthy. There is information on the disk," Edith said, "but if it is serious, call me. I will be glad to help."

Eddie accepted the package, then turned to Kaj. "Come on then, son," he said.

Kaj looked surprised for a moment, despite the lack of eyebrows; then he turned to Edith. "Thank you," he said politely. "Please thank Ben and Yin Leng for me, too."

"*Certainement*, I am in touch with them," she said. "Good luck, Kaj." She watched them leave the office.

Edith twisted her mother's engagement ring, which she wore on her right hand. *Now what did he mean by 'exploited'?* she wondered. A chill settled over her shoulders with a butterfly's touch, and she shivered.

*

The Ashrafs' house, Hyderabad, Pakistan, that evening.

"Gosht achcha hai, Davan. Khao!"

The translator told her that she had good meat before her and should eat it up.

Davan stared around the table at the adults and tried to copy them. Her foster parents and five-year-old Saliha used bread to enclose sauce, chunks of meat and vegetables. She broke a piece off. It was different from the bread at the Reception Centre.

She'd arrived at the house some two hours before, with Professor Ashraf and a JSEP marine for escort. Professor Ashraf's wife, Mrs. Jamilah, had welcomed her with a hug and a kiss on both cheeks, while Saliha clapped her hands and jumped up and down in delight at the prospect of having an elder "sister". Davan thought of Miril – *a similar age to Saliha, surely?* Fostered in a land called England, he'd been weak when he left the Reception Centre. She hadn't seen Miril since a tall, pale human had carried him out of the dormitory wrapped in a blanket.

Davan's hand clenched on the strip of bread. It shredded against her talons. *Is Miril even alive?* She looked up to see every gaze on her; Saliha with alarm, and the two adults with concern, on their features.

"Something is wrong?" asked Mrs. Jamilah.

Davan looked at her kindly round face and felt a twisting sensation inside.

"I miss my friends, and most of all my brother," Davan explained. "It isn't anything you've done – you're very kind –" She put the ruined scrap of bread down.

"Oh, it's all strange, isn't it? But you will get used to living here, and learning our ways. It won't be strange forever." Mrs. Jamilah moved to Davan's side and put her arm around her. "Look, I'll show you how to use the bread. It was thoughtless of me to assume you knew. You scoop it up like this, see?" She popped a mouthful into Davan's mouth.

Davan tasted sweetness in the bread and the contrast of hot, bitter spices in the meat sauce. It was unlike any other meal since the Long Sleep, but she liked it. She chewed and swallowed, aware that her situation had dulled her usually healthy appetite. She smoothed a finger over the scars on her arm. Some of the younger children had had problems as they adjusted back to solid food after being fed intravenously for so long. Her brother Miril was the youngest, and had been worst affected.

She brushed the thought of him aside until she could deal with it. "Show me again how you do that," she said to Mrs. Jamilah.

*

After the evening meal, Professor Ashraf wandered into the garden, while his wife led both girls upstairs. In the corner of Mrs Jamilah's sewing room, a collection of plants stood in pots on a large table. Some were made of yellowish brass, and some were a reddish colour. Davan wandered over to look at them.

"What are these made of?" Davan pointed to the red pots.

"Terracotta – a kind of clay," Saliha told her.

At the back of the table, various machines and accessories surrounded another machine with a screen. Davan thought it was a computer.

Mrs Jamilah said, "We can't let you go outside dressed like that," and cast a glance at Davan's bare legs under her knee-length skirt, then reached into a drawer in the table and brought out a bolt of material. It looked bright yellow until the light from the window fell on it and brought out a subtle sparkle with khaki undertones. Mrs Jamilah smoothed it on the table.

A pang went through Davan's stomach. The beauty of the fabric made her long to touch it.

"This is shot silk," Mrs. Jamilah told her. "I *knew* I'd saved it for a special reason – it was waiting for you to arrive!" She smiled.

Davan watched her, and realised she'd fallen among good people, however different their customs were from Zarduthi ways. She stood to let Mrs. Jamilah drape the fabric around her and fold it this way and that. "Yes, yes, I should have enough – although you are tall..."

"We Zarduthi *are* tall folk, Mrs. Jamilah," Davan told her. "I should grow to be two metres tall."

Mrs. Jamilah frowned. "When the time comes, it might be hard to find you a husband then," she murmured. "Our people are not usually so tall."

Davan stared at her in shock. "But I don't want to be married to a human, Mrs. Jamilah."

"It's the President's wish, when you're old enough."

Davan's mouth opened, but for a thousandth her anger drove any words away. Then she drew her lips together, and the argument she needed came. "Who is this President who thinks he can control everything about me? Perhaps there *isn't* a human who would want to be married to a Zarduthi. But also, Zarduthi women might not want to marry humans!"

"Perhaps not," Mrs. Jamilah agreed. "We need not worry about that now. I will take your measurements," she said. "I will make you a beautiful *salwar-kameez* so you can go to school with Saliha and the girls of your age."

Davan and Saliha watched as she took measurements with a laser probe plugged into the machine.

"Oh, you're so thin!" Mrs Jamilah exclaimed. "I'll have to feed you up a bit." Then she frowned. "Davan, do Zarduthi women have breasts?"

"Ah, Dr Chapaire explained about this. No, we aren't mammals like humans."

Mrs. Jamilah seated herself and sketched a design onscreen with an electronic stylus. Davan rested her hands on the back of Mrs. Jamilah's chair and watched over her shoulder in fascination as she fed the fabric into the slot at the base of the machine. It was ejected at the other side, cut into shapes.

Davan couldn't imagine what kind of a garment they would form. "How can you do all this?" Davan asked. "We trade for such things – please teach me how to do this!"

"I was Senior Cutter and Designer in a clothing company before I married," Mrs. Jamilah answered with a smile. "This was my leaving present. Now I only need to sew it up. Watch. Later, I will teach you both."

The two girls sat on the bed and watched. Mrs. Jamilah laid the silken shapes on the table, then swung another machine forward and fed the fabric through. The machine ejected the first seamed sections just thousandths later. It had stitched and sealed all the seams at once. Davan's new outfit was soon completed.

"Let's see what this looks like on you, shall we?" Mrs. Jamilah said.

Davan stripped off her t-shirt and skirt, eager to see how she'd look in her new outfit.

Mrs Jamilah pulled the trousers up around Davan's waist and tightened the drawstring, made from a strip of the fabric. Then she pulled the *kameez* over her head. It had a pleated bib-front with three buttons placed in a diagonal asymmetric line. Mrs. Jamilah tied the attached sashes into a bow at the back, and led her to a mirror in the corner of the room.

Davan gasped at the difference. She seemed taller, even slimmer, and more grown up.

"You look wonderful," Saliha said, and hugged her. "I'm so happy to have a sister!"

"Yes. The colour suits you very well," Mrs. Jamilah said, "and if you grew your hair you'd blend in easily." She led Davan to the window and pointed. "Look, do you see that plant there? That is forsythia." She looked back at Davan. "See? Your *salwar kameez* is the colour of forsythia blooms."

A breeze ruffled the yellow-clad branches beneath the window.

In the distance, Davan thought she heard a door slam. She trembled, but wasn't sure why.

CHAPTER 7 – Tournament

Kazid *Shuttle 4, Zero, ship's time/date: 406.156.5.52.394 AD (3rd October, 2094).*

AS THE SHUTTLE SWOOPED OVER THE SKYLINE, Omol scanned the terrain ahead through the cockpit window. And then he saw it.

In a canyon between two mountain ranges lay the area they'd noticed as the shuttles came in to land on Zero. Huge towers pierced multi-coloured sand and raised their heads as high as the mountains that flanked them. There must have been close to a hundred, silhouetted against the dim sky.

Omol had seen similar formations before on many worlds. He circled over the area above the towers, fascinated. These had subtle shades the same colours as the multi-coloured sand they pierced: reds, yellows, browns, purples, and violets, greens, and blues. "Look, Tangar!" he said. "It's spectacular."

"It is," Tangar agreed.

"We'll have to come back in what passes for daylight," Omol said. "I'll scan for water first."

There was a powerful response to his scanner command. *There must be a stream or spring here,* he thought, *but its location's not obvious.*

He switched the scan to look for metallic resources in the area. He heard the ascending whistle that indicated the presence of metals. When he ran a spectrographic analysis, he was rewarded with many lines. "Tangar, there are metals here!" he exclaimed.

"Which ones?"

"Various." He put the petrographic analysis programme to work, and within a few thousandths it had identified seven elements. “Iron, copper, nickel, titanium aluminium, scandium, and yttrium – ideal for a replacement satellite. There may be others.”

“Try the water analysis again,” Tangar suggested. “I can see openings in the towers, like caves. See?” He pointed. “Omol – could we live here in relative comfort and safety?”

“Perhaps, if there *is* an aquifer there,” Omol said. “It sounds promising, but the best way to find out what’s down there would be to drill a borehole. Maybe several – till we find the water.”

“Then let’s do that, once we’ve assessed the rocks. That way we’ll know what conditions to expect and what specialist equipment we’d need. We can 3-D print or use the synth machines to make what we need if we don’t have a drill in stock.”

*

Neoluddite safe house, Moscow, next day.

“Show me that list Zanaida sent.”

Per Lakshar handed Grigori a memory drive, which he plugged into his tablet. He selected a file and opened it. “Let’s see where the placements fit into JSEP.” A tree diagram appeared in the projection tank. One by one, the placements appeared in blue, with the children’s names in red beside them. The JSEP departments the staff members worked in and their jobs sprang up below the placement. “Oh, so Madame Jouvin has one of the children!”

“And the pilot of the Mars Run,” Per said. “Oh, he’s in Moscow –”

“Don’t get any ideas, now, Per! The Jouvin family would be a better target,” Exio Calendra said. “We could get more leverage on JSEP that way, seeing *her* role in JSEP… Incidentally, the feasibility study hasn’t even been discussed, let alone set in motion."

"Typical!" Per observed. "|Hmm…they're scattered all around the world, Africa, Australia, Britain…"

"And every placement is with a family involved with JSEP in some way," Grigori said. "Keep it in-house, why don't you, JSEP?"

"I guess there are good reasons why they'd do that," Per said. "Secrecy is one; they can keep tabs on the children, find out information from them, keep the information in-house, and spy on both families and children at the same time."

"That sounds about the right of it," Grigori snorted. "Hey, didn't you plan to infiltrate JSEP with more agents, now Zanaida's not in post?"

"I am, but it's more urgent to get Barbara back – before she spills any beans. There's a cell up there on standby."

Grigori clicked buttons on his tablet and projected a plan onto the wall. "This is Galatea Station. Obviously we can't use the safe house where Paul Morgan and Barbara Bereskova were arrested." Grigori pointed at the plan. "I'd say it'd be best to just go up to Galatea Station, locate Barbara, get her out, and come straight back. There's nothing to gain by hanging around up there, and it could be…counter-productive, shall we say?" His gaze passed over Exio seated opposite him at the table, and settled on Per. "I'm happy to head up there and see if I can't spring Barbara from wherever they're holding her." *In fact, I'm probably the best person to go,* Grigori added to himself.

"You're a valuable asset, Grigori. What if they spot you?" Per murmured. "I couldn't replace you if anything happened."

"And how would you hold up under torture?" Exio asked, one eyebrow raised. His smile was sly.

"I have a cyanide pill in one of my teeth." Grigori shrugged.

"Best be prepared to use it, then!"

*

The Lawtons' apartment, Richmond, 1st November 2094.

"You've made good progress today, Mil," Steph told him, as she helped him onto the sofa for a rest. They'd finished the morning physio session, and he was tired.

Steph had adopted Ronnie's version of his name. Mil had decided it didn't matter, though it wasn't something his people did. "Have I?"

"Yes. You can move easily now, and you walked on your own for ten minutes. Don't you think that's progress?"

"I suppose so. How long have I been here now?"

"Two months. And you've grown in that time." Mil hadn't yet grasped the intricacies of the human time-measurement system. He stared down at himself. He'd put on some weight, and his limbs had developed some muscle, though he couldn't be described as plump by any stretch of the imagination. But he could move without difficulty now. He felt better than he had since the Awakening, and improved every day.

But always at the back of his mind were the questions. *Where are my parents? Why didn't they come back to the ship? What happened to them?* Neither he nor his sister Davan had found answers, however much they'd talked about this back at the Big Place.

"Steph? Where are the other children like me?"

"Chas said they've gone to other families to live." Steph paused. "Do you miss them?"

"Zooch." Just to make sure she understood, he nodded. The English equivalent followed via the translator. Steph and Chas treated him well, and he liked them a lot. He thought they liked him too. He wasn't sure about Ronnie. *But I need to know where the others are...especially Davan. What happened to them?*

"Perhaps when you're better we could find out where they live." Steph's eyes held their usual kindness.

He thought of his parents. A mental image of a tall grim-faced man in furs and leather, bent over him as he lay in the sleepcase, came to him. He remembered the sharp pinpricks of the needles that would feed him, remove wastes, and keep him asleep...

"I think you're strong enough to learn to speak English now," Steph said.

With an effort he wrenched his thoughts back and concentrated on her words, but she'd interrupted his train of thought. The image of his father flickered before his eyes and cracked into a thousand fragments –

"Why do I need to?" he objected. "I've got the translator."

Steph nodded. "I know. But I should teach you English so that when you go to school you won't have to catch up too much. After all, you're what – seven?"

"I don't think I'm that old." Mil tried to work it out – Steph must think it was important. He thought he was about two when they entered the Long Sleep. But he had no idea how long ago that was... "I'm older than two," he volunteered.

To his surprise, Steph burst out laughing and leaned over to hug him. He giggled a bit, to be like her.

"I think your hair's growing back," she said, and stroked the dark wisps on his hair crest. "I think you're getting *much* stronger. I'm sure you could learn English."

Mil yawned.

"How about a rest before lunch?"

He was happy to have a rest. *Steph's pleased with me.* He hugged himself and turned on his side.

He was onboard the ship as soon as his eyes closed. There were children all around him. The younger ones laughed and played, the older ones hushed them so they could study. He remembered the white walls, the hard floor he'd sat on, and the noise of other children around him... Then the door opened and the grown-ups filed inside.

As they entered, the play and laughter stopped. The children looked at each other. The younger ones were as surprised as Mil. His mother Laleen bent over him, picked him up, and held him close. He felt her arms lift and carry him into another room. His fingers clutched at her fur jerkin.

As she told him what would happen next, he clung to her. "Did you leave us before?" he asked.

"Yes," she said, "but you were too young to remember."

Her words spiralled down into a sleep from which there was no escape. It held him as securely as her arms.

When he awoke, the silence that had shocked him awake surrounded him. Mil looked around the room. Its bright colours burst against his vision. Steph or Chas must have carried him to his room and put him to bed. He tried to remember the dream, to savour it, to draw from it the things that comforted him and made him feel safe...

What struck him most was, he was alone in this room. Steph had explained when he arrived that this would be his room. He'd sleep here on his own. He couldn't remember ever being alone onboard the ship. Even Ronnie – who sometimes gave him things to play with but soon took them from him – wasn't there.

"Steph!" he cried. "Steph! Don't leave me alone!"

*

Tokyo, the Kobayashis' apaato, 2nd November 2094.

"I wish you wouldn't wear trousers everywhere, Chan! It's *so* unfeminine."

Chaneg Dar felt the familiar tingle of resentment at Mrs. Kobayashi's reprimand. She didn't like having her name shortened to make it sound more oriental, either.

When she looked up, her foster-mother half-smiled at her. Chan smoothed a hand down her close-fitting trousers and answered. “I wear trousers because I’m used to them.”

Chan seldom used her translator when she spoke English now. But her Japanese was still poor, and Mrs. Kobayashi’s English wasn’t easy to understand. They communicated in a hybrid fashion, though both had improved.

“But we’re going out! Could you put on a skirt this time, just for me?”

Chan sighed. *Every time we go anywhere we have this argument,* she thought. She hadn’t given in yet, though it upset her foster-mother. “Trousers are more comfortable and practical than skirts, Mrs. Kobayashi,” she said. “Why not try them? You might love them!”

Mrs. Kobayashi’s face crumpled. “I love my boys dearly,” she said, “but I wanted a daughter. I thought I’d get one when we were chosen to foster you, but –” She lifted her shoulders, then let them slump as if defeated.

Chan spread her hands. She’d tried to explain before, with no success. “But *any* Zarduthi girl would think this way, Mrs. Kobayashi,” she said. “It’s not just because of *who* I am – it’s *what* I am as well.” She watched as moisture spilled from over-bright eyes. She knew this indicated extreme upset in humans, but didn’t know how to make her foster-mother feel better. “I’m sorry you’re so disappointed in me,” she said. “I want to be a good daughter to you, as my family aren’t here.”

“Come here.” Mrs. Kobayashi opened her arms.

Unsure what to expect, Chan went closer. The arms folded about her. She remembered the feel of her own mother: her skin leathery, bones rigid, muscles firm – quite unlike the touch of this tiny woman.

“Please put on a skirt, just this once! Give me a daughter

to be proud of," Mrs. Kobayashi whispered. "Honour me."

Chan's arms closed about her. "I do," she said. "But I still want to be the person I always was."

"Well, so you shall, inside."

Chan struggled to balance two mental images: one of herself as a slender Zarduthi child, dressed in furs and leathers, the other a human-looking child with Zarduthi features, swamped by a silken kimono, like the ones she'd seen in local museums and on HV. *Would it cost me so much to please her, just this once? After all, she welcomed me into her home and tried to make me feel like I live here, and that I'm not just a guest.* She came to a decision. "All right," she said. "I'll go and change, if it will help you to feel better."

The smile on Mrs. Kobayashi's face as she drew away told her she'd said the right thing. Chan hurried to her sleeping area and found the plain skirt she'd kept at the bottom of the drawer. It took a thousandth to change, though she felt the fine down on her bare legs rise against the chill in the air.

She returned to see Mrs. Kobayashi fuss over her sons. "Mind that kit, it's freshly pressed!" she chirped, and straightened the strap of Ojin's bag.

"I'm ready, Mrs. Kobayashi," Chan said.

"Good," she approved. "We don't want to be late. This is an important day for Ojin and Meiji."

They left the apartment and walked to the monorail stop. The transport system was something Chan enjoyed. It was so efficient, and, for her, a novelty. Chan sat back in her seat and watched the people in the carriage. They stared back at her, faces smooth with a studied lack of emotion, eyes as dark as hers as they darted to look at Mrs. Kobayashi, then her two sons, then back to Chan.

"Ay, ay, ay!" Mrs. Kobayashi whispered to Chan. "I wish it was still legal to own a private vehicle in Tokyo. People stare so when you have more than one child!"

"Perhaps it's because I look different," Chan suggested. "People are curious *wherever* you go."

Meiji watched, eyes wide, mouth open. "Have you been to lots of different planets, then?"

"A few, when it was safe."

"We're getting off here," Mrs. Kobayashi interjected.

She never wants to hear about my life before I came here, Chan thought. But then they rounded the corner of the street and a thrill of excitement ran through her.

The venue for the tournament was a large modern building; Chan didn't catch its name. Mrs. Kobayashi ushered her sons and Chan inside and explained to the receptionist that she'd come to watch her sons in the tournament.

The receptionist cast a dubious glance at Chan, then directed Ojin and Meiji through a door. "If you'd like to seat yourselves in the grandstand," she suggested to Mrs. Kobayashi with another little sideways glance at Chan and a hand gesture, "it's through this door."

The corridor brought them out into a large room with seats that climbed in curved rows towards the back. The grandstand was already three-quarters full. "Let's sit here, they're good seats," Mrs. Kobayashi whispered to Chan. "Oh, I'm so proud of Ojin and Meiji!"

Chan received more than a few stares, but ignored them or smiled back and won a smile in answer. She felt some of Mrs. Kobayashi's excitement. "What happens now?" she asked.

"They'll limber up first," Mrs. Kobayashi said. For almost a hundredth they waited, as the buzz of conversation echoed the excitement of the crowd. Chan leaned forward in fascination. The umpire declared the tournament open, and the first contestants entered the arena. She was surprised when, after bows and some ritual, the umpire shouted a command. The contestants faced each other. Even on humans, she recognised the fighter's stance in an instant.

"Sit back, Chan, it's not seemly to lean like that," Mrs. Kobayashi chided her. "You'll crowd someone else's space."

"So sorry!" She obeyed, though reluctant.

The nearest competitor grasped his opponent's jacket. With a quick movement that Chan found hard to follow, he jerked. In a thousandth the other boy hit the mat and slapped it. It sounded like a thunderclap in the grandstand. The boy rolled upright on one shoulder and along his arm. As he faced his opponent he caught his eye and bowed low. His face was impassive.

"They have to throw their opponents with the feet higher than the shoulders," Mrs. Kobayashi whispered at her side. Chan was engrossed and hardly heard. The two boys – perhaps a year older than her foster-brothers, but no taller – grappled again. A practised flick of the wrist sprawled the stockier boy on the mat. The taller boy hooked his arm around the other's neck. In the background the referee's voice counted. Then she felt a touch on the back of her hand and looked round.

Mrs. Kobayashi pointed. "There's Ojin!"

Chan glanced across the crowded arena and said, "Thank you," then returned her attention to the nearest pair. Both were on their feet and circled each other once more; the shorter boy must have broken the arm lock while she was distracted. Without warning he grabbed the taller youth by the jacket as before. There was a brief struggle – this time Chan followed the weight changes and handhold shifts – and then it was all over. The taller boy lay on the mat, chest heaving.

"The shorter one's the winner?" Chan asked, and pointed.

"Yes." But Mrs. Kobayashi's eyes were on her sons, across the arena. "Ohhh! Meiji's taken two falls now."

"That means he's lost?"

"Not necessarily – oh, yes, his opponent's been awarded an *ippon*."

"What about Ojin?"

"He's still upright."

"I want to learn Judo," Chan said.

Mrs. Kobayashi's mouth tightened. Her eyes snapped a refusal. "I should have known it was a mistake to bring *you* here," she said.

*

Galatea Station, 3rd November, 2094.

Grigori Deshanevsky strolled around the plaza in front of the JSEP detention facility on Galatea Station. The two-storey building stood apart from the residential and commercial buildings in this part of the space station. He surveyed the square and its buildings to compare them with his memories. *They haven't changed much over the years.*

Then he went to one of the three street cafés that bordered this square, drank coffee, and watched as people entered and left the building.

He returned to his hotel, and prepared to carry out his plan. He drew from his holdall a collagen-based mask which would be indistinguishable from real skin. The nose, cheekbones and chin were built up, so when he put the mask on he looked different from his normal appearance. The mask contained a voice modulator, essential to his plan. A dark blond wig and pull-on collagen gloves completed his makeover. He changed his suit and shoes and transferred the magnetic soles over.

Grigori took the autonomous tram back to the plaza. As he stepped off it, he checked his watch. *14.42. Plenty of time.* He opened the door and entered the detention facility. Ahead the male receptionist was built like a tank. "Name?"

"Yuri Bereskov." He stepped forwards, hand extended.

"Please help me! My sister Barbara's supposed to be here. I need to see her."

The receptionist stepped back to avoid contact with him. "Why?"

"Our mother is seriously ill in the hospital. She asks for Barbara every time I visit her."

The receptionist consulted his tablet. "No-one of that name here. Sorry."

"Please! Our mother is dying!"

The receptionist laid the tablet aside. "You need to leave. Now." He stepped forwards from the desk. His size made him intimidating.

Grigori had worked for JSEP here on Galatea Station, in this very building for five years. He recognised the receptionist as John Fairbairn, an ex-military man invalided out of the army after he'd experienced mental health problems. His daunting appearance was useful in this job.

Grigori had disguised himself as Barbara's brother, so John wouldn't recognise him. "Please help! Our mother is desperate to see Barbara." He wrung his hands. "I *need* your help!"

John looked him up and down. "Proof of identity?"

For answer, Grigori pulled his wallet out of the breast pocket of his suit, extracted an ID card, and offered it to John.

John examined the card, held it under a scanner to check that it was genuine, and turned to the page where the fingerprints were stored. "I'll need to check your fingerprints."

Grigori was prepared for this. He held out his hands.

John took the fingerprints on a hand-held kit that supplied ink and a card to print on. When he'd finished he inserted the second card into his computer and compared the two sets. "It's a match," he said. "Have a seat." He indicated a row of seats to one side of the reception area.

Grigori nodded. "Please can I see my sister, now?"

John shook his head. "I'm really sorry, Mr Bereskov. They transferred her back to Earth a week ago."

"Where to?" Grigori shook his head. "I came here because this is the last place she was seen. The police told me she was here. Please tell me – where has she gone?"

"A detention centre in Siberia, called Gavotska, near – but not *very* near – Lake Baikal."

"Oh – oh, my mother will be horrified to hear that!"

"Well, her daughter shouldn't have got herself into trouble with the authorities."

"What did she do?"

"She was arrested with people who were up to no good. I can't tell you more."

Grigori got up. Anger surged through him, but all he said was, "Thank you for the information. I will try to see her at this Gavotska place – though I'm not sure how much longer our mother can hang on."

"You won't be able to see her there," John said. "Gavotska is a high-security installation – your sister's in custody for information crimes. For your sake, let it drop. It will only bring you and your mother more grief –"

"I must try, even if I can only get a photo to show my mother. She is worried about her, and the stress makes her even more poorly."

"Of course. Well, all I can say is, good luck!"

Grigori thanked John and left. He returned to his hotel and changed back to his suit. He stored the collagen masks under the bottom of his holdall for disposal. Then he checked out and boarded the space elevator for the return journey to Earth, deep in thought.

*

Tower Canyon, Zero. Ship's time/date: 406.189.3.73.206 AD.

THE ZARDUTH IMPERATIVE: DISCOVERY
Helen Claire Gould

Omol and Tangar returned the next morning at sunrise. The towers were bathed in shadow, but Omol felt new enthusiasm for action course through his veins. He tucked the geological hammer from the shuttle's science supplies through his belt, and strode to the base of the nearest tower.

It rose from the sand as if from a moat. He scooped up samples of the sand and put them into sample bags for analysis. *The changes in colour reflect different conditions of deposition.* Then he concentrated on the tower itself. It was multi-coloured, like the sand. Omol brought out his hammer and used the shaped side to chip samples off the tower. He collected chips of both sandstone and the dark bands of rock, in sample bags, labelled them, walked back to the shuttle with them, and stowed them away for later examination. Then he returned to look at the nearest tower, took out a hand lens, and peered through it.

The rocks showed a wind-laid origin in the cross-bedded dunes they were carved from. *That makes sense because wind will be the major agent of weathering and erosion processes on Zero.* Omol floundered across the sands to the next tower and checked that one, then several more. In the dim light his heat vision helped him see some features. He traced the shale and siltstone bands across the towers. When he'd checked a quarter of them, he was sure what had happened, and returned to the shuttle.

"It looks like this area was initially the sandstone block the towers are formed from," he told Tangar. "Through the action of wind, occasional water ingress, and freeze-thaw action, the gaps between these towers were formed. The sand floor is tower material, reworked by the wind. The sand unit represents an unconformity, a gap in deposition while weathering took place, and it's covered up the bedrock below the towers. So we don't know what we'll find if we drill down, but it could be worthwhile – *if* we could find water and metals."

"I'll assemble a team and requisition the equipment we need from Supplies," Tangar said. "I'd be happy just to find water – metals are a bonus."

*

Eddie's apartment, Houston, same day.

Eddie stroked baby Lucy's wisps of golden hair. A rush of emotion choked his throat. "I'm so glad we're together, Juli," he murmured. His voice sounded thick to even his ears.

Juli held the baby to her bared breast, and smiled down into Lucy's eyes. She'd been home for the last four days; their daughter was almost a week old.

And Kaj had been with them for just over a week. He sat outside in the sunshine and read a book. It was a rare moment of privacy in Eddie's paternity leave; Kaj had been with them all day.

The door onto the balcony opened. It was Kaj. Eddie looked up and tried to curb his annoyance.

Kaj seemed to have settled in well. But every time Juli fed the baby, he found an excuse to come into the room, and sit with eyes fixed on mother and baby. Eddie had attributed it to simple curiosity, until it had occurred to him that perhaps Kaj sought comfort. *He's in a strange place, with strangers looking after him,* he'd reasoned. *Perhaps he lacks confidence?* So he'd resolved to be patient with Kaj, despite his own exhaustion and Kaj's stares at Juli.

"I'm hungry," Kaj announced.

"What would you like to eat?" Eddie asked.

"Anything. It doesn't matter."

Same answer. Every time. Several times a day they went through this pantomime. "I thought you were reading, Kaj."

"I finished the book."

"You're such a fast reader!"

Kaj kept his eyes on Juli and the suckling baby. His face wore an odd expression. It took Eddie some moments to realise it was curiosity.

"Kaj, do your people breastfeed?" Juli asked.

"Breast…feed? No," Kaj replied. His forehead was screwed up in a frown, as if he struggled to understand something. "I wanted to ask about it, but didn't know what it was called. But we have babies, though it's a long time since there were any in our clan. I think Miril was the last." His features drooped. "I wish I could see the others – I miss them. I don't know where they are."

"I'll ask when I send the first report in," Eddie promised. He put a hand on Kaj's shoulder. "Come on, let's go make lunch so Juli can finish feeding Lucy in peace."

Kaj followed Eddie into the kitchen area. "My mother told me she wanted to have another baby just before she and my father went to Kiai," he volunteered.

"When was that?"

"Two or three years before the last Long Sleep." His smile was sad. "I don't remember my father much now. He didn't come back from Kiai. So there's just me and my mother – and she was wounded there."

There was silence for a moment. "I'm so sorry about your father," Eddie said, and shifted his weight from one foot to the other. He couldn't look away. *I've had so little experience of children I've no idea how to deal with this. And even if I had, Kaj isn't human.* "But your mother's better – was better, I mean, before the Long Sleep?"

"Oh yes, she was fighting again before we children were put into the Long Sleep."

"Er – good." Eddie pulled a tin from the cupboard. "How about a hot dog? Or a peanut butter and jelly sandwich?"

"I don't mind. We Zarduthi can eat nearly anything, as

long as it isn't poisonous."

Eddie *felt* Kaj watch him intently.

"Why don't you just have a synth machine, like we do on the ship?"

I couldn't have asked for a better opening, Eddie thought, glad to get onto a safer topic. At least Kaj was the first to mention the ship; he'd avoided the subject of his work so far. "We aren't as advanced as that yet, Kaj. How does it work?"

"I'm not sure," Kaj said. "But whenever we win a war for someone the grown-ups bring lots of food onboard and keep it in the cold store till we're ready to use it."

"What sort of food?"

Kaj lifted one shoulder in a shrug. "Whatever a planet has to eat. A Zarduthi can eat any animal or vegetable."

"But don't you have preferences?" Eddie persisted.

"Sure, but on someone else's planet you have to eat what's available. When the grown-ups get back to the ship they can have Zarduthi food again by running it through the synth machine and changing it to what they like."

"Ah," Eddie said, as if he'd suddenly understood something. "Kaj, could you tell me exactly where onboard the ship the synth machines are?"

Kaj's eyes sparkled with excitement. "In the mess. Will you bring one here for me?"

"I – well…" Eddie shrugged. "I'm not sure… if I could do that." *Mellows is unlikely to let me. But I might be able to copy it if I could dismantle one and find out how it worked.*

"So you could make kuznatt for me?"

"What's kuznatt?"

Kaj grinned. His oval teeth were dazzling white. "It's a bit like chocolate ice cream to look at, but there's no milk in it. Not every planet has milk, or its equivalent." He lifted Eddie's hand and sketched a shape against his palm with one taloned finger.

"What's that?"

"That's the sign you must look for to find the synth machines."

"Can you write that down for me?" Eddie had to smile. "Well, this isn't making the lunch for us, is it?" he murmured. He opened the fridge and brought out a tub of ration-issue pasta salad. As Juli had just given birth their food allowance was increased for the next six months. Once weaned, Lucy would have her own food allowance, as Kaj did.

Eddie's mind raced. *These people's synth machines could feed the world,* he thought, *just as their ships could open up new colony planets where we wouldn't have to live in domes to survive.* Here lay the logic in the placement of the children in human families. *But the Zarduthi's potential benefits to humankind don't justify befriending vulnerable children to steal their technology.*

He couldn't help but sympathise with Kaj. *He's precocious, over-studious, and way too intelligent compared to a human child of that age, but he's likeable, and just a kid.*

Even if he's not human, or mine.

CHAPTER 8 – Walking the Tightrope

The Harkness' apartment, Houston, Texas. 4th November, 2094.

"I HOPE YOU WON'T FORGET to look after Lucy in favour of your – fosterling," Juli's mother said, and turned a stern face towards her.

Juli picked up the malice that tinged her voice. "I won't do that," she said. "Don't forget, before the one-child-per-couple policy came in worldwide, women coped with multiple children, sometimes with short gaps between them. And Kaj is – Kaj is good with Lucy. I admit, I wasn't keen at first, but it's worked out fine." *Except for Eddie pumping him about the ship.* "Here." She held Lucy out to her mother. "Why don't you hold her while I make us some drinks?"

Mary-Ellen Campert took the child without comment, her expression loaded with disapproval. "I don't know why you married Eddie – he's too old for you –"

"Mom, if we're to go through all that again, I'd rather you left now," Juli answered. *So what if there's fourteen years' difference in our ages? But over the last three years he's given me confidence, and it helps me stand up to her.* She surprised herself at this response to her mother's bitchy remarks. "I appreciate the fact that you came all the way from Boston to see us, but I won't allow you to criticise Eddie in his own home."

Mary-Ellen ignored her to play with the baby's fingers and tickle her toes. *Like Kaj does, as if he's never seen anything like them before,* Juli thought. She thought of Kaj's long fingers: *Maybe he hasn't.* She got up and went in search of her husband.

She found him with Kaj, on the balcony outside, as they pored over Eddie's work-issue notebook on the table. The HV projection showed a wiring diagram, with coloured lines that linked sections of it. "Do you boys want a drink?" she asked.

"Yes, please," Kaj said.

"Please," Eddie murmured. "Kaj, what does this switch do?"

Juli stood to watch them, drinks forgotten, and eavesdropped on their conversation. *He's so precocious, yet so trusting! Why can't he behave like a child for once?*

"Oh, that one. That controls the defences. See? It's called *gabbik* in Zarduthi." Kaj paused. "I don't know much about them, just what the word-symbols mean, and the gist of how they work. Each control console has a *gabbik* switch, so that the weapons control can be transferred between consoles if there are only a few people onboard. You should talk to my mother about this."

"I can't do that, Kaj," Eddie reminded him. "I only have you here."

"And I hadn't started my mature study before the Long Sleep – even Ayar hadn't." Kaj sighed. "Are you *sure* there was nobody else aboard when you searched the ship?"

"I'm so sorry, Kaj," Eddie said. "We searched it several times – only you children were there. *Should* she have been onboard the ship?"

"Well, *she* wasn't pregnant. She'd have gone to Declain with the others."

"Wasn't pregnant –?"

Kaj explained the important role of pregnant Zarduthi women during battles.

"Oh – that's very – er – interesting, I guess." Eddie sighed. "Look, Kaj, I can't tell you what happened to your clan on Declain because I don't know. I wish I could help you better. I'm so sorry! But I'm here for you."

Juli had a glimpse, then, of what Kaj and his friends had to deal with. *Not only has he lost his father, his mother's missing too.* Eddie had told her about Kaj's father the previous night. *Poor Kaj!*

Eddie's good with Kaj, Juli thought. She'd discovered his kindness and thoughtfulness before their engagement. *I'm glad he's here for Kaj. But I'm not happy about him asking how things on the ship work – after all, he's just a child!*

Kaj sniffed. "I wish I hadn't told that Hardy person she was an engineer. He might have left me alone then, but – well, he came back to ask me about several things after that."

Juli's lips tightened as she went back into the kitchen to get the drinks. *At least with Eddie, Kaj gets a chance to ask some questions. In fact,* she reflected, as she made coffee for the adults and poured lemonade for Kaj, *Eddie is good with him.*

*

Kinuta Park, Tokyo, same day.

Chan halted at an expanse of grass flanked with rows of ancient cherry trees. "Tell me again, Ojin!"

Ojin looked at Chan from under lowered lashes. "Why do you want to know about Japanese traditions all of a sudden?" he asked. "I thought you didn't like it here."

"Well, tell her anyway – she'll only keep asking!" Meiji said.

Chan stared at him, then laughed. "He's right," she said. "I do want to find out how it's like Zarduthi ways, *and* how it's different."

"Ah. Of course." Ojin met Chan's gaze. "You know, there's a tradition from centuries ago that women could defend their homes when their samurai husbands were away fighting. And while anyone can learn judo and karate, it's better if you're reasonably fit."

"I am now." Chan had worked hard at her sports and PE lessons in recent weeks, and much of her strength and agility had returned.

"You weren't when you came here."

"I was weak for a while because we'd been in microgravity conditions for I-don't-know-how-long," Chan said with an airy throwaway gesture. "I'm loads better now." She settled herself cross-legged on the grass. "Do they take girls in your club? How do you learn?"

"Well, some clubs take girls, some don't – it depends on the *sensei* and the club concerned. Ours does. As to how you learn – I could *show* you a bit of judo if you wanted. Then if you like it, you'd need to take Mother on, and try to persuade her to let you join our classes. Then if you *really* like it and become good at it, you could apply to a major martial arts academy to continue."

Chan sat forwards, eyes as wide as they could open. "Ojin, that means a lot to me –"

"But we'd have to go somewhere away from the apartment, 'cos if Mother finds out she'll be furious."

"Where could we go?"

"This park, first thing in the morning?"

"All right. But won't other people be here?"

"Of course, but who'll take any notice of three kids doing exercises?"

"True." Chan got up. "When do we start?"

"Tomorrow?"

"Sounds good."

"We'd better get back now." Ojin checked his watch. "I promised Mother we'd be back at half past five, and it's almost that now. Come on – let's run. Last one home gets to do all our punishment chores if we're late!"

*

"Hey, Eddie! Thanks to your information the defences are functional again – and we can switch them on and off now."

Eddie nodded at Mellows as he walked along the covered walkway. His magnetic soles clung to the slick surface. His team manager came alongside him.

Mellows interrupted his thoughts. "Good leave?"

"It wasn't much of a break," Eddie replied. There was a bitter edge to his reply. "I worked with Kaj most of the time. I've hardly seen my daughter. Juli's none too pleased about that."

"You *look* tired," Mellows said.

"Er – thanks… And her mother turned up."

"Oh. Mother-in-law trouble?"

Eddie wasn't fooled by Mellows' change of tack. *He threatened me before I returned to Earth; the buddy-buddy approach won't work on me now.* He shrugged. "You know how it is."

"Never mind, it'll be comparatively restful now you're back here."

"Any more news on the alien?"

"Kobayashi's team have dissected part of the thing now." Mellows shuddered. "The stuff oozes acid, even after death. It dissolves what it touches – even metal." Mellows waved a hand in the direction of the airlock. "We think *they* damaged the airlock – ate their way in."

"How did they figure that one out?"

"One of the marines, the English guy – Chas, is it?"

"Yes, Chas. We found the children together."

"He noticed droplets of brown goo around the damaged airlock. They tested it and found it was internal material from the creature."

Eddie nodded and walked on. Mellows' presence irritated him.

On the bridge, Tony Mitchins and Gaia Zwanji hailed Eddie, and Mellows waited while they offered their congratulations to him and admired the holo of Lucy he produced from his phone.

"Did Mr. Mellows tell you?" Gaia bubbled. She pointed to the box Tony had tucked under his arm. "We're about to do a complete computer reconstruction of the drive equipment..."

"Thank you, yes, Gaia, Mr. Mellows is about to update me now. I'll be along to check it out with you in a few minutes." Eddie watched them go, unable to dismiss his misgivings about the whole project. He thought of Kaj, who trusted adults much as a human youngster would. *I feel like I'm being dragged closer all the time to something I don't want to do,* he thought, as Mellows told him about the drive reconstruction.

Then he remembered the synth machines. *That at least will be of use to everyone; and it'll revolutionise space travel.* He mentally recalled the glyph Kaj had shown him. I won't say anything until I've found out how they work –

Mellows' clap on his shoulder interrupted his thoughts. "Well, on with the good work!"

*

The Lawtons' apartment, Richmond, 5th November, 2094.

"Mil, are you ready?"

Mil's gaze was on the HV's cartoon channel. He'd been pleased to find Steph's people had this technology. It resembled the communication devices aboard the ship, and he'd spent a lot of time watching distorted, brightly-coloured figures interacting with stylised landscapes until he'd become strong enough to walk again. He still enjoyed Hoppity Hobnob, even now he was better. He secretly identified with Hoppity, who didn't fit into in his cartoon society.

"Mil, had you forgotten we're going swimming?"

"No-o," he said, "but I want to watch this first."

Steph checked the time. "All right," she said, "there's only a few minutes left. But we don't want to be late. Lily's picking us up at two."

"Mmm," Mil answered.

Moments later the doorbell rang. "We are still going, aren't we?" he heard Lily say.

"Yes, of course," Steph replied. Neither of the women came into the lounge. The murmur of their voices faded as Mil became engrossed in his show once more. As soon as the programme had finished, Mil murmured, "Computer – switch HV off," and pulled on his shoes.

It had been hard to find shoes for him. His feet were slender at the toes and high at the arch. *I'm never the right shape for human clothes.* He yanked the laces, then tied them firmly. They were still loose, but Steph had insisted he must have strong shoes to go outside in; the plimsolls he wore at home, she said, weren't enough protection. Mil couldn't remember what clothes or shoes he'd worn on the ship. But he enjoyed the laces, which he'd soon learned to tie.

This would be his first visit to the local Sports Centre. He'd been out a few times with Steph now, and mostly received curious stares from people they met, though everybody she'd spoken to had been nice to him, and a lot of them had remarked on how quiet and well-behaved he was. Mil had basked in approval from Steph at this, too.

When he joined Steph and Lily, they carried bags made of stiff fabric like Ronnie's schoolbag. "I've got your things in with mine," Steph told him. They went outside. She pressed her hand against a metal plate set into the door to lock the apartment. Mil found it strange to lock doors, but when he asked Steph about it, she explained that if she left it open anyone could enter and steal the family's possessions. Mil was secretly shocked.

In the car, Lily turned to Steph and murmured, "What about the translator-thingy? Won't it rust, or let the water in?"

Steph shrugged. "We haven't had any problems with baths

or showers. It's sealed to his skin, and Chas said it's made of a light alloy, or it would stretch his skin." She turned round in her seat harness and smiled at Mil. "I don't think there'll be any problems."

Mil smiled back, and looked through the window at the world outside. It never ceased to fascinate him; it was so different from everything he remembered.

The Sports Centre was huge. A woman sat behind a glass screen near the entrance and watched everyone come in. Mil didn't like the look she turned on him. He listened as she asked to see Steph's and Lily's passes. In addition to this, Steph and Lily had to give the woman "money" to let them in.

Steph had explained about money a few days before, while they shopped via the HV. Mil breathed in and hunched his shoulders. He was sure his people went wherever they wanted without the use of money. "You didn't have to *pay* for me then?" he asked. It was a new word; he enjoyed showing Steph that he remembered things she'd told him. He didn't know of a Zarduthi equivalent.

"No, because you're under ten. But we need a pass for you next time – she gave me a form to fill in."

They went down a long corridor and through doors into a room where there were lots of women. Their bodies were free of the clothes everyone wore all the time, but encased in tight-fitting one- or two-piece garments which left arms and legs, and sometimes much more, bare. Some of the women stared at him as people did when he was out with Steph. Mil wanted to look at them, but Steph caught his wrist and marched him into a cubicle with her. There, she undressed him, folded up his clothes, and pulled a pair of bright red shorts on him, similar to the ones he wore under his trousers, but looser. She tightened the drawstring about his waist and tucked it inside the shorts.

"These are your swimtrunks, Mil," she said. "Do you

remember, we ordered them the other day?"

He nodded. Steph had got cross with the woman on the shopping channel. She'd told her off for being prejudiced and complained to the manager, who'd had to calm everyone down. Mil had felt uncomfortable because he knew the argument was about him. It had been sorted out in the end, and he and Steph had received an apology, but it all seemed to be because Steph had asked for advice about which size would be best for him.

Mil watched as she undressed. It was the first time he'd seen her without any clothes on. Her skin was pale all over, just as his was dark all over. As she wriggled into her swimsuit, a pretty green and blue patterned one, the fascinating triangle of brownish hair at the bottom of her tummy disappeared before he could ask what it was.

"Come on, or Lily'll beat us to the other side of the pool!" Steph said. She put their bag in the locker in the cubicle and sealed it after them with a handprint, just like at the apartment.

Mil trotted after her, unsure what to expect. The tiles under his feet felt cool and damp. They splashed through what Steph explained were dis-in-fec-tant footbaths (to kill germs, she said). Mil had no idea what germs were, but he enjoyed the splash of the water. *This is going to be fun*, he felt sure, *like having a bath or shower, but better.* He didn't remember direct contact with water before the Big Place.

When they'd finished splashing in the footbath, which Steph seemed to enjoy almost as much as he did, she led him into the biggest room he'd seen since going to live with Steph, Chas and Ronnie. And the pool in it was full of water.

Lily waited for them. Her swimsuit was a pale pink. *Not as pretty as Steph's,* he decided, *but quite nice.* It was cut lower than Steph's. "Come on," she said, and held out her hand to him. He took it, and let her lead him down some steps into the water. Steph held his other hand.

Mil took the steps slowly. The water felt and smelled different from bathwater. *It's cool and warm at the same time, and there's so much of it!* He shut his eyes to feel the way the liquid swirled and sloshed around his legs, higher and higher. When he opened them again, the water was up to his waist. It felt strange and wonderful.

The two women swam from one side of the pool to the other with him between them. *I like this,* he thought. *I never knew there was so much water.*

"Now you can learn to swim on your own, like that lady over there, Mil," Steph told him. Mil looked over to where she pointed. Then Steph showed him how to use his arms and legs to propel himself through the water. He copied her movements.

I like this! Mil was so excited that he'd managed to stay afloat for a few strokes that he forgot to move his legs. As they sank he grabbed for Steph in alarm. But she laughed, so he copied her.

"Another swim across between us, and you can have a rest or practice while we swim – how does that sound?"

"Zooch." Mil liked that idea almost as much as the swimming. He looked around. *I never knew there were so many people, either. And none of them are like me.* A sadness came to him, then, that his parents and sister Davan weren't here to enjoy the water as well.

*

Neoluddite safe house, Moscow, ten minutes later.

Per Lakshar sipped from the black tea at his elbow from time to time and listened with attention as Grigori explained what he'd discovered on Galatea Station and how he'd acquired the information.

"I was shocked that she wasn't still in custody on Galatea," Grigori added.

"Me too. You did well to find all that out, Grigori," Per Lakshar said, "though I have great respect for your talent for disguise and acting."

"Thank you." Grigori's voice always rasped, but he sounded gruff with emotion this time. "Do I have permission to go to Gavotska Detention Centre, to try to free Barbara? I feel we owe her for her loyalty."

"Yes, we do. But before I give permission – since I value your talents so much – I need a report on the place. How easily can you gain access? You went to considerable lengths and some expense, only to find out Barbara's no longer being held at Galatea Station."

"I thought you might say that," Grigori said, "so I've prepared a report. Take a look at this. It looks like her extraction could be urgent." He handed him a memory drive.

Per inserted it into his tablet. A photograph of the target building popped up in the projection tank, and a holo played. Per toggled the 3D setting off, and the image became a plan of the establishment.

"Gavotska Detention Centre is based at an ex-Cold War site near Lake Baikal in Russia. It was taken over by JSEP as a remote site for the relocation of sensitive prisoners in 2075, after the food and climate change riots, which led to the eventual formation of the Neoluddites.

"Surrounded by a 20-metre-wide concrete perimeter path, the centre has electrified fences and observation towers at all four corners. Towers are equipped with machine guns, and staff are trained to use them. Escaped prisoners can be shot with stun guns, rubber bullets, or live ammunition, and the observation towers are manned twenty-four hours a day. The perimeter path concrete is kept in good repair to prevent vegetation cover encroaching from the woods nearby.

"Most of the prisoners are held in basement cells. No

prisoners have ever escaped alive, although an attempt to tunnel *in* twelve years ago reportedly left a potential way in and out again, but nobody has located it."

"I take it you intend to find this tunnel and use it?" Per said.

Grigori nodded. "I have a team at work on that at present," he said.

"If you can find it, I give you permission to use it. If not, I can't support an assault from outside the building. Too risky."

"I agree. That would make a bad situation worse. We don't know what Barbara's told them, or Paul Morgan for that matter, but it wouldn't make sense to lose even more people."

Per rose from his seat. "Well, I have a date with some young Muscovites," he said. "We always need more recruits…"

*

Upper Richmond Road Primary School, Richmond, after school.

"He's really coming to school?"

"Is he better, then?"

"When? When can we see him?"

"A real live alien!"

Ronnie wasn't sure which of them to answer first, but his heart swelled with pride. Even the hateful Annie Vereker seemed interested.

"Has he got green skin and tentacles?" she asked. Today, her nose seemed to turn upwards more than ever.

Ronnie laughed. "No, he's brown – like Boris, but maybe not so dark. And he has arms and legs, just like us." He wrinkled his nose. "But his fingers are longer, with extra joints, and his feet are sort of webbed."

Steph had taken both boys to the Amphibizoo in the city, that summer. When she'd teased Mil that his feet were like frog's feet, Ronnie hadn't been able to resist constant reminders. But the good thing that had resulted from Mil coming to live with them was that Ronnie's schoolmates had stopped teasing him about Chas not being his real dad. They were curious about Ronnie's alien foster-brother, and had forgotten their previous attitude towards him. *It's OK. Sometimes.*

"Anyway, they said he'll be fit enough to start school next month," Ronnie said. He'd learned to keep them waiting while the suspense built up. The attention it brought was balm to him. In recent weeks he'd felt excluded from the triangle of Steph, Chas and Mil.

Annie hopped from one foot to the other until she stood beside him with her arm through his. "D'you want a gobstopper?" she asked, and pushed a bag under his nose. It contained sweets of the sticky, old-fashioned sort. Thanks to the rationing laws, sweets were a rarity for children.

Ronnie took one, a great yellow globe with swirly red patterns. He relished its stickiness. But he couldn't bring himself to thank Annie. She'd been too horrid to him in the past.

*

Mil was glad to return to the apartment. He'd enjoyed his swim, but was tired. He took up his favourite position on the sofa. He recalled Hoppity Hobnob's latest episode before sleep fluttered down and alighted on him.

His dream was different this time. He became aware of the sensation of floating in the water; the warm-cool rush of wetness on his skin, and how it entered his mouth when he forgot to close it. He heard laughter: his own, as he spat out the water. His arms flailed in the water as he realised where he was. Then Hoppity Hobnob streaked past him, a brilliant swirl of colour against the water, and passed from Mil's sight.

He looked down at his hands. They were like Steph's and Chas' and Ronnie's, with short stubby fingers which bore only two joints instead of three. Pale. Human.

Mil panicked and tried to cry out, to tell Steph, but not a sound came from his throat. *Perhaps the translator's switched off.* He reached for it with stubby fingers.

It's gone! I'm dumb.

CHAPTER 9 – Perfect Storm

Tower Canyon, Zero, ship's time/date: 406.196.4.15.938 AD (8th November, 2094).

THE SHUTTLE STIRRED UP A FRENZY OF SAND GRAINS as it landed.

Omol licked his forefinger and tested the wind. It blew faster and harder than usual. He tramped across the sand to meet Tangar, who jumped down from the open hatch, floundered towards him, and brushed sand from his clothes as he stopped at Omol's side.

"Cabin instruments indicate the approach of a storm," Tangar said. "Whether it'll bring rain to swell the spring after the onslaught of the Thirsty trees is anyone's guess."

It's about time we cut them back again, Omol thought. But between the search for water, food and minerals, everyday considerations like teaching, and the exploration of the rock columns, every man, woman and child was occupied. "Well?"

"Nothing to report, Omol. There's no sign of any surface water or minerals in the area *we've* searched, though we've identified potential food animals. The infrared search was a good idea, but so far it hasn't yielded anything useful." Tangar sighed as he ran a hand through his hair crest. "We're moving on to the next sector. We'll have results in three days' time."

"Show me the sector on the map."

Tangar nodded and led the way back to the shuttle. They climbed aboard and entered the cabin. Tangar touched the controls, and the map they'd constructed filled the simtank. Trapezoids extended around the area of the canyon in a clockwise pattern to mark the search grid.

"Which sectors have you searched so far?"

"These three north of the towers and two south, west and east each. The next adjoins today's." Tangar pointed to the eastern side of the canyon. "We did come across another spring here – with its complement of Thirsty trees, of course."

Omol's mouth tightened, but all he said was, "You've worked hard, Tangar. Rest now. Start your next search at the usual time tonight."

Tangar nodded and beckoned to his men. They left the shuttle together, but while Tangar and the others tramped back towards the encampment, Omol headed towards the towers.

The sandstone columns soared above him, draped with ropes by the exploration party. Someone scrambled down them. He hurried forwards to meet Zarcor Brend just as his feet touched the ground. "What is it?"

Zarcor pointed west. "Up there – you can see it coming – a huge sandstorm. It's vital that we get everyone under cover beforehand – the shuttle, too. The towers are the only safe place." He paused. "I know we thought it might have been a settlement, but it's just a natural formation shaped by weathering and erosion. But it'll have to become a city – for us."

Omol nodded. "It makes sense."

"Only I don't know how we'll get everyone inside in time. It takes hundredths to climb up one of these things by rope."

"Why not fill the shuttle with people, hover close by, and let them walk across into the columns? We'd need to do that four times to get everyone inside, then bring the shuttle in." Omol felt a pang as he remembered the lost shuttle and Ghaneem.

Zarcor nodded. "We'll need several chambers to accommodate everyone. There are cavities of different sizes in most of them that we can use." He looked thoughtful. "I know of at least two that would be large enough for the shuttles."

"Let's do it!"

"I'll organise everyone if you can pilot the shuttle."

*

Juli and Eddie's apartment, Houston, same day.

Juliet carried her tea into the living room of the apartment. Lucy slept, but she'd allowed Kaj to stay up half an hour later to watch *Funky Tunes*.

He'd quickly picked up some nursery rhymes to sing to Lucy and learnt the movements that went with them. Juli had been pleased to learn that Kaj enjoyed music, although he didn't play an instrument, so she assumed the Zarduthi took pleasure in music and dance, and had let him watch the programme he'd mentioned that other boys in his class liked.

He tapped his long fingers on the arm of his chair and enjoyed the sound it made – if his grin was anything to go by. On the next song he tried out finger-beats on objects made of different materials in the apartment. He kept perfect beat with the music as he moved around, and listened to the sound textures the various surfaces made. Some of the time, his gaze fixed on the programme and the bands as they played and sang in the projection tank. Sometimes he stood up and jiggled about as if he itched to dance.

At the end of the programme, the music that had introduced the show came on again, and Kaj retreated to his seat.

"Did you enjoy that?" Juli asked.

"It was jinky!" Kaj said with a grin.

That's something he's picked up at school, Juli thought.

"Now I can be like the other kids – I watched the bands, noted which ones I liked, and listened to their music," Kaj added.

"That's great, Kaj!" Juli said. "Time for bed now. Don't forget to clean your teeth!"

Kaj took himself off to the bathroom, and Juli switched over to the news channel. She sat and sipped her tea and relaxed.

And then an item came on that made her sit bolt upright.

"The hardest-hit drought areas in the world could benefit from our contact with aliens. Engineers have discovered a food production technique onboard the alien ship that could revolutionise famine relief in remote areas. It requires an electrical supply, but climate change has ensured most areas have solar panels or wind turbines."

This must have something to do with Eddie and his work, she realised. *I don't want to know how Eddie found that out from Kaj. I don't like this situation at all. If Eddie uses Kaj to get information about the ship, it gives my mother ammo against him. And if she has that, she'll use it to bully me.*

*

Galatea Station Observatory, next day.

Vimal Ashraf grinned when he saw Malik Sindram cross the observatory towards him. "How is it with you, then, Malik?" he asked.

He was disconcerted when she didn't reply but walked past him to her desk, face expressionless. She pulled a pile of paperwork forward and immersed herself in it.

"Malik? We've always been friends, ever since we've worked together." He got up and went to her. "Have I done something to upset you?"

Malik turned to face him at last, and her eyes blazed. "Yes, you have," she said. "How could you accept a foster-child, knowing we'd applied for one because we're desperate for a child and couldn't have our own? How *could* you?"

Vimal stepped backwards. "I didn't realise you felt like that," he said. "We actually had no choice –"

"Well, you should have realised – we discussed it often enough. And you were supportive before."

"I know you weren't happy about Jitindra's infertility, yet he won't let you use an 'unnatural' method of fertilisation to fulfil *your* licence allowance –"

"Yes. So I'd have thought you'd have shown some sensitivity towards my feelings. Now let me get on with my work. I don't want to discuss this with you again."

Vimal took a step towards her again. "But –"

Malik banged her hand down on the workstation. "No! I do not want to hear it. Excuse me, I have work to do."

Vimal returned to his own workstation. Thoughts tumbled around inside his head. *She's jealous!* Unbelievable! The cool Malik Sindram, jealous of him because he had an alien foster-child. Before her marriage she'd been a career woman with no interest in children. But Jitindra had changed all that. And Vimal was sure that their Neoluddite membership was one major reason why Malik and Jitindra had been rejected as potential foster-parents.

He shrugged. If that was how it was to be in future, then so be it. But he hoped it wouldn't spoil his work here on Galatea Station. He'd enjoyed his eight years here, and now that enjoyment felt sour and empty.

I suppose I could always ask for a transfer if things get too bad.

*

Tower Canyon, Zero, ship's time/date: 406.198.9.21.045 AD, a tenth later.

In complete darkness Tangar swung down the rope onto the level below the tower void that now housed the shuttle. There wasn't even enough light to use his night or heat vision modes. This chamber had no opening onto the outside world, and could only be accessed by rope. He played his torch around the space.

Bebb lowered himself down to stand beside him. Bored now everything was stowed away, they'd decided to explore the tower.

The room was an irregular oval. Tangar's visual exploration revealed a further down-passage at the opposite end of the chamber.

Something embedded in the sandstorm struck the outside of the tower, and its walls resonated like a bell. But the structure stabilised after a minor wobble.

It wasn't long before he came level with Bebb.

"Look what I found!" Bebb held out his palm. On it lay a small black object, its shape an elongated oblate spheroid. "I think its power source may be a perpetual battery."

"What is it?"

"If you press this –" Bebb thumbed a catch on it. "– it crackles, as if with static. I think it's a communicator. It doesn't work, but it suggests we aren't the first to come here."

"Then keep your eyes peeled for other artefacts and signs of life." Tangar played the torch over the smooth sandstone walls of the chamber. They continued their exploration of the passage, but their torches found nothing else of interest. They moved on to the next level down.

Tangar played the light over the walls, but stopped when he spotted a dark pile at the other side of the room. "What's that?"

They approached with caution.

As they approached the pile resolved into familiar shapes. Tangar stood close enough to make out legs, arms, heads, and bodies. The black material wasn't clothing; it was a skin-tight all-in-one suit. The three corpses huddled together. Their flesh appeared mummified.

"It doesn't look like any spacesuit I've ever seen," he said.

"Could they be diving suits?" Bebb suggested. He walked round the corpses. "What if they discovered water here, under the towers? We haven't looked here yet."

"What indeed?" Tangar mused. "Our excursion here may

have provided us with the means to slake our thirst. We should tell Omol about this."

*

The Kobayashis' apaato, Tokyo, same day.

Squares of light appeared on the floor as the sun emerged from behind the clouds.

Chan stared at the window shapes on the floor for some thousandths. Instead of them she saw again the scene between Mrs. Kobayashi and herself, Ojin and Meiji earlier that afternoon, after they'd returned from school.

"Just what did you think you were doing this morning at the park?" Mrs. Kobayashi's voice had been as sharp as a Meldathari flash-whip. "You disobeyed me!"

Chan had never seen her so angry before, and was afraid for a thousandth. Then she remembered that if the human woman did anything to her she had only to tell Josie Carter, the social worker, and she'd be removed from harm. She drew herself up to her full height and said, "I'm learning judo, Mrs. Kobayashi."

"I expressly forbade you." Mrs. Kobayashi stood with her hands clenched into fists on her hips. "And what do I find? Mrs. Otashi saw you disobey my instructions when she walked her dog in the park today. You even encouraged my boys to disobey me. I'm *so* disappointed in you, Chan."

"I never do anything but disappoint you," Chan retorted. "Mrs. Kobayashi, I choose to learn the way of the warrior, since my own culture is inaccessible for me at present. I must be true to the instincts bred into me. I wasn't made for peace, or to be someone's tame stay-at-home wife. I was born to fight, and fight I shall!"

Mrs. Kobayashi stamped her foot. "And I say you won't learn fighting. It's unfeminine."

The pitch of her voice indicated the level of her temper,

Chan had discovered. "Zarduthi women fight alongside their comrades and partners," she retorted.

"You're not on your spaceship now, Chan – you live here, with me, and what *I* say goes. I want a daughter, not a ruffian." She opened Chan's backpack and pulled out her school tracksuit. "You don't even have the correct clothes for it!"

"Then let me use some of my allowance to buy a *ghi*, if it's so important!"

"No." Mrs. Kobayashi's voice rose to a bellow. "I'll tell you what'll happen. All three of you will be confined in your bedroom areas and do your homework – you for persistent disobedience, and Ojin and Meiji for encouraging you."

"What about *Hoppity Hobnob*? It's on this afternoon –" Meiji began.

"No HV. No supper, either."

"What? We'll starve!"

"Not for one day, you won't," Mrs. Kobayashi had said, as she moved the screens around the bed areas to divide the boys' area from Chan's. "You won't disobey me again."

As Chan raised her hands and slashed at the air with claws extended, she wondered when Josie Carter would make her next visit. *I'll ask to go to another family,* she thought. *If Mrs. Kobayashi doesn't want me as I am, she can't have me at all. And although I like Ojin and Meiji, they'll soon forget about me if I'm not here to get them into trouble any more –*

Chan crossed to the window, opened it and stared down into the communal garden below. Once she'd learned it was a place of peace, she'd spent hours there. It had helped her get over upset, anger and missing her friends. She followed with her eyes the contours of the raked gravel, the shape of the boulders set into it, and the green of the larch tree in the corner of the garden. It bore cones; she lost count of them when she got to about fifty, and was about to start again when she heard another window open. She stuck her head out. Ojin and Meiji watched her in silence.

"Are you all right?" Ojin murmured.

Chan sighed. "I am, but I'm sorry you got into trouble too."

Ojin waved that away with a gesture. "I enjoyed showing you. We both did, didn't we, Meiji." He nudged his brother.

Meiji stared out over the garden at the road beyond. Chan noticed his eyes looked glittery.

Ojin continued. "You're good, Chan. You've picked it up fast. You shouldn't give up." He nudged Meiji again. "Should she?"

"No," Meiji said. His voice was a whisper, and as he turned his face towards Chan his eyes glistened with moisture.

Chan made the Zarduthi sign of incomprehension – hand under her chin – but there was no chance to ask Meiji what the water in his eyes meant, because Ojin's next words took the conversation in a different direction.

"Is it true about Zarduthi women fighting?"

Chan nodded, "Except when they're pregnant, and then they have the most important job of all." She explained.

"But Dad said you children were alone onboard when they found you."

"Yes. Which means that something happened to them. And I don't know where the rest of the clan are, or my friends from the ship."

"The other children?"

"Yes. But I'll find out, some time."

"I've no doubt of that," Ojin smiled. "You're a determined person."

"I was trying to work out when Josie Carter's next visit is. I think it's a few weeks away." She turned her head away. "I thought I should ask if I could go to live with a different family, where I'd be allowed to learn judo and karate."

There was a shocked silence and the smile faded from Ojin's face. After a thousandth, he said, "You must be very unhappy to even think of that, Chan."

"It's bad enough that I lost my parents and all my friends, but you and Meiji have helped to make up for that. But I find Mother hard to cope with."

"You mustn't think she's a bad woman, Chan." Ojin's smile was back, but his expression was sad. "I know you don't know human ways, but she was *desperate* for a daughter. When first I, then Meiji, were born, despite the fact Dad pays extra tax for having two sons – she was really upset."

"That's hard for *you* to bear." Chan thought for a moment. "I know she says she wants a daughter. But I think what she *really* wants is a doll she can dress up to display to her friends, and that's not what I am."

"But you are important to her – maybe more important than Meiji and me."

"It's an obsession – and she wants to force me to go against my natural inclination! It's harder to cope with that on top of the other things. That's why I thought Josie might help me. It isn't anything personal – I like you and Meiji very much, and I love learning martial arts with you. I know your mother isn't a *bad* person. She's just the wrong foster-mother for me. No Zarduthi girl would be the right foster-daughter for her."

"If you could learn judo and karate, though, would you be happy enough to stay with us?"

Chan spread her hands once more. "How can that happen?"

"Because I've just realised how Josie *can* help you. Maybe she can persuade Mother to let you learn with us. If she thought you'd be taken away if you couldn't learn, she might give in. But you might have to learn something *she* wants you to, to please her."

Chan thought about that for a thousandth or two. "I suppose that wouldn't be too bad. I could practise the exercises you showed me to keep strong and supple in the meantime, just in here."

"You should have been born a boy, Chan!" Ojin said, admiration in his voice.

"No," Chan said. "I *like* being female, thank you! I just want to learn judo and karate, since I can't learn my own people's martial arts. I don't need to be a boy for that. I just need to be free to learn."

*

Tower Canyon, Zero, third day after the storm began.

"The wind's dropped. Should we look outside?"

Omol recognised Tangar's voice and swung to face him. His body heat made him a block of colours that shaded into one another in the gloom. Around them, the clan members' skin appeared orange-yellow, and their clothing red. There were twenty or thirty of them.

"The wind quietened down some time ago. We could try," he agreed, and together they approached the wall. Even with part of a shuttle bulkhead for protection, sand had sifted between metal and rock.

It took several thousandths to open the improvised metal shutter. Light flooded into the chamber; Omol's sight adjusted within thousandths and he looked down onto the landscape.

Where before the towers had reared up from the floor, mounds of sand now resembled waves that licked between the structures. He looked over to where the spring had lain: he could just see the Thirsty trees' green tops, but except for a depression where some water had soaked through, the spring was submerged under a deluge of sand.

"That was some sandstorm!" he said, and hoped his voice didn't betray his fear.

"All three days of it," Tangar agreed. "I hope they don't happen too often around here. Otherwise we're done for."

"We might be anyway," Omol said.

CHAPTER 10 – Victims and Perpetrators

The Kobayashis' apaato, Tokyo, 15th November, 2094.

"ANYTHING YOU WANT TO SAY, you can say here in the house!"

"I don't wish to share it here," Chan said.

"And I don't wish you to leave the house to talk. I *won't* allow it!" Mrs Kobayashi stamped her foot.

"Sorry," Josie said, "but Chan can speak privately with me whenever she needs to."

"She's not allowed –"

Josie turned and faced Kobayashi. "If Chan wishes to speak to me, it's fine, because it helps me do *my* job, which is to help her. Even if JSEP didn't permit it, which they do, I would be happy to listen."

"But –"

"Mrs Kobayashi! Please don't interrupt. I must speak privately with Chan. If she has a problem, I need to know about it so that I can work out how best to deal with it."

Fury rendered Mrs Kobayashi speechless.

Josie turned to Chan. "Now," Josie suggested, "shall we walk through the park together while we speak?"

With a glance at Mrs Kobayashi, Chan stood up, chin lifted in defiance. "Yes, please. I'll get my jacket."

Josie said nothing as they left the house to walk to the park, but it was only twenty thousandths' walk away. As they entered the park she asked, "What did you want to speak to me about?"

For a thousandth, Chan wasn't sure where to start. Then she said, "I want to learn judo and karate, but Mrs Kobayashi just wants a doll she can dress up in fancy clothes and show off to her friends – not someone with their own personality and needs." The words came out in a rush, because she expected Josie to either laugh, or tell her she was silly or ungrateful.

Josie did neither. Her expression was thoughtful. "I didn't know you wanted to learn martial arts, Chan, and I should say, Mrs Kobayashi may not be the only one who wouldn't want you to learn."

"What do you mean? Who else wants to bury me alive?" Anxiety licked the edge of Chan's emotions. *To be told this, now, when I've stifled my true nature for so long to try to make home life bearable –*

Josie looked troubled, as if she wanted to tell her but didn't think she should. After what seemed like many thousandths, she said, "I don't think President Langrishe would like you to learn, either, Chan. I think he'd feel it would make you an unknown quantity, and therefore dangerous."

"He's *afraid* of us?"

The wind snaked around the park, rustled branches and prised petals from the cherry trees. The sky snowed pink and white particles.

"I think so. We all do." Josie sighed. "You might just have to be patient."

"How long *for*, though? My life's trickling away." Chan clenched her hands. "I was born to fight. That's what we Zarduthi do – we fight under contract."

"Like mercenaries?"

"Exactly." Chan wanted to scream with frustration, but she drew a deep breath instead. The park was as serene as ever. *How many secrets can it keep?* "I need to develop my muscles, strengthen myself for an adult life as a Zarduthi warrior. I can't leave it too long – I've already lost several years."

"World Presidents are elected every five years. President Langrishe only has a couple more years of his term left. If you can be patient…"

"Patience, patience, that's all anyone ever says to me!" Chan slapped her hands against the sides of her face. "I feel as if I'll explode if anyone says it to me again!"

Another gust snowed blossom on them.

Josie sighed. "It might be the only way, Chan. Although…"

"What?" Chan sensed Josie had had an idea. Her eyes fixed on Josie in search of inspiration.

"Well…why don't you make a deal with Mrs K? You learn something *she* wants you to learn as long as she lets you learn judo and karate."

Chan watched Josie's face and tried to decide whether she was on her side or not. But it seemed like a sound idea. "OK," she agreed. "Ojin suggested that too. Will you speak to Mrs Kobayashi and fix it up? You saw what she's like with me."

"Yes, of course. And you can *always* ask to speak to me in private away from the house if you need to. What you've asked for seems reasonable in the circumstances. I know you're sensible."

Some of Chan's anger faded. Then she thought of what Ojin and Meiji had said to her, and added, "You understand, don't you, that I don't want to get Mrs Kobayashi in trouble? She isn't a *bad* person. She just doesn't understand me, and puts her needs before mine."

"I understand that, and she wouldn't have been allowed to foster you if she were a bad person. We want to do the best we can for you, though of course it won't be the life you'd have had with your biological parents."

"Ojin said his father was involved with the discoveries on the *Bekel* – our ship – so maybe that's why they sent me here?" Chan hesitated, then added, "Josie, do you have *any* idea where our *real* parents are? Have JSEP said *any*thing to you about them?"

Josie shook her head. "I'm afraid not, Chan. If I hear anything, I'll be sure to let all of you know. But they don't talk to me about it. I'm just expected to get on with making sure you children are all right." She shivered. "This wind's chilly. Let's go back to the apartment, and I'll do my best to persuade Mrs Kobayashi."

*

Tower Canyon, Zero. Ship's time/date: 406.200.4.55.135 AD, same day.

Omol leant on his spade for support. The sweat had dried on his face in the stiff breeze. Low light levels made the work harder, but the clan compensated with their heat vision.

As they'd shifted the sand, they'd found a system of burrows: a vilnossi colony, with occasional sandstars. The creatures had suffocated in the sandstorm. The provisions team had gathered them up and sent them for butchery and freezing. They'd keep the clan fed for some time, and their frozen blood would provide extra nutrients to the children.

Omol and his team had piled the sediment in a ring around the spring. For once, the Thirsty trees' breakneck growth had helped the clan pinpoint the position of the spring. They'd worked with a will to uncover it. *For now, it's our only chance of survival, along with the condensation films.*

Omol surveyed the scene. They'd cleared a space of about seven square spons in two days. The spring had been at least as large as the *Kazid's* Control Room. They'd now uncovered it in two spots, but runners choked both. *There's a long way to go,* Omol thought.

He called everyone over. "I want two volunteers from the group to cut back the trees. The rest of us will clear the sand."

Faril and Jonep put up their hands to volunteer. Omol nodded. "The rest of us can work on this new section." He indicated a sector to the left of the trees. "Let's get on with it!"

*

Upper Richmond Road Primary School, England, 17th November, 2094.

Ronnie sensed that Mil's non-appearance at school had made his association with one of the alien children less exciting. *But what I've got to tell them should get them interested again.*

As soon as the bell went for the start of break, Ronnie rushed out into the play area, and called, "Hey, Annie, Boris, guess what!"

"Dunno," said Boris. He didn't seem interested.

Annie Vereker skipped over to him. "What?"

Now that he had an audience, it was time for Ronnie to reveal all. "I had a shower with Mil last night, and I saw his willy."

"So?"

"Well, it's – it looks weird. Not like yours or mine."

"I'll get the others," Boris muttered.

"What's it like?" Annie's voice was as clear as she was persistent.

"It – well, I don't know, it just doesn't look like one of ours."

"I think you're lying, Ronnie Lawton! I don't think you've seen his willy at all."

"But I have, I *have*!"

Boris arrived with Stevie and Mark, the other members of the gang. "Well, what's it like then?"

"He doesn't know!" Annie shrieked, and stuck her tongue out at Ronnie.

"I *do*! I just can't describe it. It's – I dunno, *wiggly*." Ronnie fluttered his hands.

Annie pulled a face. "He's not sticking that in me!" She

gave a shudder, then added, "All right, I believe you. But I want to see for myself."

"Yeah, like you've seen everyone else's," Stevie said. "And everyone else has seen yours – and not just in our gang."

Annie turned her back on him.

"But how can he have such a strange willy, Ronnie?" Boris's face was full of curiosity.

Ronnie realised his ploy had worked. "Because he's an *alien.* Their faces are different, so everything else is, too." He pushed the image of Mil as he'd first seen him to the back of his mind – and the memory of the fear that went with it. He was ashamed that he'd screamed now, especially as Mil was self-contained and well-behaved. "Honest!"

"Does he still pee like boys do?" Annie wrapped her skipping rope around its handles.

Ronnie shrugged. "Seems to." He wondered if she had any rhubarb-and-custard sweets today.

"And what about the other thing – you know –"

"What?"

"You know – fuck. Do they even do it the same as us?"

Ronnie shrugged again. It hadn't occurred to him to think about that. "I dunno. Perhaps you should ask him when he comes to school."

*

Toshima ward Ikebana Society, Tokyo, Japan, 20th November, 2094.

Chan wedged the stick of contorted hazel into the centre of her arrangement and frowned in concentration. She looked at the other displays. *Most of them look really artistic, if you like flower arrangement. Mine's just a lot of bits and pieces stuck together,* she acknowledged with a sigh. *I wasn't cut out for this.* She fiddled with one of the flowers, and hoped the arrangement wouldn't fall apart, as her last attempt had.

She'd attended the Toshima Ward Ikebana Society's classes for several weeks now, and hadn't made any progress. The rest of the group were all better at this than she was. She only came because she'd promised Mrs. Kobayashi –

The room swayed for a full five thousandths. Chan grabbed the table, and thought she was dizzy. Then she realised the table moved too.

She must have looked scared, because Mrs. Tanaka, the instructor, murmured, "Minor earth tremor, Chan. Nothing to worry about." The room stilled and settled back to its previous calm.

But when Chan looked back at her arrangement, the hazel stick lolled in an indecorous fashion, and the twig of cherry blossom buds had fallen from its mounting and rolled to the edge of the table. A bud had detached itself from the stem, which lay on the wood, petals smudged and ruined.

*

Upper Richmond Road Primary School, 22nd November, 2094.

The school building looked ever bigger as they approached it.

"This way," Steph said, and caught Mil's hand. He trotted beside her. She was tall, yet familiar and reassuring.

They crossed the open space before the school, which Steph told him was the playground. They entered the building, and a woman came out of a doorway. She looked at Mil for a moment, then greeted Steph. "Hi, Mrs Lawton."

"She's not Mrs. Lawton, she's Steph," Mil objected.

The other woman laughed. "Is this your new family member that we've heard so much about from Ronnie?" she asked.

"This is Mil," Steph agreed. Mil didn't understand why,

but she didn't look pleased; but then he thought about what the woman had said. *Ronnie tells people here about me! Is that good or not?*

"Come with me, Mil. I'll take you to your class. Say 'bye till lunchtime."

"'Bye, Steph." It felt strange to watch Steph wave and walk away through the door, but when she'd gone, Mil turned and followed the woman along the corridor to a room where many human children played.

It felt familiar, yet strange, to be among other children. Mil looked around the group. He was the tallest. There were eighteen other boys and girls. The woman introduced him to the class, and told him the teacher's name, Mrs. Parks.

Mrs. Parks had light-coloured hair like Steph's, and looked almost as kind as her. She introduced him as Mil and made the other children say their names to him.

They all stared at him. He didn't like that. He felt uncomfortable, and wriggled on his chair.

"We'll do art next," Mrs. Parks informed everyone. "What would you like to paint a picture of, Mil?" she asked.

"Paint a picture?" Mil looked back at her.

"Yes, look, like these." Mrs. Parks pointed to the pictures on the walls.

"Oh." Mil thought for a moment, then said, "Spaceships."

"All right." Mrs. Parks turned to the rest of the class. "We'll paint spaceships today," she announced. There was more noise and chatter as the paints, brushes and paper were handed out, then the class became quiet.

Mil looked around at the other children to see what they did, then gripped the brush at one end like them. They dipped their brushes into pots of paints and splashed colours and shapes onto the paper. Mil tried to do as they did, but his movements were awkward. Steph had taught him letters and numbers and he could speak the language well enough without using the translator now; but she'd never taught him to paint or draw. He looked at the other children's pictures to see what he was supposed to do, but couldn't see much.

And there wasn't any white paint. He was about to ask Mrs. Parks about it when he noticed that there were two girls at his table who looked exactly the same. He'd never seen such a thing before.

"Why do you look alike?" he asked.

"We're twins," one of the girls said.

The other said, "Ronnie's mummy and daddy get extra money for you to live with them." She sounded cross.

Mil stared at her. "How do *you* know?" he asked.

"Ronnie said so. But my mummy and daddy have money taken away from them because there are two of us. Mummy wouldn't have an a-bor-tion to get rid of one of us, so now she and Daddy always argue about money."

Mil didn't reply – he couldn't think of anything to say. He reached for a pot of blue paint, stabbed at it with his paintbrush, and splashed colour onto the white paper. Then he decided to add stars. Yellow, orange and red for them. He splashed the colours on top of the blue and ignored the other children.

Mrs. Parks came to look at his picture when he'd finished. "It's very good, Mil, but where's the spaceship? I thought you were going to draw one for me."

Mil looked up at her and gulped. "Can't. Don't know what it looks like. I've only been *inside* it."

Mrs. Parks' face creased into a gentle smile – which surprised him. He'd thought she'd be upset with him. "Oh, so this is looking out from inside?"

"Through the sightport," Mil said. "But there was no white paint for the walls."

"So that's why there's only a picture in the middle of the

paper! Next time, come and ask me – I'll find you what you need. Well done, Mil! I'm sure Steph will be pleased to see what *you* see in your ship – thanks for sharing." She moved on to the next table.

"I don't see why Ronnie's mummy and daddy should get extra money for *you* when we get less," one twin said. Her face was red, and her voice sounded crosser than ever. "It must be because you're a – you're a – not-human."

The room suddenly felt huge, and full of children as horrid as Ronnie often was. Sound filled the air. Mil shivered. *I didn't know about the money,* he thought, and wished that Steph hadn't left him on his own here.

*

Outside Gavotska JSEP prison, Russia, 23rd November, 2094.

"Sir! We've found it."

Grigori looked up from his phone, where he'd copied the plan of the tunnel. One of his team of volunteer excavators watched him. "Excellent, Viktor. What's its condition?"

"We'll need timber to shore up parts of it, and there's a flooded area. We'll need to pump the water out – the noise could alert locals to our presence."

Grigori stood up. "Show me," he said. "And get Voronovich. He'll know what we need, and how and where to get it."

*

Two days later.

In the tunnel, Grigori stripped to his underwear and put on the prison guard's uniform he'd procured. He'd already fitted on a collagen mask. "What do you think, Viktor?" he asked Voronovich.

"Perfect, Grigori." came the answer. "You look quite the

business!"

They'd passed through the tunnel without difficulty. The pumps for the flooded section had been noisy enough to draw attention from the locals, but Grigori had had his story ready. "I'm from the Russian branch of the World Environment Consultancy," he'd told a farm worker a few days ago. And the man had swallowed it whole.

"Right, I'm going in," Grigori announced. "I'll probably be a few days, so don't panic if you don't hear from me. But take all the equipment out of here, except the pumps, and take Voronovich with you. He's too valuable to lose." He picked up his gear, sketched a salute to them, and set off.

*

The Jouvins' villa, Nice, 26th November, 2094.

Thwack!

This was the noise she'd often heard before – but always when Papa Jouvin was home on leave. Halka Mozada shivered in the sea breeze on the lowest terrace, and pulled her dressing-gown more closely around herself as she crept into the garden. The Moon resembled a torn-off fingernail, but her heat vision still operated in the scant moonlight. Tonight, she couldn't contain her curiosity about the noise.

Thwack!

Halka couldn't see much, but she'd checked; Robert's room was empty.

Thwack! The noise came again. This time a low moan accompanied it.

Halka crept in silence towards the noise, a skill Zarduthi children acquired early. She hadn't had to use it on Earth before. *Although Earth people give the impression they don't like to fight, they seem to have the same capacity for violence as in my people. At least* some *of them would make decent fighters –*

Her slippered foot caught against a paving stone she'd forgotten protruded, and Halka hit the ground with a *thud.* As she tried to sit up, footsteps approached.

A thickset figure blotted out the thermal landscape of the garden. Papa Jouvin's face glowed red as he loomed over her. "You! What are *you* doing here?" he demanded.

"I – I fell –" She rubbed her toes where she'd tripped against the paviour.

"You were spying on me!" Papa Jouvin thundered. In the dim light his brows stood at right-angles to the droop of his moustache.

"I wasn't, Papa Jouvin," Halka cried. "I wasn't! I thought I heard someone creeping about out here –"

"You were spying!" Papa Jouvin insisted, and he yanked her to her feet so hard she thought he'd dislocated her shoulder. He grabbed her arm and hauled her up the terraces to the top one, where the fruit trees and bushes grew. It was gloomy there, and when her night vision kicked in she saw the reason for her unease about Robert.

He crouched on the floor, hands pressed against his face. He looked up at her for a thousandth, then started up, and his expression changed from shame to anger. "Halka – no!"

"Shut up, Robert!" Papa Jouvin snapped. "Unless you want more of the same?"

Papa Jouvin stood right behind her, his huge hands hot on her shoulders as he tore the dressing-gown from them. Halka smelled wine on his breath. She remembered its sharp taste, which lingered in her mouth after she choked the thick liquid down at dinner.

Robert sniffled and stayed crouched. His body radiated pain. Halka thought she saw blood, red as wine, on his pyjamas. She looked away in time to see Papa Jouvin lift his heavy belt with its ornate brass buckle from where he'd left it in the arbour.

THE ZARDUTH IMPERATIVE: DISCOVERY
Helen Claire Gould

"I'll teach you to spy on me!" Papa Jouvin muttered. His teeth were gritted. His anger awaited its violent release. "My papa taught me many a lesson and it never did *me* any harm. Children should be obedient –"

She looked up at him, then squeezed her eyes shut and clenched her hands.

When the first blow fell, it came as pressure rather than pain.

When she lay in her bed and shivered, many belt-strokes later, Halka asked herself why Papa Jouvin should do such a thing, either to her *or* to Robert. Her shoulders smarted where the buckle had fallen so many times; but she didn't think they'd bled, as Robert's had.

All right, she admitted to herself at last, *I suppose I* was *spying. But that isn't why he belts Robert.* She thought back to her arrival, when Papa Jouvin led her inside by the hand. At fourteen, her foster-brother was about a year older than she thought she was, but so pale and withdrawn that when she'd first met him she thought he must be younger. *Robert's eyes bulged then, and he looked white and sick. For a child to fear his father – that didn't make sense at all, back then. But it must be why he looks so frail and scared...*

The house was quiet, but sleep eluded Halka. She lay in bed and stared into the darkness. After a long time there came a tap at the door.

"Halka?"

Every muscle in her body went rigid. *It could be Papa Jouvin, come to hit me again –*

"Halka? It's me, Robert. Let me in."

She recognised his voice. Halka climbed out of bed, though her bruised muscles protested as she moved.

Robert's whisper came again. She opened the door and he stumbled into the room. He recovered his balance and pulled her against him, but was careful not to touch her back. "Are you all right?" he asked. "I was worried about you, and couldn't sleep. I had to see you –"

"I'm all right, but I can't sleep either." Robert's hug surprised Halka, but she returned it, though she kept her hands away from his shoulders to avoid causing him more pain. "What does *Maman* say about this?"

Robert disengaged himself and slumped onto the side of the bed, his face in his hands. "She doesn't know. He –" He bit his lip, then started again. "I just wanted to tell you. If he does it again, cry. He'll only hit you till you cry. He wants the power to control you."

"But I can't. I mean – we don't. It's not physically possible."

"He won't know that – so pretend, Halka! Save yourself a lot of pain."

*

Mr Noguchi's dojo, Tokyo, 27th November, 2094.

"You're tall, Chan," said Mr. Noguchi, the *sensei*. "So hip and leg throws will probably work better for you. That's what we'll concentrate on when you've been with this club a while. Ojin and Meiji taught you how to break your fall well."

Chan acknowledged that with a slight lift of her head, as she adjusted the jacket of her judo whites. Since Josie Carter's visit two weeks before she'd eagerly awaited today. Without her support and Ojin and Meiji's protests she wouldn't have been able to attend their martial arts club.

Mr. Noguchi clapped his hands and raised one arm. When all the children had quieted and he'd got their attention, he introduced Chan and announced that they would begin the class with their usual warm-ups. These consisted of simple exercises such as she'd practiced with her foster-brothers, and aboard the clanship long ago. *That* seemed like a dim dream now. The reality was here, now, on Earth, and she must push herself hard to get fitter to reach her goal. Her muscles, softened by the Long Sleep, were now adequate for everyday purposes, but to learn mixed martial arts she must become stronger. It had been easy keeping up with Ojin and Meiji. This would be harder.

After a couple of hundredths the *sensei* drew a taller boy forwards to help him demonstrate a throw. "This is what we'll cover today," he said. "It's called *taiotoshi*. Grip your opponent's lapel and sleeve." He demonstrated each move as he explained the sequence. "Your opponent half-turns away on the lapel side. Keep your weight on your rear leg, place the other one in front of your opponent's ankles. Continue to turn, follow your arm round in front and down. The counter-throw is the same." He stepped back. "I'll demonstrate it again, then you can work on it with a partner."

Ojin moved to Chan's side and whispered, "Work with me."

Chan nodded, eyes fixed on Mr. Noguchi and his young assistant. It looked simple, but she wanted to be sure she understood what she had to do.

At first Ojin blocked every attempt she made to throw him. She did the same. Ojin made a slight turn, and the next moment the world revolved around Chan, and the mat was at her back. At the last thousandth she remembered to slap the mat to convert the energy of her fall into sound, then bounced upright to face him again. "Now I get why you insisted I spend so much time learning how to fall," she said. "But I'll throw *you* this time!" When she did, she had a suspicion that Ojin had allowed her to throw him, and said so.

"Not at all."

Chan turned as Mr. Noguchi said, "That's coming on well, Chan. Work on it for the next five minutes, then we'll do another throw. I teach two each session."

By the time Mr. Noguchi raised his arm for attention Chan had learned a second throw. Her breath came in gasps. "All right. *Randori!* Now you can put into practice what you've learned today."

*

Gavotska, Russia, three days later.

It had taken Grigori three days to locate Barbara, once inside the prison.

She was in a bare underground cell, disoriented and barely awake. He assumed that was due to too much truth serum. There was a bed, on which she lay; a chair and a bedside table, which bore the remains of a meal. She wore nightdress and a cardigan, both grubby. Her mouth hung open and she didn't seem aware of much.

"Prisoner Bereskova," he said, "how is it that you're in this inebriated state?"

"No' ineb – ebri –"

"No? Please follow the straight line along the floor." He helped her upright.

He could see how hard she tried, but she stumbled or stepped off the line several times, either on one side or the other, in an effort to stay upright.

"Prisoner Bereskova," he said, "come here." He explained in a whisper, with great patience, that in he was in charge of the medication for the next two days, and that she must trust him. "I'm here to get you out of this place," he whispered. Then, more loudly for the benefit of observers, he added, "I find this inebriation inexcusable."

"Not drunk," she whispered. "They drug me."

*

Two days later.

"Prisoner Bereskova," Grigori said, "come with me." He unlocked the door with keys obtained from his section leader that afternoon. The door clicked open. "And keep acting drunk, in case anyone comes" he whispered.

Barbara wobbled and stumbled towards him as if she'd drunk a whole bottle of vodka.

He needed her back to her senses and with her wits about her, but also sober enough to act as if affected by the drugs. He'd injected her with saline instead of the medication she'd been given since her capture on Galatea Station. "Well done, Barbara, I'm proud of you," he murmured outside the cell.

"Thank you," she said. "But who are you? I overheard them say there were new guards, but –"

"Later, when we're out of here," he said, and held a finger to his lips.

She nodded and acted more drunk than ever.

They passed a series of cells, all similar to Barbara's, on the way out. Some were empty, but most were occupied.

"What is this place?"

"JSEP outsource their interrogation here." Grigori halted at the corner. He peered around it in both directions, nodded and continued along the corridor.

At the exit, Grigori spotted a camera on a swivel mount. It did periodic sweeps of the area of view. He took a can out of his pocket, stood unseen beneath it, and sprayed white paint on the lens.

"We haven't got long," he said. "They'll know something's up now. Can you run?"

"Yes, where to?"

"Across the yard, under the wire fence, and into the tunnel that looks like the biggest drain you've ever seen." He gestured towards the watchtowers on the outer walls. "We just need to avoid their line of fire."

"I can manage that," Barbara said. "Thanks for coming for me."

"No problem, let's go." Grigori used his key and the door opened.

They sprinted across no man's land to the wire fence. Barbara kept up with him – just.

He lifted the section of wire fence he'd cut through to gain access to the building. They wriggled underneath it and pulled it down again behind them.

Now they must cross the waste ground space between the wire fence and the perimeter wall, a no man's land littered with broken glass, weeds and undergrowth. They were half-way between two watchtowers. There was enough cover from the undergrowth that they'd make it back to the tunnel, but as they edged past the bushes, Barbara's cardigan snagged on a thorn.

She let out an exclamation. The slight sound brought the watchtower guards alert. They strafed no man's land with machine gun fire.

Grigori felt a sharp sting on his left arm and checked it. A bullet had penetrated his arm. "Get down!" he exclaimed. "They're onto us." He caught her hand and pulled her to the ground with him as he dived under a bush. "Under here!"

Barbara wriggled, snake-like, along the ground. The periodic bursts of fire didn't come near enough to worry him. Progress was slow, in order to keep their concealment, but within minutes they were opposite the tunnel.

"Go in, and keep going. It's me, your cousin Grigori. I recruited you, remember? I'll follow." He gave her a little push, then ducked his head as another burst of gunfire peppered the bushes. It was clear that the guards in the watchtower had no idea where they were, but an eruption of machine-gunfire from the other watchtower pinned them down.

"Where does this come out?" Barbara asked when the fire had died away.

"In the forest. Wait for me at the other end. I won't be far behind."

Barbara nodded and disappeared inside the tunnel. Grigori sat up and checked his arm. Blood flowed freely. He pulled a handkerchief from his uniform pocket, folded it into a wad and tied his necktie over it to hold it in place. Then he crept into the tunnel.

Another barrage of fire sprayed bullets around its mouth.

*

Zero, same day (2nd December, 2094).

"Hey, Omol!" Tangar squatted beside him to read a document on the computer. "Thanks for giving the children the water from the condensation films." He had a son, Kweelor, and a daughter, Bronska.

"I thought it was vital they got pure water. I wish we had more of those condensation kits."

Tangar nodded. "Me too." He hesitated, then added, "Omol, we think those aliens we found tried to mine the ores."

"Oh?"

"Yesterday we found abandoned tools and marks on the ore body that suggest an attempt to mine it – and they probably also drank water from the aquifer without realising its toxicity." He sighed. "You've got to wonder whether they were trapped here as well, or whether they came to look for mineral resources. We'll never know for certain."

*

The tunnel was dark. Grigori pulled his phone from his breast pocket and switched on the light. At least he could see where he was going now. *Barbara has no such luxury,* he remembered. He made good progress up the tunnel, and soon reached her. She hugged him. She seemed glad to see him. Outside, all was quiet.

"How's your arm?" she asked. "Oh good, you've bandaged it now."

"I'm OK," he said. "I wasn't going to leave you to JSEP's tender mercies."

"If they outsourced their incarceration, you might wonder whether they even know what goes on here," Barbara said. "They think it stops them from looking bad, I guess."

"Ever the investigative journalist, little cousin!"

And then the world erupted into a jumble of timber, tree roots, a choke of earth and rubble, and a sound like a clap of lightning.

"They're shelling us!" Grigori yelled above the din. He grabbed Barbara's hand and pulled her along with him. They clambered over the piles of rubble to seek the further stretch of the passage where no shells had yet struck.

As they jogged into its shelter the second shell fell. The air subsided and the tunnel walls collapsed around him.

Grigori realised he no longer felt the weight of Barbara's tug on his injured arm. He turned his torch light on Barbara's arm.

It was severed. He dropped it in horror. *No time to find her body.*

He stood stunned as another shell fell nearby. The timbers on one side of the tunnel shattered.

His sense of self-preservation roused. *I must leave or die,* he realised, and scrambled for the end of the tunnel. He kept on the move but his chest heaved with effort. His legs and feet ached as he clambered over rubble and debris. And his arm was agony.

He had a vague memory that he should keep it elevated above his head until he could get first aid. But that was impossible in the dark tunnel. He needed his injured hand to hold his phone torch to light his way. The other supported him wherever the wall permitted. *I'm sure I've got splinters from that rough timber we used to shore up the walls.*

Ahead there was light, but he didn't think it was from the exit into the forest. The tunnel was about half a mile long, but he was already half-way through it. The light he saw was well ahead of him.

When he reached the topographical low where Voronovich had set up the pumps, he could no longer hear their mumble. *They must have failed when the shells fell. Nothing for it – I'll have to wade through the water.* He located the water's edge with the torch on his phone and stepped in. The water was only about a foot deep, but rose as he waded. The cold soon invaded his whole body, thanks to the shock from the bullet wound. He couldn't feel his feet as he stepped out where the passage sloped upwards again. But he was glad to be on dry land.

As he neared the patch of light his heart sank. The light entered through another breach in the tunnel roof. He continued to move, wary. Ahead lay a body. He turned it over. It was Voronovich.

He left the engineer where he lay. *No time or strength to do anything else, and to close the engineer's eyes would give away my survival. At present, any pursuers might well assume I was also killed when they shelled the tunnel.* He pressed on, trying to suppress his gasps for breath.

He surveyed the scene as he approached the tunnel mouth. He saw no troops with machine guns. *Perhaps they're hiding.* He scanned again. It was an obvious place to set a trap for him in case he'd survived. He smelled vanilla. Before long he spotted a couple of uniformed guards lurking behind a bush, vaping.

I can't just stay in the tunnel until they leave. Yet it was what he should do to make good his escape. The only other option was to kill the two guards. He didn't want to do that. For one thing, he wasn't sure he could take on both of them with an injured arm. And he recognised one, a lad of eighteen. *He'll recognise me too*, he reasoned, as he stepped back into the shadows.

The decision was out of his hands when the older guard put his radio to his ear. They held a short discussion, then edged into the dark tunnel. One had a flashlight.

Bad news. Grigori took out his pistol and gripped it by the barrel. The lad he knew by sight ventured closer. He crept up behind the two of them. The pistol flashed down once, then, as the other guard turned, twice.

Grigory left them in the tunnel, and headed for the hut in the woods where his clothes were stored. The nearest train station was three days' walk from the prison.

*

Three days later.

With only a couple of miles to go now, Grigori's main problem was that his feet were rubbed raw from his sodden shoes, and from walking so far with wet skin. With no towel, he'd used his guard uniform and left in in the hut, and had been walking ever since. But he'd found his wallet and other personal effects in the hut, and had bought food and hot drinks from time to time.

He was so exhausted it was hard to keep walking. He felt inside the pocket of his coat for his ticket. He daren't stop to rest. *I can do that in the train.*

It had rained for most of the day. Grigori pulled his coat around him and turned the collar up. He didn't mind a wetting under normal circumstances, but his feet were agony, and his arm hurt a lot too.

He limped into the station, hobbled over to the nearest seat and sat down. *Back to civilisation at last,* he thought, and looked around to see what the station offered. Opposite was the departures and arrivals board. The next Moscow train was due in minutes. He stood up, though his feet felt as if they were on fire, bought a coffee and a doughnut (he rather liked them, a relic from his JSEP days) to tide him over, showed his ticket, boarded the train and collapsed into a seat.

Although tired, he kept a wary look-out for uniformed guards or police on the platform. Once he thought he saw a politsiya push through the crowds, but the man soon moved out of sight.

The carriage was empty, so Grigori put his feet up on the seats and laid back. It was bliss to just rest. He had nowhere to walk for a while.

But he froze as there came a knock at the window outside. He forced himself to relax and pretend to be asleep. After several minutes, he opened one eye enough to see that there was nobody there.

He felt in his pocket for his painkillers and swallowed two with a gulp of coffee. Then he took off his coat, laid it over himself, and drifted into an exhausted sleep as the train pulled out of the station.

*

Safe house, Moscow, three days later.

"Where the hell have you been?"

Grigori's mouth dropped open. Per Lakshar had always been polite to him. He respected his contribution to the movement. But his leader looked to be in a bad mood. "I went to the other safe house for medical attention. I came as soon as I could walk again."

"You'd better come in and sit down. What happened to you? Where's Barbara?"

Per must have realised things had gone wrong. Grigori told him everything. “She was my cousin, and because she helped us, she’s dead. I really regret recruiting her now.”

“I told you it wasn’t sensible to recruit family members, didn’t I?”

Grigori sighed. “I know.” He heard the resigned note in his voice. “But she had the investigative skills we needed. And I knew it was risky to try to rescue her, but I had to try. I think I’d have felt even worse if I hadn’t tried to get her out of there.”

“You lost Voronovich, too. He was a good engineer.”

“The team?”

“All back safely.”

Grigori nodded. “And my effects were still in the hut, for which I’m grateful.” He moved his arm and pulled a face. “I got shot. The bullet’s out, but it’s very sore, especially as I couldn’t get medical attention until yesterday. And my feet are blistered all over. The pumps failed when the shelling started – that’s when they got Barbara – and I had to wade through the water. But they’ve been dressed and will be OK soon.”

“I’m glad to hear it. But that’s the last time I let you carry out such a hare-brained scheme!”

Grigori looked at the floor and apologised.

CHAPTER 11 – Power Play

Upper Richmond Road Primary School, 15th April, 2095.

MIL HAD FINISHED HIS LUNCH. He wandered around the play area, with the rest of the midday break to fill, watching the human children. Their shouts filled his ears, but he felt empty. He wished he was back on the ship.

Or with Steph. Schooldays seemed long and empty without her. Although he was at least as advanced as any child in his class in most subjects, and had learned a lot in since he'd come to school, he looked forwards to the evenings and weekends when he could be with Steph – and Chas, when he was on leave. Ronnie was no substitute. Mil had soon learnt that any time he did spend with him at school was occupied in him boasting about his alien foster-brother.

His legs ached. He was tired. He sank down, and leant back against the sun-warmed playground wall. He closed his eyes, and the calls and laughter of the human children drifted away.

A giggle roused him, then a jumble of words buzzed against his tympanic membranes: a girl's voice. It was moments before he processed her words. He opened one eye. A girl he'd sometimes seen with Ronnie stood before him, skipping rope tucked under her arm.

"D'you want to play with us, Mil?"

"Play?"

"Come on – we're going over to the chestnut tree there." She beckoned him with one hand and pointed to the tree on the green with the other.

"OK." Mil grinned his pleasure at the invitation – from human children older than him – and climbed to his feet.

She walked quickly; he had to run to catch her up. “You’re Ronnie’s friend, aren’t you?”

The smile slipped from her face. “I’m in his class.” She quickened her steps. “Nearly there. Come under the tree. The others are already here.”

“Others?” Mil felt apprehension’s shadow block the sunlight. “Is Ronnie here?”

“Just our gang. Boris and Stevie and Mark. And me. I’m Annie Vereker.”

The shadow became real as they stepped under the low boughs. As his vision adjusted to the gloom and slipped between normal and thermal vision mode, three figures became visible: a tall, thin boy with skin darker than his, and two paler-skinned boys, seated cross-legged.

Annie pointed to the trunk. “Sit down and lean back against that.”

Mil obeyed.

“Undo your trousers.”

“Why?”

“That’s the game.”

Mil looked at the other three boys. Each of them had unzipped their trousers. Annie lifted the hem of her dress and wriggled to pull her briefs down. Mil caught a glimpse of bare skin until she sat down. It puzzled him; he remembered the triangle of hair in the same place on Steph at the pool.

“Come on, undo them!” Annie’s forehead creased in impatience.

“Why?”

“It’s the game. You know – we look at your willy and you look at ours. Well, mine’s not a willy, but – same thing –”

Mil’s reluctance to play this game surprised him, but he let himself to go with it. He stood up. “I don’t know why you want to look at my willy,” he said. “I only pee with it.”

"Don't you do the other thing?"

"What other thing?"

The boy Annie had introduced as Boris spoke. "You know – fuck."

"Fuck?"

"Yeah, you know, where one of us puts his willy in her thing."

"Oh," Mil said. "I didn't know you could do that." He moved away from the trunk of the chestnut tree, and headed for the light.

Annie Vereker's hand caught his wrist, then dropped it. She let him go.

But as he stepped over one of the white boys, he caught sight of what peeped out of his trousers. A vivid mental picture of Ronnie's thin freckled body as Steph towelled him dry came to him.

Then he realised. *Ronnie must have told them about the shower.*

*

Eddie's apartment, Houston, next day.

"Time for bed, Kaj," Juliet told him. "You've already stayed up later than you should." *He looks tired,* she thought. *It's not surprising.* Since Eddie's return to Galatea Station, Lucy had slept poorly. She often woke up crying, as if she missed her father. She'd kept them both awake the previous night.

Kaj nodded, ejected a book disk from the computer, and put his schoolwork into his school bag. "Goodnight, then, Juli," he said, and turned towards the door.

"Goodnight, Kaj. I'll bring you a drink in a few minutes. Computer, put the news on HV." The projection tank filled with the holoimages and Bonnie Smith's voice burst from the monitor.

"...JSEP engineers at Galatea Station have made a breakthrough in their exploration of the alien spacecraft brought back to Earth eighteen months ago."

Juli locked gaze with Kaj, who stood, framed by the doorway.

The report continued: "Engineering Team Manager Terry Mellows says he's received information that has helped to identify machines onboard the ship which could revolutionise astronaut food, eradicate famine worldwide, and be useful in the Moon and Mars bases…"

Juli got to her feet.

Kaj stood open-mouthed, an expression of dismay on his face. Juli's stomach churned. She crossed to Kaj, who stood like a statue as he scanned the HV for further information. But the newscast had moved on to a serious earthquake in Japan.

"That's about me," Kaj said. "Me and my friends. But mostly about me."

"Yes… Terry Mellows is Eddie's boss. I only met him once. He's a slimeball."

"Eddie said he was an engineer," Kaj continued. "It was him that gave them the information about the foodsynth machines, wasn't it?" His voice was a whisper. "He got it from me, didn't he? He got me to betray my people, and I didn't even realise!"

Juli guessed he was in shock. She realised he was furious and put out a hand to him. "Kaj, Kaj! How can they find out what happened to your people if they don't know how the ship works?"

Kaj struggled out of her embrace. "They can't. Only *we* can do that. All of us kids have a right to know what happened to our parents. But they're keeping us apart from each other so we can't find out. None of us knows where the others are." His fist thudded against the coffee table. "They're scared of us, and they want the drive. They won't look for our parents, even if they can get the drive to work!"

He turned and fled. His footsteps thumped on the laminate.

Juli stayed where she was, even when a door slammed. After a moment or two, Lucy's cry reached her.

I'd better go to them. They both need me. But I'll let Kaj cool down first.

She trudged towards Lucy's room. Lucy lay in her cot, face red, eyes slits. Her screams punctuated the silence as she waved her arms back and forth.

Juli picked her up and held her. She rocked her to try to quiet her.

"Juli? I'm sorry – I didn't mean to wake Lucy!" Kaj said from behind her. "I'm just *so* angry! I thought Eddie liked me – you know, that he liked talking to me about technology and stuff – but he just wanted information!" His face was full of bitterness.

Juli drew him against her and rested Lucy between them. The screams subsided. "I understand," she said. "And I think Eddie does like you."

"Then why would he do this to me?"

"Maybe he had to, for his job. I thought it was strange when he called me to say that we'd been selected to foster you, but Lucy was due, and I didn't have time to worry about it." She smiled at him. "*I* like you, Kaj. I know you didn't mean to upset Lucy. But it must be scary for her when someone thunders about in the house."

"Yes." Kaj took a deep breath, then said, "Let me hold her."

He lifted her up and held her in the air, her legs kicking. "She's getting heavy." He looked into her storm-washed eyes, now fully open in the wide-awake way she had. "Lucy, I'm *so* sorry. I wouldn't scare you for anything. Please forgive me, and go back to sleep."

I don't believe I'm hearing this, Juli told herself. *But she really is quieting down, just as if she understands what he says.* She'd noticed before that Kaj had a calming effect on the child.

"Kaj, do you like young children?" she asked. "You're good with Lucy."

"I used to play with the youngest kids on the clanship, and help teach them to fight." Kaj shrugged with one shoulder. "We grow up communally. There was a boy called Miril, the youngest, only two before the Long Sleep. I don't know how old he'd be now – and unless we can go back to the ship and consult the computer, we'll probably never know! I don't even know how old I am, though from my height I think I might be twelve or thirteen in Zarduthi years." He offered Lucy back to Juli. "Here. She's gone back to sleep."

Juli looked into Lucy's face. The angry colour had faded from her cheeks, and she smiled in her sleep. She laid the toddler back in the cot and tucked her in again.

"Go to bed, Kaj, and I'll bring you a hot chocolate drink. Rest, even if you can't sleep. We'll talk about this tomorrow."

Kaj dipped his head in a nod. "All right. But I'm still angry with Eddie. The worst part is, I really like him."

"Me too," Juli sighed. "I liked him enough to marry him and have his child." *Mom always said I shouldn't have married him. Perhaps she was right.*

*

Holiday Inn, London, UK, 19th May, 2095.

"I don't want to go to any stupid circus." Ayar folded his arms across his chest. "I'd rather stay in the hotel on my own." *I wish they wouldn't try to make me like their things,* he thought with a resentful frown. *I'm Zarduthi, not human, and I don't like it here. Not Russia, not Britain, nor anywhere on Earth.*

THE ZARDUTH IMPERATIVE: DISCOVERY
Helen Claire Gould

"Don't sulk so, Ayar! This holiday has cost us a lot of money, and I won't let you spoil it for all of us, especially Natalya." Irina's mouth hardened into a straight line. "She's been looking forwards to coming to England."

Natalya's face was a magnet for Ayar's gaze. She stood with her arms folded across her chest and leant on the windowsill to regard the city spread out below.

He smoothed out the creases in his expression, got up and went to her side, where he copied her posture. "You can go without me, Natalya," he said. "I know it's important to you, but I'm just not interested. It doesn't mean anything to me. I feel trapped on Earth."

"I'm sorry you feel like that, Ayar. But I *want* you to come with us," she said. "It won't be as much fun if you aren't there."

He saw the tears swell along the inner edges of her lower eyelids.

"I want us to be a family. After all, you live with us as my brother. I want you to be a real brother for once. I can't have one, except for you, and I want you to –" The tear bulged over her lower lid, broke amongst her silvery lashes, fell onto her arm, then dripped down it and onto the sill.

Ayar watched in fascination. He saw he was hurting her in some indefinable way.

She stamped her foot. "Can't you just *try* for once? *Surely* it wouldn't hurt you?"

Natalya's burst of anger astonished Ayar. "I thought *I* was the angry one," he murmured. He watched the storm-clouds gather in her grey eyes. "Look, if it means so much to you...then of course I'll come with you."

Natalya hugged him and smiled up at him through her tears. "Thank you, Ayar," she said. He stepped back, half-surprised and half-embarrassed.

"You'd better tell me about this – *circus* – I suppose," he said with a sigh.

"I'll tell you on the way," she said, and took his hand as if she didn't trust him to follow. "Get your coat." As they left the hotel room, Natalya held on to his hand as if she had no intention of letting go.

"Listen. 'The circus was kept as a monument to tradition, preserved for future generations,'" Natalya read to him in the train. "'The performers who staff it train rigorously to maintain the highest standards of their art. There are clowns, jugglers, trapeze artists, and a range of other performers, and in the fair next door there are various old-fashioned rides and features...' You're not listening to this, are you? Look, there's a Hall of Mirrors –"

Ayar shook himself and refocused his attention on her. "Who wants to go look at themselves?" he asked.

"I do," Natalya retorted. "I'm not going to let you spoil my holiday!" And she wouldn't free his hand, even then.

*

Richmond, same day.

"Don't want to go, don't want to go, don't want to go!" Ronnie chanted.

"Don't be so childish and ungrateful. You're on course for a time out!"

Mil stood quiescent at the bus stop as they waited for Chas.

It's not fair *on Mil when Ronnie behaves like this,* Steph thought. *Perhaps we should see if they can find him a home where he won't have this sort of behaviour to contend with.* Her heart gave a little lurch. *But I don't want to lose him – I love him, human or not. He's my other son, my stranger son. But it's Ronnie* who's behaving *like a stranger!* "You won't spoil anyone's day except your own!"

"Where are we going?" asked Mil.

The interruption of her thoughts was welcome. "The Tower of London, then the circus, as it's nearby."

Chas hurried to join them at the bus stop outside the apartment block. "Piccadilly, is that?" he asked with a grin. "Sorry I kept you waiting – I had to send off that report."

"Oh, you did it? Good. Can you sit with Mil? Ronnie's misbehaving." It wasn't that she wanted to deprive Ronnie of the privilege of sitting next to Chas; she would have liked to sit with him herself, but Ronnie wasn't to be trusted to sit with Mil. *They'll be scrapping in five minutes,* she told herself, *and that can't happen on public transport.*

"Sure. Here's the bus. In you get, Mil."

Steph watched Chas climb aboard the bus. Mil sat down beside him. *He's still too tall and slim to be a human.* If Chas had forgotten to send that report... *I don't want to lose him,* she realised. *I know there'll be a time when he has to grow up and leave, but I don't want it to be yet. Even if it does cause problems for him to be here.* She climbed in and the door closed behind her.

It was a moment or two before the sound reached her again. "Don't want to go, don't want to go, don't want to go!"

With a supreme effort of will, Steph ignored Ronnie.

*

"Well?" Natalya asked. "Did you enjoy it at all?"

"Oh...I thought the trapeze artists and jugglers were very skilled," Ayar said, with a gesture, which he recognised with surprise as a human shrug. "What do you want to do now?" He'd decided to go along with Natalya's plans, and had bargained with her to go to a museum the next day. She'd agreed with such grace that he'd mumbled an apology for his earlier behaviour and made up his mind he would match her manners.

They'd received curious glances in the ghost train. Although their clothes and speech were different, the stares were mainly due to Ayar's appearance. He'd ignored them. "Where to now?"

"I want to go to the Hall of Mirrors." She pointed. "Over there."

They walked over to the sign. Natalya giggled and pointed again. "Here we are."

Ayar's English had always been better than his Russian, and he struggled to read in Russian, though he was now a fluent speaker of both languages. But it was easy enough to read this sign, in English characters, painted in bright colours. "Hall of Mirrors," it announced. They climbed the three steps that led to the entrance.

Even he had to smile as they passed from one distorting mirror to the next, as his slim shape grew taller and thinner still, while Natalya's head still stayed at chest level beside him.

"I didn't know you meant this kind of mirror!" he said. He looked around for Alexei and Irina. He couldn't see them anywhere. *Perhaps they didn't follow us. Good.* He pointed at their hands, still clasped together. "Black – white, Zarduthi – human." And he leaned down and kissed her.

Natalya stepped back in surprise as his lips touched hers. "Ayar?"

Ayar opened his eyes. He wanted to ask whether it had been surprise or distaste that had made her move away, but couldn't find the words. Even if he'd been able to, they'd have stuck in his throat. He watched her in an intense silence. When he could no longer bear it, he looked away, to stare at his distorted image again.

The image drew his attention to a figure behind him in the mirror. A tall, slim, dark figure; that of a *gyargh't*, a Zarduthi boy-child.

For a moment time froze. Ayar couldn't draw breath. He noted details he'd never expected to see again: the gleaming black hair-crest on the bare-sided head; dark skin, a leathery mirror-image of his; the lobeless ears that quivered as they processed the sounds in the pavilion; long, slender, quadruple-jointed fingers.

He must be very young, only six or seven, Ayar thought. But before he could move, the *gyargh't* was gone. His heart restarted. He pulled Natalya after him and headed for the entrance.

"But we've only just come in!" she protested.

He ignored that. "Got to get outside," he grunted in reply.

"Why? Are you ill?"

"No," Ayar said, as he pushed past the attendant and dragged Natalya after him. "I've just seen one of my people." He stumbled as he stepped onto the ground.

Natalya steadied him with a hand under his elbow. "Careful!"

Ayar stared around him. The crowds were denser than when they'd entered the Hall of Mirrors. The press of humans was great, their scent strong even in the fresh spring wind. "*Grusken!*" he muttered, as anger rose in him. "Where has he gone? I *must* find him."

"You know who it is?"

"I'm not sure. The only one of us young enough would be Miril, though he was very young when he left the Reception Centre. He might not remember the rest of us."

"Did he come to England?" Natalya asked. The pupils were dilated in her eyes.

"They didn't tell us where any of the others were sent, only that we were all going to families in different countries. But we needed to stay together. And now I can't find him."

Natalya hugged him. "At least you know he's alive –"

"I'm pretty sure JSEP knows where everyone is. Maybe I should talk to them." The balm of her embrace soothed Ayar. He returned the hug, but continued to scan the crowds for the boy-child.

There was no trace of him. He might as well have been swallowed alive by the humans who swarmed about them.

CHAPTER 12 – Manipulation

Richmond, 19th May, 2096.

"BUT MUMMY, HE'S YOUNGER THAN ME. Why should he go up a class *again*?"

Steph met Chas' gaze. *I'm glad* he's *home on leave right now.*

"Because he's learned fast," Chas murmured with a sigh. "In eighteen months he's gone from an estimated developmental age of two or three to seven. There was nothing more for him to learn at Reception level, and nothing more for him to learn at this level."

Ronnie snorted. "Just because he sucks up to the teachers!" he growled. "I don't *want* him in my class."

"Sorry. It's already arranged. You'll get used to it." Chas' tone held no compromise.

"That's what you said when he first came here, but I haven't. Why can't I go up a year too?"

"Because you're not ready. You'd struggle with the work," Steph said. "Come and have your tea. Chas goes back to work tomorrow – don't spoil his last evening here with arguments." She ushered her son towards the table, then went to the door and called Mil. In moments he appeared. He rubbed grass stains from his knees and elbows and laid the book he'd just closed on the table beside his place.

Steph wondered if he'd grown again overnight. He was already taller than Ronnie, though less sturdily built.

"Is it tea-time? Mmm, I'm hungry!" Mil yawned.

Steph noticed again his sharp, oval-shaped teeth.

"Yes, and you'll be up half the night reading, no doubt," Ronnie muttered. "No wonder you're going up a level again!"

"Well, p'raps if you did your homework instead of playing football and cricket *you'd* have the chance to go up," Mil retorted. Then he caught sight of Chas's expression and subsided into his seat.

"Boys!" Steph hated it when they bickered. "I won't have this from either of you. Behave – or go to your rooms."

Steph saw Mil stare down at his food for a moment, then risk a glance at Ronnie. Anger had congealed on her son's features, and she wondered if Mil realised that Ronnie's desire to shine at sports was connected with him.

"Sorry, Steph," Mil mumbled, and examined the food on his plate again.

The redness left Ronnie's face as his mouth reconfigured itself into a smirk.

*

Eddie's apartment, same day.

Kaj lay awake. *I feel stupid,* he thought. *Why didn't I realise Eddie only wanted to find out how the ship works? I shouldn't have told him anything.* He pulled the duvet up around him, as if to hide from the sense of betrayal. But the feeling was still there in his head. He couldn't escape it, no matter how he tried. *I won't tell him anything else,* he resolved. But his thoughts still wouldn't let him sleep. He shifted position. His neck ached, a sign of stress or emotional distress ever since the bout of Mimso Fever at the age of six.

What hurt worst of all was that Eddie had treated him as a Zarduthi adult *should* treat a child. Kaj had been taken in by it. Yet instinct told him Juli was right. Eddie did like him, or would he have trusted *him* to live here with her and Lucy? *Human grown-ups can be so tricky! And what if he had no choice?*

Juli says she likes me too. But can I trust her now? I'll think about it in the morning. It hadn't occurred to him to wonder about that before. His mind drifted as he slipped in and out of sleep.

A sound alerted him as Juli left her bed to feed Lucy, and in an instant he was wide-awake again. *I should have said I'd tell him if he told me where all the others are. We Zarduthi trade information, weapons, or our fighting skills for food and clothes and other goods. Why not information for information? Had I traded in that way, I might not feel so bad. But it feels like Eddie took advantage of me.*

A short while later, Juli's footsteps across the landing told of her return to her bed. He threw back the cover, tiptoed across the room and opened the door.

"Juli? I can't sleep," he said.

"Do you want a drink?"

"Please."

Juli nodded. "I'll have one as well. Get back into bed so you don't get cold – I'll go get them." Her shadow, illuminated by her heat trace, went downstairs. He slipped back into bed and pulled the cover up around him.

He blinked awake again as Juli put on the bedside light. "Here." She handed him a glass of juice and sat on the bed to sip her mug of tea. "Are you still worrying about that news article?"

Kaj nodded. "I feel so stupid."

"I should have stopped it when I felt uncomfortable about it." Juli stopped and a frown settled on her forehead. "You shouldn't blame yourself either, or feel stupid, Kaj."

"I betrayed my friends. My people," he answered.

"But Kaj, you didn't know. You're just a child."

"I'll be an adult in a few years' time," Kaj said.

Juli drew in a breath. "You can't blame yourself for this, Kaj. People like Mellows, up on Galatea Station, are *really* to blame." She took the glass from his hands and placed it on the bedside table. "Rest now. You shouldn't have to worry about it.

I'll speak to Eddie."

*

Richmond, two days later.

"Steph said we should go home this way!"

"We always go home that way. It's boring." Ronnie scuffed the toe of his shoe as he kicked at the kerb. "Do you always do what people tell you?"

Mil shrugged, a habit he'd picked up from Ronnie. "I don't know. I can't remember much before I came here."

"That's what you always say. It's *really* boring."

Mil thought back. What Ronnie said was true – he'd never been able to remember much about the time before the Long Sleep. The hunger for knowledge gnawed at him. He schooled his face into impassivity. "You were happy to boast about me being your foster-brother before I came to school…"

Ronnie turned away. "Scared to go this way?" he asked over his shoulder.

"I'm not scared of anything."

"Prove it!"

Mil ran to catch Ronnie up.

The footpath wound down among trees. Leaves clustered on their branches blotted out the late spring sunlight as the boys passed into the shadows under them. Ronnie strode ahead. Mil saw him shiver.

Mil took off and pocketed his sunglasses. Ahead shadows became heat traces that moved among the trees that grew around the footpath and the stream the bridge crossed. A ripple of fear spread out in his mind, despite his assertion. Perspiration gathered on his skin, chilled by the cooler air in the shadows.

If Ronnie's not scared, then I can't let him think I am. Even if he is older than me... I won't be called a coward! He stepped onto the footbridge as the sense of wrongness increased.

Shouts split the air: the cries of hunting animals.

"Get him!"

Boys burst from the trees like a swarm of hornets and made for Mil.

"Get his clothes off!"

"Hold him down!"

Mil shrank back against the bridge's scaffold-pole handrail. He clung to the pole and swung beneath it. He thought he might overbalance but tried to duck under the barrier anyway.

A dozen boys surrounded him. Somebody grabbed his arm and tugged. Someone else grabbed his other elbow.

He glanced at the boy. He was a head taller and well-built. Mil wriggled, then tried to shove the older boys off him. But he was too strong.

More hands gripped Mil. On his arms. His blazer. Around his neck. He kicked out, not aiming at anyone in particular. He thought to create a distraction so he could get away – and if that meant hurting someone, so be it. "Ronnie!" he yelled. He was nowhere to be seen.

Someone yanked at his blazer sleeve. Mil shut his eyes, and dared not move. *Rrrip!* The underarm seam split. *"GET OFF ME!"* he yelled. The words came out in a throaty roar.

"Hold him down!"

Mil opened his eyes. His captors had ripped his shirt open, heedless of the buttons that popped and rolled in all directions. Ronnie stood over him; his face wore a sly smile. In his hand he held a willow switch. It dripped icy water onto Mil's bare stomach.

"It hurts more if it's wet!" Ronnie said, and leant over Mil. "You three – hold his arms and head. Jack – sit on his legs!"

Mil shivered.

Mil wasn't sure if he'd addressed this to him or the other boys. They still held him down. Beneath him the paviours were hard. Something under him – perhaps a loose pebble – ground into his spine. He wriggled for a more comfortable position.

Mil tried to turn his head, but someone held it.

"You go first, Ronnie," Jack said. "This was your idea."

What will they do to me? Mil stared up at Ronnie and tried to read his expression. The pause stretched time like elastic as if Ronnie couldn't make up his mind.

"Go on! Alien bastard –" Jack shouted.

Thwack! The willow came down on Mil's bare stomach; wet, flexible, and sharp as a whip. Mil jerked with the shock of it. His leathery skin recorded the impact, though not real pain.

Ronnie watched him in silence and tried to gauge his reaction. Mil held his gaze. His eyes, engorged with hatred, never broke their gaze at Mil's face. Now they blazed emotion at him. That hurt more than the impact of the willow switch.

The switch sliced the air again. Mil's body did its reflexive jerk. But he kept silent.

"Can't make him cry? Let me try." It was an older boy. None of them had ever spoken to him, but Mil had often seen them look and point.

The boy shoved Ronnie out of the way. He raised his willow switch for the blow.

It fell on Mil's exposed shoulder. He heard a giggle from Ronnie. Someone else joined the game. The next moment a switch slammed against his stomach, the herald of a rain of blows from all around him.

"Let me, let me!"

"Kill the alien bastard –"

The pressure on his legs and arms released. Mil tensed, ready for action, then sprang up through the crowd. Out of the corner of his eye he noticed an old couple step onto the bridge. Their dog trotted between them.

Mil lunged at Ronnie, arm raised. His shirt flapped around

him. He ignored the sound and the chill air as his talons slashed Ronnie's cheek. A blaze of joy streaked through him to see red blood spurt.

The others stood as if turned to stone. Mil shot across the bridge. Footsteps pounded behind him before something thudded against his back.

Mil's head jutted out over the rest of his body and his feet skidded on the dusty bridge. For a moment everything went into slow motion. The concrete post that supported the railings loomed.

He approached it in slo-mo, as if in a dream. His forehead connected with it bit by bit. This time, the pain hit at once.

Then everything snapped back into real-time. Mil's knees buckled. He slid to a halt on them. Grit abraded them, as the post against his shoulder broke his fall into the water. Dazed by the impact, it was several seconds before Mil moved. He eased back into a crouch amid an intense silence. His teeth clenched on his lip. He laid his open palms flat on the dusty paving and pushed himself upright, then turned and looked behind him.

Ronnie stood nearby. His hands hung at his sides. Blood welled from the scratches on his cheek, but the fight had gone out of him.

The other boys approached in a semi-circle, as if they didn't dare get too close –

"Look at that cut!" Jack whispered. Awe and shock made his voice quaver as he added, "His blood – it's purple..."

Anger filled Mil. He wanted to swipe his claws across Jack's face too; but his body signalled his hurts. He stood as if frozen to the ground and clung to the post for support. The volume of the *tap-tap* and *slap-slap* of heels, and the *click-click* of claws on paviours increased. He turned to look as the couple and their dog approached.

Ronnie turned to the boys behind him and waved his arms

at them. "Go on – get away!" He faced Mil again. "Are you okay? I didn't mean..."

Mil's balance returned, accompanied by pain that peaked and subsided by turns. Every step required concentration. He couldn't see for the blood that dripped into his eyes. He ached all over.

He ignored Ronnie. *He can wait.* He made it off the bridge and stepped past the astonished old couple and their dog.

*

Zero, same day; ship's time/date: 407.385.8.23.924 AD.

Tangar Derren zoomed in on the co-ordinates Omol had followed from the shuttle's logs. A solar system popped up in the simtank. "Planet in the habitable zone, one large moon. Perfect!"

"Talking to yourself, Tangar?"

"It's how this planet gets you!" Tangar squinted into his simtank. "Eh? That's odd."

"What is?"

Tangar leaned over the main simtank to show Omol.

"Where's this?"

"It's that system you told me about – and I've just zoomed in on it. There isn't just a *moon* in orbit around the habitable zone planet – there's a huge artificial satellite as well." He pointed.

Omol stared. "Why didn't *I* see that when I looked?" A thought occurred to him. "I suppose I did use my console monitor rather than the main simtank!"

"*And* I've pushed the resolution up really high, though I can't see the *Bekel* itself though this is updating in realtime. But this is a massive space station. The *Bekel* would only have gone there because it's next in line for attack by the Voth, so either they went to warn them or to ask for help…or maybe something happened on the way?"

"Most likely the Voth. But you're right, the *Bekel* could dock there. Not that *we* can do anything about it. We can't even warn them." Omol pulled a face. Then he remembered he'd been interrupted when he searched. "Computer, show the last recorded position of the *Bekel* on universal co-ordinates."

A white marker appeared beside the habitable zone planet, at the co-ordinates of the space station.

"So it *is* there," Omol murmured. "Not that we can do anything about it."

"Incidentally, is Garchon doing a post-mortem on the aliens in the suits?" Tangar asked.

"Yes. I've asked him to take a look at them and try to work out what killed them, in case it was something in the water."

"Sensible precaution."

"We can't rush in and use the water just because it's there. We need to know it's safe first."

"Ah, you're in here, Omol." Aldor Zevin, who'd taught Omol everything he knew about geology when he was a boy, entered the shuttle. "We wanted to let you know. I can confirm that there *is* an aquifer, several strata below the base of the sandstone these towers are formed from. We did a shot or two to see how they reflected – you might have heard it? Do you want us to proceed with borehole drilling?"

Omol felt a wave of relief wash over him in spite of his cautious explanation to Tangar. "Go ahead."

*

A clatter at the door disturbed Steph as she started the washing machine. She hurried to see what the noise was.

Mil fell through the door and collapsed.

Steph helped him upright. "What's happened? Where's Ronnie?"

"Don't know." Mil shook his head, then screwed up his

face as though the effort hurt him.

"I'd better have a look at you." Steph supported Mil to the sofa and knelt beside him.

He held his shirt closed with one hand. She drew back the cloth when he half-sat, half-lay on the sofa. Purple welts had appeared on his skin. Appalled, she demanded, "How did this happen?"

"Fight. Some boys."

"Which boys?"

"Older boys. One called Jack, I think." Mil's face wore a closed expression.

"Ronnie should have taken you back to the school if there was a problem. He could have phoned me –"

"Ronnie was one of them."

Mil said it in such a quiet voice that Steph wasn't sure she'd heard aright. She stared at him for a moment, then tightened her lips, unsure what to say. At last she managed, "You mustn't tell fibs about things like that, dear."

"I'm not."

The desperation in his voice convinced her. She turned his face to the light to examine his forehead, and saw the anger in his eyes.

"Why would Ronnie attack you?"

"I don't know. But he doesn't like me. He made me walk round the other way – you know, by the stream –"

"Mil, nobody can *make* you do anything! I've told you *both* not to walk that way unless I'm with you..."

The door opened again. Steph got to her feet as Ronnie walked into the room.

"And what happened to *you*?" she asked.

"There was a fight. Mil scratched me." Ronnie put his hand up to the blood on his cheek, but Steph stopped him.

"No – I'll clean it up in a minute." She leant closer, and

realised that tears had mingled with the blood as they dried on his cheek. Steph pointed to a chair on the opposite side of the room. "Sit over there and tell me what's happened while I patch you both up. Then you can both go to bed without any tea. I will *not* have fights from you."

Ronnie glowered at Mil from the other side of the room.

Mil ignored him.

"The bruises will hurt for a day or two, but the thing I'm worried about is this cut on your forehead, Mil. It's deep, and hasn't stopped bleeding yet – it must have hit a vein." Steph said. She pressed lint hard against the cut until the flow stopped. "I'll put some butterfly stitches on it. Sit still."

Steph cleaned the wound, then squirted surface anaesthetic into it. "That's cleaned it up." She pushed the flap of skin back into place, then pressed the first adhesive stitch against his forehead, to hold the flap in place.

"Ouch." But Mil kept still for long enough for Steph to get three adhesive sutures in place.

Steph turned her attention to Ronnie. She had to perform a similar operation on him – except that his scratches were on his cheek, and less serious.

Steph went to call the school when she'd finished.

*

"I don't want you for my brother any more!" Ronnie hissed as soon as Steph was out of earshot.

Mil turned his back on Ronnie and stared out of the window. He wouldn't be drawn into another fight. *He used to tell the other kids about me,* Mil thought, *and he was excited about it. What have I done that changed him? He wanted to play with me when I first came here. Now he gets bigger kids to attack me. It doesn't make sense.*

He turned to look at Ronnie. But his foster-brother was either asleep, or pretended to be.

*

Steph returned a few minutes later, lips compressed together. And once Mil and Ronnie were confined to their respective bedrooms, she pondered on what the boys had told her, as well as the Head Teacher's response.

Did I make a mistake, taking Mil in? Should I have seen that there'd be trouble? Should I have said no? I did know it wouldn't be easy, particularly with Chas away from home for three months at a time...

I'll drive them both to school myself tomorrow. Ronnie's not mature enough to be trusted with Mil's safety, even though he's older. Nor are any of the others. I'll just have to drop them off in plenty of time for my first physio client.

Steph sighed. She had a meeting with Mr Hansen booked for the morning, and it was one she didn't expect to enjoy.

*

Villa Jouvin, Nice, same day.

Robert leant over the terrace railing.

On the foreshore below, Halka picked her way over the boulders on her return from a walk on the beach. The sun faded, and Robert stilled a shudder at what he could expect later. *I hate it when Papa is home on leave.* He'd returned from Galatea Station that afternoon.

Robert knew his mother had interceded on her second husband's behalf again, following another indiscretion on the space station. *He'll return there on Monday morning for disciplinary action.* He glanced back at the house. The patio doors were open, and his parents sat at the table. Their conversation continued, and Robert could hear most of it.

"Oh, Denis? Mademoiselle Carter is coming to see Halka sometime soon – I have the date on file." Maman manoeuvred her wheelchair away from the table. "I'll check it now." And her wheelchair swished towards the hall and disappeared from view.

Robert thought she might need his help and entered the dining area.

"That bloody social worker!" Papa Jouvin muttered. He swilled the wine in his glass, then took a swig. "She can keep her nose out of my business!"

"Papa, she's just doing her job," Robert protested. "She's here to look after Halka."

His step-father set the empty glass down on the table with an audible clink. "Shut up!" he said, and grabbed Robert's arm. "If you tell that nosey social worker anything, I'll kill you!" he snarled.

Robert couldn't help an indrawn breath at the threat, but knew better than to allow his thoughts to escape.

Papa Jouvin took a swig from his glass and wiped the back of his hand across his mouth. "And I'll finish the job I started on your mother," he growled. "We'll soon see how your little alien friend Halka stands up to me *then!* They should have put the alien kids down when they had the chance!"

"Excuse me, Papa," he said. "I've just remembered Maman needs my help with something." And before Jouvin could say any more Robert left the room.

But instead of going to assist his mother, he crossed the garden and went to the peacock gate, hyperventilating as he hurried to meet Halka.

"Robert – are you all right?" Halka asked.

"We need to talk," he said. "Come with me."

"What's –"

He held up a finger to his lips. "Not here," he warned.

They headed up the road out of Nice, towards Monte Carlo. A few moments later, he held out his hand for hers, and took it. He still didn't speak. He waited until they were perhaps a half a kilometre from the villa before he stopped and said,

"Papa just threatened me. He threatened all of us. I need to tell you just what happened here before you arrived."

"Why? What do you mean?"

"In case anything happens to me. Then you can tell the authorities – if you survive and I don't."

Halka gasped, but again, he held his finger against his lips.

He led her along the alley that ran behind the houses. It was steep in places, but it gave him a vantage point from which he could look into the gardens and villas below. "Papa Jouvin is not *my* father – he is my mother's second husband. *He* put her in the wheelchair. Five years ago, he tried to kill her. I saw him."

"You mean – you're a witness to the attempted murder of your mother?"

"Yes. That's why he belts me. To keep me quiet."

"Why are you telling me now?"

"I think you're in danger. He threatened to kill me tonight. It's not the first time. He thinks I'll tell your social worker, Josie, about what he did. He made threats against *all* of us as well. I think you should ask for a transfer out of here, Halka. It's not safe for you to stay. And he means to finish off Maman – he said so."

"But I can't just leave you, Robert! You are my only friend, and if I leave here, I'll be sent to another country to live – and we'll never see each other again." Halka looked more agitated than Robert had ever seen her look. "Tell me about it now. Then we'll go back, and tomorrow we'll think about what we should do about it."

Robert beckoned her into a small space behind the back wall of the Jouvin property. There was a little gap in the wall they could watch through. "Come in here, then if he's followed me, he won't be able to see us."

Halka squeezed in beside him.

"Papa Jouvin was jealous of a man she knew. He thought

Maman was attracted to him, and was going to leave him, so he attacked her with a crowbar." Robert heard Halka's gasp. "She lost her memory, so she doesn't remember what he did. She just woke up unable to walk or remember what happened."

"That's terrible!"

"Yes. But *I* saw him do it. But he saw *me*, too. He was always jealous of her because she has a better job than him. JSEP had just promoted her before the accident – she's Deputy CEO. He, meanwhile –"

"– is a complete waster and spends all his time drinking!"

Robert nodded, but added, "Wait, there's more. He was going to claim on her life insurance, but because she lived, he couldn't."

"He threatened me, too," Halka said. "He said he'd kill *you* if I asked Josie for a transfer or breathed a word of what he's done. He is a hateful man."

"He is, and I'm utterly ashamed of him," Robert said. "But I don't know what we can do about it. You don't deserve any of this."

"Why are *you* ashamed? *You* can't help it, and nor are you responsible for his actions."

"I know this sounds weird, but I'm ashamed because you came to *our* house and family, and Maman took you in to help you, and now this has happened. Not everyone on Earth behaves like him!"

"I know that, Robert! Josie and Dr Chapaire are kind, and so are you and your Maman. Does she know he hits you?"

"No, of course not."

"Perhaps we should tell her."

"It would put her in even more danger. And us."

*

Upper Richmond Road Primary School, UK, next day.

"In view of yesterday's events, we've reviewed our decision to put Mil up a year. Clearly," Mr Hansen said, "Ronnie planned his actions yesterday, to the point that he taunted Mil into disobeying your instructions. Had he not done so, the attack would never have happened."

A vast disappointment gathered in Steph's heart and mind. *My son betrayed Mil.* Steph bowed her head as tears dripped from her eyes. "I'm so sorry," she said. "Ronnie had no right to behave like that, and we certainly haven't encouraged him to be nasty to Mil."

"It's not just you that's disappointed in Ronnie's behaviour," Mr Hansen said. "We pride ourselves on producing excellent students with a good grasp of social skills. Just think what would happen if Mil's biological parents turned up tomorrow! Nobody knows where they are, and therefore that literally could happen. How would they feel?"

"I know," Steph whispered. "I feel terrible. Ronnie is *my* son, and the responsibility for his behaviour is mine."

"Well, the incident occurred out of school time and off the premises," Mr. Hansen pointed out. "I will deal with the bullies by withdrawing *all* privileges from them – that includes Ronnie. They'll have extra work at break-times and lunchtimes for the rest of the term. But I'd suggest Mil stay put in his current class."

"Why should Mil be punished? It wasn't *his* fault!"

"I think Ronnie's jealous of Mil. Think about it. Up until Mil's arrival, Ronnie was the only child at home. After Mil came to live with you, staff members saw him use Mil's presence at home to get attention from other children. He may feel you've spent time with Mil and ignored *him*, though the reason for that's probably because Mil was, as you've told me, in need of your physio skills when he arrived. But there's no sense in stoking the fire."

"You could be right about that," Steph admitted. The thought had crossed her mind a few times.

Mr Hansen interlaced his hands. "You can't take all the blame for Ronnie's behaviour. The fact that so many kids joined in on this incident shows there's ill-will against Mil in school, so my staff and I have decided to run a campaign against bullying by promoting inclusiveness in the classroom. We're planning it now, and will implement it at the start of next week." Mr Hansen sought to meet Steph's gaze.

Steph wiped the tears away with her fingers. "Thank you."

"But Mil should stay where he is for a while. Although he's a very bright lad, perhaps he needs more understanding of human interactions. We'll give him extra life skills training, in short sessions during his best subject lessons. Hopefully that will help him settle in more. It's early summer now. Then he'll move on to new work with his peers in his class in September."

Steph opened her mouth to protest, but nothing came out. She felt unable to even express her feelings at that moment.

Mr Hansen waited for her to compose herself.

"I – thank you," she managed at last. She couldn't decide which was worse, feeling indirectly responsible for the conflict that had torn her family apart, or shame that her own son had attacked his foster-brother. Either way she felt humiliated and ashamed.

Mr Hansen must have had a good idea of her emotions just then, because he said, "Please don't think we're criticising your parenting skills, or Mil's interpersonal skills, Mrs Lawton. But Zarduthi families may interact in a very different way from human families, and we want to support *all* our students. This is a way in which we can help Mil *and* you – and the whole family. And please –" He met her gaze. "If you have *any* concerns that we can help you with in the future, talk to me. We want the school to function for everyone, and that means children –

wherever they're from – and their parents, and the staff and local community."

Steph muttered a last "thank you", shook Mr Hansen's hand, and stumbled out of the room. She was blind to her surroundings as she replayed their conversation. Mr Hansen had addressed Mil's wellbeing and Ronnie's as well as the older boys' punishment for what they'd done. But she wasn't happy with the outcome.

Ronnie's got his way after all, kept repeating in her head. *He manipulated all of us.*

*

Alexander Pushkin School, Moscow, same day.

"All right, everyone. Break for fifteen minutes. No drinking or eating in the classroom, remember."

Ayar got to his feet. His face felt as if it had frozen into a scowl ever since he'd arrived in Moscow. *I miss my friends from the clanship,* he realised. He wandered out of the classroom and into the corridor, looking for his foster-sister. Although Irina and Alexei were kind, and keen to help him settle in, Natalya was the only bright light here for him. He spotted her in a knot of girls just as her eyes flashed with laughter.

I won't go over there if she's with them! Ayar told himself. His body reminded him of its needs, so he turned towards the cloakroom. He headed for the nearest cubicle, only to find the door shut and the red "engaged" sign in place. He stepped back to try the next cubicle, but the same sign showed on all five doors. The urge to urinate became intense.

He looked at the white fittings mounted on the wall, which he hadn't used so far. Pipes ran from them down the wall and into an open channel on the floor which drew the liquid waste away. The smell was overpowering: sweet, sharp and rancid. They didn't resemble other toilets he'd used – on the clanship, the toilets were partly enclosed behind bulkheads, with only the seating exposed.

Two boys from his class stood before them. Ayar didn't want to upset them so he averted his vision. But he didn't want to make a fool of himself either. The nearest boy glared at him; Ivan Razich was a known bully. Ayar managed a small smile and nod, and stepped closer to the row of mountings. He tried to breathe shallowly through his mouth, and peered down and across to see how Ivan used the urinal.

Ivan directed a jet of yellow urine at the mounting.

Ayar couldn't see much, but it was enough to tell him he'd guessed right. He unzipped his trousers.

"What're *you* looking at?" Ivan's voice was a growl Ayar hadn't realised a human voice could make.

"Nothing," he said, and directed his own stream into the mounting. Sheer physical relief mingled with apprehension.

"You're looking to see if my cock's bigger than yours!" Ivan sneered.

Ayar began, "I was trying to see –"

But Ivan ignored him, shook himself so that droplets sprayed out in Ayar's direction, then tucked himself away and zipped his trousers up. "Well, let's have a look at yours, Mister Ayar-the-alien!" He leaned closer, then recoiled. "Christ! It looks more like a fucking screwdriver with worms crawling all over it than anything else! You'll never pork anyone with *that*, never mind Natalya!"

His crudity startled Ayar. *How do they know…?* He clamped his lips together and stared down at himself. The stream's urgency waned; the liquid was colourless. He wanted to finish, wash his hands, and leave.

But Ivan Razich stood there beside him with an expression of disgust on his face, and the other boy, Nicolai something-or-other, hovered behind him. Ayar knew their reputation; he was sure they wouldn't let him leave without trouble. There was no other reason for them to stay. And though he was taller, there were two of them. He shook himself and zipped his fly closed. Then he turned to face the bullies. The stench of urine filled the confined space. "I wasn't looking at you," he said. "I just hadn't used these –" he indicated the mountings "– before, and wasn't sure how to –"

"Well, we can show you, Ayar-the-alien," Nicolai said. A smile lurked on his lips. "Can't we, Ivan?"

Nicolai's other name came to Ayar. *Tchenkov.*

"We certainly can," Ivan agreed, as he grabbed Ayar's arm.

Ayar dropped into close-combat stance at once. Nicolai stepped back a pace in shock. Ayar was gratified to realise that neither Ivan nor Nicolai had expected his reaction. He cast a glance around the washroom. *There's not much room for a fight, but I have to make a stand now or I'll have no peace from these two.* He kept his chin tucked down to protect his translator as he laid his hand on Ivan's arm and squeezed like a vice. Ivan released his grip. A jerk of Ayar's wrist had him on his knees, arm behind him.

It only occurred to him to wonder where Nicolai was when he felt sharp bones thud into his back and drive him off his feet. As he leant forwards, his head hit the urinal. He sank to his knees, dazed.

For a moment he couldn't think for the pain in his head. Hands seized him, pulled, and forced him downwards. The smell of human urine was overpowering. His balance had gone. He opened his eyes. The channel which took the waste away was directly under his nose. He tried not to breathe.

"You stink, shitface!" A shove brought the porcelain into sharp contact with his cheekbone.

Ayar's face went numb. "Don't think human shit and piss

doesn't stink!" he grunted. Pain replaced the numbness in his head.

Another shove. The pain in his cheekbone grew worse. He put his hand up to cover his face and block the smell. His head cleared and he drew his feet under him for a final effort to stand up. He was sure they wouldn't leave it at that. His father had drummed it into him – all of them – that until an enemy showed it in his eyes, he wasn't beaten.

Though he couldn't see their eyes, he knew they weren't beaten. But nor was he. With an effort that made his thighs tremble he surged upwards and twisted, fists balled. He got in a strike at Nicolai before Ivan caught his arm, then kicked upwards as hard as he could. He could only guess at how much damage he could do. Ivan doubled up and clutched his crotch. Ayar settled back into the close-combat stance again, ready to serve Nicolai the same if he made a move. He forced a smile of satisfaction to his lips.

Nicolai took Ivan by the arm. "Come on," he muttered. "We'll get him later." He hauled Ivan after him.

Ayar sank to the floor when they'd gone, his back against the door of one of the cubicles. His whole body trembled. *I must have been weaker than I thought after not fighting for so long,* he thought. *I'm going to start working out.*

The adjacent cubicle door opened and a stocky figure emerged. Ayar recognised his face but couldn't remember his name.

"Have they gone?" the boy asked.

"Think so," Ayar gasped. *Oleg, that's it, Oleg's his name.*

"Are you all right?"

"Maybe." Ayar pulled his feet under him and tried to stand. Behind him, the cubicle door opened and another of his classmates emerged and went to the washstand. "Did you all stay in there because of them, Oleg?"

Oleg nodded. "Everyone keeps out of their way. We've all been bullied by them. Especially in here – the teachers can't see what they're up to. They should put cameras in here." He looked at Ayar. "You'd best get that cut cleaned out and dressed."

Ayar hobbled to the nearest washstand and regarded himself in the mirror. Purple blood oozed from a cut on his cheekbone; the area was swollen. He washed his hands carefully with soap, then bathed the cuts, though the soap stung.

"They won't let you get away with besting both of them," said Oleg. He still hovered beside Ayar, and watched him. "You've made an enemy. They won't let you forget this."

"I know." *And Ivan Razich and Nicolai Tchenkov know about my unbrotherly attraction to Natalya. As if it's not difficult enough –*

Ayar felt the hot surge of resentment again. *Just eighty days off adulthood when my father left the* Bekel. *I wish I'd been old enough to go with them. If only...*

CHAPTER 13 – One Step Forwards…

The Lawtons' apartment, Richmond, 23rd May, 2096.

MIL DREAMED.

He stood in a circle of boys and the circle was closing in on him. They reached out for him with short blunt fingers. There was nowhere to run, but he couldn't fight them all. Just as the nearest laid a hand on his shoulder and drew back his fist for a blow, Mil saw his face: Jack towered over him, an impossible giant. Behind him stood Ronnie.

Jack's features melted. His hair went first. It revealed something lurked underneath his scalp as it melted into a pale mess. Tears of blood – light red human blood, the colour of wine – streamed down his cheeks. Runnels of spoiled parchment festooned his features as Jack's true face was exposed. It wasn't a proper face, like Mil's or Ronnie's, but plates of armoured material. From between the curved plates, tufts of coarse grey hair sprouted.

Jack's eyes dissolved. Tissue peeled away in drapes of rotten membranes, layered like clothes. It was as if he removed a coat. But Jack had no control over what happened, yet he wasn't scared. He smiled as his face dissolved, and the smile contained absolute cruelty.

But the coat is his skin! Mil shuddered. He feared *his* flesh would rip and spoil like Jack's. He couldn't hold back a cry.

Now Ronnie melted behind Jack. But Mil couldn't look away at him. He was afraid to even look at himself. His arm itched. He shut his eyes, afraid to scratch it. The itch spread up his arm. Mil's stomach somersaulted in dizzy terror.

The Jack creature approached to embrace him. Although he'd squeezed his eyes shut, he could still see Jack's body, all curved armoured plates, and grey-white whiskers. It touched his shoulder. He screamed again.

The metamorphosis began again. Terrified, Mil tried to shut his eyes again, although he knew he'd just done so. The faceless creature peeled open again, to reveal the human underneath, with wicked red poison spurs at his knees and elbows. Jack was new and perfect –

"Mil, what's the matter?"

He awoke to find his fingers at the new scar on his forehead. His arm had gone to sleep where he'd lain on it. Steph held him, and her hand touched his shoulder where the thing had touched him in the dream. He shuddered.

"Bad dream –" he croaked.

"It's okay now, you're safe. You know I won't let anything bad happen to you." Steph stroked his head, smoothed hair-crest and bare scalp alike. "D'you want to sleep in with me for tonight?"

Mil gazed up at her. She'd never suggested that before. He associated her as only sleeping with Chas, when his foster-father was home on leave. Ronnie always slept in his own bed in his own room, though he was probably a couple of years older than Mil. *I'm sure he'd have plenty to say about this if he knew,* Mil thought. *But the dream was really scary...*

"Please," he nodded. "I'm not big enough to fight the Voth yet – or the Kiai –"

He was half-aware as Steph carried him into her room and laid him in her bed. Moments later he felt her warm body against him, and the protection of her arm around him.

"It's OK," she said. "You're safe. Go to sleep now..."

*

Mr Noguchi's dojo, Tokyo, next day.

"You're next, Chan," murmured Mr. Noguchi. Chan

tightened her belt and advanced a step. She'd gone up a grade after the last examination, and had made good progress in karate, too. Mr. Noguchi had been so impressed with her progress that he'd suggested she enter the next competition.

Her opponent came forwards too. His eyes flickered as they exchanged bows. He was from another local club, a stocky lad of twelve or thirteen – at least a year older than her.

He looks strong, she thought. *He'll be hard to beat.*

The boy circled her warily, fists raised to block an attack. Chan copied his posture and circled until he presented an opening. Then she stepped forwards and gripped his tunic with both fists. Her elbow slid into *his* hold, but Chan had expected that. She looked into his impassive face. His breathing was shallow. *I think he's ready to make a move –*

His hand swung out in a straight punch aimed at her face.

Chan raised her free forearm. The blow slipped off-course. She shifted position and adjusted as if his shadow. A lunge off her back leg gave her the momentum to deliver a glancing blow to his chin. She followed it up with a twist of the hips. The pressure of her arm across his back at the same instant flipped him over her hip. He landed flat on his back.

In a trice he recovered.

Chan stepped back, chest heaving. The next fall was hers, but she bounced upright as if by reflex.

They circled again. The light flashed off Mrs. Kobayashi's necklace. *I* must *prove this isn't a waste of time!* Chan thought. She tried to take hold of his cuff to throw her opponent, but he moved it out of her way, shuffled his feet to change the dynamic and threw her instead.

Okay, no need to prove anything. The honour's in competing. Look out, here he comes again!

Chan's slight advantage was in her long limbs – though they carried less power than her opponent's stocky frame. His punch came at her fair and square. She eluded him with a body drop, and followed it up with the manoeuvre she'd tried earlier, the hip throw.

The boy stared up at her from the mat. She saw in his gaze that he knew she was the victor, though narrowly so.

Afterwards, he bowed deeply and said, "You fight well."

Chan returned the bow. "So do you."

He said, "You're one of them, aren't you? The aliens. I had no idea I would be matched with one."

Chan grinned back. "On the other hand," she said, "there was every indication *I'd* be matched with one!"

*

Zero, same day (24th May 2096), ship's time/date: 407.10.3.76.024 AD.

Omol got himself a drink from the synth machine, then returned to his computer. Before he had time to immerse himself in his work again, Aldor entered. He looked pleased with himself. "Omol! We've got something to show you." He led him through the tower they occupied. Lights and cables followed the walls everywhere now. Thanks to Fenalt and his team, and a reactor from one of the shuttles, electric lighting was provided to each chamber now.

At the exit, they clambered down the rope ladder that festooned the outside of the tower. Aldor led Omol to the tented compound where the latest borehole had been drilled, with another computer nearby, which had software for geological mapping on it. The power supply came from a shuttle reactor and solar panels switched to infrared mode.

"We used resistivity studies to distinguish between salt and fresh water, so it should be safe to drink the water from the aquifer."

"Can we get the water out via the drill borehole?" Omol

asked.

"We can just pump it up."

"Fantastic!" Omol exclaimed. "Good news at last. That's what we needed."

*

The Kobayashis' apaato, Tokyo, 25th May, 2096.

"You did *what?*"

"I wrote in the report that Chan has been learning martial arts and won her latest competition," Mrs Kobayashi said.

Dr Kobayashi stared at her. "Why ever did you do that?"

"Kaito, you know I don't want Chan to learn! It's not something females should do, in my opinion."

"Yes, well, I've now received an instruction from JSEP that she's not *allowed* to learn any more. Have you any idea how frustrated she feels? Your attitude makes her miserable."

"She shouldn't be miserable about something she shouldn't even want to learn!"

"You need to take into account that she's Zarduthi, not human, Minato. She was *born* to fight. It's everything to her to learn. Whose side are you on?"

"Mine. She should be a good girl and learn the feminine arts."

"You've always had a bee in your bonnet about that – and it's irrelevant in Chan's case." Kaito Kobayashi threw up his hands in despair. "When are you going to abandon this outdated idea?"

"Never. I want a daughter, not a warrior-woman. President Langrishe must have realised I'm right at last, and supports my view –"

"Nonsense! He doesn't care about your opinions! It's obvious he's scared that the Zarduthi children will plot against him, but he hasn't thought about what happens if their parents turn up and want to know why they were separated and forbidden to communicate with each other, not to mention why they were prevented from learning any form of combat training, or working as soldiers. When that happens, and they find out that he's effectively committed human rights crimes against those kids –"

"But you yourself said that the kids aren't human, they're Zarduthi, so how can it be against their human rights?"

"Stop splitting hairs! If the kids' parents attack Earth, there could be an interplanetary war because of his mismanagement. He either hasn't thought of that, or he's ignored it and hopes it'll go away." He spread his hands out in an appeal to her. *I can't believe you're so dogmatic about this. You're my wife, and I love you, but you're being blatantly stupid over this.*

Minato never let up. "I don't care what the other children do, or their parents, and I don't care what the president does either. I just want Chan to be a daughter, instead of a tomboy."

"You know what? She'll *never* be a daughter in the way that you want her to. Stop being so hard on her. Give her a bit of leeway if you want to earn her respect. Or carry on with this outmoded fantasy of yours, and totally lose her respect, and maybe her as well. She's perfectly capable of asking for a different placement."

Mrs Kobayashi's face went white.

He wasn't sure at first if it was from anger or fear. "See, you wouldn't like that, would you?"

"N-no. No, I wouldn't."

"Well then, you need to consider how you deal with her." Dr Kobayashi went and got his coat. "I'm going out for a walk. I'll be back shortly."

He stepped out into the rain and walked briskly for half an hour.

When he returned, he'd made two decisions. *They might*

get me into trouble, but I'll see them through. I will ensure that I file the reports from now on. Minato will have no access to them.

And Chan will *continue to learn martial arts, even if she can no longer compete.*

*

Eddie's apartment, Houston, 29th May, 2096.

Juli looked around the room to make sure the apartment was empty and she'd remembered to pack all but Eddie's possessions. Then she walked across to the table and laid her note on Eddie's placemat.

She put Lucy into her stroller, and called to Kaj to come with her.

He came to her side. "Are you OK?" he asked.

"Yes, Kaj. I'm fine."

"You don't have to do this for me," he said. "I know you love Eddie, and I'm pretty sure he loves you."

"I know, Kaj, but I won't compromise my principles and see you exploited."

"I could go back to Dr Chapaire," he said.

"But you'd just be placed with another JSEP family," Juli said. "And they'll be given the instructions to exploit your knowledge of the ship again. It will never end if you go back to JSEP."

Kaj drew a deep breath. His features drooped. "I won't see my friends and kin from the ship ever again, will I?"

Juli rubbed his shoulder with her thumb. "We don't *know* that, Kaj. It's my guess that when you're older they'll find out what's happened, and come to look for you. I think that's what will happen." And she rubbed his shoulder again.

She knew that once she did this, she'd never see either Eddie or her mother again. She wheeled the stroller, with Lucy and her bag of clothes and necessities, out of the apartment for the last time. The removals truck had already left. Her effects would go into storage until she could use them again.

Kaj followed her out, and she locked the door behind them.

*

The White House, Washington, 12th June, 2096.

"What do you mean, disappeared?" President Langrishe's fist thumped the desk.

"Just that, I am afraid, Monsieur le Président." Dr Chapaire paused. Her frown accentuated the angularity of her features, and the holoprojection from the phone in no way softened it. "I received a report from the family two weeks ago as usual. The children's social worker made a visit a week ago, but when she arrived the apartment was empty. She investigated, in case they were on holiday, or the mother, our usual contact, was ill. Neighbours said they hadn't seen the family for a couple of weeks. Nobody knew where they were. It seems the family disappeared the day after she sent in the most recent report. The social worker continued her investigations, but hasn't discovered their whereabouts, or anything further, except that the foster-father is at work at Galatea Station, and doesn't yet know of his family's disappearance."

President Langrishe's hand clenched on the mug of coffee beside him on the desk. Veins stood out on his pallid flesh and pulsed with rage.

"I would not," said Dr Chapaire. "It will probably cut you!"

"Damn you!" roared the president. "Don't tell me what to do!" He picked the cup up and flung it. It shattered with a satisfying sound against the wall opposite, and stained the expensive paper. He ignored the sting of hot coffee against his palm. "You can't even keep your own house in order!"

"I beg your pardon, Monsieur le Président," Dr Chapaire answered, "but I think it would be unjust for you to lay the blame for this at *my* door.

"*What?*"

"I have spoken to our social worker today, and she reported to me that on her initial visit she was disquieted to see the foster-father discussing the principles of the alien ship's drive with the boy. When she spoke to the foster-mother, Madame Harkness seemed angry about it as well. Mademoiselle Carter, our social worker, got the impression the boy was being used."

President Langrishe sat bolt upright. "What *could* she mean?"

"Actually, Monsieur le Président, I think she thought *you* would be able to answer that question. I certainly do. The foster-father is an engineer, working for JSEP at Galatea Station, on a project to strip out and copy the alien ship. On *your* instructions."

"You can't prove that."

"Are you sure?" A smile appeared on Edith Chapaire's face. "It rather confirms my own impression of the foster-father when I met him. And he was *not* willing to exploit the child. These children are my responsibility, and I do not wish to see them exploited further." The smile disappeared. "Evidently Kaj's foster-mother thinks as I do."

"You've conspired with her," the President snarled. "Before we know it there'll be alien whelps everywhere, and they'll take the Earth over."

"Oh really, Monsieur le Président! This is nonsense. You should talk to the children. All they want is –"

President Langrishe flicked the switch to cut the transmission. Then he leaned back in his chair, hands behind his head as he thought. After some moments, he stood up. His expression had cleared, and his features were now set hard. He leaned over the desk towards the videophone, thumbed the switch on, and spoke to his secretary.

"Get me another coffee, Hayley," he said. "I want a clean-up crew in here as well."

"Yes, Mr. President," Hayley responded.

"And set up a teleconference with Hardy Brencher for me, will you? Tell him I have an assignment for him."

*

Eisenhower Reception Centre, Texas, same day.

Hardy Brencher settled into his office chair and signed into the teleconference programme on his computer.

The president answered. His face resembled a thunderstorm.

Hardy felt ill at ease. *That expression bodes no good for anyone.* Working with Langrishe was not straight-forward; he felt as if he trod on eggshells every time he dealt with him. "I've had a conversation with Dr Kobayashi, as requested," he said, "about the implications of the dead Voth's presence onboard."

"Oh, I'd forgotten about that," President Langrishe said. "What did he say?"

"They've discovered something weird about the creature's DNA," Hardy said. "They did a *post mortem*, and –"

"Yes, yes, I know about that," Langrishe said. "He told me that as well. But what I'm interested in is what he thinks it was doing aboard the ship. Was it friend or foe to the Zarduthi?"

"The children don't seem to know it was onboard," Hardy said. "I spoke with all of them at the start of this project. Not one of them mentioned it. And it's impossible to introduce the subject without letting them know it was onboard. But taking into account that it's omnivorous – even down to it dissolving the metal of the ship using only enzymes from its body – as the

English marine, Chas Lawton spotted – it's unlikely to be friendly. If we run with that interpretation, it follows that it was there for aggression. And if it showed aggression to the Zarduthi, it will probably show it to us, too."

"I was afraid you might say that," Langrishe said. "What's your assessment of these creatures' threat?"

"Until we know more, I'd suggest we assume that if the Zarduthi were on a war footing with these aliens, *we* should be, as well."

Langrishe nodded. "I agree. I'll speak to Jim Martin about it. We don't want to get sucked into an interplanetary war." Langrishe paused for a deep intake of breath. "Now, I must discuss with you the way these children are managed. I hear from Japan, via the monthly reports, that a female Zarduthi child has been learning human martial arts. You told me the Zarduthi were space mercenaries, so that should never have happened."

"Uh – no, Sir!" Hardy sat up very straight in his chair. "When did this happen?"

"When I spoke to Kobayashi he told me that this girl – I think they call her Chan – has made great progress in martial arts, which she recently started to learn. But I want you to go to Japan and explain to the family that I won't allow these children to learn martial arts, join our armed forces, or practice fighting in any way, shape or form. Is that clear?"

"Yes, Sir," Hardy said.

"Oh, and while you're about it," President Langrishe interjected, "I want you to give Alexei Petrushenko a verbal kick in the bollocks for taking the Zarduthi boy he's fostered to England on holiday. England is one of Petrushenko's black-listed countries."

Hardy turned an enquiring expression on the World President. "I'll call him and find out why he did that."

"You'll go there in person and explain why these countries

are black-listed," Langrishe said.

"On which budget?" Hardy asked. "JSEP's? Yours? We have sustainability practices we have to adhere to. Flying isn't one of them. Teleconferencing is considered sustainable."

Langrishe knew that was so because he'd introduced the policy, but barked, "Since the problem pertains to Project Revive, you'd best get your ticket from that budget."

"That's the JSEP budget. Mr President, Sir, if you can clear this with Jim Martin, I'll go to Russia and speak to Alexei Petrushenko."

Langrishe just nodded. "I'll get it cleared. All the foster families need to understand this. That's part of your assignment, too."

Hardy nodded. "I'll get on it, Mr President, Sir."

"I'll wait to hear from you on that, then. Now, there's another matter."

"What's the deal?"

"The deal is, Dr Chapaire informs me that one of the kids has disappeared, along with his placement family. I need you to find him again. Can't have them running about on the loose, can we?"

What did I tell you? Hardy thought. *That they all ought to be together at the Reception Centre!*

"I want your best man on this case, mind!"

"Sure," Hardy drawled. "No crap. No sweat. What information do you have on him?"

"I've sent you a file."

He opened his tablet, found the e-mail, and briefly studied the dossier. "No real leads, then," was his only comment.

"No," President Langrishe agreed. "It's up to you to find those." He leant back in his chair and blew smoke rings into the stale air. "I'll leave you to deal with the boy's disappearance."

"I'll send someone to talk to the mother first. That's the

first place women head to when there's trouble. I'll be in touch as soon as there's any news of Kaj." Hardy closed the dossier, turned off the tablet, and finished the call. He leaned back in his chair and interlaced his hands behind his head. He tried to relax the knots in his shoulders.

I need a coffee, he thought. He checked all his security systems, then left the room, locked it, and strode along the corridor to Edith Chapaire's office.

He knocked on the door. "Edith! Can I scrounge some of your excellent coffee?"

Josie Carter answered it. "Edith's not here at present," she said, "but you're welcome to come in and get a coffee."

"Thank goodness for that!" Hardy finger-combed his hair back off his face, though it was short enough to stand on end when he did that. He snapped his fingers. "You know, you're just the person I need to talk to."

"Oh?" Josie became wary of him. "Why?"

"The girl in Japan – Chan. Is it true she's learning martial arts?"

"Yes. Why?"

"Langrishe is spitting bullets about it. I think he's afraid of the children – he's decreed that they aren't allowed to learn martial arts, join our armed forces, or practice fighting either, for that matter." Hardy sighed. "Mrs Kobayashi reported it."

"That woman has a warped mind. In my opinion it isn't a suitable placement – especially for a girl."

"What d'you mean?"

Josie explained about Mrs Kobayashi's obsession with having a daughter.

"That was one of the placements we had to re-arrange in even more of a hurry than the first lot." Hardy sighed. "Well, I have to go to Japan now, and tell Chan."

"I have every sympathy with Chan. She's being prevented

from learning something she really wants to learn because her foster mother has a fantasy about having a daughter. Now you tell me the president is a cranky old bitch who's afraid the children will acquire power over him!"

"And – they're only alive now because the Neoluddites held the President to ransom over his intentions towards them."

"What do you mean?"

Hardy explained the president's original plan to dispose of the children before their presence became known to the general public. "Don't even *think* of repeating that, though," he added, and sighed. "Sometimes you have to accept the hand you're given until the mood of the moment changes."

"Chan won't accept that. But *we* could protest on their behalf."

Her eyes were dark with passion, her nostrils flared. Hardy sensed that adrenaline pulsed through a body rigid with the fight-or-flight instinct. *The girl's a firebrand, but gorgeous with it!* "I think you'll find that would only make our jobs more difficult!" He sighed. "I've worked for three presidents. They were all different, but none has lasted more than a few years. We'll see what happens in the upcoming elections. A new president may have different views."

"Well, I have a plane to catch," Josie said. "I'll leave you to think about it. Oh, and I need to lock up the office."

"Point taken," he murmured, and gulped down the rest of his coffee. He rinsed the cup under the tap and up-ended it on the drainer. "Thanks for the coffee, I must go too."

*

The Jouvins' villa, Nice, France, next day.

Josie nosed the rented BMW into one of the few spaces in the layby opposite the Jouvins' villa, turned off the engine, and reached for her notebook. It was the main tool of her job; it went everywhere with her, a lightweight substitute for the piles of paperwork social workers had dealt with in the decades that followed the birth of their profession.

The atmosphere inside the car became clammy once the air conditioning was switched off. As she opened the door to climb out, the whoosh of incoming air brought heat to her already damp skin.

For a moment she stood and looked out over the sunbaked view. The Jouvins' villa was ideally placed. Sunlight glittered off the water. She reached inside the car to retrieve her sunglasses, pushed them onto her nose, closed the car door, and approached the wrought iron gates.

The villa, like others in the area, shared its main entrance with several other dwellings. To her right, a path led up to the Villa Jouvin, flanked by massive squat palm trees which Josie guessed must be many years old. Their leaves fountained into the air in all directions, like the sails of windmills. The only function they could usefully perform for humans on such a hot, windless day was to provide the villa with privacy.

As Josie approached the peacock gate, the synthesised voice of the intercom said, "Please state your name and business."

Josie did so, conscious of the Brooklyn twang that distorted her French accent.

"Please wait. I will inform Madame Jouvin."

Josie remembered that artificial voice from previous visits. Because Madame Jouvin was an invalid Halka had been placed here on a trial basis. Josie suspected the placement owed its existence to Madame Jouvin's position as Deputy CEO of JSEP.

"Please enter." The gate opened. She entered and walked through the cool of the garden behind the villa. She stepped into the kitchen when the door clicked open.

Inside it was cool. She removed her sunglasses, folded

them, and tucked them into the breast pocket of her off-white linen blouse. She walked on into the lounge. A regular squeak came from the terrace, and through the patio doors she saw the hammock move in time with the squeak. Halka and the Jouvin boy sat at opposite ends. Halka looked to be asleep, propped up by cushions.

She turned her attention back to the lounge. A half-scale bronze statue of a classical naked athlete stood in a sunlit patch in the corner of the room, about to fling his discus. Josie approached it and gave it a thorough appraisal. When she reached out a hand to touch the head sculpted into tiny curls, it was burning hot. Josie snatched her hand back from the statuette, wrapped her uninjured fingers around the burned ones, and turned in time to see Madame Jouvin enter the room.

The woman's face was, as usual, a pale shade of winter. But Josie had been prepared for that. What she hadn't expected was that she was still in her wheelchair. *"Bonjour, Madame Jouvin,"* Josie greeted her and extended her hand, which had cooled down. "I'd hoped to find you fitter by now."

Madame Jouvin clasped her hand with her own limp one. "I know," she said. "My operation was rescheduled, so I'm two weeks less fit than I should have been." A pallid smile at her own joke crossed her face. "But it shouldn't be long before I can be up and about more often."

"I'm *so* pleased to hear that," answered Josie. "I've come to see Halka."

"Of course. She's outside with Robert," answered Madame Jouvin. "Why don't you go onto the terrace and speak with her? Robert can bring you some drinks."

"Thank you," said Josie with a nod, and, replaced her sunglasses as she stepped through the patio doors. The heat beat at her again at once.

She crossed the terrace to the hammock. Halka slept in

peace, but Robert turned in his seat as Josie approached, a finger against his lips.

"You're very protective, young Robert," Josie whispered with a smile.

"Of course!" he said. "Halka is my favourite sister." He grinned at Josie.

"You have your mother's sense of humour," Josie murmured. "Does Halka always sleep in the afternoon?"

"She always has a nap after school." A faint bleep sounded from Robert's wristwatch. "Excuse me, I have to go help my mother."

"Sure." Josie watched him as he hurried into the villa. *He doesn't look much healthier than Madame Jouvin,* she thought, *always so thin and pale*. She stopped the hammock's movement to lower herself into his vacated seat. As she did so, Halka stirred.

"Robert?" Halka asked as she blinked awake. "Ah no, it's Mademoiselle Carter!"

"Robert's helping his mother with drinks. I'm sorry if I woke you." Josie looked at Halka. As she became more awake, Josie saw that her features had changed over the last eighteen months. Her eyes were huge dark orbs, and her features had taken on a sharper, more adult appearance than the childish quality Josie remembered. *But the Zarduthi aren't so different from us,* Josie thought, *at least in some ways.*

"It's fine," Halka said, and checked her wristwatch, which Madame Jouvin had given her. "I usually wake up about now."

"So tell me, Halka," Josie said, "how do you like it here?"

"I – Robert's very kind to me. He's my best friend."

"He seems to like you a lot. And he helps his mother a great deal. You like her?"

"Oh, yes!"

"And how about Monsieur Jouvin?"

*

Josie had asked the question Halka dreaded. *I don't want to tell a lie,* she thought. *I hate him. But I love Robert and Mama Jouvin. What can I do? He'll hurt Robert even more if I tell the truth.*

"Well?"

Halka came to a decision. "I – Papa Jouvin is a strange man," she admitted. "I don't know what to make of him." In the background, she had spotted Robert's approach.

"You see," Mademoiselle Carter said, "Your teacher could only see me *before* I came here. She is – concerned about both of you. She says that although you've made better progress in recent weeks, your work – and Robert's – suffers whenever Monsieur Jouvin is on furlough."

Halka studied the crazy-paved terrace with intense concentration. An ant emerged from between two paviours. Its feelers waved from side to side. Halka's skin crawled whenever she saw them; they reminded her of images she'd seen in the Control Room simtank on the *Bekel*; yet they were easy to crush underfoot – much as Papa Jouvin's violence crushed her and Robert.

Josie switched to English. "You can speak English if it's easier, or more private." She paused. "I'm worried about you, Halka. If there's anything you want to tell me, you can do so without fear. I'm here to protect you, to be someone you can confide in if there are problems."

Mademoiselle Carter had finished, but Halka still held her breath as Robert placed the tray on the ground and handed cool drinks of fruit juice and ice to them. Her glance met and locked with his for a second. *I can't let Robert be hurt any more,* she thought. "There are no problems," Halka said at last, as Robert sipped his drink beside her. "I am very happy here, with Robert and Madame Jouvin."

CHAPTER 14 – …And Two Steps Back

Tower Canyon, Zero, ship's time/date: 407.40.5.35.394 AD, (14th June, 2096).

OMOL STOOD AT THE ENTRANCE to the settlement tower, and looked out. The scene below was neat and tidy. To one side, Aldor had set up a core analysis desk in the shade of the main tower, and a team of three – a petrologist, a mineralogist and a metallurgist – checked each core from the borehole. Their borehole log gained more data every day. But the work was slow and painstaking, and required careful analysis and accurate records.

Further afield, the spring showed some regrowth, after their attack on the Thirsty trees thirty days ago. But the plants were yellow and wilted, even in the dim light. He frowned. *Not that I miss them, but…*

That observation made Omol cease to ponder and clamber down the tower's newly-installed metal external ladder. He set off for the Thirsty trees.

As he approached, he saw the leaf tubes had a greyish-yellow tinge. Usually fresh green, they looked unhealthy. He closed the gap between himself and the trees, and immediately noticed the metallic reek that filled the air. The smell alarmed him.

I'll get Mahyonar to look at this. Omol didn't have the knowledge to investigate further, but his chief botanist would, and could liaise with Aldor. *To work out what's really going on underground,* Omol realised, *we'll need to drill more boreholes.*

He headed over to Aldor and explained his observations.

Aldor scratched his hair crest. "To get a good picture we'd have to drill in a grid pattern over the whole area. It will take time, and we'd need more help with the analysis."

"Vordan and Charime are approaching maturity and would benefit from assisting you and your team," Omol said, "I'll send them to you."

Aldor nodded. "Thanks, Omol. I'll enjoy training them, and it will help a lot."

*

The Bekel, *Galatea Station, same day.*

Eddie Harkness watched in silence as his team piled diagnostic equipment in an empty area in the engineering section. All the fittings had been stripped out of the ship. They were investigating the controls now. *The ship's yielding up its secrets one by one...*

Despite having never found out from Kaj how the Zarduthi made *kuznatt*, the food-synth machines had been a huge success – they'd already mitigated some of the worst effects of the ongoing famines. But for all Eddie knew, the company that had licensed them from JSEP used shit to feed the millions.

And how did the Neoluddites respond? Per Lakshar had issued a statement which had played over and over on news channels. Several of them had been fined because they'd given him air time. "My researchers tell me these machines will take the pressure off the Committee for Resettlement and Colonisation," he'd said, "which I take to mean that the knock-on effect will be to slow down colonist programmes."

But the Neoluddites are probably right, at least in the short term, Eddie thought, then brushed the thought away. He continued to work on the ship's drive, and was still employed. But Juli and the children had gone, and he had no clue where they were. He remembered their last argument – not even face-to-face, but over the airwaves via his laptop. And in his heart, he knew she was right.

By the time he went home for leave, she'd gone. He found her note on his place at the table. He hadn't seen Lucy since she was three weeks old. He sometimes wished the ship had never been found. He half-blamed Kaj, though he knew it wasn't his fault. *I should have stood up to them,* he told himself, on the dark mornings of leave periods. *I shouldn't have let them manipulate me like this.* He'd ignored the irony that he'd allowed it to happen because of love and fear for his wife and child.

And then his conscience would whisper back. *But if not you, they'd have found someone else. Kaj would* still *have been exploited.*

While at work he tried to think of nothing but the task in hand. So he shoved back all the thoughts that tried to escape, and tried to look pleased and encouraging when Gaia came to him in the Control Room and said, "We think we've found the drive system controls, Eddie."

"Oh?" He followed her over to the partly-dismantled control column.

"The controls link back to the nuclear reactor Roy's team found at the heart of the ship, Eddie. It's an ion drive of some sort, similar to those our own ships use, but much more powerful."

"No," Eddie said. "That's not what Kaj told me. He said it was a hyperdrive ship. It travels faster than the speed of light between star systems, but the drive can't be used within a system because the gravity well's tidal forces would tear the ship apart. They have to rely on the ion drive within solar systems. This is probably part of *that* system." He knelt beside the control column to examine the wiring beneath the enamelled metal casing. "I'm afraid you'll have to keep looking."

Gaia's face fell. But all she said was, "All right, Eddie. You're the chief."

Eddie bent to trace the paths of some of the wads of wiring

down the column. There were the cables for the ion drive which Gaia had pointed out, backed up twice as usual. *But what's the other set of cables for?* There were three of *them* as well. He followed them up the column again, using his gloved finger to follow where each led.

"Yes!" Excitement flowed through Eddie's veins. "Gaia!"

The African girl returned to squat beside him.

"Where do these cables go?"

Gaia stood up and played her handheld sensor over the upper face of the column. "Each one goes to a switch," she said, "but some of the switches are linked to each other on the underside of the column – a kind of toggle system."

"Can you trace which ones?" Eddie asked. "I think I'm onto something. Let's get the top off this column." He pointed to a fastening. "Release that for starters," he grunted.

Gaia released it with the special tool he'd designed and had made for the purpose. The Zarduthi used these fastenings throughout the ship.

"Okay, another here, and one at the back." Gaia followed his finger. In a few moments the head of the column was off. Eddie stood up awkwardly and stamped his feet to get the circulation going again. The two of them followed the tracer diagram on Gaia's sensor, and compared it with the maze of wires exposed in the column.

"I think we've found it," Eddie said. "These three switches are linked to these three." He indicated the red cables. "This looks like an automatic relay – for toggling between systems, I'd say. See, it's duplicated here again." He looked at Gaia, and wished he had the heart to grin back at her with the same delight.

But a voice in his head whispered and the smile never reached his face.

Was it worth it? The voice asked.

*

Mr Noguchi's dojo, Tokyo, same day.

"*Sensei*?"

Mr Noguchi turned to face Chan and smiled. "Chan. You did so well in last week's tournament – I'm very pleased with your progress."

Chan bowed her acceptance of his compliment. "I'm afraid you're not going to be very pleased with me now, Mr. Noguchi. Dr Kobayashi has received orders from the World President that I'm not to represent the club any more."

"Why ever not?"

"My foster-mother reported that I had been asked to represent the club, and won my tournament, and the orders came back by express. I'm not allowed to enter any more competitions, and they don't even want me to study mixed martial arts any more. I..." Chan cleared her throat. "I just wanted you to know that I feel happy to have won for the club."

"And what does your foster-father say about this?"

"Dr Kobayashi said I should carry on, if you agree, but just not go in for any more competitions. He knows I would be unhappy if I couldn't continue as your student."

Yuma Noguchi put a hand to his head. Thoughts raced through his mind. *Chan's a natural. She shouldn't give up*, just *because the President says so. It'd be a crime to forbid her to learn more.* "Chan," he said, "there's so much more I could teach you. I wish all my students were as eager to learn and gifted."

Chan stared back at him. He noticed, as he had before, that her eyes weren't the dark brown of his people's. They were a pale brown with darker spikes of colour running from pupil to the dark outer rim of the iris, which was larger than in a human. The specks of amber light in them became more noticeable when she was excited or upset about anything – as now.

He sighed. "Perhaps I should speak to President Langrishe on your behalf. I don't understand why he would refuse to let you learn."

"*Sensei*, I don't think he'd listen," Chan interrupted. "He wouldn't understand at all. I think he only accepts me and the other Zarduthi children, on the basis that if we don't learn to fight, we aren't a threat to him. Look, *sensei*," she said, "I'm a stranger on this world. I *have* no power. Any that I might have had was taken from me. So I only want to regain a little of it, as if I'd grown up on my clanship. If you can help me in that, I'd be more than happy to continue as your student. Dr Kobayashi wondered if you might be able to teach me privately, away from the others, so that they don't have the responsibility of keeping my secret. He thinks I should continue learning." She took a deep breath and added, "But I can't go in for any more tournaments at present. That's what I came to say. I'm so sorry."

"So am I, Chan, believe you me!" answered Mr. Noguchi. "But if that's how you want it to be, I shall be honoured to retain you as my student. You can study with the adults, and it will be our private arrangement. They'll keep quiet about it."

*

Villa Jouvin, Nice, 23rd June, 2096.

Papa Jouvin arrived home on leave again late on Saturday night. A storm raged outside. Furious sheets of water slapped against the windows. Wind funnelled between the hillside houses, and droned loudly enough to dig fingers of fear into the cracks between glass and brick.

Halka heard him enter the house; his footsteps vibrated the floorboards as he stalked into the kitchen. *Even without cause, he's angry!* she thought, and half-wished she'd had the courage to defy his threats and ask to leave. *But there's Robert...*

She couldn't hear further against the groan of the wind

outside, but she imagined what might happen next. Apprehension sent pangs through her stomach. *If Papa Jouvin's been drinking on the flight home, he'll be in a bad mood. If he hasn't, all will be well. Until tomorrow night, or even later tonight.* A lull in the storm reassured her, as she could hear nothing, not even a conversation. She closed her eyes and slipped sideways into sleep.

CRASH!

Halka jerked awake again.

A weak cry followed.

Something's happened downstairs!

Footsteps thundered up the stairs. The door into Robert's room slammed back against the wall with a thud. Robert's shriek, quickly silenced, was a shrill alarm against the vicious winds renewed outside.

Halka sat up in bed. Her heart beat at her throat as if trying to escape. Nausea engulfed her.

Papa Jouvin's voice carried through the door. "Did she say anything?" he screamed. "Did you?" The familiar sound of his belt on Robert's body followed.

Halka huddled down in the bed. Her hands covered her ears.

"No!"

"Good!"

The door slammed shut with a crash. Microthousandths later, Halka's bedroom door swung open. Halka was afraid to open her eyes as huge rough hands dragged her out of bed. She dared not look at him, but out of the corner of her eye she was aware that Papa Jouvin swayed on his feet. His heat trace was the purple of Zarduthi blood, and his breath was thick with sour wine.

"You, girl! What did you tell the social worker?" Papa Jouvin backhanded Halka round the face, hard enough to send her reeling against the wall. An ornament fell off the mantelpiece and shattered.

"N-nothing. Nothing."

"Louder, girl!"

"*Nothing!*"

"That's better!" Papa Jouvin mumbled. He seemed even more drunk than usual. He swung round to grab Robert but lost his balance as he did so.

Robert danced out of the way.

Halka seized the moment and picked up a vase from the dressing table while he wasn't watching. *If I've calculated right, the alcohol he's drunk has affected his balance*, she thought, as she swung the heavy glass vase. It made contact with the back of Papa Jouvin's head with an audible *crack.*

He collapsed on the floor.

Stars, I think I've killed him! she thought.

Robert stepped across the room to her side, and Halka felt his arms go around her. She hugged him back, careful not to touch his shoulders.

"I'm worried about Maman," he said. "I heard her scream."

"I thought I heard a scream too," Halka said, "but I was half-asleep at the time – I wasn't sure if it was you."

"No." Robert shook his head.

He seems worried. "Shall we see if Maman is all right?" she asked.

"Yes. Will you – we'll go together, shall we?"

"Yes, of course." Halka caught the note of fear in Robert's voice. It was infectious. *I must be strong. I must help him. He's my best friend.* She swallowed and took his hand. "Come on."

They crossed the landing and groped their way down the stairs, and clung to each other for warmth and support. Outside, the storm moved inland as it abated, its legacy an unseasonal chill.

At the foot of the stairs Robert put on the light. His hands shook.

Halka couldn't decide whether cold or fright was responsible.

They crept into the kitchen together. In the shadows in the hall a figure slumped on the floor. There was a slight noise as one wheel of Madame Jouvin's chair spun slowly. An occasional flash of chrome reflected off it in the dim light.

"It's Maman," Robert whispered. Halka sought his wrist with her fingers.

"Is she alive?"

Robert felt her throat. "No," he whispered. "He's finally finished the job."

Halka's nausea returned. She put her hands over her mouth, afraid she'd disgrace herself there and then. But Robert's next words drove even that thought out of her mind.

"We need to leave," he said. "Otherwise they'll think we did it. Or he'll come to and kill us as well."

CHAPTER 15 – Mission to Nice

Villa Jouvin, Nice, 24th June, 2096.

THE PHONE'S RING WAS DISTANT, but insistent. Denis Jouvin groaned as it penetrated his unconscious state. That took several minutes. *My head hurts like blazes. One hell of a hangover,* he thought, and then remembered that it wasn't. *Oh shit, the kids!* He felt his scalp. There was a definite bump there, just on his bald spot.

The holophone still rang; it must be several minutes already. That meant the caller was intent on an answer. He groaned again and pulled himself upright. The room spun. He held on to the wall to reach the instrument of damnation. "All right, all right, I'm coming!" he told it. It continued to ring. Finally he swayed and stumbled to it and pressed the answer button.

The face of Jim Martin, his wife's boss, appeared before him. "Is Marie available?"

"I'll just – check," Jouvin mumbled. He turned away, trying to buy time. *I need an excuse for her absence. I must get rid of the body, of course, but what about the blasted kids? Where are* they? *They could easily have phoned the Gendarmerie – or JSEP headquarters – and reported Marie's death. That would scupper me –*

He went outside and looked around. There was no sign of Robert or Halka in the garden or on the terrace. *Good.*

And then an idea presented itself. He swayed back to the phone. "Sorry – you've just missed her," he told Martin.

"Missed her?"

"Yes, didn't you know? Oh, you probably wouldn't. She had a communication from her specialist a couple of days ago, and has gone for further treatment for her back."

"Oh? When was this?"

"You've just missed her." Jouvin warmed to his cover story, though it registered that to make it stick he'd have to post the non-existent message himself. "If you like I'll call the clinic later on and ask them to get her to phone you."

"Thanks. Though it seems rather strange that she didn't call and let us know –"

"The weekend," Jouvin interrupted. "She didn't get the message until Friday, and had to travel today – there was a cancellation. I'll ask her to call you. Goodbye." He ended the communication and stumbled towards the drinks cabinet, then changed direction and headed for the kitchen. *Coffee's better for clear thinking.*

He averted his eyes as he walked past the wheelchair and its occupant. Marie had bled out on the floor. *Those are the next things to deal with. If the kids aren't here, I've got no witnesses and no worries,* he told himself. *Although JSEP will come looking for them – and I'd better not be here when they do. One thing's certain, I won't be going back to work for JSEP.*

All I have to do is post that fake message on the computer, clean up the blood with bleach, get rid of the body, then disappear. His idea opened up many possibilities…

Several cups of coffee later it occurred to him to search the villa for Robert and Halka.

*

The beach, Nice, half an hour later.

"Are you going to carry that backpack around with you the *whole* time?"

Robert's enquiry roused Halka from her thoughts. "Of course. I wasn't going to leave it for your papa to find. It's my inheritance." She shifted the pack on her lap.

"What do you mean, your inheritance?"

"My Zarduthi clothes for when I'm grown up. My weapons. My identity, I guess."

"I didn't know you had anything like that. Especially weapons."

"They were in here all the time." She laid a hand on the backpack. "We all had one of these. I presume the humans recovered them from the Sleep Room for us." Halka gazed out over the seafront, glad they were hidden below the villa. "I couldn't leave it behind. We must find Josie and Karak Chapaire. They'll believe us. They'll understand."

Robert sighed. "I suppose that's the best plan. But what will we do for money?"

"Why?"

"Well, we can't just get on a plane and go there. They won't let us on unless we've paid for tickets."

Halka stared at him. "I didn't have to pay for a ticket when I came here."

"Of course not. JSEP provided transport. But this isn't the same situation." Robert's face creased into a frown. "Have you any idea how much a plane ticket costs?"

"No-o," Halka murmured, "have you?"

"Not really, but I think it's a lot of money. More than we have with what I took from Papa, and Maman's market money. She doesn't keep much cash at home."

"And in any case there are two of us, so –"

"I could stay here. You're the one that needs to go to JSEP."

"I'm not leaving without you. What would you do here? You can't go back to the villa – your maman is dead and your papa would kill you as soon as look at you! I won't let that happen."

Robert shrugged. "Fair enough. We still don't have

enough money for even one ticket."

"Maybe we should phone JSEP and ask them to come and get us."

"We'd still need money for that."

"What's the number?"

"I don't know. Maman had it at the villa."

"We can't go back." Halka thought for a moment, then said, "Look, Robert, we should be wise with our cash. We should keep it for food for you, and buy it in markets because it'll be cheaper – though not here where we're known. I can eat most things because I'm made that way, and with my weapons I can hunt animals, so we won't starve."

Robert gaped in admiration. "Halka, how do you know all this stuff?"

"Because I'm Zarduthi, and we have to know it. Now, what about you? What special skills do you have which might help us?" She considered him for a moment. "You speak the language better than me. Though…that won't help much – we need to avoid people who know us."

"I know about plants," Robert said, "and how to garden. Maman taught me."

It's true, Halka realised. *He does – did – all the gardening at the villa.* "Do you know which things are edible? For you, I mean. I'm all right to eat most things."

Robert nodded. "I know enough to get us by, I think." He stared into her face for a moment. "Halka, you're different. More…" He hesitated. "More alien, I suppose – and more purposeful."

"I've always been like this, Robert. It's just that you're learning more about me now." She sought his hand, and then when he went to hold it as if for a handshake, formed a grip around his thumb instead. "Zarduthi thumbclasp. Like this."

He gripped her thumb back. "Thank you, Halka," he said.

"I'm honoured that you shared that with me."

"That's OK," she said. "You're my best friend."

*

The Oval Office, the White House, Washington. 10.00 am, 25th June, 2096.

"'Morning, Hardy." President Langrishe gave Hardy Brencher a perfunctory handshake.

"Good morning, Mr. President, Sir."

"Come in, sit down. How did Moscow go?" Despite his welcoming tone, Langrishe's eyes were hard as stones.

"I made it very clear to Alexei and Irina that holidays in Britain or any other black-listed country would be problematic for them."

"Good. Now tell me what's happening on the Kaj Kalinga disappearance."

Hardy seated himself and crossed his legs. "Not much, Sir. The Harkness woman failed to call in with her monthly report the next month and hasn't been seen since. I talked to her mother, but she's seen neither hide nor hair of Juliet since she and the children disappeared." He paused. "I've spoken to all the other friends and relatives, but none of them have seen her. I put a watch on the house of the mother, and the husband, Eddie Harkness, is under surveillance up on Galatea Station. He reported them missing – he found a note when he came home on leave."

"That she'd left him?"

Hardy nodded. "He's had no contact with his family since. He was distraught when we spoke – he'd cancelled his leave and returned to Galatea. There's not much else I can do for now. They're bound to re-surface at some point, but –"

Langrishe's face was the purple of stormclouds. "Shit! Why am I surrounded with incompetents?" His fists slammed onto the desk. As he lifted them, Hardy saw the wood was dull with a layer of oil and sweat, as if the President often thumped the desk. "You can't even find one alien child, a task that shouldn't be difficult, considering his appearance!"

"We're all doing our best to do that, sir. I've got the best agents on the job –"

"Find him, Brencher!"

"Sir, with all due respect, had the kids been kept together it would have been a hell of a lot easier to keep tight security on them. My whole department's worked like Trojans to monitor all of them. As regards Kaj, I've had people trace through house computer logs, school computer logs – you name it, I've had it done! Nobody's found a thing. You can take it from me, Mr. President, sir, that if somebody wants to disappear, and they don't want to be found, ain't nobody gonna find 'em." He straightened in his chair.

"I want them found, or you'll pay for it with your job!" Langrishe's steely eyes glinted at him. "I should sack you," he hissed. "You're JSEP's most Senior Special Investigator – not some poxy private eye from an HV soap. If you can't do the job properly, move over and make way for someone who can."

Hardy crossed one ankle over his knee and settled back into his chair. *I won't be intimidated,* he told himself. *I'm in deep shit here, but I can still bring this situation round if I play my cards right.* "Now just one minute!" he said, and his voice lowered, to slide through the air like a snake on the attack. "I'm sure you wouldn't wish it leaked to the news programmes that it was *your* plan to do away with the children, and then to spy on them by placing them in JSEP families, while you had their ship plundered for its star-drive and food technology – which led to one of them disappearing –"

"You wouldn't!"

"You'll only find out if you sack me, won't you? And I

don't think you want to do that, since the elections are next month. You might *just* get a second term if you can avoid any scandals –"

The President's eyes flickered. His teeth clenched. Nerves jerked along his jawline. But all he said was, "Brencher, you reveal that and you'll be out for definite."

"But I'll take you with me...Mr. President. Sir." Hardy leant forwards and laid his hands on the edge of the table. "You stick to presidenting and I'll do my job."

President Langrishe's eyes darted pure venom at Hardy. But before he could say anything else, the intercom buzzer sounded at his desk. He leaned forwards and thumbed the channel open. "What is it, Hayley?"

"Sorry to interrupt, Sir. You have an urgent call from Jim Martin."

The President drew in a deep breath and let it out again. "Put him onscreen."

After so many years as a JSEP intelligence agent, Hardy felt no compunction about listening. *Besides, if it means I might have to do something, I need to know about it.*

Jim Martin's face filled the holoscreen. "There's something funny going on with Marie Jouvin. I had important work to check out with her, but when I called she wasn't at the villa. Her husband said she'd had a call from her specialist about a treatment," he said. "But she'd have left a message if that was really the case – she always lets me know if anything crops up especially healthwise."

"She's in a wheelchair, isn't she?"

"Yes – since her accident five years ago. Of course I'd have given her sick leave, particularly for something that could improve her quality of life. It can't be easy, being confined to a wheelchair when you've been an active person, and a mom." He shook his head. "The thing is, Jouvin said he'd get her to call me from the clinic, but when she didn't, I phoned them. Not only is she not there, but they know nothing about any appointment or treatment. I think it requires investigation."

Langrishe shot a sideways glance at Hardy. "She's got one of the youngsters from the ship, hasn't she?"

"Yes." Jim looked down at a sheaf of notes he held. "Halka Mozada, a female. Age early teens, as far as Dr Chapaire could tell –"

The President held down his secrecy button as he turned to Hardy. "Anything connected with the children is sensitive. You've got a chance to redeem yourself here, Brencher. Get onto it!"

Hardy got up and left the room.

*

Reception Centre, next day.

Hardy's footsteps echoed on the floor as he strode through the Reception Centre. He found Josie Carter in Dr Chapaire's office.

"So," Edith said. "What can we do for *you* today, Monsieur Brencher?"

"I've been asked to look into a problem in the South of France."

"And how does that concern us?"

"The problem involves the possible disappearance of Madame Jouvin."

Josie sat upright in her chair. "That's odd… I've been concerned for several months now."

"How d'you mean?" Hardy focused on her.

"Oh – poor school reports from *both* children, not just Halka. The fact that the boy, Robert, has to do almost everything his mother can't, including intimate day-to-day care. That's not fair on a child. I don't know *why* – perhaps Jouvin won't have anyone in to nurse her or help with the household. But mostly just a sense that something's wrong there. And once, when I visited when the father was home on leave, both children were withdrawn – scared of him, I'd say. I'd like to know who authorised the Jouvins to take Halka in – it's not a suitable placement, in my opinion."

Hardy still stung enough from his encounter to mutter, "President Langrishe." He'd argued against it, and been overruled.

Josie's only reply was to raise her eyes heavenwards.

Edith Chapaire was more vocal. She tutted, then added, "What does he know about the children? He's never even been to see them!"

Hardy turned back to Josie. "Why didn't you do anything about it?"

"Because when I asked, Halka herself told me she was very happy there. On that basis, there wasn't anything I *could* do."

"Well, there's something wrong now. Jouvin went home on leave five days ago. His wife was due for an online conference with Jim Martin on Monday, and failed to check in. When Martin phoned her, Denis Jouvin told him she'd gone for further treatment for her back injury. The clinic know nothing about it. I've been assigned to go to Nice to find out what's going on."

"Madame Jouvin was supposed to have an operation some time ago," Josie remembered. "It was on that basis that the placement was approved. But I don't think she ever had it in the end – it was rescheduled."

"Then I need to check out the situation with her specialist. But first I should to go to the villa. I've got an idea. We could both go, under the pretext that it's a rescheduled visit."

Josie smiled. "I visited only four months ago, but if

something weird is happening that could affect the children, we need to know about it."

"Good. Get your things ready for a week's visit. I'll arrange transport." Hardy got up, nodded to Edith and left.

It was easy to make the flight arrangements and hire a car in advance, and plenty of good local accommodation was available. Hardy met Josie outside, drove them to the nearest airport, checked in their luggage, and got them onboard without any fuss, before the other passengers.

"How did you manage that?" she asked.

"It helps to be a JSEP Special Investigator," he grinned.

"Why did you say to bring enough stuff for a week's stay?"

"I'll need to have a good look around the villa and nearby. The short visits you have to make don't give you much chance to observe the children's behaviour. It's a superficial process, although things like school reports do help."

"You mean you'll watch the house or something?"

"Something like that."

"Don't secret agents have to have cover stories?"

"That's right. Mine is, I'm another social worker."

Josie smiled at this, and Hardy responded, as he realised she regarded his investigative role with some amusement; he hadn't seen it in that light before. "One good thing about this is that Halka and Robert already know and trust you," he observed.

"I hope so, especially if there is something strange going on. Er – you mean they don't trust you?"

"As I was responsible for debriefing them when they awoke, I'm not sure if they trust me the same way they trust you."

They arrived at Nice Airport in the late afternoon. Josie dozed on the plane, to her embarrassment when she awoke.

"Don't worry," he assured her. "I might take a nap too –

I'm jetlagged! I had an early flight back from Moscow yesterday."

"What took you there?"

Hardy sighed. "President Langrishe sent me to discuss something with Alexei Petrushenko."

"Couldn't you have phoned him, or teleconferenced?"

"I suggested that, but Langrishe was adamant that I should go."

"Why?"

"He demanded that I give Alexei Petrushenko a bollocking for taking Ayar to London for a holiday –"

"How petty!" Josie's tone matched her expression. "I know the children aren't supposed to meet, but that holiday was booked a while ago, and they struggled to shoehorn Ayar into it as well."

"See, I knew you were the right person to bring with me for this mission! You know all about the children and their families –"

"Don't change the subject. And don't get too excited about it. I'm still bound by JSEP's Non-Disclosure Agreement, just like you!"

When they'd booked into their hotel, Hardy suggested they unpack and meet in the lounge to discuss strategies. He'd already ordered coffee when she sat down on the couch beside him.

"How far away is the villa?" he asked. "I have a feeling we should go there soon. Say after dinner."

"I've got a map." Josie brought out her notebook and opened the app. "Where are we now?"

Hardy took the notebook and pored over it for a moment, then stabbed a finger at the position of the hotel. "Here." He looked at the rest of the map. Josie had marked the position of the Jouvins' villa. "Close enough for an after-dinner stroll. I don't plan to *call* there tonight, but a recce would be good – we can go in the morning."

"Good plan. We should check out the latest reports from school." She pointed. "It's here on the map."

"That's a good idea – their teacher might have noticed something." Hardy handed the notebook back. "I've ordered a table for seven."

"Fine. It stays light till nine-thirty or so at this time of year." Josie finished her coffee and stood up. "I'd better get changed if we're to have dinner at seven."

Hardy yawned. "Yes, a shower wouldn't come amiss. I'll meet you here in an hour."

A shave and a leisurely shower later they met in the restaurant. For dinner she'd changed into a column dress with a draped cowl neckline. They ate an excellent dinner of *moules marinières*, lobster salad, and fresh strawberries, washed down with a bottle of crisp, chilled Sauternes.

"I always like to sample the local cuisine," Hardy told Josie. He sipped the last of his wine, checked the time, and added, "We'd better go for that stroll."

The villa was ten minutes uphill from the hotel and commanded the same sea view. Josie was out of breath when they reached the gateway that led to the Jouvins' home, but Hardy laughed. "You need to get fit!"

"I don't have time."

"Whereas my job demands that I'm in good condition." He crossed the road to the layby that overlooked the cliffs above the Bay of Nice, looked around, then crossed back. "Fancy having a garage built into the hillside under your house!"

"I suppose that's the only place they could put it," Josie said. "How the other half lives, though, eh?"

"You can say that after that dinner?" He grinned at her for a moment, then something occurred to him. "It seems very quiet.

I'd have expected the youngsters to be outside at least."

"Don't forget that Jouvin's on leave. I guess he's strict – the children were very quiet when he was around."

"There's something odd about that guy." Hardy hesitated. "I think you should know his work history. He does have an alcohol problem."

"That doesn't surprise me. But fancy placing Halka in this family!"

Hardy sighed. "Yes, it wouldn't have been my idea. But then I always thought we should keep the kids together."

She looked at him in surprise. "*Did* you?"

"Of course. It's better from a security point of view. But Langrishe had made up his mind."

"Is that your brief, then, the security of the children?"

He nodded. "*And* anything they're connected with."

"So, you're more like a bodyguard than a secret agent? I'm *so* disappointed in you, Mr. Brencher!"

"Just 'Hardy' will do. And your first assumption was correct." He paced back to stare up at the villa through the peacock gate. "I want to get a look up there. It's too quiet."

"You're working on a hunch now," she smiled.

"I am, and it's not a nice one at all. I'll only be satisfied when I get a look-see."

Josie pointed to the mountainside. "A path goes up behind the houses."

"Only one thing: I'm not good with heights. I suffer from vertigo." He shrugged. "Never mind. You're right – a view from above will tell us a lot." He gestured towards the road and they walked uphill. After the next group of houses they spotted a path that curved back behind the various developments.

"That's the one, then." Hardy hoped he wouldn't make a fool of himself in front of Josie. He ushered her along the alleyway between the houses, and tried to look as if it made no difference to him at all that he had little or no sense of balance.

The path climbed when it reached the backs of the houses. Most of their gardens clung precariously to the mountainside. Hardy could already see that they would be able to look into the house itself from above. It made the struggle worthwhile, and gave him an excuse to take her hand.

Josie struggled too. "Wrong dress and shoes," she gasped, as if she'd read his thoughts. "I imagined a little gentle after-dinner stroll!"

Hardy permitted himself a grin – that felt more like a grimace – and led her on. He often worked alone, but in this instance was glad of her company, and hoped she hadn't noticed how sweaty his palms were.

A few moments later they were above the Jouvins' villa. He took out his folding binoculars and peered through them.

"Can you see anything?" Josie asked when she'd got her breath back.

Hardy scanned the house and garden. "Ye-es," he said. "There's someone in every garden except the Jouvins'." In the house next door a woman hung out washing. In the next garden, nearest the mountainside of Mont Boron, the family clustered around a barbecue. The fourth house had a man on its side patio, about to leave to walk his dog, while in the garden of the house opposite the Jouvins' villa, two boys of about nine or ten played together. The villa, however, was deserted. "Take a look for yourself." He handed her the binoculars.

"Maybe we should ask at the other houses if there's anyone there?" suggested Josie.

"I think that would be appropriate in the circumstances," Hardy agreed, and pointed to the rockwall behind them. "Look, these houses were built into an abandoned quarry. See how the mountain forms a sheer wall behind this footpath?"

"Yes." Josie leaned forwards and peered. "What's that

oblong of darker ground there?"
She handed him the binoculars.

Hardy trained the binoculars where she pointed. "The soil's disturbed there." He patted her arm and gestured back down the hillside path. "Come on. We're going in. And we may call on the neighbours."

By the time they'd retraced their steps the sunset had faded. That didn't deter Hardy. He marched up to the wooden communal gate, opened it, and strode over to the elegant black ironwork one – the peacock gate – which led to the villa.

"You have to press the buzzer and speak through the intercom," Josie said behind him. He pressed the white button and asked for Madame Jouvin.

[Please wait,] said the house computer through the intercom. [Please wait.]

They waited for a couple of minutes. Nothing happened.

"I'll climb over," said Hardy, and scaled the gate. "Wait here while I let you in." He strode towards the terrace. It was as deserted as it had looked from the hillside path. He tried the patio door. It was locked. He walked around the side path which led to the back of the property. The kitchen door was also locked. The garden was silent. He took a tool from his pocket, inserted it into the lock, and within seconds the door opened. He stepped inside.

He found himself in the small kitchen. In a few paces he'd crossed it and the threshold into the lounge. In the corner stood the statue of the discus thrower. A door led off the corner of the lounge. He looked through it into what might be an office; the orange telltale of the house computer glowed. The machine was on standby. The password was on a sticky note beside it.

Every room in the villa was empty. A dried lacquer of coffee at the base of a mug on the lounge table suggested fairly recent occupation. Hardy switched the house computer back on and opened the gate for Josie.

"I'll check the garden," he said to Josie. "There's nobody here at all. I've opened the back door – see if you can find anything useful inside. But give me a few moments before you put the lights on."

She nodded.

Hardy went back out through the kitchen door and crossed the terrace towards the beach. The palms stood like eerie sentinels opposite the wall at his left. Their fan-shaped leaves rustled in the sea breeze. *Nobody here either.* He returned to the back garden and passed the rotary washing line in the lower yard. The patio pots of colourful flowers stood three layers deep below the steps. The next level was wider, more like a traditional garden, with grass and borders. White flowers glared at him, luminous in the dark. He made for the spot Josie had pointed out earlier.

It's an amateurish job, done in haste! Flowers lay dying beside the disturbed earth, which smelled damp. Even if they hadn't spotted it from above, he'd have found it in the morning. *But who's in it?*

A light sprang on in the kitchen. Hardy regarded the makeshift grave in the fading light, took a flash photo on his phone, then walked back to the villa.

Josie met him at the kitchen door. "Halka's backpack is gone."

"Excuse me?"

"Sorry, I know I'm not making much sense, but I'm very worried about her and Robert."

"OK, explain again."

The breath Josie drew trembled. "All the children had a leather backpack, full of clothes and stuff, when JSEP's personnel found them. The children all took theirs with them to their placements. Halka's is missing."

"Then the body in the garden's unlikely to be hers –"

"Body? In that disturbed ground?"

"Yes." *She's clearly rattled by all this.* He wanted to reassure her. "Which means the children are elsewhere, but hopefully safe. But where's Jouvin?"

Josie shook her head, then pointed to the study door he'd left open. "What's that?" Her face went white.

A slight rusty stain smeared the skirting above the black and white diamond-chequerboard tiles. Hardy stepped forwards to examine it. "Might be blood, I think –" He turned just as Josie slumped to the floor in a faint. "Oh, hell!"

She stirred as he rearranged her limbs into the recovery position. "Come on, Josie – on your side for me." Her eyelids flickered open, but she didn't respond. "Josie!"

"Not sure I can in this dress," she mumbled.

He hitched the tight-fitting dress up, and at last she did what he wanted. "This is no time for modesty. You've got two kids to find, and they need your help, Josie!"

As she came round properly he helped her up and led her over to the nearby sofa. "Lie here till you feel better. I'll get you some water." He did so.

"Thanks." She managed to sit up and take a few sips. "How silly –"

"Not at all," he said. "It's not every day that you encounter something like this, and I know you're worried about Halka and Robert. But we'll find them." He sat down and waited while she recovered, then added, "It's time to talk to the neighbours, if only because they may wonder who's in the house, with the lights on."

She nodded. "Shall I come with you?"

"I would, if you don't want to stay here on your own. When you're ready."

"Hardy – should we call the police?"

He drew in a breath. "We'll have to inform them, but right now I need to talk to the neighbours, and tomorrow you need to speak to the school. I'll have to visit Madame Jouvin's clinic, too. And as soon as we call them they're likely to want us to stick around as witnesses."

"True." She hesitated. "I've had an idea. The school reports are probably on the house computer. I could check it out now."

"Excellent idea," he said. *She'll be better off doing something useful, rather than sitting and worrying, and besides, she's been helpful.* "Do that. It's your specialism."

She nodded.

"I need to deal with this." Hardy took out his phone and took a photo of the droplets of blood spatter. Then he extracted his pocket knife, scraped off some of the residue, stowed it in a plastic sample bag, and put it in his pocket. He also used some tape to get a DNA sample from the coffee cup in the lounge.

"Will you be all right if I go talk to the neighbours?"

She nodded again.

"Okay. It would make sense to call the police right after, though you may not get to bed early tonight."

"I realise that." She got up and went towards the study.

Hardy watched her. "Sure you'll be OK?"

"I'm sure. Go talk to the neighbours."

He left the villa and turned towards the other dwellings. *There might not be anyone in the house with the dog, but the woman hanging out her washing is there, and so are the other two families.* He knocked at the first door.

A woman opened it.

"*Bonsoir, Madame*," he said, and introduced himself and showed her his ID.

"JSEP Special Investigator?" The woman regarded him with some suspicion. "I suppose you're here because of the girl?"

"Yes."

"I don't have much to do with the Jouvins. That man –" She pulled a face. "It's not right. A child shouldn't have to look after his mother. Jouvin should give up his job and stay at home to look after her. And he always drinks a lot when he does come home. We've heard them argue."

"Have you seen or heard anything unusual within the last few days?"

"He was home again last night. Usual thing – drunk, a lot of noise – me and Guy, we always reckoned we could hear Jouvin hit the boy or something at night. Anyway, last night there was a bad storm, but it was quiet today. Haven't seen the children, either."

Hardy thanked her and moved on. He drew a blank at the other villas. Nobody had had much to do with the Jouvins. He returned to Josie.

"I've got it," she told him. "The latest reports were transferred directly to the house computer. Neither of them have been doing very well, yet they're both bright kids. Their teacher was concerned about them last time I was here." She hesitated. "I've downloaded copies of all the reports into my notebook, plus some things I found on the computer."

"Good work, Josie. And now, it's time to settle with the local *gendarmerie*."

CHAPTER 16 – Escape

Hotel Riviera, Nice, 27th June, 2096.

JOSIE HEARD THE ALARM GO and ignored it. She was warm. But when she tried to turn over she couldn't move any further. Something blocked her movements.

She opened one eye to see what the obstacle was. A man lay there next to her, his hair so pale as to be almost white.

Abruptly it came back to her. Halka and Robert's disappearance. The body in the garden at the villa. Hardy Brencher, who'd slept on top of the bed beside her because she was too upset to lie there alone. They'd been exhausted after several hours of police interviews on top of their flight and the activity of the evening.

"Hardy." She put out a tentative hand and shook his bare brown shoulder. "Wake up, Hardy!"

"I wouldn't want to miss breakfast, now, would I?"

His eyes crinkled up at the corners as he smiled at her. He hadn't tried to take advantage of her, but had just laid on the bed beside her and put an arm around her. In fact, he'd been a tower of strength just when she needed it. *Of course, he's used to this sort of thing,* she remembered, *being a secret agent. Sort of.* She smiled. *What is it he calls himself? Special Investigator.*

"Are you OK?" he asked.

She nodded.

"I'll meet you downstairs at breakfast, then." He jack-knifed upright off the bed and left the room.

After a shower and coffee Josie felt better, despite the lack of sleep; and more alert than usual. She ordered ham and eggs and poured coffee from the pot on their table, then regarded Hardy. He wore a navy suit and bootlace tie, though today his shirt was an icy cobalt blue that made his eyes look like clear glass. "What's the plan for today?" she asked.

"To the villa to find out progress on the excavation first – can you stay there and liaise with the police while I'm gone? Then I'll talk to Madame Jouvin's specialist in Switzerland – I have a flight at twelve am."

"I'd rather not be there on my own," she said. Her reluctance to return surprised her.

"The police will be there too. And I need you there in case the children turn up," he pointed out. "Book a table for dinner at eight. I'll be back by then."

At the villa, the police had made rapid progress.

"You said last night that you'd met Madame Jouvin several times, Mademoiselle Carter." It was Inspector Dubois.

"Yes, four times."

"Then I'm afraid we have a body for you to identify. Please come this way."

Josie clutched at Hardy's arm. "I didn't realise *I'd* have to identify her. Must I?"

"You've met the lady, I haven't. But I'll come with you." He put a hand under her elbow.

The Inspector led them to a tent erected over the shallow grave. On one side of the hole in the ground lay a woman. Although dirt still clung to her flesh in places, Josie saw she was human, and in her forties. She breathed a sigh of relief that it wasn't Halka.

"Is this the body of Madame Jouvin, Mademoiselle Carter?" asked Inspector Dubois.

"Yes," she said. "Oh, yes!" Tears sprang to her eyes. "Excuse me!"

"Easy, Josie," Hardy murmured, and led her away with an arm about her shoulders. "It's a shock for anyone who has to identify their first body."

"It's not just that. I feel so guilty for being relieved it wasn't Halka!" she sobbed. "Poor Madame Jouvin!"

His arms went around her then. "That's understandable," he said. "Halka is young, and Madame Jouvin is older. But remember that life in a wheelchair must be difficult."

"Yes, though she was only about fifteen years older than me." Josie's voice cracked.

"I know." For an instant Hardy's arms closed tightly around her, then he said, "You need a coffee. So do I, come to that." He steered her towards the kitchen. "Madame Jouvin strikes me as a lady who would keep coffee handy for visitors. Sit here and try not to touch anything."

Josie perched on the couch, numb with dread and anxiety. *What about the children? And where's Denis Jouvin?* She'd been shocked and horrified when Hardy had told her the neighbours thought that Jouvin had abused Robert, the more so that she'd not acted sooner. And his disappearance suggested he was responsible for Madame Jouvin's death.

Hardy put a mug of coffee into her hand.

"Jouvin's got to be found before he does the same thing to someone else," she said.

"The police are on that. They'll catch him at the airport if he tries to leave the country, and his mugshot's up on the European police network. They'll get him."

"I feel guilty that I didn't discover what was going on before this."

"How could *you* have known? *I* might have discovered something, but you had no cause to discuss it with me, and you don't use my methods." He gestured towards her mug. "Drink your coffee. I'm sorry – the milk had all gone off. The children must have left when this happened."

Josie sipped at the brew. "Black coffee's probably what I need right now. I'm worried about the children. If we knew when they left we might be able to work out how far they could've gone, but –"

"They won't get far without money, and cash is all they can get at their age. While I talk to the police, go over everything you downloaded from the house computer last night. See if there's anything unusual logged, and when it was shut down. That sort of thing. Oh – and try to find out if any money's missing from their account, and who took it."

"OK." Josie finished the coffee and took out her notebook. *Hardy might have given me something to do so I'll be occupied; but maybe I'll turn up some useful information.* She looked up; Hardy watched her from the door. He smiled ruefully, as if caught out, and turned and strode towards the garden. She sighed and opened the files she'd downloaded the previous evening.

The police had control of the house computer, but the household accounts were also in their own folder on her notebook. She soon discovered a funds transfer logged just over twenty-four hours earlier, with a pick-up scheduled at the airport. She highlighted it in the notebook version.

She turned her attention to the message-log function. It was easy enough to scan all messages received and sent within the last five days. There was indeed a message from a Dr Kelfer in Switzerland, received at 4.32 p.m. on the 23rd of June, 2096. Jim Martin's message to Madame Jouvin followed it, at 9.48 a.m. on the 25th of June.

But JSEP said the clinic didn't know anything about a message or treatment, she remembered. *So let's just see what it says.* She opened the message and read.

'From: Dr T. Kelfer. To: Madame Marie Jouvin. A new treatment might benefit you. We have a cancellation for Monday afternoon. No need to send your acceptance – we will expect you at 1 p.m.'

'No need to send your acceptance.' That looks suspicious

in itself! Josie tracked through the screens until she found the code for the message-log function.

Hardy had told her to look for anything unusual. She was no programmer, but the whole message looked out of place. And there it was…

She checked the dates of the entries. They were listed in date order. The last addition was at 11.23 a.m. on 24th of June. "Open file," she ordered her notebook.

"File already open," it told her.

"Identify open file."

"Message from Dr Kelfer."

That was it. The message was posted after its log date and time. She highlighted the evidence.

She became engrossed in her task, and she didn't hear the door open. But when she felt the warmth of another person close by, she turned and saw that Hardy stood beside her and read over her shoulder.

"I found this – and this – and Jouvin must have gone to the airport to pick up the money there. At some point he must also have picked up an air ticket in her name. If we alert the airline and the police, they should be able to intercept him."

"Good work!" he said. He indicated the notebook and added in an undertone, "We'll have to tell the police about this, but you did the right thing to keep an extra copy of the evidence – we'll keep quiet about that…"

Josie beamed at his approval. "I thought that was what *you'd* do."

"Absolutely right. We'll make a special investigator out of you yet!" He grinned. "Now listen. The police and I have searched the villa – we have a joint operation. The family car is missing from the garage; so is Madame Jouvin's wheelchair, a wig she owned, her handbag and cosmetics. There is no sign of the children, but some of their clothes and possessions have gone. There's also no sign of other bodies here, so the children are probably alive. The police found blood in a couple of the bedrooms. I couldn't get any separate samples, so I want you to liaise with Inspector Dubois on this, and of course on what you've found on the computer. They're preparing their samples for analysis now. I'm going to talk to Dr Kelfer." He walked towards the door, then turned. "Are you contacting the children's school this morning?"

She nodded.

"Afterwards, go back to the hotel and try to get some rest. The police say they'll call you if the children turn up."

*

Zero, same day, ship's date/time: 407.57.4.49.725 AD.

Omol flipped back the tented fabric covering they'd used to protect the rigs from sand and crossed the drill enclosure to Aldor. The borehole was awash with cold, fresh water. It looked wonderful. "How much is there?"

"More than enough for the clan, and for decades," Aldor said. "We're analysing it now."

"I hope we won't be here *that* long!" Omol waited while Aldor and his helpers calibrated the results, checked them, and checked again. "Is there a problem?" he asked.

"Maybe." Aldor ordered another check. "We'll sample all the boreholes again and check them against each other." To Omol he said, "I'll give you the final results as soon as possible."

"Thanks. *I* need to check something, too." He went outside.

He spotted Mahyonar Gelwa, the ship's botanist, near the Thirsty trees, and hailed her. "So what's your take on the Thirsty trees?"

"Something is contaminating the water – probably the ores?" Mahyonar suggested. "Whatever it is, it's doing for them, and it'll do for us if we don't deal with it."

Omol nodded and returned to the tented area. A glance at Aldor's face told Omol it wasn't good news. "Well?"

"The water contains variable levels of chemicals which are harmful even to us," Aldor said. "I've prepared a map, and a chart which corresponds to the boreholes on it." He connected the tool to the computer and pressed a button on it. "Here's the map. Just to get your bearings, these are the towers, including ours." He used a coloured circle to locate various areas. "Here's the stream, and the Thirsty trees." He zoomed in. "And here's the excavation site. This," he scrolled down the document, "is an approximate geological map." Strata ran diagonally across the surface map. He pointed to another diagram below the map. "This is the cross-section." Under the surface the strata lay level. "The impermeable rocks above and below trap water here. It's a good place for a settlement – apart from one thing."

"What's that?"

Another layer slid into place above the base map. "This geological section shows the levels of chemicals at each borehole. See how they peak closer to the volcanics either side of the canyon on the map?" Mountain ranges with volcanoes flanked the canyon where the towers lay. "The most likely explanation is that an ore body has intruded the strata beneath the towers." He gestured at the mountains each side of the canyon where the towers were. "It's very possible, with volcanic activity on either side. The various sand colours should have told us that the water might be contaminated; volcanic soils and sands can vary in colour with the chemical environment at formation."

"True." Omol leant over the table to read the results. There was a second peak at the location of the Thirsty trees. He drew Aldor's attention to it.

"They've probably taken up some of the chemicals since

they've been here," Aldor said. "I spoke with Mahyonar – she was doing checks on them."

"She confirmed that the Thirsty trees have taken up contaminated water, which is the cause of their die-back. But if we can use them as an indicator of water health, can't we also use them to drink up the ore and clean the water for us?"

"Potentially, yes," Aldor said, "but they'd take longer to clean it up than *we* have before we die of thirst. They look terrible, so we need to investigate thoroughly. We don't want to end up like them!"

"Or like the aliens we found. I received the autopsy report this morning – I've just read it. Garchon concluded not only that they may have tried to manage on reduced water once they discovered the contamination – hence their dehydration – but also that some of the minerals dry out body tissues. We'll never truly know what happened, but we should learn from them."

"We'll need extra boreholes to get further information. Hold off releasing the water for use until they're drilled and the results from them are in."

*

Nice, that evening.

Josie checked the time: *7.43 p.m. Hardy won't be back in time for dinner.* She tried to dismiss the need to tell him the latest snippet of information. *He'll be back later, of course. I can tell him then. But dinner won't be the same without him.*

She brushed her hair and added her rose quartz, rose gold flower stud earrings. She felt let-down, and the disappointment wouldn't go away. *Hardy won't see me in my favourite dress.* The coral pink shade complimented her fair hair. She felt a sense of loss at his absence –

Stop! She reached for her handbag, grabbed the keycard from the bedside table, and flung open the door to leave.

Hardy Brencher stood there, hand poised in mid-air to knock. "Well," he observed, "you *do* seem to be in a hurry."

"Oh, it's you!" she laughed, as her knees turned to jelly. "I didn't think you'd make it back."

"I never break dates," he said, with a smile, "especially when I know the other person's relying on me."

She couldn't deny it. "Shall we go down?" she asked.

"Sure. I didn't have time for lunch." He tucked his hand under her elbow and led her to the elevator.

"Busy day, then?"

"Satisfyingly so." He dropped his volume and leaned closer. "I've found out loads."

"So have I," she countered, with pride.

"Any sign of the kids?"

She shook her head. "Perhaps they think *we* think *they* killed Madame Jouvin."

"That's crazy."

"Not so crazy," she said. "Have you seen the children's talons?"

"Lots of times, but –"

"I'm not kidding. They're genetically engineered –"

"To be the perfect soldiers. I know. Ayar told me as much."

"Not that I think for a minute that *they* did it," Josie said. "But the fact remains that the Zarduthi are interplanetary mercenaries." They continued down in the elevator to the ground floor.

After they'd ordered their meal Hardy said, "Did you find out anything from the children's teacher?"

"Not much," Josie admitted. "Just what she told me before – that their work standard drops a couple of weeks before Jouvin returns, and stays low until his leave is over. What I did find out though, was that the blood from the study/hall is Madame

Jouvin's – I put the police in touch with Edith Chapaire – while blood samples on the clothes and bedlinen in one room is probably Robert's. And we know it's not Halka's – Zarduthi blood is purplish."

Hardy looked up as their pâté starter arrived. When the waiter had gone, he said, "Oh, right. It looks as if the neighbour was right about Jouvin abusing the boy."

Josie sighed. "Yes," she said. "I could kick myself for not being certain enough to do something about it. One's instincts are always right first time. But Halka told me she was happy there. And there's no sign of the children yet. I'm certain they're too scared to come back." She forced a smile to her face. "Anyway, what about you?"

"Dr Kelfer was most helpful. And I dug around a bit at the airport." He chewed a mouthful of pâté as he composed his thoughts. "Apparently Madame Jouvin's injuries at the time of her accident included both head and spinal trauma. She lost her memory for some weeks. And Dr Kelfer discovered, prior to the scheduled operation you mentioned that although it would restore sensation in her lower half, it wouldn't have benefitted her ability to move and she would have more pain. On that basis he decided not to proceed. That's why she never had her operation. There was nothing more he could do for her."

"So he wouldn't have called her to suggest further treatment anyway?"

Hardy shook his head. "No." He sipped his wine.

"I suppose Madame Jouvin didn't say anything because she didn't want Halka to be removed as the children got on so well together," Josie mused. "Robert told me he was lonely before Halka came. You said you found out something at the airport."

"Yes, a woman corresponding to Madame Jouvin's description – using a wheelchair – was seen at Nice Airport yesterday evening, at about the time we were at the villa. She purchased a ticket to Switzerland in the name of Madame Jouvin, but didn't get off the plane. I lost the trail at Geneva, but someone there's doing further checks. Oh, by the way." He passed her a small package. "I hope you like these. I got them in Geneva for you."

Josie opened the parcel. It contained dark Swiss chocolate with stem ginger pieces.

"Thank you very much!" she said. "Candy's a weakness of mine."

"I thought it might be."

The rest of the meal passed without incident. Hardy was attentive towards Josie's wants. She wondered whether he'd bought the candy for her because he liked her or if he'd wanted to reward her for helping him. Then she decided that wasn't the sort of man he was, and that he probably wanted to help her relax after the horrors of the last day. At any rate, it was a nice gift.

After the meal he said, "I think we should relax this evening. But first I need to send a report off. Shall I meet you in the lounge in half an hour's time?"

"Fine," Josie said, and hoped he wouldn't notice her hands tremble. He always had this effect on her now. "No after-dinner strolls this evening, then?"

"In the garden, maybe. See you soon." He strode off.

Josie wandered into the lounge and watched the HV without really taking it in. She felt too enervated to settle to anything, and couldn't contain her impatience to see Hardy again. When half an hour came and went she was as disappointed as she'd been at the thought of not having dinner with him.

Just then he came into the lounge and settled himself beside her on the couch. "Sorry I'm late," he said. "I had a call from the Inspector. The autopsy has established the time of

Madame Jouvin's death as Saturday night, at 11.47 p.m., the day Jouvin returned home on leave."

"Oh. Thank you for letting me know."

"I wasn't sure if it was the right thing to do," he admitted. "I thought it might upset you again."

"I'm not so much upset as not used to making decisions in this kind of situation," she pointed out. "Any sign of the children?"

"No. The police are on the look-out for them, of course, but they don't know *where* to look." He paused. "You know them both. What would you do if you were Halka or Robert?"

"I don't know them that well," Josie warned. She thought for a moment, then said, "If I were Halka – I'd want to contact someone I knew, like one of the other children – or even myself." She turned to him in excitement. "Perhaps I should put out an HV appeal for them to contact me?"

Hardy shook his head. "President Langrishe insisted I put a news blackout on this for the moment."

Josie frowned. "He doesn't make life easy for his employees, does he? Are there any local JSEP offices?"

"Why?"

"Because Halka might try to contact me or Edith through JSEP."

"Good thinking. I'll check." He brought out his own notebook.

"I didn't know you had one of those."

"Never go anywhere without it." He checked the European directory. "The nearest office is at Rouen, north-west of Paris. It'd be a long way for them."

"If they even know it's there."

"They can't have much money between them, and what they have they'll need to use for food. I don't see how they can get far." Hardy brought up the maps on his notebook.

"Me neither."

"Now we know the time of Madame Jouvin's death, we can assume the children left the villa after 11.47 on Sunday night – probably no later than an hour after that." He pressed a switch, and the notebook drew a circle around the environs of the city. "So this is where we need to search tomorrow." He closed the notebook and tucked it back in his pocket. "And now – we should relax." He gestured towards the garden.

How does he have so much energy? Josie wondered, as exhaustion infiltrated her whole body. "Just a short stroll, then," she agreed.

The gardens were pleasant. Hardy walked beside her, not touching her. The air was still warm. It wasn't long before Josie knew she had to get some sleep, and said so.

"I'll come up too," he said. "Today feels as if it's lasted about three days."

"It almost *has* lasted two!"

They re-entered the hotel.

"I'll see you to your room." At the door to her room, he asked, "Are you all right tonight?"

"I'm fine," she said. "Just tired."

He smiled a rueful smile. "Looks like I missed my chance last night, then," he said.

The breath congealed in Josie's throat. She hesitated. *He's very direct about it.* Her exhaustion vanished. She felt mentally and physically alert again. "The chance is still there if you want it," she said.

Hardy was nonplussed. For a heart-stopping moment she thought he'd back out, or that she'd said the wrong thing. Then his face cleared, and he said, "I do."

"You'd better come in, then."

Hardy was surprisingly hesitant and self-conscious at first. "Out of practise," he murmured, when she made a comment. But once they'd got over the initial awkwardness, his lips and fingers were swift and sure.

"Take your things off," he whispered.

She didn't protest, just did as he asked.

"What about contraception?"

"I'm on the pill."

He ran his hand over the slight swell of her stomach. "Hey, what's this, Josie?" He touched the faint mauve line above her pubic bone.

She looked at him, troubled. *He won't want me now.* "Caesarean scar. I had a baby, but she got into trouble during the birth. They operated, but she was stillborn."

"Were you married then?"

"I've never been married. I was sixteen. As soon as the boy found out I was pregnant, he dropped me like a hot cake."

"He wasn't ready to be a parent," Hardy said.

"No, and the other man I met wanted a child. You know the population laws..."

Hardy didn't say anything. But he laid his lips against the scar and squeezed her hand. Just as if it didn't matter to him.

*

Nice, next day.

"JSEP must be looking for us."

"And probably the police too." Halka snuggled closer to Robert. "This doorway's hard to lie on. I think I preferred the park – at least the ground wasn't so cold and hard."

"It's out of the rain here, though." It was a light shower, but they had limited clothes and couldn't risk getting soaked. Robert thought hard. "They have HV shops – we could see if there's any news about us when the rain stops."

"Good idea." Halka was silent for a moment or two, then added, "I'm hungry. I like fruit but I need something more substantial."

"We could get some cooked sausage or cheese tomorrow."

"How much bread have we got left?"

"Half a stick."

"And how about money?"

"Hang on a minute." Robert unwound his arms from around Halka's shoulders, removed his step-father's wallet and checked the cash. "Not much – a hundred and fifty ED." They'd been on the run for three days now, and it was much more expensive to live than they'd imagined. "We'd better make the bread last another day."

Halka agreed, though her digestive system protested its emptiness. She peered out of the doorway. "I think the rain's just stopped – shall we have a look at that HV shop?"

"Which one?"

"The nearest."

They got up and left the doorway. "This way." Robert darted down an alley, pulling her after him. They came to another main road. "Cross here." She followed. On the opposite side of the street lay a string of shops with lit windows.

"Just in time to catch the news," Robert said. They watched through the iron shutters. It was all disasters. A maglev link train had been derailed in an accident with a plane. The Neoluddites had bombed yet another building in protest against their members' failure to get clearance for the colonisation programmes. The latest heavy storms in China had led to serious flooding.

Then the local news came on. A car crash had killed three people on the coastal road. Scientists working at a company in Marseille had made a breakthrough in treating animal retroviruses transmitted to humans during transplant operations. A woman's body had been discovered on the beach in Italy. Robert and Halka held their breath, but it wasn't Madame

Jouvin.

The murder at the villa wasn't even mentioned. "What if it's been in the newspapers, or posted on the internet?"

"We can't afford to find out," Halka reminded him.

"No," he agreed. "I think we have to make a point of watching the news in the HV shops every night, and in the meantime assume that they haven't made any announcement about it. If they don't, nobody will be looking for us and we can try to get some casual work. That way we can earn some money to live on and build up enough cash to send you to America."

"Robert, you're brilliant! But I'm not going without you. What sort of work can we do?"

"I don't really know, but – washing up in cafés? Building sites, anything like that, where automation hasn't come in. We can give false names, just as a precaution." He considered her carefully. "But I think you need a hat or something, so you won't be recognised." So far they'd avoided that by staying in the park, but the rain had driven them to seek shelter. "You could probably pass for a boy with your height."

"I'm not a boy!"

"I know, but we don't want you recognised."

"I suppose not. Well, I might do it sometimes, if I have to."

"We ought to find other homeless people who could suggest where to go to earn money."

"Good idea."

"And we should leave Nice as soon as we can. We'll stow aboard a maglev cargo-link tomorrow."

*

Hotel Riviera, Nice, 3.17 a.m., 3rd July, 2096.

Hardy Brencher turned on the bedside light and sat for a moment, his gaze on Josie as she slept.

Four days before, baggage handlers had found Madame Jouvin's wheelchair in the cargo hold of the plane Jouvin had travelled to Switzerland in. Hardy had a flight booked back to Geneva in the morning, though he didn't want to leave Josie just now. The last few days they'd driven around Nice to look for Halka and Robert. Once, they thought they'd caught a glimpse of Halka's tall figure, but it was someone else when they approached. The President hadn't been happy that Kaj, and now Halka and Robert were still missing, but insisted the news ban stayed.

They'd had a great week together, and it looked as if he'd get the murder of Madame Jouvin solved in double-quick time, thanks to her help. *We make a good team,* he thought.

Hardy couldn't get back to sleep. *I can't sit here all night,* he told himself. *I was going to copy Josie's files, but we've been searching for the children all day, every day. I don't want to forget tomorrow.* He padded across the carpet to where her things lay. Her notebook was on top. He picked it up, booted it, and connected it to his more powerful one, then seated himself on the chair nearby while the files downloaded. *It's fortunate that Josie's such a conscientious worker.* Everything was carefully documented.

Finished. I'll tell her in the morning.

But the connection came apart with an audible click.

Josie awoke and sat up. "Hardy? What are you doing?"

"Oh, I remembered something in the night and thought I'd forget if I left it, as I'm off to Geneva first thing –"

"I thought you must have stubbed your toe on the way to the bathroom –" She sat up and rubbed her eyes. "Hey, that's my notebook!" She got up and came over to him. "What are you doing?" She grabbed it. "You've downloaded all my files!"

"Only the ones that relate to this case. There's something I need to check and I thought while I'm on the plane –"

"You didn't have to copy them behind my back," she said. "All you had to do was ask me, but no, you have to use your *secret agent* methods on me so I don't know!" Her face filled with anger. "Get out, you bastard!"

Hardy held up his hands. "All right, I'll go." He wrapped his bathrobe around him with as much dignity as he could muster, picked up his clothes and his notebook, and left the room.

His own bed was cold after the warmth of her body. Hardy lay under the duvet, shivered, and mentally cursed himself for being all kinds of an idiot. He'd assumed she wouldn't mind, but she was asleep and he didn't want to wake her to ask.

I just didn't know her well enough. And now I never will.

CHAPTER 17 – Disempowered

Reception Centre, Texas, 4th July, 2096.

JOSIE PRESSED HER HAND against the scanner by the Reception Centre door. Her fingers trembled. She felt chilled through. Although the sun shone on her back, she hadn't felt warm since the previous evening.

She decided not to mention the business with Hardy to Edith. *She'll probably make some sarcastic comments about it. Edith and Hardy have never got on since the day he was assigned there.*

She walked down the corridor that led to their office. The coffee machine was always on, and she needed a cup. Breakfast had been hours ago, and she hadn't eaten much. Hardy's note, left in a sealed envelope for her at Reception, had removed any desire to eat and sent her back to Texas for refuge and a respite from the search for Halka and Robert. She'd fretted about them in the plane, but with no leads, she needed a break. Especially now that Hardy wouldn't be there to support and help her.

"Hallo, Josie! You are back a little early, are you not?" Edith chirped as she entered the office.

"Just a day, Edith. I needed a break."

"Thank you for keeping me informed as to Madame Jouvin and the children while you were there. But you look so pale and upset. Is there still no sign of Halka and Robert?"

"None whatsoever, and Hardy had to put a news ban on the case." Just the thought of him twisted the knife in her heart. *To think I trusted him!* She closed her eyes for a second against the tears which sprang to them.

"Oh, Josie! It is that Brencher man, *n'est-ce pas*? But he is surely not worth your tears."

I might have known I couldn't keep anything from her, Josie told herself. "I just need a coffee –"

Edith went to the coffee machine, filled a cup for Josie and brought it to her. "I will not say 'I told you so'," she said, "since that is the last thing you want to hear right now. If you want, you can tell me. I will just listen. If not, we will just work."

"Thank you, Edith. You're a true friend." Josie hugged her.

"Steady, now!" But Edith smiled as she straightened her jacket.

"I think – perhaps I should tell you now," Josie decided, since Edith had promised not to comment. She sank down into her chair and the whole story tumbled out between sips of coffee and the occasional sob. He'd been a caring lover, and it hadn't mattered to him that she'd already had the only baby she could ever, legally, have.

"He probably is not the sort of man who wants children," Edith said.

"I suppose not." Josie made no attempt to follow up that line of thought, as she'd already realised that. "It wouldn't have worked, then, because I still long to have a baby."

"Listen. Millions of women worldwide are in the same position as you. What about those who have miscarriages, or can't get pregnant at all? IVF and other treatments are only available at clinics with a dark web presence. "

"I guess." *Dear Edith, she always talks common sense.* "When Sophie was stillborn I knew I had to work with children," Josie said. "At least I have our Zarduthi children to look after, so I'm lucky in that way – even though it's not quite the same." She looked up at Edith. "I thought Hardy was the answer to all my prayers. You know, Edith, he seemed like an angel sent from heaven to love me against all the odds! I think that's why I'm so disappointed in him."

Edith digested this in silence, then asked. "Does he know you've come back here?"

Josie shook her head. "I left him a note. But when I left it at Reception, I found he'd left me one as well."

"What was in it?"

"Just that he thought I'd prefer not to see him this morning so he left early for Geneva." Josie knuckled moisture from her eyes. "Obviously, he couldn't face me."

"No apology? Nothing else?"

Josie shook her head. "He seemed so nice – shy even, and I find that a big turn-on in a man."

"It was probably an act to get you hooked," Edith said. "Do not forget, he lives lies for his job, and it is easy to transfer what you *want* to see onto someone, and believe in them, when you are vulnerable." It was the closest she'd come to criticism of Hardy. Josie hated to admit it, but she was probably right. "Come on. Let us work. You feel disempowered because several relationships have not worked out, but the children have even less power. But we are both on their side, and always have been, and we have to find Halka and Robert. Kaj as well, if we can. Think how good you would feel if we found them while Monsieur Brencher was still searching!"

"I did suggest going on HV to appeal for them to come forwards," Josie said.

"And he would not hear of it?"

"Apparently the President wouldn't *let* him put out an appeal," Josie said.

"Well, of course! He has an election next month. But whatever – it makes life difficult for us, and you do not need that at present. But if the President caused this problem, then he should put it right, *n'est-ce pas*?"

"What do you mean?"

"Let us contact the President and ask him to lift the news

ban!"

It seemed such a simple idea that Josie wondered why they hadn't thought of it before. Though she'd had a lot on her mind over the last week. "Better still," she suggested, "we could ask him to let the children contact each other. They're miserable living apart, though they try to make the best of it."

"That is an even better idea. I am sure it would encourage Halka and Robert to come forward. I will call him now," Edith decided. She managed to get through the four layers of staff designed to protect the World President from unwanted calls in only fifteen minutes, as Josie watched.

"Well, Dr Chapaire?"

"*Monsieur le Président*, I am calling on behalf of the children," Edith said. "And also on behalf of my colleague here, *Mademoiselle* Carter."

"What can I do for you?"

"We think it vital that you lift the news ban on the Jouvin case."

"Well! You're nothing if not direct, Dr Chapaire." The president stared back at Edith's holoimage. "I'm afraid that isn't an option right now."

"*Monsieur le Président*, I believe you want the children from the Jouvin household found. Your news ban makes finding them very difficult."

This is a tacit acknowledgement that Hardy might still be searching, Josie realised.

"Nevertheless, it stays."

"Then will you not at least allow the children to communicate with each other?"

"Absolutely not. It's vital they be allowed to settle into their placements."

"But they will settle much better with regular contact –"

"I'm sorry. I absolutely forbid that." The president's face

was set like concrete. “And now, if you’ll excuse me, I am a very busy man.”

*

Zero, ship’s time/date: 407.67.7.58.672 AD, same day.

Omol trudged across the twilit sands to Aldor’s makeshift workstation in the site tent. He opened the entrance flap, stepped inside, and closed the flap. “What is it, Aldor?”

“I have the results of the extra boreholes we drilled.” Aldor brought up the borehole results map, sprinkled with the crosses of borehole locations. A section below the map represented the strata underground, with information from the boreholes to confirm depths. Coloured areas showed where the strength of the contamination increased, peaked, decreased, and died away on the map.

Next, a table of borehole results, with dates sampled in the leftmost column. “Over the last few days we’ve tested the water in all the boreholes daily. There’s a contamination gradient close to the towers that decreases with distance.” Aldor sighed. “Our first samples were from a location with low heavy metal contamination. “Where we abstract our water will make a difference. It’s more heavily contaminated in some places than others.”

“Where do these impurities come from?”

“Look closely at this line on the section below the map.” Aldor traced it with his finger, “A hard cap rock – shale, in this case – lies above the aquifer, and below it there’s a granite layer – perhaps a sill. But an ore body from the granite has intruded into the aquifer, below some of the towers.”

“You’re sure of that?”

“This is the borehole data,” Aldor said. He brought up a real-time wireline log chart which showed composition along the depth plot, along with resistivity, density and porosity, spontaneous potential difference, magnetic resonance, and spectral noise logging for leak detection purposes. "We went down 1500 tondors, and used cores and cuttings from the drilling process to assess the composition. The drill stopped at the level of the ore body we found, but we can confirm that there's iron, copper, tungsten, vanadium, and many other metals down there."

"And the ore body is below the level of the water?"

"No. It's *in* it. And there's something else you should know," Aldor said. "Once we start mining, the ore will potentially contaminate the water during extraction, and any shaft casing leaks will increase the contamination."

Omol saw from the section that the ore body bloomed like a fungus into the aquifer. He met Aldor's gaze. "Good thing we haven't taken any water out yet then."

"Yes. We older people can cope with small amounts of contamination with our mature zosas. But the children's are immature and their body weight lower. They'd be at high risk."

"Then we should protect the children. We'll give *them* the pure water from the condenser kits." Omol sighed. "I have to balance up whether we mine that ore body or protect ourselves and our families. If we don't mine, we may never get off this rock. If we mine and build our satellite, we could cause ill-health to our families and friends, especially the children. And if we don't abstract at least some of the water for drinking and everyday uses, we'll die anyway."

"But Omol, to get at the ore body we need to remove some of the towers. Do I have your permission?"

"Which ones?"

"These three," he indicated them on the map, "and we don't want to destabilise the rest."

"How will you remove them?"

"We only have explosives," Aldor said, "but we can set

the charges so they don't fall into the rest of them and cause *them* to fall."

An idea coalesced in Omol's mind. "I need to think about this. I'll come back to you on it shortly."

Aldor nodded. "I understand."

Omol returned to his computer and worked on it for over a tenth. The idea bubbled away in his at the back of his mind like a volcano about to erupt. He made calculations and drew charts to compare datasets. When he was sure he'd covered all eventualities he returned to Aldor.

"We must minimise the harm and maximise the good these discoveries will bring us," he said. "I've done a cost/benefit assessment of the energy required for two potential routes to bring more water here. The amount required to produce a pipeline from an as-yet-unlocated source of water is huge, even if the water's uncontaminated. We have to mine the ore body for the satellite construction, and if we mine and refine the ores from that ore body, and use some in condensation kits, we would save time, personal energy, and electricity, *and* produce more and more pure water from the air as we do now, perhaps eventually all we need."

"Won't the manufacture of each kit use some energy, though?" Aldor asked.

"Of course, but look –" Omol showed Aldor his calculations. "It's a much lower energy requirement than a pipeline would use, and our feedstuff can still be the sand – there's enough of it! All we have to do is identify the chemical substitutions required to produce the right materials for the kits."

"There's a design for them on the shuttle's computer," Aldor said. "The information we need for that should be there." He met Omol's gaze. "I'll still need to remove those towers to get at the ore body, and it still has to pass through the water on its way up."

"Do it. We need those minerals." Omol nodded. He'd made his decision. "And in the meantime, we'll only abstract water from the boreholes that consistently show the lowest contamination values."

*

Hotel Riviera, Nice, same day.

Hardy Brencher hurried through the doors of the Hotel Riviera and over to Reception. "Any mail for me?"

The clerk hesitated, then held out an envelope and said, "Mademoiselle Carter checked out the morning you left. She left you this note."

Hardy didn't know whether to be glad or sorry. He'd realised what an idiot he'd been over the last two nights, but had convinced himself that by the time he returned to Nice she'd have calmed down enough for him to apologise and make it up with her. *I've misjudged her again. But surely she's not* that *upset with me?*

Hardy took the envelope and thanked the clerk, thrust it into his pocket and made for the lift.

In the privacy of his room he opened the envelope. The note carried a drift of Josie's perfume. He breathed it in, pulled out the note, and hoped she wasn't as mad with him as he'd thought.

'Hardy,' he read, 'I need a breather and am going back to base for a few days. I will come back to the south of France to look for Halka and Robert as soon as I can. In the meantime, perhaps you can continue in my stead. Josie.' He re-read it, and hoped to pick up something other than the cool tone which signified her withdrawal from their relationship. He failed.

Oh you bloody fool! he told himself. Yet he knew *he* wasn't yet ready to face her.

He put the envelope away in the bedside drawer. *I'll think about this later, when I'm ready. For* now, *I have a job to finish, and the need to find the kids just puts extra pressure on me.*

Switzerland had gone well; and he and Don Harris had tracked Jouvin to Belgium and arrested him there. Don would bring him back to France tomorrow. They'd guessed he'd stay within the French-speaking countries so that his accent wouldn't mark him out as a stranger. This assumption had been correct, as had their idea that he had disguised himself as his own wife to get out of France itself. Now all Hardy had to do was pull together the evidence that Jouvin had killed his wife. If he could do that the President might lift the news ban and allow him to instigate a proper search for Halka and Robert. He supposed it was inevitable that Langrishe would slap a news blackout on their disappearance; he'd done the same with Kaj.

Hardy had always been loyal to the president, whoever it was. But Langrishe liked to label anyone who failed to do what *he* wanted as incompetent, and refused to consider advice he'd asked for. He was a man it was hard to feel any loyalty to. *In fact, he's a control freak and an utter bastard.*

Hardy didn't know why he was so angry. But he knew Langrishe would be displeased with him regarding Kaj, Halka and Robert, although the Jouvin murder was solved. *A shower should relax me,* he thought.

It didn't. When he emerged his mind was still in turmoil.

He took himself down to the lounge and ordered coffee. Then he sat for an hour or more, and forced himself to go through the files he'd downloaded from Josie's notebook, though it unsettled him. But she'd copied useful material. The time-date logging anachronism was highlighted; so was the routine Jouvin had written to allow the fake message to be inserted at the correct time and date. The children's school reports and grade-tracking dovetailed with the diary of Jouvin's leave periods, which she'd compiled with his help. Combined with the bloodstains on

Robert's clothes and bedding, they would convict him for child abuse as well as murder – especially if they could find the youngsters. The scheduled pick-up of cash at the airport was the final link in the chain, and connected him to Jouvin's air ticket to Geneva in his wife's name.

Hardy called Inspector Dubois next.

"I'm at the villa Jouvin," the Inspector told him.

"Fine, I'll come over now. I have some information for you."

When Hardy arrived, he handed over to the inspector a copy of the evidence he, Don and Josie had gathered. "Jouvin is in custody, and you have a strong case against him on several counts," he said. "My work here is finished – apart from finding the children. Any word yet?"

"None, I fear. I do not think they want to be found. However, we will keep a watch out for them, and a talk with the street people of Nice may help. But it would also help if the news blackout on this case were lifted."

"You're not the only one who thinks so," Hardy told him. "I've argued against it myself but the President won't budge on it."

"When is the election?"

"Two and a half weeks' time."

Inspector Dubois nodded. "Where is your young lady friend?"

"She…had to return to the States for work."

The Inspector nodded again, this time as if he didn't believe a word of it, and Hardy went to talk to Nice's homeless. Time was of the essence. But he only found only a possible sighting on the road to Marseilles. He'd follow it up in the morning.

At dinner, he had no appetite, and couldn't decide whether it was because meals weren't so much fun on his own, or because he had failed to find the children so far. He told himself he'd kept faith with Josie, though it *was* his job to find Halka and Robert, and so far he'd had no success. He had to report to President Langrishe that evening, and didn't relish the interview.

But the president was preoccupied with campaign matters, as he fought for his political survival, thanks to a renewed campaign against him by the Neoluddites; the story they'd removed from their site in anticipation of the feasibility study they'd asked for had been reinstated. But after they'd spoken, Hardy thought he'd managed to convince Langrishe he was hopeful that his street people lead would bear fruit. And at least he'd solved the Jouvin murder.

The search kept his mind occupied. By the time he went to bed, however, he'd exhausted all the possibilities of search-related ideas, read the newspaper, and had more than his usual quota of two beers. It was too hot to get into bed, so he lay on top for a while, and tried to blot from his memory the night he'd done just that with Josie in his arms. After some time he turned over and thumped the pillow into shape. Sleep evaded him.

He got under the duvet when the rain started. He lay there and listened to the white noise the drizzle made as it hit the ground. Tired as he was, there was no rest ahead for him.

As the dawn chorus reached a crescendo he gave in and admitted it to himself. *I miss Josie.*

*

Zero, ship's time/date: 407.129.3.62.245 AD, 7th July, 2096.

Omol began his daily round of the settlement by looking in on Faril, who was cleaning out and maintaining the missile chutes on the shuttle.

"'Morning, Omol – oh, there is something I wanted to talk to you about." Faril laid down his cleaning cloth. "You know how when we came here, you said it wouldn't be sensible to bring a child into this world, because the conditions are so difficult?"

That gave Omol an inkling of what was coming.

"I'm so sorry," Faril mumbled, "but Garchon confirmed Ensee's pregnancy yesterday. He also confirmed that her contraceptive implant had failed. And apparently he has no more implants."

That's a disaster in the making, particularly as we need all five synth machines to make the condenser kits, never mind the contraceptive implants! Omol thought. But he spread his hands, smiled, and offered his congratulations to Faril, who nodded, and resumed his work.

He continued on his round, but resolved to speak to Garchon. They could make more implants, but the synth machines would be unavailable for use on the condensation kits while they did so. *But it wouldn't make sense for anyone else to get pregnant while we're stuck on Zero.* The effect of the water shortage on the child worried him, and brought thoughts of Ghaneem to the surface of his mind again. *We might have to dedicate one machine for Garchon to use, avoiding mealtimes...*

*

The Ashrafs' house, Hyderabad, Pakistan, 12th July, 2096.

"More tea, Jafar?"

Jafar Ashraf looked up. It was the alien girl who had spoken, the one who *wasn't* his cousin. He noticed she looked taller than him. Yet she behaved much like any other Muslim girl, although her large round eyes held none of the usual shyness, assumed or otherwise, as they met his. She looked at him without the veiled coquetry he'd expected.

"Please," he said, and watched her approach. She pulled her scarf over her hair with a sidewise glance at his uncle Vimal, and refilled his cup.

She doesn't look so different from a human girl, Jafar thought. *How different would she* really *look, if she wasn't dressed in traditional Muslim clothes?* The thought excited him. He watched her as she moved around the room and refilled the cups of his father Rafiq, Uncle Vimal, and Aunt Jamilah. Saliha followed her with a tray of food: seeds, seasoned with spices, and sweet, sticky doughballs. Jafar took one, his eyes still on Davan.

She seated herself once more after she'd served the guests. But despite her confidence and bold expression, she didn't watch him back. She withdrew into herself.

I might just as well be invisible, Jafar thought. He and his father Rafiq had arrived that afternoon to stay with the family for a month. His eyes returned to Davan. *Hyderabad's a world apart from New York – how strange must it be for* her *to live here!* She wore only three modest gold bangles on her right wrist, unlike Saliha, who had many on each arm. And although she wore the same flat sandal style as her foster-sister, her feet were narrower and the toes longer, with no colour on the nails. Actually, they resembled talons, and her toes were webbed.

Jafar looked up from the floor and met her gaze. "So – er – Davan," he said, "what are your hobbies?"

"Military history and motor-cycling!" Saliha interjected, before Davan could reply. Her eyes danced with mischief.

"Saliha!" Uncle Vimal looked outraged. "Go to your room at once!"

Saliha got up and left the room, eyes downcast.

"Davan borrowed a motorcycle from a boy at school."

Uncle Vimal must feel the need to explain, Jafar thought.

"We were not pleased with her conduct, and forbade her to ride again, especially without a helmet and a licence," Uncle Vimal continued. "She has not done so since."

"Oh, but it's such a *wonderful* invention!" Davan said.

"My people don't have them – how could we, when we live on space ships?"

"Davan has comported herself with great propriety since that episode," Uncle Vimal said. His voice was firm, and he directed a quelling glance in her direction. "She will not ride motorcycles again."

Jafar sought eye contact with her once more, but her gaze was lowered. *Uncle Vimal seems very strict. That must be difficult for her too.* He wondered what the military history episode had been all about but didn't like to ask. *Saliha will tell me,* he thought. *I've always got on well with her.*

Aunt Jamilah whispered to Davan. Without a word she got up and brought round the snack tray again. He took a handful of seeds this time, and as she straightened he caught her eye.

She looked surprised for a moment, as if she hadn't expected any sympathy. Then she smiled back at him.

"Davan, your school science project deadline's the end of the week – how much do you need to do on it?" Uncle Vimal reminded her.

Jafar was sure it was because he'd seen him make eye contact with her.

"Just a bit of tidying up," Davan said. "I can finish it this evening. See you later, everyone." She got up, inclined her head, and left the room.

Jafar was disappointed. He'd expected some spirit from her.

"She wants to go to university and afterwards become an astronaut," Uncle Vimal muttered, and flung his hands wide. "I just do not begin to understand it."

"She's probably just following the dictates of her own culture," Rafiq pointed out, smoothing his beard.

"But that is inappropriate here," said Aunt Jamilah. "It makes me feel inadequate, as if I am not doing my duty as a good

Muslim, though I try my hardest to bring her up as a dutiful daughter and a young woman we can be proud of. We give her everything she needs and treat her as our own daughter. Yet she never seems satisfied with that."

"I know, Jamilah, I know you do your best with her," Uncle Vimal said. "The fault is not with you – or her. Her heart is good – it is just not a Muslim heart. She can't help it, any more than we can."

"What should we do? I would like to see her go to university. She is clever enough, no doubt of that, but astronaut training..."

"Why?" Jafar asked. "You did it when you went to work for JSEP. So did my father."

"Yes, but we are men." Uncle Vimal sighed. "We should have taken a boy. I requested a boy. Had we had a boy, this problem would not have arisen. It would be acceptable for a boy to like the things Davan likes. And what bothers me about Davan's behaviour is, she has great influence over Saliha."

"Saliha adores Davan, and I am certain Davan thinks the world of Saliha." Aunt Jamilah smoothed her *salwar-kameez*. "But her ways could dishonour our family and make it hard to find a suitable husband for Saliha later on."

"You see, Rafiq, I did not realise the problems I was taking on when I brought Davan to live here. University will be good for her, and also diminish her influence over Saliha. But astronaut training is expressly forbidden by the World President. So the only thing to do is to marry her to a steady man to calm her down." Uncle Vimal helped himself to another handful of seeds. "A dowry is no problem; there is her allowance. All the children's foster families get the same allowance, but in Pakistan things are cheaper than in some countries. I saved the money I did not need to use in a separate account. It is Davan's own money, and will be enough for a modest dowry."

Jafar listened to their clipped, formal speech and felt excluded – and stifled. *Pakistan is still more rural and old-fashioned than I expected. If* I *feel like that, how does Davan cope on a day-to-day basis?*

"The problem will be finding someone to marry Davan," said Aunt Jamilah. "It will take a very special man to take her on."

CHAPTER 18 – At the Crossroads

Provence, 3rd August, 2096.

"IT'S CHILLY WHEN THERE'S A STORM AT NIGHT," Halka said. "I'm freezing."

Robert pulled the tarpaulin more closely about her, then wrapped his arms around her waist. "Halka, can I ask you something?"

"Of course."

"No, I mean something very personal."

Halka looked into his eyes. They reflected the moonlight. "What?"

"You are – er – you are really a girl, aren't you?"

"Do you mean, am I really female?"

"Yes."

Halka considered this for a moment. "I'm female in Zarduthi terms," she said at last. "I *think* I am in human terms…"

Robert digested this in silence, as if he didn't know how to proceed. Then he said, "Would you like to find out?"

"Have sex with you, do you mean? Sintala?"

"I guess so, if that's what it means in Zarduthi."

"I'm only just fifteen – although my Zarduthi clothes fit me all right," Halka said, "but Zarduthi clothes have dimensional instability, so they can grow with a person."

"Do you have to be fifteen? We're supposed to be sixteen, but there are plenty of other boys at school that have done it – well, they say they have!" He shrugged. "I just thought it would be a way to warm both of us up."

"Oh, Robert! I don't know – I'm not sure I want to have sex with my best friend." Halka hugged him. "Though I'm flattered if you want to do it with me. It never occurred to me that you'd want to as I'm Zarduthi and you're human."

She looked around. It was quiet under the pines. Their scent filled her nostrils. The rain had stopped, though the needles were still wet. But the ground was dry and springy under their tarpaulin. She closed her eyes and imagined for a moment that she was grown up and on a different planet, with her clan in a skirmish. *I've become separated from them, that's all. We'll meet up again – soon. But I could be killed in the battle, and then I'd never know what sex was like. It can't be so different to do it with a human, can it?* She opened her eyes. "All right," she said.

For a moment Robert seemed too stunned to speak. Then he said, "Good. Here." And he slipped his hand inside her jacket and touched the mound of her pectoral muscles.

"What are you doing?"

Robert's face showed puzzlement. "I can't find your nipples," he said.

"I haven't got any. We don't breastfeed our babies like you do," Halka said. She tried to remember what she'd learned about sex in biology training on the clanship, and reconcile it with what she'd learned in school in Nice.

"What do you do, then?"

It came back to her then, from memory, knowledge of her own body, and a comparison of the two. "We have babies like you, but we have a special organ, as well as our stomachs, to digest our food – that's why we can eat most things. During pregnancy the zosa makes food available for the baby. By the time the baby's born its own food organs are mature, so it separates from the mother's. That's why my belly button's higher up than yours is." She knew this from days on the beach, and a couple of times when she'd had to dress his bleeding shoulders. "Here – feel."

Robert touched her abdomen. "Oh. So it is!" He moved his hands lower. "And do you still have babies like us?"

"From the place between your legs, you mean? I don't know what it's called in French."

"Yes."

That seemed to have answered his question, because he was quiet for a few thousandths. Then his hands moved lower to unzip her jeans. She didn't protest, although the breath left her throat for a moment that felt as if she stood on the brink of a precipice. Once she fell…

But it was pleasant, not like taking an irrevocable step at all, even though he was a different shape from a Zarduthi boy. At any rate, it felt nice to have him inside her, and once, for a few bumps against her hips, it started to feel *really* nice. She kissed him, to his surprise, and told him so.

"I thought about doing it for money," he said, "but you can get AIDS and Quetzal fever that way."

"What're they?"

"Illnesses." Robert explained them. "But you can get them in other ways too. The trouble is, once you've got them, without special treatment you're never totally cured, and you can die. Or be on medication for life."

"We'll just have to carry on as we are, then," Halka said.

"We might be able to earn some money grape-picking, if we're still on the run by the autumn..." Robert said. His voice was a strand of sound from far away.

Halka looked at him. His eyes had closed. She settled herself against him and closed her own. Robert was right. She felt warmer, inside and out.

*

Hyderabad, Pakistan, 5th September, 2096.

"Davan, your future husband is here!"

Davan crossed the bedroom to watch the short, stout figure that walked towards the Ashrafs' house through the window.

"So that's Mr. Faruq. I don't like him," she decided.

Saliha's jaw dropped. "Well, what will you do? Daddy only agreed to let you go to university if you married a man of the family's choice after your degree. He won't let you go unless you're engaged to someone."

Davan sighed. "I know. Even though I came top in my class and have *way* more than the qualifications I need to get in." She looked around the room, as she tried to think of a way of thwarting her foster-parents. "Maybe I should find someone myself – a man I don't *mind* being married to."

"That's a good idea."

"No – no. That's plan B." Her eyes fell on the backpack at the end of her bed. "I need something now – something decisive." She crossed to the bed, and ran her hands over the backpack to activate its morphometric lock. Whether or not the *right* time had come, she needed its contents now. *I'll be in trouble for this, but it can't be helped.*

She tipped the pack up over the bed, and metal clashed, furs gave off particles, and two metal-and-clearplast objects fell out among them in the hasty spill. There was even a pair of boots of a soft, supple brown leather covered in little nodules – unlike any Davan had seen here on Earth. She felt excitement course through her veins as she stripped to her underwear.

Saliha watched open-mouthed.

Davan lifted one item after another from the bed, as flashes of memory told her how to wear this, and place that. She tucked the pistol into her belt, then kicked off her sandals and pulled on the boots, which fitted well, and sat down to await a summons.

Saliha's expression was a comical mixture of shock and admiration. "You look fantastic, Davan," she said, and despite their friendship she sounded shy. "A wonderful stranger. But what will Daddy say when he sees you dressed like that?"

"I know he won't like it," Davan acknowledged. "But this

is the "me" I was meant to be."

"I know." Saliha reached for the weapon on the bed, the only thing left. It was slightly larger than the projectile pistol, a gun of silvery metal with transparent conduit tubes. She hefted it, then handed it to Davan. "It's a bit heavy," she murmured. "Will you be able to lift it?" She adjusted the scarf over her hair, a reflexive habit.

"If I could do more sports at school, I'd have no difficulty at all," Davan replied. Her tone was bitter. "Swimming and walking aren't enough. I need to do weight training and running, like the boys." She put the weapon back in the pack, and returned it to its cupboard. "Martial arts, even."

There was a knock at the door. "Come down, girls."

"Come on," Davan said to Saliha.

"No, wait a moment," Saliha advised in a low voice. "Let Mum get downstairs – if you go now she'll just make you change again."

Davan eased back onto the bed. "You're right," she whispered back.

"Let me go first," said Saliha. "And act as if nothing's different."

Davan nodded.

They waited until they heard Mrs. Jamilah's footsteps fall silent on the rug at the bottom of the stairs, then opened the door and followed her.

Davan saw the man her foster-parents wanted her to marry seated on the couch against the stairs into the living room as she reached the lower stairs. He was short and thickset. Lines on his chubby face told her he was about forty – as far as Davan could judge age in humans. She scowled. *There's no way* he's *getting anywhere near me,* she resolved, certain he wouldn't want to when he saw her.

As they approached the lounge, an intense wave of

perfume issued from the couch where Mr. Faruq sat. Davan recognised it as the scent of roses. *Huh! A man who smells of flowers can never command my respect.*

As she neared the door, Mr. Faruq turned to face the two girls. As his eyes lighted on Saliha he beamed, but when he saw Davan stride into the room behind her his expression turned to one of outrage and he jumped to his feet.

"You told me she was tall, but you did not say she was a hooligan! I cannot marry a woman who looks like a man and carries a gun," he blustered. He turned to Professor Ashraf. "I am sorry to say that our agreement must be at an end." He marched towards the door.

"Mr. Faruq, wait!" Mrs. Jamilah wrung her hands, while Professor Ashraf barred his progress to the door. "Davan is something of a rebel, but her life has been difficult – she has a respectable dowry, Mr. Faruq!"

"No, no, Professor! My mind is made up. Saliha, now, she is a different matter entirely."

Davan folded her arms across her chest and watched the scene, lips clamped together to hold in her laughter. She couldn't quell her amusement.

"Saliha is too young to be married, and besides, she cannot wed until Davan does."

"Professor, I am adamant. I will not marry Davan. Please let me pass!"

Professor Ashraf stepped aside then and lowered his head. Mr. Faruq cast one more look at Davan and hurried through the door into the dusk.

"Davan! I'm ashamed of you. How could you do that?"

"Do what?" Davan burst out. "How could you offer him money to marry me? Money that belongs to me, and is provided by the government to pay for my education and living expenses?"

Vimal and Jamilah exchanged glances. "Where did we go wrong?" Jamilah asked.

"Well, for starters, you'll never marry me off to someone I detest," Davan said. "I value myself more than that."

"Davan!" Professor Ashraf's voice was hard as a crack of thunder. "Zarduthi ways and Muslim ways may be different, but while you live here in this house you *will* conduct yourself with more propriety. It may be that we cannot find you a husband, but consider, before you disgrace us publicly, the effect on your sister's future."

"What do you mean?"

"I mean that if Mr. Faruq tells anyone else about your hoydenish behaviour tonight, Saliha may remain unwed as well as you." The Professor's face was like thunder. "And I think he'll sing like a nightingale!"

*

The Petrushenkos' apartment, Moscow, 15th October, 2096.

Ayar wandered into the lounge and flung himself into a chair. The news was on HV; he watched it idly. Government forces had fought the Neoluddites at an army munitions factory, their latest target. Ayar sighed. "I just wish I could join the army and do what I was bred to do, even if I can't leave Earth."

Irina had prepared the evening meal in front of the HV. She dropped the last few beans she'd cut up into a casserole, then made Ayar a cup of tea. "*I* wish Natalya hadn't got involved with these Neoluddite people," she said. "I don't agree with what they're doing, and I don't want my family divided because of it." She handed him a cup.

Ayar gulped it down; it was black and strong, but he was used to that, and had grown to like it. "I didn't know Natalya was a Neoluddite. She doesn't talk to me much now."

"She's been a paid-up member ever since she started

seeing that Razich boy a couple of months ago."

A pang went through Ayar.

"It's him that's got her involved," Irina continued. "Well, I don't like it. I've told her not to bring him here – I won't have anything to do with the Neoluddites, and I'm ashamed that a daughter of mine is dating one."

Ayar breathed another sigh, this time in relief that he wouldn't have to face his tormentors from school. Although both had left the previous year, he hadn't forgotten the fight in the toilet, and had no wish for a return bout, especially at his foster-family's home. *And Natalya's Ivan Razich's girlfriend.* He'd seen them together a few times, and hadn't enjoyed the way it made him feel at all –

Irina interrupted his thoughts. "Oh, listen, Ayar! It's the election result!"

"It took twelve days to count all the votes in every country, but now the results are out!" the newsreader said. "The new World President is Guido Maria Sanchez."

Ayar didn't know whether to be pleased or not. But he thought about it for a while, and decided that if there was any chance that the new president could change things so he didn't have to waste his life in enforced idleness…then, he resolved, *I'll take it!*

*

Zero, 408.523.4.95.056 AD, 23rd March, 2097.

"Omol?"

He looked up from his computer. His workspace was inside a chamber in the tower they occupied, which reduced the wind's ingress and protected his equipment from sand and windweed missiles.

The floor still acquired a daily coating of sand. Omol heard the crunch of it under boots and looked up.

Faril approached. “Ensee went into labour last night, and had the baby this morning, a little girl,” he said. “She’s resting now, but if you’d like to see the baby, Ensee’ll be happy for you to drop by this afternoon.”

“I’ll come then. Thanks for the invite.”

“We named her Shenalle.”

“What a beautiful name!” Omol pasted a smile onto his face, thanked him and wished Ensee a peaceful rest. Faril nodded and crunched away over the sand-strewn floor.

Omol’s thoughts returned to Ghaneem. *If we’d had a child together, what would it have been like?* He’d never dared explore the feelings that lurked in his subconscious, though he’d known he’d need to at some point. *I wish we’d had more time together, and that we could have tried.* But having admitted the feeling, his mind dismissed the question.

That would just have meant I had two special people to mourn...

*

Juliet’s apartment, Paris, Texas, 9th August, 2098.

“I won’t have any lunch today, Juli.”

“What, no fries or hot dogs?”

“I’m not hungry. I feel a bit sick.”

Juli tried to remember what was in the information from Dr Chapaire, but couldn’t. She knew there was no real risk of Kaj catching human ailments, since his DNA was different. In all the time she’d known him, Kaj had never been sick or caught a single cold, however ill she and Lucy were.

“Why not go and lie down, Kaj?”

He just nodded and left the room.

Juli dished up Lucy’s lunch and her own, and made sure her daughter was eating before she went to see if Kaj was all right. He lay on his bed with his eyes open. The skin on his cheekbones, chin and forehead had a whitish tinge she hadn't noticed before. *Perhaps it's lack of sunshine that's making him go pale.* She dared not let him go outside during the day, as he'd be recognised at once. They went out for walks and exercise at night, and kept themselves to themselves.

Juli often regretted that she'd left Eddie, though not the reason for it. Kaj needed protection from him – and JSEP – because he was bright and knew so much about the ship and its workings. The horror she felt when she realised JSEP had expected her to spy on her foster-child persisted. *That's no atmosphere to bring up a child in!*

"Are you OK?"

Kaj nodded. "I'll just have a rest, Juli. I feel so tired."

Not surprising, she thought, *given the restrictions our life puts on us. When we're out in the fresh air we should be asleep.* And the food Juli could afford on her wage from the library wasn't always as nutritious as she'd have liked. "How long have you felt poorly?"

"A couple of days."

"Why you didn't tell me?" Juli asked in concern.

"I didn't want to worry you, and I thought I'd soon feel better."

"In future, always tell me about anything like that," she said. "I need to know in good time so I can decide what to do about it. I can't make choices without all the information."

She thought back over the past two years. It hadn't been easy, although both children were even-tempered and well-behaved. They'd put up with a lot of hardship, relative to other children – and the life they could have had. When they'd left Eddie, she'd surrendered access to Kaj's food allowance and Lucy's State Assistance, intended to ensure that no under-five ever suffered from malnutrition again. *Still, we do all right.* Juli had found them somewhere reasonable to live and had regular work at the library. This gave her access to many books, so neither child's education suffered. And since Kaj had a bond with Lucy, and was happy to spend time with her, he looked after her while she was at the library. He was mature and responsible. *It all worked out very well. Usually.*

"Just rest, then, and see how you feel later," she said. *But if he gets really sick that'll blow everything,* Juli told herself. *I won't be able to make any money without childcare for Lucy. What then?* If necessary, she'd seek medical help for him. That wouldn't be cheap, and she had no medical insurance.

And it would make us vulnerable to JSEP's security forces. Which is just what we don't need.

*

Provence, France, 12th September, 2098.

The September sunshine was hot on Halka's back as she knelt beside the grapevine, snips in hand. They'd worked at the vineyard for the last two summers, and done fill-in work between the grape harvests in cafés and restaurants, and even on building sites.

She felt drowsy. *I must stay awake,* she thought, *the pay's too good to miss here!* She brought her wheeled trug closer, pushed the snips between the stems, and squeezed. The bunch of dark red grapes dropped into her gloved hand. She laid it in the trug.

Robert wielded a pair of snips, a few metres away. Halka caught his eye and winked. He winked back, grinned, and turned to scare away a pigeon that circled over the vine he worked on.

The pigeon circled once over the vine, released a gob of droppings, and flew off. The droppings landed on the back of his hand.

Robert had left his gloves behind today. He shook his hand in disgust and wiped it on the ground. He continued with the harvest. It was over an hour before he could wash his hands.

*

A month later.

Halka wasn't sure what had woken her. She listened for audible clues, but heard none. She checked the taste of her saliva. It had its usual indeterminate taste, though her mouth was dry. She opened her eyes. The pine forest surrounded them. The light grew stronger as dawn approached. In the distance she heard the *flap-flap* of birds, and their calls. *It must have been the dawn chorus,* she reasoned. *It's not as if I'm not used to that.* She draped an arm over Robert. Then she heard it again.

Robert coughed, cleared his throat, then coughed again. It was a slight sound, but close, so it seemed loud.

"Robert, are you all right?"

"Of course." He coughed again. "At least, I have a catch in my throat, but I'm OK apart from that." He twisted on the tarpaulin, and pulled his blanket around him. "I'm a bit cold."

"Here." Halka snuggled closer and put her blanket across him. "This'll warm you up. It's luxury to have a blanket." Other than food, they were the first things they'd bought after their first payday at this vineyard. She wrapped her arms around him. "How far are we from Marseilles?"

"A couple of days' walk." He coughed again.

"Maybe we should get you some cough medicine."

"I'm fine," he said, "but there aren't any shops around here, in case you hadn't noticed!"

CHAPTER 19 – Errors of Judgement

Outside the Petrushenkos' apartment, Moscow, 21st October, 2098.

SNOW HAD COME EARLY TO MOSCOW THIS YEAR. This flurry of sleet was the latest in a series; the temperature had hovered around freezing point all day. With chilled fingers Ayar felt in his pocket for his key to the Petrushenkos' apartment, on its key-ring. *Not far now.*

He'd been to the city centre to look for a present for Irina's birthday. But he'd also pressed his face against the window of the army recruitment office. Surely they could offer him something? It wasn't as if he weren't fit and healthy. He went to the gym and worked out several evenings a week, he'd repented of his disinterest at school and signed up for a part-time Astrophysics degree at the State University and had made good progress, and he'd worked hard to improve his Russian and English.

But it was the same as each time he'd asked. Although they'd been interested in him, at the end of the interview there had been the same, "Sorry. We'd be delighted to have you, but we can't – President's orders." *I feel like I'm strangling.*

He turned the corner of the street that led to the park, and darkness folded over his head. It shut out the sleet and buildings. For a moment he thought he'd fainted. Then he reasoned that if he had, he wouldn't be *able* to think, feel, or anything else.

"Hit him!"

Ayar felt a sharp pain at his temple, then nothing more as he sank down...

When he came to, he was in a vehicle. He was warm enough, but it was hard to breathe, or move, and impossible to see. A few thousandths later he realised his hands were tied together behind him, and something over his head blocked out the light and muffled the sounds around him.

"He's coming round." It sounded like the voice that had growled the order to hit him. "Tough buggers, these Zarduthi! A human would have been out for hours."

"I'll make sure he is," someone offered.

That sounded just like Ivan Razich, Ayar thought. *But how can that be?*

"Not here. Wait till we get to the safe house."

Ayar thought to save himself from injury and let his head hang forward again as if unconscious.

"Oh – he's gone again." A new voice.

Although he couldn't see, Ayar tried to learn as much about his surroundings as he could. He thought the vehicle was large; big enough for several passengers, judging by the various voices. Even had his hands been free he couldn't have taken them all on at once. And he'd never received the hand-to-hand combat training he should have had at fifteen. *If I pretend to be unconscious I might get useful information. I'll just have to wait for a chance to escape, and give them the least information possible – whoever "they" are!*

Soon after, the vehicle pulled up. Hands jerked his shoulder.

"Wake up!" Growler ordered.

As if waking from a faint, Ayar lifted his head. As he did so, pain shot through his temple. He tried to raise a hand to it, but had forgotten his bindings. He heard the door open as if from far away, then a shove sprawled him against the wet road. The pain stabbed through his head again.

"Get him up, you fool! Don't let *anyone* see him!" That was Growler.

Someone dragged him upright. He lurched across the

ground till he heard the creak of a door as it opened. They hurried him along what seemed like a corridor, then through another door and into a room.

"We've got him!"

"Good. Tie him up in the corner and rough him up a bit. We want to show JSEP we mean business and won't take any shit from them." The new voice was harsher than Growler's, if possible.

Ayar might have relished a fair fight, but didn't appreciate being kicked in the face with no idea where the blows came from and no chance to strike back. He withdrew his genitals inside him for protection. Blows fell on his face, shoulders, the back of his head, his chest, stomach, even his groin. *Just as well I anticipated that,* he thought. A kick (he felt the sole of a boot) landed on his jaw and he heard a *crack*, and thought it was broken. The pain ground into him. The extra bone strength he should have had wasn't there; he'd spent too long in microgravity in the Sleep Room.

"All right, that's enough. Get the hood off."

Somebody yanked at his head. This time Ayar couldn't help a yelp of pain. The hood came off and the eye of a holocam glared at him.

"Nothing personal," the harsh-voiced man said. "Seeing as we've learned that Langrishe never bothered to instigate the feasibility study I asked for, we just need your ship."

"I heard it was destroyed," Ayar mumbled. His lips had swelled; his speech was indistinct. He tried to study the speaker. His chin bore a near-white beard, and he wore a black robe, like a monk. He looked to be in his late fifties.

"Whoever told you that lied. We know it's at Galatea Station, and we'll get it. "

So the Bekel *is at Galatea Station?* His attempt to forestall them had failed, but he'd learned something of interest.

But that was a small victory against the overwhelming defeat of his life here on Earth. The humans had mistreated him time after time. And it didn't look as if they were about to stop.

*

Paris, Texas, 22nd October, 2098.

"I'm sorry, Mrs Chapman, but I can't accept Kaj as a patient. I know nothing whatsoever about his anatomy." Dr Williams sighed. "I daren't help you – any treatment I might, in ignorance, give him – could kill him."

Juli had half-expected this response, but she persevered. She'd come to this doctor because he ran an unofficial clinic. "But without treatment he might die anyway. I can't go back to JSEP – they just want information about the starship's drive –"

"Mrs. Chapman, you must. The JSEP doctor who knows about Zarduthi anatomy is the only person who can help you." The doctor's voice softened. "You love him and don't want him to die, or you wouldn't be here now. So give him a chance, and realise that not everyone can live up to your high ideals."

"What does that mean? That you're going to hand us over?"

"Not at all. I'm bound by an oath, remember? But in this instance it would be in Kaj's interests to take him to see *that* doctor."

He's right, of course. Kaj grew weaker every day. She'd wrestled with herself over what to do.

"*Please,* Mrs. Chapman. Otherwise you could *cause* his death by denying him the treatment he needs."

That decided her. "All right," she said. "Thank you, Dr Williams. C'mon, you guys." She manoeuvred Kaj to the door. Lucy clung to his hand. Juli somehow got both of them out through reception and into the car.

"You said the doctor would make Kaj better, Mommy?"

Lucy said.

"I'm sorry, Lucy. He doesn't know how. I have to take him to a different doctor. But she's a long way from here. And I'll have to meet her first, to make sure it's safe for Kaj to go there."

"You can...leave her with me... I'll be OK."

Kaj rarely spoke; he hadn't the energy. Juli wanted to gather him up in her arms and hug him. Instead, she concentrated on driving. "I need to go to*day*, Kaj. I can't leave you to get worse, and now that we've been to see that doctor, he might turn us over."

"You gave a false...name and address, though...didn't you?"

That was the sole benefit to paying for third party free healthcare; no official documents were required. She'd given Dr Williams a fake Social Security number. "Of course, but he's seen you now. I don't want to get back to you and find you've been taken into JSEP custody."

"How long…will it…take you...to get there?"

"I'll be gone overnight. I'll try to bring the doctor back here, OK?"

Kaj nodded.

Back at the apartment, Juli made her arrangements. She left food available that Kaj and Lucy could prepare and eat easily, and packed a few clothes into a holdall. She checked her watch. *Two minutes to six.* Then she hugged both children for a moment. "I'll be back soon," she said. "Lock the door after me and don't answer it."

Lucy had tears in her eyes when Juliet turned to go. *She* is *only four.*

Kaj just lay where she'd left him on the sofa. He hadn't the energy to move.

Juli raised her hand, pulled the apartment door firmly to, and clamped both lips between her front teeth.

*

Reception Centre, Tom Green County, Texas, 6 pm, 23rd October, 2098.

By the time she arrived at the Reception Centre Juli was very tired. *I must be crazy,* she thought. *Why didn't I fly?*

Because they might still be looking for you at airports. And you couldn't afford to fly, her inner voice argued with her.

She'd skirted around Dallas and Fort Worth on Highway 82, then turned onto Route 59 at St Jo and passed through Montague, Bowie and Jacksboro. Highway 380 took her through Bryson and Graham, and down to Breckenridge, where she picked up Highway 183. She pressed on to Cisco and Coleman on Route 206. She stopped at Coleman for a snack and called the children to make sure they were all right. Kaj said they were fine. With less worry, she gave in to her fatigue and slept for a few hours in the car.

She awoke stiff and tired the next morning, but put her foot down and kept up the pressure, despite her exhaustion. *I can sleep when I get there,* she told herself.

At San Angelo she found a truckstop, where she ate an all-day breakfast. Then she'd turned onto Highway 87, with utter relief that the journey neared its end. A minor road took her to a long, low building, miles from any others. She hoped this was it. The perimeter fence suggested it might be. *I hope Dr Chapaire can help Kaj.*

The journey had taken fifteen hours, including stops. She dreaded the drive back.

There was a gate in the fence. As she approached it opened automatically. She parked in front of the building and sat still for several moments, too weary to get out. Then she thought of the children, and couldn't justify her stupor.

She walked to the door and pressed the bell. It sounded

inside the building. She sank down onto the wide step to wait.

It was a minute or two before the door creaked open and a woman appeared beside her. Juli saw the low-heeled leather shoes first, then the long checked skirt in pastel colours, the matching silk jersey blouse above that, and finally the angular face and brown hair with blonde streaks. She was too tired to take in much about Dr Chapaire's features; they were a pale blur. "Juliet Harkness," she said. "I need your help. Kaj is ill."

Dr Chapaire stared at her for a few moments, then said, "Edith Chapaire. You had better come inside."

"Thank you. I didn't know where else to go for help. I left yesterday evening. I need to phone the children as well, to make sure they're still OK. I had to leave them on their own."

"It is not advisable to phone them from inside if you do not wish their whereabouts to be known."

"You mean – they spy on you?"

"On all of us, I am afraid. But come in and rest. Do you have a cell phone?"

"Yes, and Kaj has one."

"We can phone the children on the way so that our dear Monsieur Brencher does not find out where your hideout is." Dr Chapaire reached down a hand to help Juli up. "I am sorry," she said, "but I will need to verify your identity after your absence from the scene for so long. And we never met, though I met your husband."

"That's all right."

"This way, please." Dr Chapaire led Juli down a corridor, then halted before a door. "I share this office with Josie Carter."

"I did meet *her* a couple of times."

"I know. But she is out on a visit at present, though I expect her back momentarily." They entered a comfortable room with couches as well as two desks, each with computers, a work surface with coffee machine and sink, a bookcase, and some low chairs. A holophone, flanked by a few plants: bright geraniums, spider plants, a cactus garden. And, on an extension to one of the desks, scanning equipment, similar to that used in banks. It was to this that Dr Chapaire led Juli. "I just need a handscan to verify your identity. Then you can tell me what the problem is, and I'll see how best to help."

"Where's Josie gone?"

"England. Place your hand here, please."

Juli did so.

Dr Chapaire seated herself at her desk and checked the monitor. "That seems fine," she smiled. "Now, please have a seat, and tell me what is wrong with Kaj."

"He lost his appetite a few weeks ago, and since then he's eaten less and less, so of course he's really weak now. He has no energy and complains of feeling sick. He's never even caught a cold before."

"All right. It sounds as if it is something related to his digestion, and probably not an illness he has caught – the children's DNA is too different for them to catch our diseases." Dr Chapaire smiled. "Do not worry. I will come with you to your lodgings and we will bring Kaj here for diagnosis and treatment."

Juli felt a ton weight lift off her.

*

JSEP HQ, Washington, five minutes later.

On Hardy Brencher's desk, a red light glowed as the auto-identify facility activated.

He lounged with his feet crossed on the edge of the desk, but came upright, then leaned forward in his seat as three-dimensional images filled the holotank. "Well, fuck me to hell and back!" he muttered, as Juli Harkness's face stared at him. "So, she's surfaced at last." To the computer he said, "Download everything to memory, then transfer it across to my notebook, but keep a copy." He plugged the notebook into the side of the computer and watched the tank. The holoimages were from Dr Chapaire's office.

It's a pity I wasn't there when the Harkness woman turned up, but the scanning equipment is wired and it's the next best thing. The installation allowed him to keep track of what was going on there. So far he'd resisted the temptation to watch it to see if Josie came into his field of view.

He'd just lifted the holdall he kept packed in a corner of the room when the holophone rang. "Answer," he told it.

President Sanchez's holoimage appeared in the tank. "Hardy Brencher? I've received a message from the Neoluddites. They've kidnapped the young Zarduthi who was fostered in Moscow."

"Kidnapped? What do they want with him – ransom?"

"Exactly. They're demanding that the Zarduthi ship be handed over in exchange for his life."

"Play me the message. I'll copy it." He gave instructions to the computer; it would copy the holovid to the notebook as well.

The holoscreen filled with Per Lakshar's bearded face. "It seems you are as unwilling to listen to our needs as President Langrishe was," he said. "So I'm doing something to make you sit up and take notice. We've got your Zarduthi, Ayar Dekkutz. We want the Zarduthi starship based at Galatea Station in exchange for his life. If we don't get it, we'll kill him and take it anyway. You have the choice." The images of Ayar at the end of the message showed his face battered and bruised, his jaw and mouth swollen. He was chained at the wrists and ankles, and looked as if he'd fall over at any moment.

"Shit!" Hardy muttered under his breath. This was just the sort of security breach he'd feared when Langrishe had insisted on his insane plan for the children. "When did you get this?"

"About fifteen minutes ago."

Hardy considered this. "Per Lakshar has always maintained he is just a priest, and dissociated himself from the terrorist arm of the Neoluddites," he said. "What changed his mind?"

"Desperation, perhaps, or the acquisition of something which put him in a strong enough position to lay his cards on the table."

"Like Ayar, maybe? Shall I try to get a fix on them?"

"The message was delivered by courier."

This time, Hardy swore aloud. "All right. I'm on it, Mr President," he said, and cut the connection. The Harkness woman might have surfaced, but Kaj Kalinga's life was unlikely to be in as much danger as Ayar Dekkutz' was, so that business must wait. He was going to the Reception Centre anyway. He disconnected his notebook, pushed it into the holdall with some things he thought he might need, and made his travel arrangements. Then he left the room, and locked the door.

*

Eisenhower Reception Centre, 25th October, 2098.

Apart from the friction between Ronnie and him, Josie mused, *Miril has adjusted to life in his new family better than any of the other children. Then again, he* is *the youngest.*

She parked her car, walked to the door, and wondered whose the third car was. It was a large, well-polished vehicle that looked like a comfortable, if expensive, ride. She shrugged and entered the building.

Her question was answered as Hardy Brencher rose and greeted her. Her stomach flip-flopped over and her heart raced.

She didn't bother returning his greeting. "What are *you* doing here?" she asked, conscious of the hostility in her voice.

"Ayar –" he began.

"There was a kidnapping in Moscow," Edith interjected. "The Neoluddites want to ransom Ayar for the starship, and Monsieur Brencher thinks he may need our help as Ayar has been injured."

"I hadn't heard any of this. Oh, I forgot, you always put a news ban on things like this, don't you?"

"A news ban could work to our advantage in this instance," he said. "This is the message the Neoluddites sent." Holovid images sprang up over his notebook.

Josie didn't think she could trust anything Hardy told her again. But the images of Ayar's bruised face horrified her. "We must do *some*thing!"

"Just what I propose, but I need Dr Chapaire's co-operation since Ayar will need treatment for his injuries." Hardy disconnected his notebook.

"What did you have in mind?" Josie asked.

"A rescue, but I don't know what or where yet."

"And did you find any trace of Halka and Robert?"

Hardy sighed. "No. I spent several more days searching for them when I last returned to Nice, but the only trace of them I could find was a potential sighting near Marseilles. When I went there, nobody had seen them." He locked gaze with her. "I did try, Josie, especially as *you* asked me to."

Josie heard his words, but the appeal in his voice stood out more. She hardened her heart against him.

"You know, I am seriously concerned about them," he continued. "Jouvin is in prison for the murder of Madame Jouvin, but the youngsters can have no money. I don't know how they can survive."

Josie shook her head. "Me neither. Though I'm glad you caught Jouvin."

"Well," Edith said, "I for one am a little less worried about *them* than I am about Ayar."

Hardy looked surprised. "Why?"

"You did say, Josie, did you not, that Halka had her backpack with her?"

"Her clothes, yes."

"And the weapons?"

"Oh-h-h." Josie raised a hand to her mouth. "I see what you mean."

"You see, I think that young lady may be more resourceful than we have given her credit for, Monsieur Brencher."

"You mean – she had weapons all the time?"

"They all do. Halka could hunt with them, so I doubt that she and Robert are starving."

The expression on Hardy's face told Josie that a light had switched on in his mind.

"And any news on Kaj?" Josie asked.

"None," Hardy said, "at present." He glanced towards Edith.

Her face was expressionless.

"Hardy, you once told me you thought the children all ought to be together," Josie said. "What's the new president like? How receptive would he be to that idea?"

He considered that for a moment. "Might be. He seems a decent man. He knew nothing about the demand for a feasibility study – but I remembered and asked him why they'd taken Ayar. He thought the feasibility study might have been the trigger." He met her gaze again. "Why?"

"What if we – Edith and I, that is – could help you find Ayar, at least? Could you try to persuade him to let them contact each other again?"

"Me negotiate with him, you mean?"

"Yes."

Hardy shrugged. "It could work. He's not like Langrishe."

"You don't feel he's on *your* back all the time, then?"

"Not so much."

"Josie, you look in need of a coffee," Edith chirped. "Monsieur Brencher?"

"Please."

"So you will help us change the president's mind?" Edith handed him a cup.

"Yes – it's worth a try."

"You won't back out once we find Ayar?"

Hardy looked from Edith to Josie. "Don't *either* of you trust me?"

"You have not done anything to engender trust in the past, have you?"

There was a silence, during which Josie thought, *That was below the belt, Edith, but he deserves it...She wants to punish him for the way he treated me.*

"I guess not," Hardy conceded at last. He met her gaze. "But I promise you I will try once Ayar is safe. Though we have no idea where they're holding him, other than probably somewhere in Moscow."

Josie had no ideas to offer, but Edith said, "Had you considered a trap?"

"What did you have in mind?"

"These terrorists want the ship for its FTL drive, is that not so? So why not let them think the engineers have found out how the drive works, and have duplicated it, and that the ship is now reassembled and ready to leave?"

"How would that help us find Ayar?"

"It might not, but – it might flush them out so that we could catch some of them and question them."

That gave Josie an idea. "And we could use the media to set the trap."

Hardy rubbed at the scar below his eye. "You know, that

might work, especially if I went over to Moscow and did a follow-up with the foster-family...so that they don't realise it's a trap. You could come with me, Josie."

"I don't think so."

"Not even to help Ayar? It would look – like a very normal procedure."

"You don't need me, and I have thirty-odd other children to keep an eye on." *And besides,* Josie added to herself, *this just shows what a pretence your whole life is.*

He looked deflated for a second; then he said, "Dr Chapaire, it's a good plan. If I don't get any information through the usual channels this should at least yield something, and if not we could still end up with some terrorists in custody."

"Which would give *us* something to bargain for Ayar with."

"Exactly. It's not perfect, but it's the best we have at present. We could even start bargaining to distract them from our rescue attempt."

"How close *are* the engineers to a copy of the drive?" Josie asked.

"As far as I know, nowhere near. Now look, ladies, don't breathe a word of this to anyone. For the scheme to work we have to keep Ayar's kidnapping under wraps. Otherwise you can kiss goodbye to him, and maybe the ship as well. But if *they* think there's any chance of grabbing the ship, I think the Neoluddites will take it anyway. After all, Per Lakshar's nailed his colours fair and square to the mast after publicly dissociating himself from the terror squad for years. I'll go next door and make my arrangements." He nodded to both women and left the room.

Edith refilled her coffee cup. "So, he tried to find Halka and Robert after he returned to France, eh?" She smiled at Josie. "Do not be taken in by him, my dear. I noticed he was quick to invite you to go to Moscow with him. I am glad you refused."

"I wasn't going to let him hurt me again, Edith."

"Just so. More coffee?"

Josie held out her cup and Edith refilled it. "Now, how was Miril?"

Josie explained how well he'd settled in with the Lawtons. Then a knock at the door made Josie's stomach turn over again. She tried not to look up as Hardy put his head around the door.

"All done. I'm leaving now. I'll keep in touch. Oh, and Dr Chapaire?"

"*Oui*, Monsieur Brencher?"

"You will let me know if you have any information about Kaj, won't you?"

"Of course. But how can I contact you?"

"Just leave a message for me next door. I check my calls every day."

"Fine. Goodbye."

Edith beckoned to Josie, and together they watched him cross the car park, get in his vehicle and drive away.

"Good, he is gone," Edith smiled. "Now, I have a patient to attend to. Come with me."

Mystified, Josie followed her down the corridor to the dormitory where the children had lived on their arrival. Inside, a woman of about Josie's age rose to greet them. She looked familiar. A girl of about four played with a couple of dolls, never used by the Zarduthi children, on the floor nearby.

"Has he gone?"

"Yes." Edith smiled her most knowing smile again. "I wonder if he ever gets the feeling all the women in the world are ganging up on him…?"

Josie couldn't resist a smile at that. Then she remembered who the woman was. "Juliet Harkness!" she exclaimed.

"Yes. And here is Kaj." Juli gestured towards one of the

beds.

*

"So that's what the illness was – a recurrence of an illness he had when he was younger?" Juli was surprised, but relieved, at Dr Chapaire's diagnosis.

"Yes, but it'll take a while for Kaj to recover."

"Is this an illness humans could get?"

"Unlikely. The children's DNA is not the same as ours, though its structure is similar, and built from the same proteins."

"Are any of the other children likely to get it?"

"Only if they have had the original illness."

"How's that? And how could it make him so weak?"

"It is a bit like shingles. After the original illness, the chicken pox virus lives in the spine, and can reactivate in the right conditions. Stress or a weakened immune system can be factors. This works in the same way – convergent evolution, if you like. Kaj could not assimilate certain proteins, which bound instead to receptor sites in his digestive organ and prevented assimilation of other foods. Effectively he has been suffering from malnutrition."

"I wasn't as ill as this when I had the original illness," Kaj observed. "This is worse, and I don't understand why."

Dr Chapaire turned to him. "Kaj, you will be fine again soon," she assured him. "Just rest for now. The tablets will help everything to settle down again, and I will give you a shot which should help build you up and give you more energy. The medication will prevent the protein binding problem, and it should clear soon."

"Thank you, Karak Chapaire." Kaj lay back on the bed and looked up at Juli. "Are we staying here?" he asked.

"I don't know. You haven't had much personal freedom since you came to Earth, and I don't know whether it's worse for you to be cooped up in the apartment all the time or hidden here."

Dr Chapaire looked troubled. "Mrs. Harkness, I do not know how long I could keep Kaj hidden from Monsieur Hardy. He has an office here, and although he is not based here all the time, he comes in often, and when he is here he sometimes –" She hesitated. "He prowls around." She shrugged. "It is his job, of course, but I do not like it!"

"Are you saying we couldn't stay here, then?"

"Realistically, yes."

"I don't want to be here on my own, anyway, Juli," Kaj said. "I want to stay with you and Lucy."

"Even though it was my stupid impulsiveness that put us in this situation?"

"You didn't know." Kaj took Juliet's hand. "It wasn't *your* fault."

"It was also your principles," Edith murmured. "You were unwilling to see Kaj exploited. So was I, and so was your husband when he came to collect him –"

"He *was?*"

"I am convinced of it. He did not want to get information out of a child. He said so."

"If that was so, why would he do it?"

Dr Chapaire put her hand on Juliet's arm. "Perhaps he had no choice. JSEP employees must do as they are told. Since the children arrived there have been things I had to do which I did not approve of."

"Why do you still work for them?"

"Because my conscience tells me I must do what I can to help the children. However little it may be, I can stand against the dictates of the government in small ways. But it is hard to fight authority," Dr Chapaire said, "when to help one must also retain one's employment."

"You mean – they would sack him if he didn't agree?"

"Undoubtedly."

Juliet's hand was at her mouth. "Perhaps I misjudged him, then." *Oh Eddie, what have I done?*

*

Walkway to the Bekel, *Galatea Station, 27th October, 2098.*

Hardy raised his stun weapon, aimed at the nearest terrorist, and fired. The man's body crumpled to the floor only metres from the covered walkway from the dock to the Zarduthi ship.

Around him, stun bolts snaked out as his men rose from their hiding places in the docking bay. There was an occasional *thung* as bolts missed their targets and bounced off the bay bulkhead or a stun shield, but for the most part the shots fell true. The Neoluddites had made a well-armed attack on the *Bekel*, with a large force, but JSEP security and a unit of marines based on Galatea Station were ready for them. And Hardy had observers posted all over the space station to see where the terrorists entered.

"Unit One! Make sure no-one gets away," Hardy instructed. "I don't want tales taken home to base." A precaution, since he'd had the passenger and freight docks sealed off as soon as the terrorists had come aboard Galatea Station, but he didn't know what their exit plan was. He counted. *Thirty-seven bodies on the ground.* Several had backed out rather than run blind into a pitched battle; his men would get them. *Seventy terrorists walked into the bay. There could be between twenty and twenty-five on the walkway or onboard the ship itself.* He turned to Don. "Unit Two – follow me!" Hardy raised his stun shield and made for the covered walkway at a run. It wobbled as he stepped onto it, despite the steel base.

A blast struck his stun shield, bounced off and sent shock waves through the lightweight metalloplastic structure. The steel-framed base clanged like a gong – he felt the vibrations through his spaceboots.

Shit! Hardy thought. *We've lost any element of surprise now.* He'd hoped to board the *Bekel* without the knowledge of the terrorists already onboard. He beckoned his men on despite the rain of stun bolts that made the structure writhe. *Got to get off this thing!*

His vertigo returned in full force, despite the Magnetix on his boots. He hoisted his stun shield higher; his upper left arm muscles strained. He gritted his teeth, sprinted, and fired ahead. Bolts thudded against the *Bekel.* The mirror-hulled ship absorbed them…but then a *GIGANTIC* wave rolled back along the walkway towards Hardy as electricity converted to kinetic energy. He made to throw himself on the ground, then stopped himself and staggered upright. *My Magnetix will keep me attached and upright.* He crouched, and clung to his stun shield and a nearby handgrip. The wave passed him. Its recoil flung him in multiple directions. Nausea pounded at his throat.

The faces clustered at the rigged-up airlock had disappeared. *It would have been useful if I'd taken them all out.* But Hardy was a realist; as he'd expected, only three or four unconscious bodies blocked the doorway when he got there. *The rest of them must be inside.* He stumbled over the bodies.

"Take these into custody – I'll question them when they come round," he said.

Don was behind him. He nodded and knelt to cuff them.

Hardy passed through the airlock. Once inside the ship, he pressed the button to open his helmet and advanced with caution. The white haze of the bulkheads merged into the ceiling.

Hardy followed the corridor, and passed through a couple of tall doorways on his way to the Control Room. He looked back to check the marines followed. Don was hard on his heels. The door to the bridge was shut.

"They've set their own trap," he whispered. "We need to get that door open."

Don nodded. "I'll short out the mechanism like Eddie showed me."

"OK," Hardy agreed. "We must rely on hand signals. Send men to cover the other entrance, and someone to the centre to relay the message and we'll short them both out together when I give the signal. We'll bottle the terrorists up in there. Then it's a matter of time before we KO all of them."

"Unless they risk projectile weapons –"

Hardy shook his head. "They won't do that – too risky in a pressurised environment, triple skin or not. And they may not know about that."

They split the unit.

"Everyone in position?" Hardy gave the order to short out the door mechanism, though it would make work for the engineering crews.

As the doors slid back Hardy and his men crouched behind their stun shields. Terrorists spilled out into the corridor, only to be cut down with flashes of stunfire. He'd found Eddie Harkness onboard on arrival at Galatea. They'd met briefly when Eddie had reported Kaj missing. He'd been willing to help set the trap.

In the bridge, Hardy stepped over unconscious bodies and piles of debris to find Eddie, roped into one of the control seats, suitless. He hugged his wrist. He smelled of singed flesh.

"A stun bolt glanced off the console and I couldn't get out of its way!" he explained as Hardy untied him.

"We can take care of that," Hardy assured him. "Let's get you out of here. Can you walk?"

"Think so," Eddie grunted.

"Do you need help getting a suit on?"

"My arm feels dead – I doubt I could get a suit on now."

"Hope the walkway doesn't leak!" Hardy wasn't entirely

comfortable with taking a suitless man through such a risky environment, but he could see it would be impractical to make him suit up. "D'you always work late?"

"We work round the clock – we need to find out how the ship works. *Someone* has to supervise the engineering crews down in the Drive Room. The terrorists didn't get that far."

"Not too much damage done in here, then?"

"Don't think so."

"Then let's get you fixed up." Hardy called Don over and explained about Eddie's current predicament.

"The medics have something they can use in injury situations," Don said, as he called for medical assistance. The medic arrived a few minutes later with an inflatable Zorb sphere. Eddie climbed inside. It was large enough that he could stand upright in it, walk normally, and protect his injured arm. The medic walked on one side of Eddie, Hardy on the other. It fitted into the airlock with room for all three of them.

When they reached the walkway, Eddie looked at him with an odd expression on his face. "Are *you* OK?"

"I don't care for the walkway. It's even worse when stun bolts slam into the ship and roll back at you." He met Eddie's gaze. "I suffer from vertigo."

"Ooh, shit! You shouldn't even be up here."

"Too late!" Hardy said. "But hopefully I'll find out where Ayar Dekkutz is when I question these guys."

Eddie nodded and indicated his wrist. "How long will it take for this to mend?"

"A few days' rest should sort it out once it's sealed off from the air," the medic replied.

"Rest isn't an option on this job." Eddie sighed. "I wish I could find out how the ship got here."

"Yes, President Sanchez called me on the way up here to tell me you'd found what might be ship's logs. I wasn't best pleased to be hauled from my acceleration couch and have to get myself to a holophone in free fall – and all for a fucking phone call!" He'd left the phone in a hurry, hand clamped over his mouth; being sick while weightless hadn't seemed a good idea. Worse still, the new President thought it was hilarious, if gross…as did Eddie and the medic. Hardy preferred to forget the rest of the trip.

They reached the end of the walkway, and the medic led Eddie away for treatment.

Hardy returned to the bridge. "What's the news, Don?"

"Nobody got away, Hardy. We arrested several Neoluddites on public transport routes on the Science Lobe, on their way back to the freight dock where they came in."

"Good work!"

"Could any of the ships in the freight docks be connected to them?" Don asked.

"We'll find that out when we question them. Make sure Station Control understand there must be *no* flights out until *we* clear them."

Don nodded and despatched a man to Station Control. "No exceptions, now!"

"Who have you got for me to question?" Hardy asked.

"We've already completed preliminary questioning. Nobody's talking, so far."

"We'll need to use truth drugs, then."

Don nodded again. "Since most of the others are either out cold or need burns treatment, there could be a delay before you can question them."

"OK, though I might get the information I need from those that are awake and unhurt." Hardy could see he was in for a long night. "Lay on plenty of coffee, will you?"

CHAPTER 20 – Interview with the World President

Marseilles, 28th October, 2098.

"ARE YOU LOST?"

Halka turned to look at the owner of the voice, a middle-aged man with a beard and moustache. "No," she said.

"Are you sure?"

"Positive." Her tone was firm.

"I'd like to show you around Marseilles."

"We don't need to be shown around," Robert snapped.

"Ooh, hoity-toity, aren't we? I wasn't speaking to you, pipsqueak!" The man made a grab for Halka's waist and caught her arm instead as she side-stepped him.

"Let me go!"

"Oh no, my alien beauty. I need a pick-me-up right now."

"Let her be!" Robert shouted. He clawed open Halka's backpack and grabbed the larger weapon. "Or I shoot."

The man let go immediately. *Probably from shock,* Halka thought. *I bet he didn't expect Robert to carry out his threat.* Her suspicion was confirmed when the man snatched at her wrist again a moment later.

Without warning, Robert fired. A crack of blue-white fire snaked out. It melted a patch of the railings outside a nearby building. "Shit!" he said, and almost dropped the weapon.

The man let go of Halka's wrist, and in a thousandth he'd vanished.

Robert made to slide the weapon back into the pack, but Halka stopped him. "It's too hot yet – it might set the backpack on fire. Give it a few – euh – minutes. And let's get out of here."

"OK," Robert said. They ran until a coughing fit doubled him up. It was the dry rasp of the cough he'd developed after working at the vineyard. "Sorry," he gasped between paroxysms.

Halka put her arm around his shoulders while he coughed. "It's OK," she said. "We don't need to move until you feel better."

"I don't know how to tell you this, Halka, but – I've felt worse and worse all day," Robert said. "My head hurts when I cough now."

"I'll get you some medicine," she suggested. "We still have some cash from the winery – and this is an emergency. But first we must find somewhere safe to leave you."

"*He* might know," Robert said, pointing to a man at the side of the street.

Halka studied him for several thousandths. He looked grubby – but then *they* hadn't been able to shower since the vineyard. His face was almost as dark as hers, from sun exposure. His clothes were torn and filthy, his sports shoes scuffed; his left big toe poked out. "Him?"

"He's a street person, I think."

"What's he doing?"

"Begging?" Robert reached for her hand. "Help me up, I'll go and talk to him." They put the gun back in Halka's backpack.

He walked steadily once upright, and they crossed the short space to the man in thousandths. "Sir, we're strangers to Marseilles. Do you know of anywhere safe to stay?"

The man regarded them in surprise. "It's been a long time since anyone called me 'sir'," he said, then considered Halka for a moment. "She's one of them alien kids, isn't she?"

Robert nodded. "Can you help us? A man just tried to take Halka away with him."

"Probably for sex," the beggar said. "There are people who would pay a great deal to have sex with an alien, particularly a youngster. Don't you go having nothing to do with them, now!"

He scratched his head and pointed again. "Go down that street there. "There's an alleyway, fourth on the left. It leads to a derelict building where there's a squatter colony. It ain't very private, you'll probably have to share rooms, but it's out of the weather and it don't cost." Then he pointed to Halka's backpack. "But don't leave whatever you've got in there lying around. It won't lie for long!"

"You mean – someone would steal it?" Halka was shocked. Although everything was shared on the clanship, nobody would take someone else's clothes or weapons. Those belonged to an individual for life, though they would be redistributed on their death.

"They'll take it to sell, maybe for drugs or whatever."

"Thanks. What's your name?"

"Everyone calls me Jacques."

"Thank you, Jacques. Goodbye." Robert took Halka's hand. "Let's go find it."

They set off down the street. It only took them a few thousandths to find the building. They stepped inside. It might once have been an office block. Numerous rooms and corridors led off the main foyer.

"What do *you* want?"

They turned. A man stood watching them. He was as dirty as Jacques, with his unshaven chin and trousers belted with string, but even less savoury; he smelled of beer and piss.

"We need somewhere to stay," Robert said. "We were told there might be room here."

The man nodded at Halka. "What's in the bag?"

"My clothes."

"There are rumours on the streets of a strange weapon."

"All true." Halka sensed a show of power might be necessary.

Robert stared at her in amazement, then nudged her. "We

don't want to be in any trouble," he whispered.

For once Halka ignored him. "I hunt with it. Now, how about the room?"

"What can you give me?"

Another man emerged from the room. "Nah, Lucius, they're only kids. Let them pass." To Halka and Robert he said, "Take no notice of him. He don't run the place." He waved a hand around. "Just go in and find yourself a room that isn't occupied. And make sure there's a lock on the door!" He guffawed loudly.

"Come on," Halka said to Robert. They moved on. The building smelled of human piss, sawdust and concrete substitute.

They found an unoccupied room on the fifth floor. All the locks were broken, so Halka decided the man downstairs must have been joking at their expense.

Robert sank down, doubled up with his cough. While it eased, Halka put her pack on the floor and stripped off her clothes.

"What are you doing?"

"Putting my own clothes on. I'll leave you the projectile pistol. Be careful with it, and don't let anyone steal it." She pulled on leather breeches. "I'll get you some medicine, and a bolt for the door."

"But – you'll be recognised."

"I know. But it might be the only way to get ourselves across the Atlantic."

"What do you mean?"

She let the fur jacket hang open over her sweat-stained t-shirt and came to squat on the floor beside him. "I'm not leaving my stuff here to have it stolen by ruffians while we sleep. Equally, I won't be fucked by a load of sensation-seeking humans. We need to leave here and go to America as soon as possible. It may be necessary to show myself and see if JSEP will come and get us."

"But what about Papa?"

"You've only got to show them your back and they'll realise he was hurting us. That might help prove we didn't kill your *maman*." Halka looked around. "I don't like Marseilles, and I don't want to stay here a minute longer than I have to. I don't feel safe here." As she said it, she realised she hadn't felt safe at the villa either, but Robert had been strong enough to take charge there. *But he's ill now, so it's up to me to keep us safe. This is the only way.*

"Now, I want you to rest. Get under this." She pulled the tarpaulin out from the bottom of her backpack and laid it on the floor. Then she tucked the larger weapon back in. "I'll bring you something to eat and drink as well." She arranged her blanket over him and put her jeans under his head. Then she sought his hand for the thumbclasp, and kissed him at the same time. "I'll be as quick as I can."

Halka strode through the building. She met a few of the street people as she went; they stared at her, but most didn't speak. One man did. She said, "*Bonjour, monsieur*," and went on her way.

At the foyer she realised she didn't know where to go for medicine. But there was a signpost on the opposite side of the street, so she crossed to it and read it, and followed its instruction to reach the main shops.

I didn't realise I'd be stared at so much. In Nice, everyone knew me, through Robert, and knew I lived at his home. They soon stopped taking notice of me. Here things are bound to be different, she reasoned. Since Madame Jouvin's murder they'd been wary of anyone who stared at them. They'd only just arrived, and hadn't had a chance to check if they were on the news, but Monsieur Brencher must have put a news ban on Robert's mother's death, so it was unlikely the police would arrest her.

She ignored the stares and marched into the nearest drugstore. She picked her way among cosmetics, perfume and baby equipment counters, sweating in her furs and leathers. At the drug counter she had to ask for help to find the best medicine for Robert.

The woman wanted to know details, though she avoided remarks on Halka's appearance. "How long has he had this cough? Is it wet or dry?"

"About a month now, and he seems really ill with it. It's – er, a dry one – I think."

The woman produced some medicine which she thought would help ease Robert's cough.

"And do you know where the nearest JSEP office is?"

"Not here. The nearest is north of Paris." The woman allowed herself to scrutinise her at last, and Halka guessed what was coming. "You're one of those children, aren't you?"

"Yes. Can I pay for this medicine?"

"Oh, of course." The woman took the money. "Are you in trouble?"

"Thank you for your help," Halka mumbled, and fled.

Back at the room, she found Robert half-asleep, gun in hand. "Wake up, Robert, I've got you some medicine."

He opened his eyes and looked up at her, groggy. He sat up and coughed again. "I feel really ill, Halka. I'm all hot and cold," he said, when he could speak again. "Oh – there's no spoon!"

"Well, just drink it from the bottle!" Halka suggested. "I've got you a sandwich and an apple."

"Are you having something?"

She shook her head. "We agreed we wouldn't spend money on food for me, remember?"

"But Halka, you can't hunt things in the city! Well, rats,

maybe."

"Robert, you don't understand." She met his gaze, and hers was troubled. "I nearly fainted when the saleswoman told me how much your cough mixture cost. I did get a bolt, but there's no money for me to buy food as well. We need the cash for your medicine." She sighed. "I'll *have* to hunt. The longer we stay here, the less chance we have of reaching America. Or even phoning JSEP."

*

Neoluddite safe house, Moscow, 31st October, 2098.

"I need the bathroom," Ayar said. He'd wrenched his jaw back into place when he realised that otherwise it would need to be broken and reset if he didn't do so himself now – and it had begun to heal. His lips were less swollen than the previous day, but speech was still hard.

"I'll take you." Per Lakshar unlocked the shackles that confined Ayar to his corner, yanked him upright, still handcuffed, and half-dragged him along the corridor. He opened the door and switched on the light, then stood and watched as Ayar fumbled with his trouser zip, extracted his penis from its internal skin pocket, and started the stream with the utmost relief. "If you wanted to go, you should've asked before."

Ayar made no reply. But the priest seemed to just accept him. After the beating when he'd arrived, they'd left him alone, though his hands and ankles were chained. They fed him once a day, and gave him water twice a day. Sometimes Per Lakshar brought him coffee or black tea instead of water. It was enough to keep him going.

When Ayar had finished, the priest took his arm and led him back to the room they kept him in. He felt shaky as the circulation returned to his legs – if not his hands. *If only they'd leave off the manacles –*

The window imploded as dark shapes burst through its dusky square. Glass flew everywhere.

"Get down, Ayar!" someone shouted. A man's voice, speaking American English. It sounded familiar, but he couldn't identify it.

He obeyed instinctively, and wrenched himself out of the priest's grip to drop into a crouch and roll into his corner. At least someone thought he was important enough to want to rescue him. *Perhaps Natalya –*

A burst of stunfire interrupted his thoughts. He opened his eyes to see what had happened, but it was impossible to tell. Humans struggled everywhere, dark uniforms mingled with the terrorists' casual clothes. Some Neoluddites had stun weapons and shields. Most hadn't. Those without guns used knives or their fists. But all the uniformed men had weapons, and it looked as though the terrorists had come off worst.

Someone had a loudhailer, speaking in Russian this time.

"The building is surrounded. You cannot escape. Surrender now!"

The terrorists ignored it. The fighting continued. Heaps of prone bodies occupied the room. Per Lakshar was down. His robe was torn. Blood leaked from a wound somewhere.

Ayar felt a thud of satisfaction for a heartbeat when he saw Ivan Razich and Nikolai Tchenkov among the fallen, certain it was one of them that had broken his jaw.

Then a familiar face was before him: pale eyes and hair, semi-circular scar under one eye. *Hardy Brencher.* He remembered him initially from his visit after the holiday in England, then from the Big Place. "Come on, Ayar," he said. "Let's get you out of here."

"My hands –" he began, holding out his handcuffed wrists.

"Who has the key?"

"Per Lakshar." Ayar indicated him.

Hardy bounded over to the priest's body to check his pockets, and returned with the key.

In a couple of thousandths, Ayar stood up and chafed the welts on his wrists to get the circulation back into his hands.

"Are you OK to take over here, Don?" Hardy asked a stocky man with ginger hair. "Ayar's safety is my responsibility."

"We'll carry on with the mopping-up," Don said. "Off you go. I'll report to you by phone when the operation's finished."

"Fine. Send me a photo of your wedding day!" Hardy's shoulder was firm under Ayar, despite the height discrepancy between the two of them. "I have a car outside." He hurried Ayar down a corridor.

"Where are we going?"

"First, to your foster-parents' apartment. I'll get a medic in to see to that jaw of yours," Hardy said as they reached the front door. It lay in halves at the threshold.

"No need," Ayar said. "It's already healing. Fortunately I knew how to click it back into place –" He stopped at Hardy's hiss of indrawn breath.

"OK. Here's the car. In you get." Hardy pulled his thick black greatcoat firmly around himself.

The chill struck through Ayar's clothes, but he ignored it. *It'll be warm in the car.* He climbed in. "Is Per Lakshar dead?"

Hardy settled beside him. "Possibly. Don will let me know in his report later."

"That solves your problem with the Neoluddites then, doesn't it?"

"It's not as simple as that, Ayar." Hardy met his eyes. "If he's dead, he might become a martyr for his cause. People will follow him because he died for his inner convictions."

"Humans are very strange."

"How d'you mean?"

"A Zarduthi's loyalty is to his clan and his current contract. Humans seem to have conflicting loyalties, and reasons why they can't be loyal to their families and friends." He paused. "They're not always loyal to work contracts, either."

Hardy laughed, but without humour. "Very well-observed, Ayar." His mouth settled back into its brooding line.

Ayar made the sign of incomprehension and wriggled back in his seat. The car was warm; he felt sleepy. Alexei was on a work spell, and he hadn't been sure about Natalya's motives for some time. Their relationship had deteriorated since he'd kissed her. But Irina was always kind; he'd be glad to see her. Although she'd never mentioned his attraction to Natalya, he thought she must know of it...

"We're here, Ayar." Hardy got out and held out a hand to Ayar. He took it, though it felt strange; he was the taller of them by nearly a head.

"In here." Ayar pointed to the lift.

"I know. I came here to try to track you down before we set the trap for the terrorists."

"Trap?"

"We flushed them out of hiding up on Galatea Station." Hardy explained Dr Chapaire's plan as the lift carried them up to the fourth floor. "I got some information from your foster-sister first, but the men we captured up there sang like nightingales." He smiled grimly. "With a little help from a truth drug."

Ayar was shocked. "You didn't use it on Natalya?"

"No need."

"She knew where I was?"

"Not exactly, but she knew where the safe houses were. It was a question of which one." Hardy slanted a sidewise look at Ayar as he rapped on the door. "She seemed concerned about your safety."

Ayar stared at the door as if willing it to open. After a few moments, it did. "Ayar!" Irina cried. "You're safe!" And she hugged his waist. "Come in, come in!" She pulled him inside despite her diminutive size, and beckoned for Hardy to follow. "Natalya, wake up! Ayar's back." She released Ayar and bustled towards the kitchen. "I'll make us all some tea."

Natalya appeared at the door to her bedroom and rubbed her eyes. She wore a short nightie. "Where's Ivan?"

Hardy answered. "He's been arrested with the rest of the Neoluddites."

"But he's done nothing wrong! I thought he'd be with you when you came back." She stared at Ayar. "What happened to your face?"

"Someone beat me up while I was chained up and blindfolded. They broke my jaw." His only satisfaction was when Growler accused them of stupidity. "Your boyfriend and his crony, I think."

"Ivan would never do anything like that."

"He already did – when I first came here. He and Nikolai Tchenkov attacked me in the school toilets, but I bested them. I suspect he did this –" Ayar indicated his jaw "– to pay me back for that." *Not to mention making sure I never got the chance to date you,* Ayar thought.

"I don't believe you!"

Ayar spread his arms in the gesture of helplessness. "I can't make you. But before you get involved with him, it's worth remembering that a man who uses violence on his enemies may also be tempted to use it on those he counts as friends. Old Zarduthi proverb."

"You do talk some rubbish, Ayar Dekkutz! Anyway, Ivan wouldn't hurt me – I'm having his baby." And she stalked back into her bedroom. As she passed through the dark doorway, Ayar saw the heat trace of the child within her, and knew she spoke the truth.

An intense chill descended on him. He saw Irina come back into the lounge with a tray of tea as if through a filter that made everything seem misty and distant.

"Here's your tea, Ayar. It's so good to have you home again!"

Ayar shivered.

"What's the matter, Ayar?" Irina's voice sounded concerned.

He couldn't draw breath to speak.

"It's probably the shock, after what he's been through. Let's get him into bed," Hardy said. "Ayar, you'll feel better for a good night's sleep. Come on." And he hoisted Ayar out of his chair and supported him into his room.

Ayar allowed Hardy to undress him, certain he'd wake up from his nightmare soon. When the night air struck his bare flesh, he shivered like a naked man in a snowstorm.

"What is it? Are you ill?"

Ayar shook his head.

"Into bed with you and I'll get Irina –"

"Want to leave here. Now," Ayar mumbled between spasms.

"In the middle of the night, and you in this state? You must be crazy." Hardy pulled a blanket off the bed and wrapped it round him. "We'll go in the morning –"

"Natalya."

"You want Natalya? I think she's gone back to bed." Hardy rubbed Ayar's back to warm him up. "I'll get her –"

Ayar shook his head again. "No. Didn't mean that." His shivers subsided. "I saw – the baby. I know she dates him, but how could she…?" He stopped and swallowed hard. "Won't sleep. Want to leave now."

Comprehension enlightened Hardy. Natalya was pregnant

with the only baby she could legally carry – and it was the child of a terrorist. *And he likes her.* "Oh, I get it. But leaving now isn't a good idea. Hang on till the morning – it'll save face and fit in with the travel arrangements. I for one don't fancy a night at a draughty airport." He felt in the pocket of his greatcoat, which he hadn't removed. "I've got something here that Dr Chapaire thought might help you to sleep. Though I don't think she had *this* particular shock in mind. Here." He handed him two white tablets. "I'll get your tea to take them with."

Hardy returned a few moments later, followed by Irina. He handed him the tea, which was at drinking temperature now. "This'll warm you up," he said.

Ayar hadn't expected him to be right, but he was. It couldn't banish the chill *inside* him, though.

"Ayar," said Irina, "Mr. Brencher says you'll leave with him in the morning. I understand that you don't want to stay here after what's happened. It's all right. I'm not offended, and neither will Alexei be."

"I'm sure JSEP can find you something useful to do in America," Hardy added.

"Like what? I doubt whether they'll let me join the marines or the army. They wouldn't let me do that here."

"Is that what you really want?"

Ayar thought for a moment. He relished Irina's kindness, but if he left, he'd never return to Moscow. He couldn't stay here now. And the kidnapping told him he must find the rest of the children and leave Earth. "No. What I *really* want is to find out what happened to my parents."

Hardy nodded. "I guess that's all you've wanted ever since you woke up on Earth," he said. "Well, I might be in a position to point you in that direction."

Ayar stared at him. "How?"

"The engineering team on your ship have found what they

think might be holovid of what happened before you came to Earth. How would you like to help them find out?"

"The President would let me?"

"It's a new president, remember? I think he might be persuaded."

Ayar's eyelids became heavy; not surprising, since he'd slept little over the past week. Dr Chapaire's drugs must be working… "All right," was the last thing he heard himself say, before darkness and blessed oblivion enfolded him.

*

Hardy's apartment, Washington, two weeks later.

Hardy Brencher's apartment in Washington wasn't as large as the Petrushenkos' in Moscow, Ayar found, and was on the seventh floor instead of the fourth. But it was comfortable, with deep pile carpets everywhere except in the bathroom and kitchen, which had expensive-looking tiled floors. The decoration was tasteful, in clean, uncluttered shades; the apartment was superbly appointed and spotlessly clean. Hardy (as he'd suggested Ayar call him now) drove a large, powerful electric car, kept in a private garage under the building. Ayar supposed he must earn a good salary.

He leaned against the window and stared out over the city. Since leaving Moscow he'd stayed here, and Hardy had made him welcome. He treated him very much as an equal, and Ayar enjoyed that; he suspected Hardy hadn't known how to deal with children, but that now he was almost an adult, in human terms, he felt more comfortable with him.

"Are you ready, Ayar?"

He turned to see Hardy surveying him. He looked at himself in the long hall mirror: shiny new leather shoes and new suit (made-to-measure, as he was so tall and slender compared to the human shape), fashionable bootlace tie, cropped hair crest brushed smooth. He wanted to look smart to meet the new president.

Such an interview had been unthinkable, Hardy had said, when President Langrishe had held office; but President Sanchez was a different kind of man altogether. 'Play your cards right,' Hardy had said, 'and you have everything to gain. Good presentation's part of it.'

At any rate, Ayar thought, it would be an interesting encounter.

Hardy smiled at him. "And just remember, it's equally important to be able to fight with words, Ayar."

"My father would agree with you. He's a clan negotiator."

"I think the President will listen if you can construct a good argument."

"I hope so."

A trip to Dr Chapaire in Texas the previous week had reassured them that his jaw was now mended; his speech was clear again.

"Come on, then. We have an appointment." Hardy led the way out of the apartment, locked it, and made for the lift. "We'll go by car."

Forty minutes later an aide ushered them into the oval office in the White House.

"Hello, Ayar. How's the jaw?"

"Hello, Mr President, Sir. I'm fine now, thank you."

"I must say, Ayar, I've been most impressed by the speed of your recovery," Hardy said. "What was it, ten days for a broken jaw to mend?"

"That *is* impressive. How did you do it, Ayar?"

He understood that Hardy had made an opening for him, which he mustn't waste. "I knew it would heal quickly, so I reset it myself," he explained. "We Zarduthi are genetically engineered to have all the qualities to make us good soldiers.

Fast healing is one of them."

"You set it yourself? Didn't that hurt a lot?"

"Of course, but I didn't want it to set wrong and have to be re-broken later. And Per Lakshar's organisation didn't appear to boast any medics, so I thought I'd better do it myself."

The President chuckled. "You have a keen turn of phrase, Ayar." He ordered coffee over the intercom. "Two white, one black. Now, do sit down, and tell me how I can help you."

Ayar perched on a seat opposite the president. *This man is the most powerful on this planet. He might be able to help me.* He thought hard before he spoke. It seemed likely there were things the humans wanted, in return for which he might get something for himself, and perhaps for the other children. He hadn't forgotten Hardy's suggestion that he assist with the ship's logs up on Galatea Station. Hardy hadn't said so, but Ayar supposed that if someone had tried to open the logs they must want to find out how other aspects of the ship worked, too. That suggested that the humans wanted to find out how the hyperdrive worked. That had been what the Neoluddites wanted – or at least, they wanted to use the ship. "I have several things I want to ask you. First, do you have any idea of what happened to my parents, and how we came to be here?"

"I understand that the engineers are working to find that out," the president said. "Apparently they've found a set of relays linked to cameras sited all over your ship, but can't find the controls for them. Do you know where they could be?"

"Perhaps." Ayar wasn't ready to admit one way or the other yet. "It's a while since I was onboard, but I might be able to remember if I went there."

"The engineers have another problem, Ayar. They don't speak or read your language." The president held his gaze. "It's possible we could help each other."

"It might be, if you could authorise marine and/or pilot

training for me, Sir."

The president regarded him through a sidewise glance over the rim of his coffee cup. "That would mean you'd be getting two things you want, while we'd only get one."

"I don't agree – you'd get the best marine and pilot in the business as well!"

President Sanchez grinned. "Touché!"

"Besides, I'd only find out for definite about my mother. She was pregnant, so she didn't go with the contracted warriors."

"Just a moment. Explain about these contracted warriors." The president's expression was troubled.

Ayar looked from him to Hardy Brencher, then explained. "That's all there is to it."

"But – your mother was pregnant, so she didn't...go with the contracted warriors?"

"The children – those under fifteen – stay in the Sleep Room, where you found us, while the warriors go to complete their contract. The pregnant women stay behind and look after them."

"To keep them from danger?" The president's face grew more troubled with every question he asked.

"And because they will fight all the harder to protect their unborn babies as well as the children in the Sleep Room."

"*Now* I understand." President Sanchez drummed his fingers on the desk. "Ayar, I think the previous World President wasn't always fair to you and your friends. I'll try to act more appropriately."

Ayar caught Hardy's eye. It seemed that *he* understood the situation better now as well. Ayar felt as if he were the only one who didn't.

"What I don't get is why we were split up, and why we aren't allowed to communicate with one another," he said. "We all grew up together. We live communally until we reach adulthood at fifteen, then we're allocated cabin space and take combat training. We also have what you would call vocational training, either in engineering, pilot skills, navigation, astrophysics, whatever interests us. With our line of business, you never know what you'll need to know just to survive. We also study academic subjects."

"I'm sure that was because President Langrishe was afraid." President Sanchez's brown eyes glowed with compassion. "Look at it this way. We have a world with limited space and a growing population – we've had a population explosion problem since at least the middle of last century. We tried many different ways to control fertility, but in the end it came down to the fact that only if every woman only had one child could we halve the population every generation. The ravages of global warming meant fertile land was submerged by the middle of this century, and the climate changes that followed did even more damage." He paused, perhaps to let his words sink in. "I think President Langrishe was afraid that if he allowed all of you to live together you'd breed out of control, and since you aren't human, what right had he to impose our population laws on you?"

"Perhaps he should have discussed it with us, then," Ayar retorted. "We understand – probably even better than you humans – the breeding restrictions limited space puts on us."

"What do you mean?"

"Once a clanship has a full complement of crew, breeding must be restricted until someone dies. If warriors are killed, say in battle, licences to breed are issued in strict rotation. It's important to keep numbers up aboard the clanships to remain an effective fighting force."

"So…women are obliged to have families when the clan demands it?"

"More or less. It takes fifteen ship's years for a Zarduthi

to grow to maturity – I know your children are considered mature at 18 years, and from living among you I suspect one of our years is a similar length of time to one of yours. But every Zarduthi woman can expect to have at least one, possibly two children, and if there's a disaster, more."

"I see." President Sanchez pondered this information for a few thousandths. "So – you might not have a problem with our population laws if you were able to live together again?"

"*I* don't, and the general view of the Zarduthi clans is that we expect some regulation of our fertility," Ayar said. "But although I'm the eldest child, so nominally our leader, I can't speak personally for the others. You should ask *them*."

"Are there many clanships?"

"Enough to destroy a planet's population if necessary and appropriate."

"Do you think your parents would consider it necessary in the case of the Earth?" Hardy had sat quietly, but the urgency of his question told Ayar that he'd followed the conversation.

Ayar didn't think for one thousandth that they were in a position to do so. If they had been, they'd have arrived on Earth by now. Most likely they weren't even aware of the ship's arrival at Earth. But he sensed that if he said that, he'd lose ground. Yet he didn't want to tell an open lie. "Possibly," he replied, "if they knew what had happened." He shifted back in his seat and forced himself to relax against its back for the first time. The humans seemed worried, so it was probably a good idea to consolidate his position, and if that meant using their body language against them, then so be it. "I know you humans want the hyperdrive."

The president's eyebrows shot ceilingwards. "Do you indeed?"

"Well, yes – I mean, why else would there be engineers aboard the *Bekel*? Besides, that was what the Neoluddites wanted, wasn't it?"

The President met his gaze. "You're in a better position to know that than I am, considering what happened to you in Moscow. But they seemed prepared to kill you to get it. Without it they have no chance to colonise other planets because membership of this organisation automatically bars people from selection for the Moon and Mars colonies. But they wouldn't want to go there anyway, because populations there must be controlled, much like here. They want a whole new planet to colonise, and one where they can live outside a life-support dome." He heaved a sigh. "You're very astute, Ayar. We do want the hyperdrive. And you see, Ayar, I think there was also another reason as to why President Langrishe had you children split up." The president's hands did a complicated dance on the tabletop.

Ayar was sure the drumming was a sign of nervousness.

"I think he was afraid that if you were together you'd plot against him –"

"Then why didn't he just have us all killed and have done with it?" Ayar asked. "It would have been simpler all round, and then he could just have helped himself to the hyperdrive."

"He considered that, but the Neoluddites got in first. They released the information to the press – that you children had been found – *before* President Langrishe could give the order to have you done away with. And once your presence became public knowledge, he couldn't kill you without a public outcry. Also, he feared what would happen if your parents learned of it."

"They also released information about the existence of the hyperdrive," Hardy interposed, "which put the World Government in a position where it had to admit that it had made contact with an alien race – namely yourselves. It meant people accepted your presence here on Earth but also expected to be able to use the hyperdrive once copied."

"I see. So that's you humans' aim – a star-drive?"

"Yes," President Sanchez said. "Ayar, I could help you and your friends, but you're also in a position to help *us*."

"By giving you the hyperdrive?"

The president dipped his head. "You've missed out on a chunk of your normal development because of what's happened – firstly by being in the Sleep Room for longer than intended by your parents, then by what has happened since you came here. It's up to *me* to make reparation for the way President Langrishe treated you, though I can't take responsibility for what happened before you arrived here."

"I understand that, and so would our parents."

The president spread his hands. "I can help you in several ways – by giving you full citizenship rights, if you wish, if you accept that if I do that you must be bound by our population laws."

"What benefit would that be to me? To us?"

"If we gave you full citizenship rights, you'd be able to vote in elections, work at whatever you wanted –"

"– Get military training?"

"If that's what you want, although I'd prefer to see you working for JSEP, where your talents and knowledge would be best appreciated."

Ayar's heart leapt, and he allowed himself to hope, for the first time since awakening on Earth, that he might one day be able to do what he wanted – desperately needed – to do: take back the *Bekel* with the rest of the children, and use it to find his clan. "And in exchange you want to know how the hyperdrive works. You want to copy our ship."

"Yes."

Ayar considered this for a moment. "If you have that knowledge you'll immediately become a target for groups like the Neoluddites."

"We know. That's why the whole project must be top

secret. That's another reason for you to enter JSEP service instead of joining the army."

"But if I join JSEP I'll still get military training?"

"Yes. And depending on which section you work in, you may also get astronaut training."

Alexei had explained the difference to him long ago: that while JSEP was an international organisation, run on military lines, individual nations also had their own military forces. What the president had suggested was better for him personally than joining such forces, and more than he'd hoped for.

"And what will happen to the *Bekel* afterwards?"

The president shrugged. "It's your ship, isn't it? But remember that some of the children are still under even the Zarduthi age of majority, and have had no military training. It would be better for all of you to stay on Earth at least until the youngest reaches the human age of majority and has done military training – if you thought to leave and find your parents."

"Fair enough. I'll help you with the hyperdrive – and with interpreting the ship's logs, as Hardy suggested – in exchange for full citizenship rights and a job with JSEP, including military and astronaut training. Is that what you're offering?"

"Yes."

"Will we be able to contact each other and meet up?"

"I see no reason why not."

"Done." Ayar held out his hand. The president shook it in the human way, but after shaking hands, Ayar said, "We do it like this, with the thumbs," and showed him, though the president's thumb disappeared inside his long fingers. "This is how we seal a fighting contract. Once made, the contract can't be broken."

"You'll regard this as binding, then?"

"Of course. Don't you?"

"I'll see to it that it is." The president stood up, so Ayar guessed that the interview was at an end. "Complete your studies before you start work for JSEP, Ayar, and assist Mr. Harkness during vacations."

"Mr. Harkness?"

"JSEP's chief engineer on the star-drive project. Mr. Brencher here will arrange your transfer to a local university."

Ayar agreed.

"Excellent idea," Hardy murmured. "You'll need a degree to enter JSEP, and Astrophysics is a great choice. It's also a good cover for this vacation project."

The president shook hands with both of them again. "Goodbye, Ayar," he said, "and good luck."

"Thank you, Mr President, Sir." Ayar followed Hardy out of the room. When they got outside, he said, "He seems very keen to help us."

"You have to understand, Ayar. The president is afraid."

"Why?"

"I think he's worried that your parents will try to exact reparation for the way President Langrishe treated you and your friends. He wants to be seen as a good man, someone who can help his people, and at the same time help you. That's why he's made this bargain. He also must avoid public unrest by letting you do as you please – so he's placed the same restrictions on you as on anyone else. He won't treat you differently from anyone of any other nation."

"I understand. That's fair. " Ayar stood on the steps of the White House and surveyed the vista before him. Winter had yet to touch Washington; the grass was still green. "I hope I'm doing the right thing."

Hardy touched his arm. "C'mon, son. You have a victory to celebrate!"

CHAPTER 21 – The Vacation Job

Zero, ship's time/date: 410.329.5.67.420 A. 12th November, 2098.

OMOL STOPPED BY the satellite build team to check on progress. They had improved on a standard design stored on the shuttle's computer, and would test it before launch this time, after the disaster last time.

"It's partly complete, but some key parts are still missing," Reven Treyk said, "mainly because the refining team haven't refined enough ores yet."

"Give me a list of ores you need, with quantities, and I'll get the refiners on it."

Reven indicated some of the parts on the diagram he'd brought up to show Omol. "Once we get some copper, gold and platinum we can manufacture these parts – for now. There'll be a further list later."

"Send me the amounts you need," Omol said. "I'll chase it up."

*

JSEP, Washington office, same day.

Hardy Brencher leaned back in his chair and requested a phone line to the Reception Centre in Texas. Within seconds Dr Chapaire's image confronted him.

He greeted her as cordially as his wary nature – and their thorny relationship – would allow, then said, "You'll be pleased to know, President Sanchez has agreed to give the children full citizenship rights. And the Thanksgiving break is coming up, so Ayar will work with Eddie then."

Dr Chapaire goggled at him, open-mouthed, for several

seconds, then asked, "How did you manage that, Monsieur Brencher?"

Hardy couldn't quite banish the triumphant note from his laughter as he explained what had happened. When he'd finished he privately congratulated himself that he'd explained it as if the advantage was all on Ayar's side. Then, while Dr Chapaire absorbed all the information, he asked, "Is Josie there?"

"Just one moment."

As Josie appeared he felt the familiar pang and wondered if he should apologise and try to make it up with her. She looked no different, though her smile was strained and her eyes guarded. Perhaps she'd listen; perhaps not. He decided to leave it since there was no indication she might have forgiven him. "Josie, I need you to do something important." He repeated what he'd told Dr Chapaire, and added, "Next time you visit each child, can you explain what this means, both to them and to their foster parents?"

"Well, yes, but – what *does* it mean? Will they come back to the Reception Centre or stay put?"

"There are some other options now, for the older children. They can join JSEP, for instance, and get astronaut training or other useful skills for working in space. Why not ask them what they prefer to do? We can take it from there."

"All right." And she smiled at him.

His lips parted in response, but then she said, "Is Ayar there?"

"Yes, he's staying with me. He's fine." Hardy paused. "Actually, I'm taking him to the HV studios this afternoon, to record a message for Kaj and Halka. It might encourage them to come forwards." He waited to see what response this would bring, since he was sure she must know something about Kaj's whereabouts – since Dr Chapaire did.

Josie's expression didn't change. "That's a good idea."

"He'll speak in Zarduthi, so only they will know what he says." Hardy permitted himself a rueful grin. "I've told him what I *want* him to say!"

"But you won't know whether he's saying that or something else?"

"Exactly. Oh, and I'm taking him up to Galatea Station tomorrow. I'll call you if there's any response to the HV message."

"Thanks."

Time pressed on him. He cut the phone connection. He stood up, collected his overcoat from its peg, and called Ayar. They left the office together. *One immediate benefit of the presidential change of policy towards the children,* he thought with relief and satisfaction, *is that I can enlist the media's help to seek Kaj, Halka and Robert now.*

The message recording went well. Ayar was calm and confident, and appeared to say the things Hardy had considered appropriate – as far as he could tell without knowledge of the Zarduthi language. Ayar had told him his language had two parts: the hard language, which related to everyday objects and actions, fighting, and practical things; and the soft language, used for emotional, intellectual and philosophical concepts and content. Hardy concentrated, and guessed Ayar's message had a high emotional content because of the soft, liquid sounds he used, with lots of hand gestures and body language. It looked like a moving appeal for the children's return.

"When will this go out?" he asked the studio manager, after the recording.

"Tonight, after each news programme. The first time will be in the *Missing without Trace* spot our news channel runs every week."

"Fine. And you'll also release it on your French subsidiary?"

The studio manager smiled. “Of course. JSEP’s paying well for the privilege! And we also have an agreement with the national media.”

“Excellent! But you mustn’t cut any of it,” Ayar told him.

“We wouldn’t dream of it.” The studio manager’s smile became rueful. “We wouldn’t know what to cut, anyway!”

With these assurances, they left. Outside it was windy. Hardy pulled his overcoat collar up around his face, but Ayar left his jacket unfastened. *Of course, it was much colder in Moscow*, Hardy remembered. *It probably feels like summer to him, especially with his lower body temperature.*

In the couple of weeks since they’d come back to Washington, Hardy had learned a lot about the Zarduthi from Ayar. And they got on well. It had even occurred to him that it would have been advantageous to have put himself forward as a prospective foster-parent at the beginning, though only existing families had been considered.

“What happens now?” Ayar asked, with a gesture towards the studios.

“The message goes out, and hopefully they’ll contact me soon. Then, if they’re in trouble, I can try to sort things out.”

“Perhaps I should go to France and try to find Halka and her friend.”

“You’ve got enough on your plate right now,” Hardy said in a gruff tone. “Leave that to me.”

“All right,” Ayar agreed, “I’m looking forwards to studying here, now you’ve made all the arrangements.”

Hardy had spent the morning calling various universities, and had organised Ayar’s transfer, with credit from his previous study. All that was left was to await signed documentation from the President to make arrangements for Ayar to enter JSEP service after graduation.

“What shall we do now?”

"I thought we could send out for some food and watch the HV broadcasts to see if there's a response. But I need to go back to the office and check something first." He hadn't had a chance to follow up the Harkness woman's reappearance since Ayar was kidnapped, but he'd reasoned that since she hadn't wanted to be found before she didn't want it now either, and therefore that an emergency had driven her to visit Dr Chapaire, whom JSEP had chosen to look after the newly-revived children due to her paediatrics background and research on the effects of space on the body, and that therefore it was likely that the emergency was health-related.

Perhaps Kaj is dead, he thought, and immediately rejected the possibility. Ayar's quick healing precluded that. But his musings had set off another train of thought, and some calls that morning had followed it up. He thought there might have been a response by now. "Ayar, can you get us both a coffee while I check my e-mails?"

Ayar set off for Hardy's favourite stall down on the street corner, and Hardy settled down to check the listings he'd requested. Every city had sick people, so there was no help for it but to go through the listings one by one. He downloaded half into his notebook and saved the rest to a file on his main computer, then closed it down just as Ayar returned with the coffees. He tucked his notebook into the pocket of his overcoat, sat down and raised the cup to his lips.

They returned to Hardy's apartment soon afterwards. Ayar packed his few possessions and some clothes into his backpack, and they settled down to watch the HV appeal. They tucked in to pizza, accompanied by pop, in Ayar's case, and a chilled beer swigged from the bottle in Hardy's.

Missing without Trace and the news slots came and went. Hardy and Ayar talked through the evening.

"It comes over well," Ayar said, after they'd watched it for the fourth time. "I'm pleased, and I really hope Kaj and Halka see it and get in touch."

"That's *exactly* what it comes down to," Hardy agreed. "If they don't see it they won't contact me, or the police, or Dr Chapaire for that matter." After much thought, as she'd already outwitted him, he'd given out *his* number at the Reception Centre as well as hers. He'd monitor the calls anyway. He rubbed at the scar below his eye. "D'you think they'll trust me?"

"I don't know. But if *they* don't see it, someone else might, and might tell them so they can contact you."

That seemed like good sense, considering the holophone had remained silent all evening.

"Ayar, if you were Kaj or Halka, would *you* trust me?"

Ayar linked gaze with Hardy. "I can't speak for them. But *I* trust you, Hardy."

"At least someone does." *Perhaps the phone call with Josie affected me more than I thought. Or perhaps I'm drunk.*

"What makes you say that?"

Hardy shrugged. "I made a bit of a fool of myself with a woman back in the summer. Now she doesn't trust me, and until she does we're unlikely to get back together again."

"Anyone I know?"

The heat in Hardy's face answered for him. *Ayar's probably curious about me,* he realised, and resolved not to give his inquisitiveness openings in future.

*

Marseilles, 17th November, 2098.

"Oh, so it's you again – dressed in your national costume, I'd guess." It was the man with the moustache and beard. "I've got clients lined up who'll pay through the nose to go with you, and they'll pay even more for the pleasure of screwing you in that get-up!" He snatched at her arm. "Come with me!"

"Let me go!" Halka cried. She was his height, but he was bulkier, with a barrel chest and blocky build. She stared into his face, and wondered if she could best him in a fight. It seemed unlikely. And she'd left both weapons with Robert. Perhaps the best thing would be to make some noise to draw attention to his attempt to kidnap her. "*Help!* This man's trying to rape me!"

"Let the girl alone, Pablo."

It was Jacques, the street beggar who'd directed them to the derelict building. He knew the area and had helped them several times. He had a knife out, and waved it about.

Pablo let her arm go, bared his teeth at Jacques and made a lunge at him.

"Go!" whispered Jacques. Aloud he said, "So, you thought you'd rape an under-age kid, did you?"

Halka didn't wait to hear Pablo's reply. She turned and fled.

One thing was certain. She wouldn't venture out on the streets without firepower again.

*

Galatea Station, 22nd November, 2098.

Ayar stepped onto the walkway that led to the *Bekel*. Beside him, Hardy gripped the handrail to walk towards the ship.

It had taken a day to get one of the spacesuits from the *Bekel* for Ayar. His tall, slender build hadn't fitted into the loan suits, so he'd had to explain to Don Harris where to find them onboard the ship. "We don't use them much," he'd argued; but Hardy had refused to let Ayar leave Earth without proper protection.

During this time the appeal for Halka and Kaj had produced no results.

They'd caught the public space elevator to get there. *At last I'm going home,* Ayar thought, as he stepped out of it onto the metal deck of Galatea Station.

The first indication that all was not as he remembered it lay before him. *The humans must have cut through the triple skin of the ship and erected a new airlock, of a different design, in the resulting breach.* They stepped into it together.

"They needn't have replaced the airlock," he said to Hardy, and waved his hand around as they waited for the air pressure to equalise.

"There was a hole in the hull here when they found the ship," Hardy said. "They had to plug it, and putting an airlock in seemed sensible as there didn't appear to be one this side."

"I suppose so." For the first time he caught a glimpse of Hardy's face when he flicked back his helmet components. He was pale and sweaty. "Are you OK?"

"Yeah, but I loathe that walkway."

"Can't Dr Chapaire give you something for your vertigo?"

"Probably – I never thought to ask! Still, I hope not to have to come up here too often."

"It's odd that it should affect you this way," Ayar mused as the door opened. "You're fine in a plane."

"I'm not in free fall in a plane," Hardy pointed out. "And I'm fine here in the ship, as long as I have the Magnetix – but the walkway wobbles about, and I can't forget I'm standing over a void! C'mon, I'll take you to meet Eddie." He set off down the corridor.

But Ayar went to the bulkhead, removed his gloves, and ran his hands over it. "I want to feel the touch of my home."

It was only when he felt the faint dimpling on the surface under his fingertips that he realised how much he'd missed it. Every memory of his life before the Long Sleep crowded into his mind in sharp focus. The dormitory where he'd spent much of his time as a child. The huge simtank in the Control Room; his father had taken him there sometimes as a treat, and twice, as he'd put it, 'to enhance his education'. The trip to Haveertel, where he'd seen the clan make contract with the people there. Fighting practice in the gym. Learning to use his translator unit, a very early memory. He turned to Hardy, his eyes full of ghosts.

"Something happened to my mother and the women with her. Something else happened to my father and the other warriors on the planet they were fighting on. I intend to find out what, at the very least." He narrowed his eyes and pursed his lips, full of determination. "Come on, let's go!" He marched off down the corridor. Hardy trailed him.

In the Control Room, it was far worse. Piles of metal panels lay where the control columns had been stripped one by one, and below some of the wall fittings. Wiring hung in skeins from them. Humans were everywhere. Ayar fought to contain the scream that rose inside him as he turned to Hardy. "All this mess because they wanted to copy the ship?"

Hardy raised his shoulders in a helpless shrug. "Sorry, Ayar. I didn't realise it would affect you like this." He led Ayar towards a human who squatted before one of the control columns with his hands on his thighs. "This is Eddie Harkness." He tapped Eddie on the shoulder.

The human looked up. He had brown hair and an open, reddish-brown face. When he saw Ayar he scrambled upright and offered him his hand, first rubbing it on the thigh of his spacesuit.

Ayar took the hand and shook it.

"Hardy." Eddie nodded the rest of his greeting and turned back to study Ayar. "So *you're* the eldest of the children."

"Yes, sir."

"No need to 'sir' me – 'Eddie' will do nicely," he said, and pointed to the column. "D'you know which system this is for?"

"Life support." Ayar leaned over and lifted some of the wiring. "Was." He let it fall. "The ship's more or less dead, then?"

"Yes, apart from the lighting, which we can't put off. We had to put in the airlock to stop atmosphere leakage. There's none from the sealed rooms, but as soon as they're opened –"

"I noticed damage to some doors on the way here."

"Oh, we didn't do that. It was already like that when we found the ship."

"The *Bekel*," Ayar said. "That's its name, and the name of our clan." He fastened onto Eddie's last sentence, and said, "You're *sure* it was like this when you came aboard?"

"Absolutely. Mine was the second team aboard, after the marines."

"Ah." Ayar glanced around the control room once more. "And Alexei told me that nobody actually went into the ship during the salvage operation to bring the *Bekel* here."

"That's right. You know Alexei Petrushenko?"

"He became my foster-father." Since he'd left Russia Ayar had resolved not to think about his years there, but it was impossible to excise them from his life. "Hardy mentioned that you thought you'd found some ship's logs?"

"Yes, when we checked out this console here." Eddie led Ayar over to it. "It connects directly into the server that runs the ship's functions. The server is functional but there's no way to play the images back."

"There is, but you'll need to move all this stuff out of this area." Ayar waved a hand at the pile of panels. "The simtank – where the images will form – extends from here to there, and back to the bulkhead." He pointed. "Anything within that space will interfere with image formation."

Eddie wasted no time. "Clear the area," he told Brad and Gaia. "And keep it empty."

Ayar stood still for a moment to look at the console. Then his hands skipped over the access panel, bringing life to the controls. In the area he'd indicated a shimmer formed. "Gezdushchee nar hudgat," he ordered.

Images played. He saw first himself, then Hardy, step into the Control Room. He turned to face Eddie and Hardy. "I'll ask it to replay the section from when our parents left the ship to complete their last recorded contract."

Images formed in the simtank area that showed his mother, as he remembered her. Her combat leathers strained across her abdomen to accommodate his sister or brother. Ayar watched her face. It was calm, serene, contented and confident. There were four other women with her: Tambur Dar, Kaylar Durana, Vinta Pril and Nam Garangey.

"Fast forward," he told the computer, as he set up the logs to use the ship's own translator for the logs.

The full-sized holo-images rushed around at several times their normal speed. It would have been amusing to watch if it hadn't been so important. Momentarily the image changed to a navigation display, then back to a view from inside the Control Room. "Stop, play." He'd seen his mother's face fill with distaste at the sight of two small solar-sail ships that approached their position as the *Bekel* clung to an orbit on the far side of one of the inner two moons.

It was all there. Ayar stared aghast at the simtank. Even Eddie's engineers downed tools to watch.

The Voth appeared in the simtank.

Someone touched his arm. He turned. "D'you know what these things are?" Hardy asked

"They call themselves Voth. My father told me about them, and I've seen holo-imagery of what they did to Kiai."

"Kiai?"

"A planet in the solar system the other side of the one the *Bekel* was in."

"We found one aboard the ship."

Ayar felt the blood drain from his face, and a bodily chill similar to the one in Russia invaded him. "Oh no, please not that! Not my mother –"

"I'm so sorry, Ayar," Hardy said. "I didn't – we none of us knew how –"

"I don't blame *you*, Hardy! I need to know."

He turned back, and watched in horror as the Voth "gave birth", and saw Kaylar leave the Control Room to try to detach the Voth bubble-ship. He gasped as she was expelled after the Voth "babies".

The adult Voth dissolved door after door until they entered the corridor to the Sleep Room, channelled there by the women.

"They set a trap," Ayar murmured, but nobody heard. They were engrossed in the images.

Near the line of disruptor nozzles that defended the Sleep Room the four women put up a tremendous fight. They took several Voth out with disruptors; two ran into the ship's defences. Vinta lured a third there.

Then the "parent" attached itself to Tambur. It devoured her disruptor in seconds. She fought the Voth with her bare hands until the feeding pseudopod coated them with digestive gel. Then she fought it with the bloody stumps. But one of the remaining "babies" attached itself to her leg. Once attached, the adult turned its attentions to Rilla. All she could do for the stricken Tambur was to fire on her shipmate and the parasite that fed on her.

Vinta and Nam couldn't help, as they lured the last tiny Voth into the ship's defences. But although the thing lacked sensory organs, it avoided the line of disruptor nozzles. They sacrificed themselves and their unborn babies and pulled it in with them so that Ayar and the other children could live.

Now it was between the Voth parent and Rilla. Her orders were to save the children or die trying. Her legs and part of one hand had gone. The creature exuded its gel onto her stomach. Perhaps it sensed the child within her; perhaps it sought revenge. Her spacesuit and clothing could only protect her for so long. With a massive effort she heaved the thing off her and dragged herself towards the intersection of the corridors, where her disruptor lay. But the digestive gel had laid her stomach bare. Layers of skin spalled off where it lay taut over her distended abdomen.

At last she allowed herself one agonised scream as her stomach convulsed. Shock expelled Ayar's baby sibling through the wound in her stomach. It lay in a rush of blood on the floor.

But the Voth parent recovered itself enough to ooze along the floor. It arrived at the congealing mass of bloody tissue on the floor and pooled digestive gel over it. That was the last Ayar saw of his sibling.

Rilla had reached the intersection of the two corridors. She gripped the disruptor with her bloodstained hand and turned to face the creature. She fired, but couldn't lift the gun high enough to aim true; the disruptor bolt hit the creature's side and burned a hole in it.

Rilla watched as its internal matter oozed onto the floor. Then she turned the weapon on herself while she had enough strength to press the trigger.

And Ayar stood in a stunned, half-comprehending silence as a double percussion and the changed view of the stars from the simtank told him the ship had entered and left hyperspace.

Ayar's heart cried out then. *My mother, my wonderful, beautiful mother, is dead. My baby brother or sister was eaten alive by that filthy thing!*

He felt as if the Voth sucked the breath from his lungs. He couldn't process what had happened. There was a moment's blankness. He thought he must have passed out for a few thousandths, because he came to and realised Hardy had an arm around his shoulders and wanted him to sit down. He struggled instead, and raved his agony aloud. "My mother! My *MOTHER!* I'll destroy every one of those Voth *bloodsuckers* if it's the last thing I ever do –"

"Ayar! Calm down!"

He hardly understood English any more. He fought by reflex. He'd reverted fully, in that instant, to what he was bred to be, and lashed out to free himself.

"My God, I didn't rescue you from the Neoluddites just to get socked on the jaw!"

He opened his eyes. Hardy and Eddie bent over him. Hardy rubbed the side of his face, but they both looked concerned. Behind them, two engineers argued about something.

"Ayar! How do you turn this thing off?" Eddie asked.

Ayar came back to himself enough to give the voice command, and the simtank emptied of images.

*

Marseilles, 25th November, 2098.

Halka sat with her back against the wall and stared at the coins in her hand. Robert's medicine was low again, but there was no money to buy more. It didn't even help him much now. When awake he could barely draw breath between coughing bouts; his sleep was disturbed. His clothes were soaked with sweat from the fever. The mattress Halka had rescued from the rubbish dump, so he'd have something to lie on, was rank with the stench of it.

Shadows gathered in the room as dusk fell. The chill of night deepened around Halka. It echoed the hopelessness she felt. There was nothing to do now except lie down beside Robert and try to sleep. She didn't even want to leave him to hunt or scavenge for food. She was afraid, each time she did, that he'd be dead when she came back.

She'd lain on the floor for some time when someone knocked on the door. She got up and crossed to it.

It was Jacques, the street beggar. "Halka! Halka! You must come – there's an appeal on HV for you!" He started off down the corridor and beckoned to her to follow.

"I can't leave Robert!"

Behind her Robert muttered to himself in his sleep.

"You must – it's really important. There's a young man – just like you – and a number to call."

Halka was undecided. The nearest HV shop was nearly a hundred thousandths' walk away. "I'm distraught about Robert," she said. "He's very ill, Jacques, and there's no more money for his medicine."

"Then all the more reason for you to come and get this phone number! There's just enough time to get there before the next news bulletin."

That decided her. She pocketed the pistol, pulled the door to and set the bolt on, via a concealed hole in the wall, and followed Jacques.

The streets of Marseilles were dark, wet and cold; a mist had settled in off the sea. People's shapes loomed out of it. Halka startled some of them in her leathers and furs.

The HV shop was closed, but behind the security shutters the sets still display-ran. As Jacques had said, the next news programme was about to start.

He took a scrap of paper and a pencil stub from his pocket and pushed them into her hands. "Look!"

The newscaster on the nearest HV said something about a very special appeal. As Halka watched, Ayar Dekkutz appeared. He spoke mainly in the soft language. She listened as he explained that he wanted both her and Robert, and Kaj Kalinga, who'd gone missing two and a half years ago, to contact him via one of three phone numbers. He feared for their safety. In the case of Halka and Robert, her foster-father had been arrested for the murder of his wife, and the children were in the clear. Would they please contact one of the following numbers and let him know they were safe and well. Halka scribbled the numbers down as best she could. It was good to see Ayar's face and hear his voice, but she wasn't sure what she could do about it. "I haven't got enough money to phone him, Jacques," she said.

"Then go to the police and ask them to put you in touch with him."

It all sounded so simple. "What about Robert?"

"He'll understand that you're trying to help him."

Of course he was right. "Come with me," she said.

"I'll see you to the *gendarmerie*," he said. "And then I'll sit with Robert till you get back." And there, at the police station, Jacques left her. His encouragement and good wishes rang in her ears.

The building loomed out of the mist above Halka. For a moment she wondered if her French was good enough to explain everything, but then she decided it had been good enough so far, and she had her throat translator. She took a deep breath and opened the door.

At the reception desk a man half-dozed away the evening shift.

Halka crossed to it. "Excuse me," she said.

The man jerked awake, saw her and clutched at his chest.

"Are you OK?" she asked.

"Oh, you did give me a fright!" He stared at her. "You're that –"

"That's right." Halka was relieved, for once, that he'd recognised her. "I'm Halka Mozada, and I want to speak to Ayar Dekkutz. I can't phone any of the numbers he gave out because I don't have any money."

"I'll call the *commissaire*."

Halka waited on the seat he waved her to, and looked around. She'd never been in a *gendarmerie* before. The place was bright and clean – unlike the squat they lived in. It smelled of polish and air freshener. At a noticeboard she spotted a holoprint of herself with Robert, and one of Kaj.

When the *commissaire* arrived she stood up and held out her hand. "I'm Halka Mozada. Please help me," she said. "I need to phone JSEP in America, where Ayar Dekkutz wants me to contact him." She heard herself speak faster and faster. "But I haven't got any money because my foster-brother Robert is ill, and –"

"Slow down, slow down!" The *commissaire* patted the bench. "I know who you are. Sit down and tell me calmly."

Halka tried to do as he said, and the *commissaire* listened with great attention. When she'd finished, he asked for a line to the first of the numbers.

The blond man from the Big Place appeared above the holophone. "Hardy Brencher," he said.

She'd forgotten his name. It didn't matter. She'd been afraid of him when he used to ask everyone questions at the Big Place, but now she was just glad to see a familiar face. "Can I speak to Ayar?"

"He's not here right now, Halka. Are you safe?"

She shook her head. "We're in a squat in Marseilles, and Robert is ill."

"I'd better come and collect you both – if you want?" He explained that he and the police had taken Monsieur Jouvin into custody, and that they had proof that he'd murdered Madame Jouvin. "They know about the way he treated Robert," he added.

"And me. He belted me too. He threatened to kill me if I told Josie about it."

Monsieur Brencher sighed. "I'm so sorry you've had to go through all this, Halka. But we have a new World President –

would you like to come back to America to live?"

"Yes, please."

"What's your address?"

"I don't know – we squat in a derelict building in Marseilles."

"I came there to look for you again back in the summer. How did I miss you?"

"We only arrived here in October. We worked in a vineyard in Provence during the autumn, like we have for the past couple of years."

"Tell him to come to the Marseilles main police station," suggested the *commissaire*. "We'll collect your friend in a moment."

Halka smiled gratefully at him. "He's very poorly – won't you need protection?"

"We'll have that covered, don't you worry." The *commissaire* said. "Just wait here."

"And I'll be there first thing in the morning," Monsieur Brencher said.

CHAPTER 22 – The Voth

Eisenhower Reception Centre, Texas, 27th November, 2098.

TO HALKA THE VIEW OF THE RECEPTION CENTRE from Monsieur Brencher's car was the reverse of that she'd seen when she left for France. *I hope I can put that all behind me now,* she thought. *The nightmare's gone on long enough!*

She glanced back at Robert, asleep on the back seat.

Monsieur Brencher had been horrified to find Robert so ill. "I'll take you both back to Dr Chapaire," he'd said, "and hopefully she can find out what's wrong with Robert and make him better."

That was good enough for Halka. She'd decided there and then that Monsieur Brencher wasn't so bad after all. He'd brought them from France to America by JSEP jet, and then across part of Texas by car – though from what he'd said he hadn't slept at all.

"Monsieur Brencher?"

His eyes met hers in the rear-view mirror. "What?"

"Can I talk to Ayar?"

"He's up on Galatea Station right now. You'll need to phone him there." He hesitated. "He's had rather a shock recently – his mother looked after all of you and the ship before it drifted into our solar system –"

"That's right," Halka said. "And Nam, Vinta, Tambur, and Kaylar –"

Why didn't you tell me all this when I asked you?"

"Maybe you didn't ask the right questions!"

Monsieur Brencher sighed. "Obviously not." Hardy sighed. "I'm afraid the pregnant women are all dead." Hardy explained about the ship's logs. Halka was very quiet for a few thousandths while she took in the implications of this news. "Anyway, he found out how she died and was so upset that we had to sedate him."

"Is he all right now?"

"He seems to be coping, and I've no doubt that having something to do has helped. I spoke to him on my way to collect you. I think he'll be pleased to speak to you, but be aware that he's in shock, and grieving."

"I know about that," Halka said. "It's one of the first things they teach you on the clanships, because nobody knows when they'll lose a friend, or a relative, or even a partner. I'll be gentle with him." She rested her eyes on Robert. "Will Robert die? He's just got worse and worse."

Monsieur Brencher sighed again. "I don't know, Halka. He seems very poorly to me, but if anyone can help him, it's Dr Chapaire."

"I hope so."

Monsieur Brencher parked the car and opened the door to lift Robert out. His eyelids fluttered open and he said, "I can manage," but succumbed to a coughing fit. Monsieur Brencher sent Halka on ahead to ring the doorbell.

When his coughing subsided, Robert allowed Monsieur Brencher to support him to the door. Karak Chapaire appeared there.

"Please make Robert better," Halka begged her.

"I will try, Halka. Shall we all go inside?"

To Halka the inside of the building was more familiar than the outside, and she wasn't sure whether to be glad or sorry that she was back. Once in the dormitory again, Robert lay on a bed while Doctor Chapaire examined him and Halka looked on, flanked by Monsieur Brencher. At the end she looked up from keying information into her notebook and said, "I am sorry, Robert, but you have Quetzal fever."

"What does that mean?" Halka asked.

"Quetzal fever is a retrovirus which has crossed the species barrier and infected humans. Originally it only affected birds, and their faeces are the most likely cause of infection. But once a patient has it, they can pass it on during sex and other situations where body fluids are exchanged."

Halka's hand was at her mouth. "Is it serious?"

"I am afraid so. There is no known cure, although we can immunise people against it."

"I have been," Monsieur Brencher said, "as are all JSEP personnel."

"I bet I caught it at the vineyard," Robert murmured. His voice sounded cracked and broken. "It was after we left there that I became ill."

"That sounds most likely, Robert." Doctor Chapaire stood and regarded him for a moment. At last she spoke again. "The first thing is to reduce the inflammation to your throat and lungs, and makes you cough so much. I will get you some medicine which will help." She turned towards the pharmacy at the side of the dormitory. "There is also an anti-viral I could try, which will also boost your immune system."

Halka followed her. "Karak Chapaire." She couldn't keep the concern from her voice. "Can I ask you something in private?"

"Of course, Halka."

"You said people can get infected during sex."

Karak Chapaire's pupils dilated. "What are you saying, Halka? That Robert is your lover?"

"I – yes." Halka stared at the ground. "I know it was wrong, that we're not old enough, but – he's my best friend, my partner."

"Oh, Halka, you do not have to explain! I was young once, too – strange as that may seem!" Karak Chapaire smiled. "But I suppose you are worrying that you could also become infected."

Halka couldn't speak, so she nodded.

"It is only dangerous if you exchange body fluids, remember?"

Halka nodded again. Then she thought of something else. "Our friend Jacques, one of the street people in Marseilles, sat with him while I was at the police station, waiting to talk to Monsieur Brencher –" She thought for a moment and added, "He helped us a lot. He saved me from rape and trafficking, and told me about Ayar's message. I'd like to help him."

"I will try to trace him and help, Halka."

"The villa has no-one living there now – perhaps he could live there. I'll ask Robert."

"An excellent idea. Now listen. It is possible that you might eventually become infected, but because your DNA is so different, it would take years. I would not worry about it if I were you. You could be immunised, although we will not know what the effect of that on you might be. What we *must* do is bend our minds to helping Robert fight the disease."

"Will he get better?"

Karak Chapaire reached for a bottle of medicine and some capsules. "I hope so, Halka. This medicine will certainly help. But I can only do so much. I can also give him drugs which will keep the disease at bay for a time, but eventually the viruses will multiply to the point where they will take over his body. Soon after, he will die."

*

Zero, ship's time/date: 410.239.5.05.782 AD, same day.

Omol seated himself at the controls of the shuttle, fastened himself in, closed the door, and ran the usual take-off checks. Then he started the shuttle's engines and lifted it off the ground in a test flight prior to the satellite launch.

It was a while since the shuttle had flown, but Omol's mechanics teams had carried out regular cleaning, maintenance and repairs. He swooped above the tower settlement and looked down on his people as they worked. On the dunefield below, a copse of condenser kits trapped water from the atmosphere. Every day, a few more joined them. They'd increased the daily water ration for all of the clanfolk over the last half-year or so.

He took the shuttle up as high as they'd calculated they needed to be to release the satellite into low planetary orbit for it to complete its work. All the while, he kept a wary eye on the shuttle's performance monitors and the life support parameters within it. All was well. With the satellite built, all that remained was to deploy it. It was now safe to do just that, and the technicians had also tested the satellite itself.

At low planetary orbit, Omol cast a glance in the direction of Zero's dark star. It was about to pass behind the planet but for the moment he could see it. The brown dwarf's aurorae sparked and crackled at its poles, and clashed with the magenta star with the orange cloud bands. In the sky above Zero, they danced and twirled in shades of cobalt, viridian and scarlet, a beautiful – if bizarre – ballet in the sky.

Omol returned to the settlement and landed. Garchon met him as he stepped from the craft. "Omol, I just wanted to tell you that Keran and Ludar have died of multiple organ failure. I'm so sorry. I couldn't do any more for them, even with the medmachines from the shuttles. Their partners have organised a joint vaporisation ceremony at sixth today."

They'd lost three more clan members in the last twelve days, mostly miners or refiners. Several more were ill, but stayed functional on medication.

"I'll be there to pay my respects. They were brave fighters who kept battling to the end." He took a deep breath. "I reached low planetary orbit. And the satellite is ready for launch."

Garchon dipped his head. “That’s good news, Omol. But it may take some time for its message to be picked up on the commgrid. Let’s hope it’s not too long.”

I hope so too, Omol thought. *The longer we stay here, the more clan members we lose.*

*

The Bekel, *same day.*

“Look.” Ayar pointed. The simtank showed the ship had approached a yellow-star system. “I think this is how we arrived here.”

He was grateful that Eddie, armed with a list of recorded commands for the various functions, had re-recorded an edited version of the ship’s log while he was under sedation. They watched it now.

“Can you increase magnification?” asked Eddie.

Ayar gave the computer the appropriate instruction. The yellow-star system resolved into a multi-planet system with many moons encircling the largest few of its outer planets. “See? This is your solar system, isn’t it? I’m sure my mother mentioned it. Wait, I’ll get a transcript of the conversation.” He requested it.

“Oh – it’s in your language!” Eddie exclaimed.

“Of course, but I can translate for you.” Ayar scanned the densely-printed pictograms. “Here. ‘Take us out of this system, Tambur, on a heading for the yellow star system at bearing two hundred and seventy-four degrees. Make it look as if we’re making a run for it.’ That’s my mother, Rilla. She was in charge. Then Nam says, ‘Their system’s directly in the line of the Voth advance.’ Now my mother speaks again: ‘Precisely, and Eren says they’ve developed a form of spaceflight based on chemical fuel.’”

“Who’s Eren?”

"Clan leader – Miril and Davan's father."

"I'll get someone to check that bearing," Eddie said. "There are astronomers based at the space telescope unit here."

Ayar felt hope rise in him. "There's something else we could try." He requested a local star map. It appeared in the simtank. "Re-orient from position of third planet from the yellow star."

The map circled and swooped about in the simtank, then settled.

Eddie watched in admiration. "This is brilliant."

"It has to be," Ayar said. "If necessary, just one person could pilot this ship – making heavy use of the auto-systems. Mostly, though, it requires a crew of at least five, preferably seven." He leaned forwards to inspect the star map, and traced the approximate position of the source system. "That means *this* is probably the planet my father and the other warriors fought on. Zoom out." At this command the simtank showed the Earth's solar system, the system the *Bekel* had travelled from, and beyond it, the Kiai system. They lay almost in a straight line. "Shit, we must warn Hardy!"

"What about?"

"We fought the Voth on Kiai – I was eleven. Within about three years the Voth had overrun Kiai and enslaved the people there. We Zarduthi lost the equivalent of a whole clan on Kiai – about two hundred and fifty people. The planet's a barren desert now. The Voth went on to this system here. Wait, it's called –" He peered into the simtank again. "The people on the planet call it Declain. Oh, I remember – we went there for rest and relaxation after Kiai, and because they were next in line we left them a means of communicating with us. Not long after, they asked us for help. That made Declain even more our fight, so we went. My clan was the first to arrive. It may be that the other clans never did." He pointed at a dotted line which joined the human and Declaini systems. "The next nearest inhabited system is yours."

"I'll call Hardy."

"Wait – look, we may have a bit of time. It all depends on how long it the *Bekel* took to arrive here after it left hyperspace.

"Ayar, this records in real-time, doesn't it?" Eddie waved a hand at the simtank.

"Of course."

"Then wouldn't that tell you how long since the ship left that system?"

"Better than that, we can just ask the computer how long it recorded for, since what happened was so sudden that they didn't have time to switch off recording. Hyperspace doesn't count because you're in and out in a flash, and back into realspace," Ayar explained, and asked his question.

[After the hyperspace jump, the *Bekel* drifted for three point two ship's years before it entered this system,] the computer supplied.

"Calculate in human years." Ayar turned on his throat translator for the benefit of the audience.

[Ship's years are five days longer than human years. It was approximately three point four ship's years from the last hyperspace jump to salvage, three human years.]

"That means I'm nearly a year *older* than I thought," Ayar said. "And that means we have about a year *less* than I thought. Call Hardy now!"

*

JSEP Research Facility, Galatea Station, Earth, 5th December 2098.

"Are you all right?"

Ayar nodded. He didn't trust himself to speak. He wasn't looking forwards to what lay behind the metal door at one end of the changing room. It would bring back the memory of how his mother had died.

He'd been sedated for two days after they'd played back the logs. Hardy had insisted that he take the medical aid on offer, and he and Eddie had been supportive of him. Hardy had had to leave Galatea Station to collect Halka and her friend from France, but he'd returned the day after that. Today he'd brought Ayar to view the dead Voth at the JSEP research facility on Galatea where Dr Kobayashi worked. Since the probable threat to the humans was now known to be real and credible, they wanted to learn all they could about the creatures. Ayar had promised to help.

"Come on, then – put this protective clothing on. Then we go in." Beside him, Hardy put on his own PPE and turned to face a newcomer to the room. He introduced them. "Ayar, Dr Kobayashi is also Chaneg Dar's foster-father."

Ayar felt the tension leave his face. He greeted Dr Kobayashi politely and shook hands with him, and then asked after Chaneg.

"Chan's fine – she's progressing well with her martial arts studies now that she's finally allowed to learn."

Ayar resolved to try to speak to her later by phone. He donned the protective gear Hardy had given him and stowed his clothes in the locker Dr Kobayashi indicated.

"Mr. Brencher tells me you've seen these creatures before, Ayar."

Ayar explained that the clan had fought them on another planet before being called to Declain. "We don't know much about them," he said, "not even where they come from, but my father thought they may have a kind of collective consciousness."

"How did he know this?"

"From their speech and behaviour." Ayar made a

throwaway gesture with one hand. “If you do something to one of them, the others often know about it even if they weren’t there.”

“I suppose that would tie in with the fact that they reproduce parthenogenetically.” Dr Kobayashi spun the wheel on the door to open the vault where they kept the creature. “But that suggests that only new creatures budded from the same parent would share that parent’s knowledge. From the start we thought each cell contained all the information each creature has ever garnered, and we now think their DNA is used as information storage – in lieu of a brain, since there’s little internal differentiation, and no major organs.”

“I read your preliminary report on the creature three years ago. Have you learned any more about them since then?” Hardy asked.

Dr Kobayashi bowed his affirmation. “We have, and I’ll tell you that later. Such a creature, by rights, should live a sedentary life, perhaps attached to a rock, just feeding on whatever comes past.” He shook his head. “That’s what I don’t understand.” He gestured for them to enter. “Perhaps you’ll be able to shed more light on it, Ayar?”

Hardy stepped through the door first. Ayar followed. It was cold in the vault, even for him. This was the first time he’d seen a Voth up close. He looked around.

The room was lined with glass jars: tissue samples, Ayar guessed. He identified various human organs and body parts from memory; he was good at biology. There were machines he didn’t recognise, cupboards and a computer terminal, and that was about it.

The creature lay on a table, in a large glass vacuum jar. Ayar averted his eyes from it and allowed them to range around the rest of the vault first. He didn’t feel ready to face this foe yet.

Outside in the corridor, the Voth had seemed distant and

unreal. As he confronted it, hatred and rage welled up. It had, after all, consumed his baby sibling and part of his mother.

He stepped closer to the table. Disgust rose in his throat. He felt a great reluctance to look at the Voth, but knew he couldn't stall any longer.

Even through the glass he could see the individual bristles of greyish hair that bushed out between the surface plates. The wound in its side faced him. *This is the one my mother killed.* The armour plates formed a rind on the creature, and from the blackened, shrunken scar protruded colourless filaments of internal matter, and lumps of brownish sticky goop, the digestive juices.

Ayar remembered then that he didn't even know what had happened to his father. He was somewhere on Declain – either alive or dead. He had to turn away as his emotions rioted out of control.

"D'you want to go outside, Ayar?"

He nodded, and allowed Hardy to support him back through the doorway. He sank down onto a bench with his head in his hands. "I'm sorry, I can't go back in, not yet –"

Dr Kobayashi dialled the door shut behind them. "Ayar, I understand your reaction. You don't have to go back in, but is there *anything* you can tell me about these things that will help destroy them?"

Ayar nodded. "Wait," he said. He needed time to deal with the raw emotions that pulsed through his veins. He leaned back against the wall of the locker room, allowed himself to go supine, and breathed in and out deeply several times. Only then did he open his eyes. "I need a shower," he said. He wanted to wash all emotion from himself, along with the sense that contact with this creature had sullied him.

"Not yet, Ayar. What if you slip? You're in a bit of a state there," Hardy said.

"I'll get changed and get us some tea," suggested Dr Kobayashi.

"Good idea, but please make mine coffee." Hardy watched Ayar with concern.

Ayar was relieved when Dr Kobayashi left. "I also don't know how to tell him," he murmured.

"Tell him what?"

"If Chaneg is his foster-daughter – her mother was with mine on the *Bekel*. You saw her in the ship's logs. She'll be pretty upset as well."

"Oh shit! Why didn't you tell me before? I could – I could get Josie to tell her, or – or go myself, or something. Look, don't worry. I'll explain it to him in private before we leave."

Ayar nodded. "That's probably the best way. Ask him to tell Chaneg I'm very sorry, and that I'll call her soon."

Some minutes later the locker-room door opened. Dr Kobayashi entered with a tray. He set it down on the bench beside Ayar and passed him a beaker of green tea. "Made in the traditional Japanese way," he explained. "Are you feeling better, Ayar?"

"Yes." Ayar kept his head lowered. "But you do realise we have no idea what happened to the *rest* of our parents?"

"Chan told me that." Dr Kobayashi put a hand on Ayar's shoulder. "Are you ready to tell me what you know about these creatures?"

Ayar nodded. "You can't use projectile weapons," he said. "Their armour's tough – though bullets can penetrate it – but the creature just absorbs them and uses them as fuel. And the lack of surface differentiation is a definite advantage for these things – there are no obvious sensory organs to target." He hesitated. "Only I don't know whether I should pass over our weapons technology."

"Why not, if it works on these things?"

"I'd hate to be responsible if it fell into the wrong hands."

Hardy and Dr Kobayashi exchanged a glance.

Ayar couldn't read it.

"It *is* important that we be able to duplicate that weapons technology if we're to defend ourselves should these things come our way," Hardy said. "You see, Ayar, the stakes have just been upped. From making contact with you Zarduthi children there are now several players in the game. And some are distinctly unfriendly, and may already be on their way here."

"Yes – though we don't know that for certain."

"No," Hardy conceded, "but I'll recommend to President Sanchez that he take steps to find out PDQ. Otherwise the Earth could be totally defenceless against them."

Ayar felt as if he were poised on a knife-edge. Hardy was right, but he'd lived too long among humans to disregard his fears of what some might do with the weapons. *Yet if they go into space using the hyperdrive – and perhaps other Zarduthi technology – they'll soon encounter the Voth anyway.*

"All right. I'll co-operate. The weapons we use disrupt cells at a molecular level and cause implosion and vaporisation. It works efficiently on the Voth, even with a partial hit. On a human, a Kiai or a Zarduthi that would vaporise the body part hit, and cauterise the wound left. On a Voth it causes death – as you saw on the creature there. But – I want a written guarantee from the President that these weapons are never used except against the Voth. I've lived here long enough to know that some of you humans are too dangerous for us to just give you such power."

He stared at Hardy and Dr Kobayashi. "But I don't want my foster-family to suffer like my mother and her friends."

*

Outside Juliet's apartment in Paris, Texas, next day.

"Is everyone in place?"

"Yes," Don said.

"All right. Here she comes." Hardy Brencher stepped forwards and intercepted Juliet Harkness as she approached the door to her apartment. "Mrs. Harkness?" Hardy took out his ID and showed her. "Hardy Brencher, JSEP Security. You're under arrest."

She stared back at him aghast. "You've got the wrong woman," she managed after a moment. "I'm Lori Chapman."

"A.k.a. Juliet Harkness." Hardy pulled his phone out of his jacket pocket and showed her a holo. "This *is* you, isn't it?"

She examined the holo, especially the name below it. "What's this about?"

"The safety and security of the children and any matters relating to them is my responsibility. Now, could you please come with us? I don't want to have to use force."

He thought she'd crumble then, but instead she said, "On what authority are you acting, Mr Brencher?"

"That of World President Sanchez. You disappeared more than two years ago with one of the alien children, Kaj Kalinga. Your husband Eddie –" he pointed to the holo "– has been worried sick about you and the children, and you've given me a lot of headaches over Kaj's disappearance. Now I'm arresting you on charges of kidnapping."

"My daughter is in the apartment." She gestured towards the door. "How can I look after her if I'm under arrest?"

"I'll make sure she's looked after, and Kaj. But if you don't come with me, I'll have you charged with resisting arrest as well."

Mrs Harkness's shoulders bowed. She reached into her bag and got out the keys to the apartment.

But Hardy seized them with an abrupt, "I'll take those," and signed to Don to handcuff Juliet. Then he handed the keys to Don and told him to enter the apartment and get the children.

"I hope you've got a warrant to search the apartment," she said.

"I have." Hardy took it out and showed her.

"How did you find me?"

"You took Kaj to your local doctor for treatment for his recent illness," he said. "Then when he couldn't help, you contacted Dr Chapaire." He held up his hand. "Oh no, neither of them let on. But the handscan machine in Dr Chapaire's office, unbeknownst to her, is connected to the computer in my office next door, and that in my office in Washington. As soon as you surfaced, I picked up the trail. In the last week I've traced you to this apartment. My men have kept a watch on it, and I decided that today was the day to pick you up and take you in." *She doesn't need to know it's my first opportunity.*

Don came out with the two children. Kaj held Lucy's hand, and had her teddy bear tucked under his arm. Lucy cried and reached for her mother when she saw her handcuffed.

"It's all right, young lady," Don said. "There's no need to cry." He patted her hand, to no avail.

He's a family man, Hardy remembered. "Let's go," he said. "Dr Chapaire will have plenty of things for the youngsters at the Reception Centre, and Halka and Robert are already there." He ushered them down the stairs towards their vehicles.

Kaj spoke for the first time. "You've found Halka? Is she OK?"

"She's fine. You knew she was missing?"

"We saw Ayar's appeal on HV, but Juli wouldn't let me answer it. She thought you were trying to use Halka as bait."

"I suppose in a way we were," Hardy admitted, "though we *were* genuinely concerned about your safety."

"Yes, because you want him to spill the beans about the way the ship's drive works!" Juliet Harkness burst out.

Hardy stopped and regarded her. "That's irrelevant now, Mrs. Harkness," he said. "Ayar Dekkutz is assisting Eddie with his work, and has been ever since I got him away from the Neoluddites, when they kidnapped him in Moscow." *She wouldn't have heard about that,* he remembered. "The net result of that episode is that all the children have received full citizenship rights. You had no need to disappear like that."

"You can't use that to justify treating me like a criminal," she said in a fierce tone. "That wasn't the case four years ago. Kaj was desperately unhappy that he'd been separated from his friends, and equally so when he realised JSEP just wanted him to tell you about the ship."

"Just so," Hardy agreed. "Take Mrs. Harkness into custody, Don. I'll deliver Kaj and Lucy to Dr Chapaire."

Lucy still cried and clung to Kaj. Hardy helped them into the car, fastened their safety belts, and settled himself behind the wheel.

Then he heard Kaj whisper, "I'm sorry, Lucy. I'm so sorry. It's all my fault for being ill. But I won't leave you."

CHAPTER 23 – Message in a Bottle

Zero, ship's time/date: 411.79.4.60.267 AD, (15th December, 2098).

TANGAR HELD THE SHUTTLE STEADY in its orbit while Omol prepped the satellite for release. He'd checked all the satellite parameters were optimal.

"I'll do a countdown," Omol said. "Hold her stable." He began a countdown from ten.

Tangar held his breath as he remembered the last time they'd done this. Everything had seemed fine then, too.

Omol's countdown ended, and he pressed the launch button. The satellite slid smoothly out of its chute and spun away into the void. Its solar panels extended after some thousandths. They'd convert the infra-red and radio emissions – the products of deuterium-lithium fusion – from Zero's dark star, into electricity.

"Fire thrusters."

[Thrusters fired.]

The satellite settled into its orbit.

Tangar exhaled with relief, as he tracked the satellite in the simtank. "The satellite's in its programmed orbit," he confirmed with relief.

"Excellent. Let's locate the other ships," Omol said. "Then we can monitor whether they receive the message."

"Good idea," Tangar said. "And I'd like to look closer at that planet the *Bekel* headed to."

Omol ran through the steps he'd followed before and soon found the planet with its moon and large artificial satellite. "Zoom in."

[Resolution increased to highest available.]

Tangar nodded. "Sweep for the *Bekel*."

[Sweeping for the *Bekel*.] A white dot appeared beside the artificial satellite.

"Well, we've found them, but there's nothing we can do about it." Tangar sighed. "Computer, sweep for the present position of the *Kemeen* and the *Velakta*."

[Sweeping for the *Kemeen.*] A white dot appeared in the simtank near the Haveertel system. [Sweeping for the *Velakta*.] Another white dot appeared nearby.

"They're together," Tangar observed. "Perhaps they're working together. But they're in range of our message, unlike the *Bekel*."

"Looks like it." To the computer Omol added, "Sweep for other Zarduthi vessels."

One by one, seventeen white dots winked into being in the simtank, scattered around this sector of the galaxy.

"Return to base, Tangar," Omol said. "The *Kemeen* and the *Velakta* are nearest. We'll trigger the broadcast from Zero's surface."

*

Control Room of the Bekel, *Galatea Station, 23rd December, 2098.*

"Is Hardy Brencher here?"

Eddie looked up. "He's back on Earth."

"Oh, that's a shame," the man said. "I wanted to thank him for visiting Chan to explain what happened to her mother. It was kind of him."

Ayar looked up too and offered him his hand. "Dr Kobayashi? I'll pass the message on," Ayar said. "I stay at his apartment when I'm not up here or at college."

"Thank you."

"Is Chaneg all right? I was totally in shock, so I can

imagine she –"

"Chan has been quiet since Mr Brencher's visit, but she has coped well with her loss," Dr Kobayashi said. "She learns martial arts, and it helps her deal with her problems."

"We have some footage you might find interesting," Eddie said. "Ayar, could you get us some drinks?"

Ayar realised that Eddie wanted to show Dr Kobayashi the log with the Voth on it. "Sure," he said. And when he returned with tea for Dr Kobayashi and coffee for himself and Eddie, the doctor had seen the footage and had a better understanding of the way the Voth behaved.

"I *was* told the Voth was found floating in microgravity," Dr Kobayashi said after a sip of his tea. "But I don't understand why."

"I can answer that one," Ayar said. "When either drive is on, the ship revolves around the central axis, and simulates gravity. You can only use one drive at a time, and if they're both off, there's no gravity," Ayar explained. "We now know from the ship's logs that the Voth were already aboard. But after a hyperspace jump, the drive auto-switches to ion drive mode, during which time the housekeeping machines cleared up after the fight, but some of the doors were sealed, so they wouldn't have been able to enter those. And with no further input from the crew, the ion drive powered down, so the ship went into orbit around Titan. Hence there were no bodies left but the single Voth found after the door was cut open."

"Now *that* makes sense," Dr Kobayashi said. "And we've discovered something about the creature's DNA."

"Are you allowed to tell me this?"

"No, but I'm going to anyway, because I think you've just solved several mysteries for *us*. And you deserve to know." He drew a deep breath. "It has a different mathematical code from human or Zarduthi DNA."

"That's because they're from a different bubble universe," Ayar said. "That's why their DNA is so different from ours."

"We figured that. But Zarduth is in *this* bubble universe, isn't it?"

"You mean – our DNA has the same mathematical code as yours?"

Dr Kobayashi nodded. "The Voth are *really* alien. But you Zarduthi and we humans could be distant cousins. The proteins are the same in Zarduthi and humans, but completely different in the Voth."

*

Zero, ship's date/time: 411.151.4.21.094 AD, 27th March, 2099.

Omol hovered near Perik's workstation. "How's the project progressing?"

"We've located the design and are working on synthesising the chemicals for the various components of the condensation kits. We should be able to produce the first ones soon. And your calculation of how many we need, and can produce over time, was spot on, Omol."

"Excellent. And how long do you estimate we'll need to produce them?"

"We can make between five and eight a day, allowing for the time and the amount of energy the matter conversion process takes, so it will take approximately half a year to produce enough to give everyone a basic water ration each day. Continuing the project until the water ration is *fully* adequate will take another year."

"Then that's how long we need to continue for. And we'll still need spares in case of malfunctions, and maintenance will be ongoing."

Perik nodded. "I'll get back to you on those things, Omol."

*

Hyderabad, 29th March, 2099.

Josie settled herself beside Davan on the sofa in the Ashrafs' lounge. "How are you, Davan?" she asked.

"I'm fine. But can you speak with Mrs Jamilah and tell her I don't want to get married to a human?"

"Are they *still* pressuring you about that?" Josie asked.

Davan nodded. "She keeps on about it. It does my head in."

"Well, I have some news for you *and* Mrs Jamilah. The new president disapproves of what President Langrishe tried to do. He asked me to tell you that they don't need to marry you off to a human. I just wanted to tell you that before I speak with the Ashrafs."

"Thanks, I really appreciate that," Davan said. A smile lit up her face, and she relaxed visibly.

Mrs Jamilah bustled in with a tray of seeds and tea. She put the tray on the coffee table and poured them each a cup.

"I have some news for you, Mrs Jamilah," Josie began.

"Oh, and we have some news for you too," Mrs Jamilah said. "We're going to America for a holiday with my brother Rafiq in a couple of weeks."

"How lovely!" Josie said. "I just want you to know, President Sanchez says you needn't worry about finding Davan a husband any more. Hopefully that will take the pressure off you."

Mrs Jamilah didn't look as pleased as Josie expected. "Hopefully Davan will behave herself now," she murmured.

*

Eisenhower Reception Centre, Texas, 4th April, 2099.

"Have you been here before?" Ayar asked.

"Once, when I came to collect Kaj," Eddie said.

"I thought it looked like you knew your way around. What did you make of Dr Chapaire?"

I thought she had Kaj's best interests at heart." Eddie smiled at Ayar. "And I think it's worth using some of my leave to help you. To tell the truth I haven't taken any for the last few years. I've had no reason to."

"Yes, what happened to you was awful," Ayar said. Not wishing to dwell on it, he added, "I hope Dr Chapaire and Josie can help us."

"They have access to the other children, you have access to the *Bekel*. All we have to do is persuade them, and from what you've said, they should be receptive."

Eddie spoke into the intercom.

"I will collect you," Dr Chapaire replied. She arrived a few minutes later. "Hello, Monsieur Harkness, Ayar. How is the jaw?"

Ayar rubbed a hand over it. "Not bad. It aches sometimes."

"We will discuss it indoors. In the meantime, if you have another reason for coming, do not mention it inside the building."

"Oh…OK," Ayar said, and thought, *I know your ways, Hardy!*

"Where *can* we talk?" Eddie asked.

"Outside – it is such a pleasant day."

Ayar nodded. "That makes sense."

Dr Chapaire held the door open for them to enter. They followed her down the corridor and entered Dr Chapaire's office.

"The ache in your jaw will pass as you become stronger, but I will give you some exercises." Dr Chapaire went to her desk and sat down. "Monsieur Harkness, I am so glad you are here. I must tell you that Kaj and your daughter Lucy are here too. Would you like to see them?"

Eddie gaped. "I – uh – of course. But how –?"

"I am afraid Monsieur Brencher is responsible for that. He traced your wife after she contacted me about Kaj, who was very poorly. I brought him here for treatment and then returned him to their lodgings when he recovered, but Monsieur Brencher found out where they lived, and yesterday he had Madame Harkness arrested –"

"Arrested? But –"

Dr Chapaire held up her hand. "He had her arrested for the kidnap of Kaj. She is in custody, awaiting trial. Meanwhile, Kaj and Lucy are staying here, along with Halka Mozada and her friend Robert, who is also seriously ill, though now stabilised."

Ayar was pleased that Kaj and Halka were both there, but sorry about Eddie's upsetting news. "Can we see them?" he asked.

"I was just about to suggest that." Dr Chapaire led them through the office to a heavy black door.

"We came to see you and Josie about something," he said. "I didn't realise any of the others would be here, but I'm pleased they are."

To Ayar's surprise, Dr Chapaire switched to passable Zarduthi. "What did you come to see me about? Josie is in Pakistan at present – but I expect her back soon." She took them into the dormitory. Eddie spotted Kaj and Lucy straight away, and went to speak to them.

"I'll tell you when we can talk in private," Ayar said in Zarduthi.

"It is so hot – I will get some juice." She went to the fridge, and switched back to Zarduthi. "I cannot vouch that the building is free of listening or recording devices, so let us go outside for refreshments."

"That sounds good," Ayar said. "I stayed at Hardy's

apartment for several weeks, so I know how his mind works. I don't want him to know about this, partly so that he can't stop us, and also so he can't get into trouble for not doing so."

"You get on well with Monsieur Brencher," Dr Chapaire commented.

"He's been supportive of my problems, as has Eddie."

"And now I think we should support Eddie and *his* problems." Dr Chapaire switched back to English and nodded in Eddie's direction. "He will have enough of them."

Eddie walked back towards them. His frown creased his whole face. "Lucy doesn't know who I am," he said. "And because Kaj won't speak to me, she won't believe I'm her father."

"I will speak with them. It must be as big a shock for them to see you as for you to learn they are here." Dr Chapaire pointed towards another door. "Ayar, Halka and Robert are through there, using the computers to catch up on what they missed while they…travelled. Why not take Eddie with you to talk to them?"

"Good idea," Ayar said. "C'mon, Eddie." He took his arm and led him through the door. As Dr Chapaire had said, the teenagers were seated before a bank of computer terminals, working hard to catch up on their studies.

When Halka saw Ayar she jumped up. "Ayar!" She caught at Robert's hand. "This is Ayar, from the clanship. You know, he made the appeal for me to return –"

"I remember," Robert said. He stood up, moving as if in slow motion, then extended his hand. Ayar went to shake hands the way the humans did, but to his surprise Robert gripped his thumb with his fingers. "Halka's taught me some of your customs," he said with a self-conscious grin. "And a few words. Shulai!"

"Shulai, Robert!" Ayar remembered Dr Chapaire had said Robert was ill. That might explain the slow-motion movements.

"Fight well and bravely."

"I am."

"I need to speak to you, Halka."

Dr Chapaire beckoned to them from the fire escape door, a jug of fruit squash in one hand and beakers in the other. Kaj and Lucy followed her. Dr Chapaire led them to a bench with attached table.

Ayar settled himself on the bench, aware that everyone watched him and unsure where to start. After a moment to compose his thoughts, he began, "You may know that Eddie and I have worked on the ship's logs and the hyperdrive. That's now vital in the light of what we discovered." His gaze rested on Kaj for a moment. "You may also know that the crew are dead. A Voth boarding party killed them – they died so we could live. But we don't know what happened to the rest of our parents, who went to Declain to fight the Voth. So I want to go find my father and the others."

"Yesss!" Halka hissed. "I want to know what happened to *my* parents, although I know what we find there could be difficult for us."

Ayar held up his hand. "I'm not suggesting we leave straight away. Eddie still has work to do on the hyperdrive. I'm helping him with that."

"I thought we weren't supposed to trade technology with other species!" Kaj put in, his tone hostile.

"Not usually, no, but this is a different situation. Eddie and I have checked back with the ship's logs and discovered where Declain is. If it has fallen, once the Voth have sucked it dry they could well be on their way here – this is the next system in the line. Declain was a detour. I want to go there *before* that happens." He paused and looked at Halka and Kaj. "Are you with me?"

"Of course we are," Halka said.

"Yes." Kaj looked concerned. "So Juli got into trouble for no reason?"

"Absolutely not. Everything she did was right for you at the time," Ayar reassured Kaj. "But I've taken the decision to share our technology with the humans so they might have a chance if *we* fail – for all we know the Voth could already be on their way here. It will take them some time to reach the Earth without a hyperdrive, but they will come here eventually."

"I won't leave without Robert," Halka told him. "He's my partner."

"I guessed that. Discuss with him how he feels about coming with you, but he's welcome."

"Where does Eddie fit into all this?" Kaj asked.

"When we take back the *Bekel* he'll come with us. By then he'll know enough about the drive to be our engineer."

"I see." Kaj was not pleased. He hoisted Lucy onto his knee.

"Ayar, what about Josie and myself?"

He turned to look at Dr Chapaire. "You know where the other children are. I don't. We may have full citizenship rights now, but if we don't know where our friends are, we can't even phone them."

"So you want us to put you in touch with all the other children?"

"Exactly." Ayar hesitated. "Would Josie help too?" He couldn't see the car park, but he'd just heard some cars arrive.

"I'm certain she would."

"When do you expect her back?"

"Later today."

"Then who's that?"

"She *could* have got an early flight," Dr Chapaire said.

Ayar relaxed.

"In a war zone you may need a doctor," Dr Chapaire said,

"especially one familiar with both human *and* Zarduthi physiology."

"That sounds like a good idea. Are you applying?"

"I may well do."

"Applying for what?"

Ayar swung round.

Hardy Brencher watched them from the door, Josie beside him.

"My job will soon come to an end," Dr Chapaire said. "I saw a job in the internal news."

Hardy nodded as if he understood. "All outside?" he asked. "This is a bit of a security breach, isn't it?"

*

"Eddie? What are *you* doing here?" Hardy demanded.

"I presume I'm allowed to visit my daughter on furlough?" Eddie countered.

"Of course, but how did you find out she was here?"

"Conversation with Dr Chapaire," Ayar muttered. "I had an appointment for her to check my jaw. What are *you* doing here?"

"Just because I got you away from the Neoluddites once doesn't mean they won't make another attempt on you. Your security is still my responsibility, Ayar."

For that read, I'm following you to see what you're up to, Ayar thought. *I know your ways, Hardy.*

"I understand my wife is in custody," Eddie interrupted. "I want to see her."

"Get your work copying that drive finished and you *can* see –"

"Damn you, man!" In a trice Eddie was up and had Hardy in a half-Nelson. "Let me see her *now* – and drop the charges!" He yanked at Hardy's arm. "Juli's no criminal. She did what she thought was the right thing – at the time – to protect Kaj from exploitation. As it happens, I agree with what she did. Now drop the charges, or I'll destroy everything I've done so far on the hyperdrive!"

"You wouldn't!"

"I damn well would!" Eddie brought a small black device with buttons on out of his hip pocket. "See?" He stowed it away again. He'd positioned his other arm so that it was right under Hardy's chin, and jerked his arm up.

"*Urk!*" Hardy said.

"As a matter of fact, Monsieur Brencher, I do not agree with the children being exploited for the hyperdrive either," Dr Chapaire said.

"Nor me," Josie said, "and I don't like the fact that President Langrishe wanted the foster families to report back on things the children said and did, or the way they were split up and not allowed to communicate with each other, or learn certain skills." She folded her arms and looked hard at him, as if trying to outstare him.

"And as Ayar has voluntarily shared his people's technology with JSEP," Dr Chapaire added, "there's no need for it now. They could *all* come back in-house here."

Hardy made a strangulated noise in his throat, as if trying to speak, and flung out a hand in appeal.

Eddie released his grip fractionally.

"Josie, you know I – *urk* – didn't like them being split up either."

Josie snorted. "Only because it made your job more difficult."

"Free her and drop the charges!"

"First let me go."

"Not on your life!" Eddie looked across at Dr Chapaire. "Your personal phone, please, Doctor."

Dr Chapaire brought it across.

"Tell them to release her now!" Eddie yanked at Hardy's arm again.

Hardy yelped in pain. "You've dislocated my shoulder!"

"I will if you don't get on that phone *now!*" Eddie met Dr Chapaire's glance. "Hold it near and dial for him."

She did.

"Free Mrs Harkness," Hardy said as the holograms sprang up, "and bring her to the Reception Centre in Texas."

"On whose authority?"

"Mine," Hardy gritted out. "I've just – er – discovered a material fact that – negates the case against her."

"What material fact?"

"The child in question…went willingly with her. There's no case of kidnapping – to answer."

"Very good, Mr. Brencher. Mrs. Harkness should be there in about –" Don consulted his wrist watch. "Four hours."

"Send her things here as well. I think she'll stay a while."

When he'd finished the call, Hardy turned a face full of bitter defeat and anger towards Eddie. "Are you satisfied?"

"That'll do for now." Eddie released Hardy.

He stumbled over to the bench where he sat and rubbed his shoulder. "I've got a bone to pick with you, Dr Chapaire. I knew Kaj was here when we set up the trap for the Neoluddites. Why didn't you tell me *then*?"

Dr Chapaire's cheeks flamed, but she shrugged. "Kaj was ill. I treated him for a recurrence of a childhood illness. He and his foster-family were vulnerable. And we can never be sure where we stand with you, Monsieur Brencher, and I had promised Madame Harkness that Kaj would not be exploited further on recovery." Her eyes flickered across to meet Ayar's. "We could not have known at that time that Ayar would decide to share his people's technology with JSEP."

"Besides, in the past you haven't exactly shown us you can

inspire trust." Josie folded her arms across her chest.

Hardy leaned forwards on his elbows and put his face in his hands. "I do try to do the best job I can, but I can't do it if nobody trusts me."

Ayar regarded him. "Where I come from, trust has to be earned," he said. "I guess it's the same for humans."

It was Hardy's face that burned this time. "It's my job to work in the way I do," he said after a pause. "I guess I'll just have to work harder to earn everyone's trust," he added, exchanging glances with Josie and Dr Chapaire.

"Let us all go inside and have lunch," Dr Chapaire suggested. "You too, Monsieur Brencher. Josie and I will make it." She led the way back towards the Reception Centre.

Ayar and Eddie followed at a slower pace.

As the others disappeared inside the building, Ayar asked, "Would you really have destroyed the copy of the hyperdrive?"

Eddie grinned. "It's a good job I had the car remote in my pocket," he said, as he took it out and flipped it up in the air. It spun back into his hand, and he pocketed it again.

*

Seattle, America, 10th July, 2099.

"What time are we collecting Uncle Vimal and his family from the airport?" Jafar asked as he tried again to squash down his excitement, which again threatened to burst forth like a Jack-in-a-box.

"Well, *I'm* going to meet them," Rafiq Ashraf replied. "Everything's ready for their stay."

"They might need help with their luggage. Can I come too?"

"I guess."

"When are you going?"

"Soon. You're suddenly very keen to come with me!"

Jafar felt his face grow hot. "I – kind of like Davan," he admitted. "Actually, I can't wait to see her again."

"Oh! Well, they may have married her off to another human by the time she arrives here," Rafiq said. "The last time they mentioned it, that was the plan."

"I do hope not." Then Jafar noticed his expression.

Rafiq teased him often; he regarded him intently. "You *do* like her, then?"

"Somewhat," Jafar said, "and I know she wants to go to college. I figured if we were engaged, Uncle Vimal might let her go, and then we could join JSEP together."

"Well, this is a shock," Rafiq murmured. "I take it you'll want me to drop a hint or two of that?"

"Perhaps..."

"Then let's just see how things work out while Vimal and his family are here," Rafiq said. "Leave it with me."

*

Four days later.

"Come for a walk with me, Davan," Jafar invited.

"No way, they'll make me marry you!"

"Would that be so bad?"

"I don't want to be married to anyone." Davan tossed her head so that her plait, which was now down to her waist, swung about. "I can't understand their obsession with marrying me to a human. Can't they just let me be myself?"

"It seems not," Jafar said, secretly pleased. "Don't Zarduthi women get married?" He walked along the garden path, and noticed she'd followed so as to answer him.

"There's no ceremony involved," she said, "but it doesn't mean Zarduthi women are less true to their partners – we just don't need ceremonies. Everyone knows when two people share a cabin."

"I guess you would, in a closed community," Jafar said, after several more steps. "Tell me about your people."

She stared at him. "Why?"

"I'm interested to know." He remembered the other thing he'd wanted to ask her. "And tell me why your hobby is military history."

"It isn't a hobby," she said. "I did a school project on it, that's all."

"But why? All the girls I know like boys, make-up, music, and dancing. You're different."

"I don't suppose I'd be allowed to like boys and make-up even if I did!" Davan retorted tartly. Then she sighed. "Sorry, Jafar. That wasn't intended as a criticism of your culture. It's just that it gets me down a bit at times. I need to be free."

"I understand," he said. "I've thought that ever since I first met you." He shrugged. "I like your straight-forwardness, Davan. So I'll be honest with you: I'm not a devout Muslim. Neither's Dad. It's more difficult to keep to the old ways here. I know enough about my family's culture to understand the things my uncle and aunt talk about, but I live my life as an American. It would be hard for me to live in Pakistan." After a pause he added, "I heard you'd joined a gym and taken up weight training, too."

"Who told you that?"

"Aunt Jamilah. And Uncle Vimal stuck up for you. He said it wasn't anyone's business but yours!" He met her gaze.

She regarded him intently. "Don't be offended at this, Jafar. You said you like my straight-forwardness. Well, one of the things I like least about humans is their deceptiveness. Saliha and I are expected to be quiet and demure – but we're real people and want to enjoy ourselves. My culture is based on honesty and is straight-forward."

"Is that why you refused to marry Mr. Faruq?"

Davan regarded him sideways through her lashes. "You know about that too?"

"Uncle Vimal told my Dad the first evening you were here. That *really* upset him."

"I know." Davan stared at her toes and sighed. "Of *course* I don't want to spoil Saliha's chance of marriage, as long as it's someone nice." She looked up and locked glance with his. "But I wasn't going to let them force me to marry an old man. He was really old-fashioned and pompous – and besides, he smelt of roses!"

Jafar smothered a laugh.

"Luckily he didn't like me. If I must marry a human, it has to be someone I can get on with, someone who won't expect me to be a decorative, useless appendage."

"I'll tell you what, Davan. Why don't you go and put on your Zarduthi gear? You have got it with you?"

"Of course." She hesitated, then added, "I half-expected them to produce a prospective suitor while we're here!" She permitted herself a grin.

"I know a few friends who would love to meet a Zarduthi girl, especially one wearing her war gear! We could meet them at a café."

"An irresistible suggestion," Davan murmured, "but I'd better take my things with me and change while we're out. It'll be less hassle, though it means *I'll* have to be deceptive, too."

"Tell Saliha to come too. We'll go skating first. It's fun!"

"Sounds interesting! There isn't a rink near where we live."

"I'll go phone my friends. Meet me outside in twenty minutes."

She nodded, and walked back towards the house.

Jafar noticed a spring in her step that hadn't been there before. He hugged himself, then took out his phone and dialled.

In seconds the face of a good-looking youth appeared above the phone. "Zip? It's working. Meet us at the skating rink in half an hour. Phone Dave and Chico and get them to bring their girlfriends."

"Okay. Did you organise the sister to come?"

"I did, but I should say I haven't any sympathy whatsoever for you – serves you right for making two dates for the same night! By the way, how's that scratch?"

Zip grimaced. "Improving. Ciao."

Jafar waited in the car – with some impatience, by the time Davan and Saliha put in an appearance. "What kept you?"

"Dad wanted to know where we were going and who with," Saliha said. "I told him you were taking me skating, with Davan as chaperone."

"I think the boot, if you'll excuse the pun, is at least half on the other foot," Jafar murmured from the window, "but never mind. That'll do. Got your stuff, Davan?"

She nodded.

"You can change when we get there. Jump in, then."

They got in. Jafar was disappointed to see them climb onto the back seat together, but he shrugged and backed out onto the road. "We're lucky to live out here in the suburbs," he said, and turned the wheel. "I'd hate to have to live in one of those poky apartments in the centre of town. And there are still plenty of entertainments close by."

"Yes, you're lucky," Davan said. "We've got s*ome* entertainments nearby, but we aren't allowed out on our own."

At the skating rink Jafar pointed out the women's changing rooms and Davan and Saliha hurried off to change. When they returned, not only was Davan a magnet for Jafar's gaze in her Zarduthi clothes, but Saliha was wore light blue, tight-fitting jeans, a crisp red and white gingham shirt, and a red cotton sweater. She'd applied mascara and red lip tint, and looked older than eleven.

"Put these boots on," Jafar said, "and I'll show you how to skate. Oh, by the way, this is Zip, David, his girlfriend Lorna, and Chico, and his girlfriend Marcia."

"What's this, Jafar, revenge?" But Zip laughed as he spoke.

"I don't know *what* you mean!"

"Partnering me with a babe in arms – I won't forget this, you know."

Jafar grinned. "I sure hope she's safe with you, you rake. Let's skate!" He took Davan's hand and led her towards the rink. Their skates clomped on the wooden floor. "It's easy. You won't fall over if you're with me."

An hour later he'd taught Davan to skate with some confidence. "You learn fast," he said. And then, because he'd been wanting to say so ever since she'd changed, "You look great." He looked around. "I guess I'm not the only one who thinks so, either." She'd had admiring and curious glances from other skaters.

"It's a good job I'm not trying to scare you off marrying me, then!"

"Er – quite." Jafar wondered if she realised what he was up to and baited him, but decided that wasn't the case. Although far from stupid, she was, as she'd remarked earlier, straight-forward in her dealings with other people.

Later, as they sat in a café, drinking coffee and Coke, he asked her if she'd enjoyed herself.

"Very much." She sounded enthusiastic, and a smile lit up her face. "I hope I'll be able to study in America. People are freer here."

"It would be great if you could," Jafar agreed. "I'll ask my father to try to persuade my uncle."

"Thank you. He might be glad to get me out of the house

so he can marry Saliha off without my harum-scarum ways putting suitors off."

"Can't you just say no to whoever your foster-father wants you to marry?" asked Marcia.

"That's included in the harum-scarum ways!" Davan said. "A Muslim child is expected to be obedient to their parents' wishes. So are Zarduthi children, but nobody would arrange a partner for their child, much less force them into a sexual relationship with that person."

"Ah, but you're all expected to enter the family business, aren't you?" Jafar countered with a sly smile.

"Become a warrior, you mean?"

He nodded.

"Yes, but it's bred into us. Though I suppose that if someone *really* objected they'd just be left wherever they wanted to be dropped."

Not long after, they left, so as to be home by Uncle Vimal's 10 p.m. curfew. The girls changed back into their traditional salwar-kameez and sandals and left the café. After Jafar had parked the car and Saliha had gone inside, he caught Davan's hand. "So – do I get a goodnight kiss?"

She tut-tutted. "I bet you're not going to mention it to your father if I let you kiss me, and that's just the kind of deceptiveness we talked about earlier."

"It'll be our secret," he agreed, "but even if Dad knew, he wouldn't mind. This time I've got permission to court you. They wouldn't let me when we came to stay in Hyderabad."

"Oh, killing two birds with one stone, are we?"

"What d'you mean?"

Her laugh was bitter. "Get me out of the way and salve the family pride at the same time?"

"It isn't like that, Davan. I – I like you a lot, and I *really* want to kiss you."

He was never sure what it was that made her mind up – whether she liked him anyway, or there was a note of appeal in his voice as he confessed that he liked her. What she said was true, since those were the grounds of his offer for her. But what he hadn't admitted to Uncle Vimal and Aunt Jamilah were the feelings he'd had for her since their first meeting.

At any rate, she lifted her shoulders and murmured, "All right," with an odd gesture, and let him kiss her. He had to stand on tiptoe, but decided it was worth getting cramp in his toes.

She kissed him back. "I thought if you saw me in my own clothes, you'd be put off me, like Mr. Faruq was!"

"Oh no, Davan. I like you *because* you're so different from women in my culture. I think you look even more attractive in your Zarduthi gear." Jafar's enthusiasm carried him away. "I'm determined to marry you, and happy to follow you to college and for us both to work for JSEP. I want to do astronaut training too. And I'm not afraid of what you'll do, because I know it's right for you. And for *me* to be with *you*."

"Why, Jafar, I didn't realise you liked me as much as that," she said. "I don't know about *marrying* you, though."

"Oh, admit it, Davan, I'm the best offer you'll get! I'm young, reasonably good-looking, and I understand your needs better than Uncle Vimal and Aunt Jamilah ever will." He paused to see what she'd say, and when she said nothing, added, "And you'll have more personal freedom with me than without!"

"Well," Davan observed, "This must be the strangest proposal any girl *ever* got!"

"Oh, so you're not going to take me *seriously* –"

"Davan! Jafar! Isn't it about time you came in?" It was his father.

"I'm…just locking the garage, Dad."

CHAPTER 24 – Invitation

Zero, ship's time/date: 413.129.3.62.245 AD, 18th March, 2101.

OMOL LOOKED UP as Faril approached. His boots were dusted with sand, his clothes and hair crest dishevelled. His breath came in gasps. "What is it, Faril?"

"It's Shenalle. Can you come?"

Omol felt dread gather at the nape of his neck. "Sure, Faril." He got to his feet and followed him to Garchon's office, with its sick bay and meds store.

In the sick bay, Shenalle, now three, lay in a portable medmachine. Although a cut-down version, it swamped her tiny frame. But that wasn't what Omol focused on. Her whole body was in constant motion. "How long has she been like this?"

"Since late last night. I've given her a low dose medication, but it hasn't worked," Garchon admitted. "I think it's to do with the contaminated water."

"But she's had the pure water from the condensation kits, like all the other children. Are there any tests that would shed light on this? I'm sure Faril and Ensee would want to know."

"Understood. I need to find out what's going on. I have a few options and tests, though Shenalle's body weight is so low, for a child of her age, that I can't use all of them."

"Could the dissolved metals enter via our skin, through clothes and bedding cleaning and personal washing?" Faril asked.

"Unlikely," Garchon said. "But what occurs to me is, metallurgy is one of Ensee's specialisms. She works in the refinery area, processing the metals. There are other women working there too. They should either stop now, or wear more protective clothing. We don't want to compromise their future fertility. And it might affect males as well."

"Now we've topped up our implant supply, and the condensation kit project has moved into the maintenance phase, we can spare a synth machine – perhaps two – for that. Garchon, do the tests. Try to find something to help Shenalle. I'll organise the protective clothing."

*

Richmond, England, 8th May, 2101.

"Mil! Phone call for you."

"For me? Who is it?"

Steph smiled at him. "Surprise!"

Mystified, he followed her to the holophone. And there was Davan's projection.

"Shulai, Miril-madar," she said, and smiled.

He'd hadn't seen her for so long, he'd almost forgotten he had a sister. "Are you all right?" he asked. He studied her for a moment. She looked different. She'd grown her hair-crest long and it framed her face in sleek waves, covered by a long scarf of turquoise silk that shimmered under the light. Her hands peeped from the cuffs of her turquoise satin tunic. She looked very human.

"I'm fine, I just wanted to talk to you, now that we can, and find out how you are," she replied in Zarduthi. "I thought about you a lot when we couldn't keep in touch."

Mil was taken aback to find his hand had strayed to the translator catch. "I'm – er – fine." He couldn't think of anything to say, although it was good to see her beam at him. She looked just as if she stood beside him, though he only saw her upper half.

"Er – good. But I didn't expect you to answer in English."

"I use it all the time. Nobody here speaks our language.

I'm used to it now."

"Miril, I'm at college in America."

"Oh? What are you studying?"

"How to avoid being married off to a human, I think!" she said, and her eyes danced with mischief.

They sparkle like that when she laughs, Mil remembered. "No, *re*ally?"

"Astronomy and astrophysics," she said. "But they want me to marry someone when I leave. Even though Josie explained I don't have to now."

"Josie's coming to see *me* next week." Mil frowned. "But wouldn't it – er – be better for you *not* to marry a human?"

Davan sighed. "I know, Miril. But my foster-parents are determined, and so is the boy concerned." She paused. "He's nice, and fun, but the human idea of marriage for life seems so – final. I don't want to be tied to anyone. Besides, if we ever go back to the clanship I'll be expected to have babies with a Zarduthi at some point, even if I stay with my human partner. I'm not sure how Jafar would feel about that."

"Does he know?" Mil shrugged. "I don't know about this stuff, Davan. I'm only ten. I want you to be happy, but I can't advise you."

"Sorry, I shouldn't have put my worries onto you. You're right, I should tell Jafar about that and see what he thinks. I'll do that." Davan stared at him, in silence for a moment. "You look so different – *apart* from being more grown up, that is."

"So do you. You look very…*human*."

The conversation grew stiff and awkward, and seas of silence flooded between islands of speech.

Then Mil heard a door open, and Davan drew a younger girl into the holophone's field of view. "This is my foster-sister, Saliha," she said.

"Hello, Saliha."

"Hello, Miril," Saliha said, and chuckled as she related how Davan had frightened Mr Faruq off with her Zarduthi gear. Mil had to laugh.

Eventually Davan said, "Miril, it's been great to talk and see you after all this time, but I have some work to hand in tomorrow, so I need to go now. But will you come to my wedding, if it happens?"

"Of course."

"Call me," Davan said. "I'm at Washington State University. JSEP's sponsoring my course." She gave him her personal phone number and they said goodbye.

Mil returned to his homework, but couldn't settle to it. It didn't have to be in the next day, so he admitted defeat and watched HV for a while, then went to bed. It took him some time to settle there, too. He heard Ronnie go to bed soon after, and then, later still, Steph's footsteps outside his door.

He wasn't surprised when the door opened.

"Steph? I can't sleep."

She came and sat on his bed. "Are you thinking about your sister?"

He nodded. "I'd forgotten I even *had* a sister!"

"Shall I get you a drink?"

She brought him hot chocolate, waited while he drank it, then settled him for the night again.

Sleep came, and with it, vivid dreams.

Mil was in a place he didn't recognise. It was full of people: humans, Zarduthi, Declaini and others. He recognised them from memory, men, women, and creatures with no apparent sexual attributes: Voth, Haveertel, Yelvai.

Davan passed him without recognition, and when he tried to call out her name his voice didn't work. She was gone in a trice. He saw other children from the ship; one, a grown man in fur jacket and leather trousers and boots. Again the familiar face disappeared.

Then he saw his parents. They stood together and held hands. His father never spoke, but his mother did. She reached out for his hand, but just as her fingers were about to touch Mil's hand, his parents became transparent, and in another thousandth they vanished.

*

Richmond, 27th September, 2101.

Ayar pressed the doorbell of the Lawtons' apartment and stepped back to wait for an answer. Miril was first on his list.

In a couple of thousandths the door opened. An attractive human woman stood there, her lips poised to frame a question until she glimpsed his face.

"I'm Ayar Dekkutz, Ma'am. Can I speak to Miril Gharm?" He'd worn his own clothes, though they'd drawn curious stares on public transport. He'd thought Miril might feel more comfortable with him dressed as he might remember him.

"Of course." She invited him into the apartment. It was about the same size as Hardy's, but with smaller rooms and more of them, Ayar noted as she called Miril.

"You must be Mrs. Lawton."

"Yes, I'm Mil's foster-mum, Steph." A man accompanied Miril into the room. "This is my husband Chas, and here's Mil."

Ayar shook hands with Chas and Steph.

While Steph went to make drinks, he turned his attention to Miril. He was about ten now. He'd been two, Ayar remembered, when they'd entered the Long Sleep.

Miril's hair crest was cropped short, and resembled a human schoolboy's hair; he wore a black-and-grey school uniform, and had a couple of books tucked under one arm.

"You're from the ship," Miril said, as Steph put a mug of hot chocolate on the coffee table for him, and coffee for Ayar.

"Yes." He switched to Zarduthi. "Do you remember me? I'm Ayar Dekkutz. I was due to start my combat training when the Long Sleep began."

Miril nodded in just the way the humans did. He stared gravely at him, then said, "I remember you now, Ayar. But you were older than me so I don't think I ever knew your family name." His speech was hesitant, as if the vocabulary was unfamiliar to him. He drew in a sharp breath and exclaimed, "It was *you* in my dream last night!"

"You dream about the ship?"

"Often, but I don't know *who* I dream about. I was too little to know everyone's names."

"You must be ten now. I'm twenty-two. I'm in my last year of college and I'll work for JSEP when I graduate." Ayar prized open a memory he'd kept shut. "I came to England with my foster-family a few years ago. I saw you at the circus, in the Hall of Mirrors – but when I followed, you disappeared into the crowd."

"I *did* go to the circus. But I didn't see *you* there."

"I know." Ayar shifted his position on the chair. "Miril, I've come here to ask you what you think about going to find our parents."

Miril stared back at him. "I have my parents here."

"I mean our biological parents. I had a foster-family too, but it's not quite the same thing, you know." Then he added, "What the hell's up with your name?"

"My brother Ronnie couldn't say my name, so I became Mil." He flung out his hand in a throwaway gesture. "I quite like it."

"I see." Ayar got up and went to the door. Steph and Chas sat together, holding hands, in the kitchen. Ayar suppressed a twinge of envy. "Do you think it would be unrealistic to try to find our biological parents?"

It was Chas who answered. “Not at all, Ayar. We know it’s important for anyone to embrace their heritage, and so far you’ve been denied that opportunity. I take it you’re here to persuade Mil to go along with you?”

“Yes – at some stage in the future. I’ve worked with Eddie Harkness during vacations, and we think the Voth are either on their way here, or soon will be. President Sanchez has even ordered SETI to trace their planet.”

“I heard about that. Any luck yet?”

Ayar shook his head. “Not as far as *I’ve* heard. You work for JSEP too?”

Steph and Chas exchanged glances. “I’m in the marines. Eddie and I found you kids. But you were the victims of a cover-up by the World Government. Langrishe was going to do away with all of you, but luckily for you, the Neoluddites got hold of the story and threatened to make it public.”

“Why would Langrishe want to kill us?” Ayar wondered if he’d ever understand human motivations.

“Because of the FTL drive.”

“Everyone wants the drive,” Ayar observed. “Even the Voth.”

“*And* because the World President was afraid you’d plot against him if you stayed together, and that you’d breed out of control. You know we have a galloping population explosion here on Earth?”

“Yes.”

“So you were revived instead, fostered with JSEP families, and those families briefed to report back any useful information you came up with.”

“Did you?” Ayar asked. He was both curious and angry.

“As far as I know, very few foster families reported anything at all, either because there was nothing to report, or because, like us, they didn’t approve of spying on you, and felt you should be protected." Chas took his own refilled mug from Steph. "I don't approve of the way Langrishe and JSEP handled the situation, though we love Mil and don't want to lose him. But there have been times when he was desperately unhappy here, and was too young to realise why. We'd encourage him to find his heritage."

"I didn't know all this," Mil said. He stood behind Ayar, having followed him to find out where his visitor had gone. "I wanted to go to the JSEP Academy too, but now I'm not sure. But I want to be a pilot, like my father was."

Ayar twisted round to face Mil. "I'm going to do that. I could teach you everything you need to know."

"How?"

"I thought we'd take back the *Bekel* – after I've finished my astronaut and pilot training."

The front door opened. The kitchen door was open, and Ayar saw a boy in Scouts uniform enter the hall. In the background Ayar heard Steph say, "Don't go in the lounge, Ronnie – Mil has a visitor and wants to be private with him."

"Why? *I* live here too." Ronnie entered anyway, and gave Ayar a thorough appraisal. "You're one of them."

"That's right. I'm Ayar."

"This is Ronnie." Miril shuffled the books lying like a barrier on the table between the two boys.

Ronnie stuck out his tongue at Miril. "You're so clever – all those kids hanging around you, getting you to do their homework for them!"

"I don't do it *for* them – I just help them if they're stuck. Anyway, *you're* good at sports."

Ronnie scowled. "So?" As he left the room he wiggled his bottom at Ayar. It seemed he wanted to make a point, because he left the door open behind him.

Ayar guessed Ronnie's behaviour embarrassed Mil. "Is he

always as rude and badly-behaved as that?" Ayar asked.

Mil made a throwaway gesture. "Pretty much. He's not quite so bad since I dropped out of the school football team. I guess he needed something to feel important about."

"What Mil doesn't say is that he was going to represent the county in a national competition," Ronnie chimed in, as he popped his head back round the doorframe.

It occurred to Ayar that Ronnie was proud of Mil and jealous of him simultaneously.

I encountered mixed emotions as a result of my foster placement, too. But I *never had the feeling I fitted into the Petrushenkos' family circle.*

*

The Kobayashis' apaato, Tokyo, Japan, same day.

"Why didn't you tell me it was OK for me to compete in martial arts competitions?"

Minato Kobayashi spread her hands. "I didn't want you to continue with those studies, since you gave up on ikebana."

Chan supposed that was fair enough, on the basis of their bargain, but she wouldn't admit it to her. "I gave that up because I was so awful at it. It's not pleasant to always be a failure."

"It's not pleasant when your daughter always makes you feel a failure as a parent."

She's not pleased that I found her out, Chan thought. "There were lots of competitions I could have entered and won, and then I wouldn't have felt so bad about the ikebana."

"But you continued to learn martial arts even though I asked you not to continue."

Chan lifted her head. "I *need* to learn them. I will suffocate if I don't. You concealed the new president's permission to study them to wrongfoot me. I *won't* be put in the wrong."

"You are a disobedient daughter."

"I am not your daughter. I am not even human. You are trying to mould me into something I'm not. I won't stand for it any more. If necessary I will ask for a different placement." *I should leave her to consider that.*

Chan stalked out of the apaato. She wasn't sure where she was going, but she wouldn't return until she'd made some decisions. Her interview with Josie that morning had made her realise she must take control of her life while the opportunity was there.

She wandered through the park where she'd practised falls with Ojin and Meiji so long ago. There were the rows of cherry trees, their blossom long since over, their fruits gone, their leaves the colours of fire. They overlooked the lake, and reflected in its serene waters.

Chan threaded between the cherries to stand on the bridge and stare at herself in the water. As she watched the flow below she became calmer. *If I were a speck of dust in the lake,* she thought, *I'd be content to float wherever the waters took me. I'm not that speck of dust, but I can become as content as one.*

A drizzle fell, and broke up the images on the surface of the lake. *The reflections are just hidden. They will return, when the rain passes, just as my actions and Mrs. Kobayashi's were hidden and have resurfaced now.* Her arms were wet; but she felt no need to take shelter.

She understood then that they played out a power struggle. She was determined to win. *I'm fighting for my survival as an entity in my own right. But I know what I must do to find my way.* She straightened and allowed the wind and rain to guide her to the *dojo*.

"Come in, Chan. You are *always* welcome here."

She followed him inside. "Mr. Noguchi," she began, "I've found out something which alters the basis of my studentship again."

"Just so," he said, and smiled. "You are allowed to compete now."

"Yes, but – how did you know that?"

"You don't think your social worker cares enough about your happiness to visit me and explain the situation?"

Chan felt like whooping with joy, but permitted herself only a smile. Of all the things she'd learned since studying under Mr. Noguchi, self-control was the most important. "I'm sure Josie does. She is very diligent."

"As are you. I am pleased for you, Chan."

She acknowledged that with a small inclination of her head. "I think if I must live on Earth for the rest of my life, I would prefer to spend it doing the thing I do best and enjoy most. Mr. Noguchi, do you think I'm diligent enough to become a *sensei* like yourself?"

"I'm certain you are." Mr. Noguchi beamed. "And I shall enjoy teaching you all I know."

*

After Ayar had left, Mil sat for a long time and thought about what Ayar had said. He explored his feelings about those thoughts. It had been clear to him for some time that the human way of life had absorbed him. *But is it* really *what I need*? *Is it the best thing for me?* Somewhere out in space his real parents might be alive, and need him now as they may never have imagined they'd need him, on the day he was born.

Much as he loved Steph and Chas, and much as he knew they loved him, there would come a day when he would have to go and find his biological parents, and try to help them. *Only then can I find my true destiny.*

He remembered the backpack under his bed, and went to investigate it. He hadn't been curious about it before.

*

A faint clash of metal made Steph turn.

Mil stood in the doorway. He looked utterly alien. The only other time she'd seen him look like that was when he'd arrived at their home. As he leant, one hand against the door jamb in a casual stance, he resembled a barbarian stranger. His face was flushed with excitement.

"Well," he asked, "how do I look?"

For a moment, Steph couldn't speak. Her heart filled her throat. Then she managed to croak, "Different. Zarduthi." *This is the moment when your baby grows up and leaves home. Except that you never were* my *baby, Mil.*

She crossed the room to stand beside him, and touched awed fingers to the fur jerkin strapped in place around his chest. Her eyes followed the line of his body. She noted the breeches of dark leather, tucked into boots of paler brown leather. A wide suede belt cinched his waist. Tucked into its left side was an object that resembled a gun, though of no type she'd ever seen before. It had metal and clear plastic parts. In one hand he bore a smaller gun. Mil looked impressive, not to say lethal, in the intensity of the change in him; and nothing seemed too large on him.

"You don't approve," said Mil. He sounded disappointed.

"No, no – it's not that!" she exclaimed. "It's just that...You're almost grown up now, and every chick flies the nest at some stage. I'll miss you when you go."

Mil was touched. He blinked and hugged her. "I'm not going just yet," he said, "Mother."

"You've never called me that in all the time I've known you," Steph said. Tears welled up in her eyes.

"You're my human mother," Mil said. "I'm lucky enough to have two mothers."

Steph smiled, but her face was wet.

"Don't worry, I'm not going yet," Mil said. "Ayar isn't ready to leave. But when he goes, I will too – but I'll never forget you."

*

Café Balalaika, Moscow, next day.

Per Lakshar strolled into the café, ordered black tea at the counter, and selected a table opposite the door. He didn't have long to wait before Blanko arrived for their meeting. As the door opened to admit him, the thrum of traffic and footsteps leaked in. As it closed, silence settled back around the café. They weren't the only occupants of the bar; its peculiar acoustic qualities made it ideal for secret meetings.

Blanko went to the counter and ordered a drink. Then he ambled over to Per Lakshar and sat down. He leaned back in his chair and adjusted the black beret he wore to an even more outrageous angle. "What's your fancy?" he asked.

"The White House computer system."

That brought Blanko upright on his seat. "Well, well, well," he purred. "What's brought this on, then?"

"I need to remind President Sanchez of our presence," Per said. "I spoke directly with Langrishe, but this guy apparently knew nothing of that conversation, or any of the reminders we sent, except for the kidnap of Ayar Dekkutz. We need to let him know we're here, and still have a goal. My understanding is that since Ayar returned to America, reverse engineering the Zarduthi ship has proceeded at speed, to the point that there is now a small fleet of replica ships. That being the case, we want some of the action. My goal is still to establish a colony on a pristine planet where we can build a low-tech civilisation. That's where you come in."

"In what way? I have no plans to leave Earth, even if new technology *is* on the horizon."

"There's no need for that. But I want to issue a reminder to President Sanchez. Let him know that we still want what I asked for from President Langrishe."

"OK," Blanko said. "I'd be up for that. But I have a price…"

"I know, but I think it would be worth it to achieve our goal."

CHAPTER 25 – Upsetting Information

Zero, ship's time/date: 414.56.8.39.456 AD, (24th February, 2102).

FARIL TRUDGED THROUGH THE SAND towards the tower settlement, now shadowed with true twilight. His footprints sifted away in the sharp breeze the instant he made them. *The synth machine team have created many new condensation kits,* he reflected, *and are making spare parts for them now. Soon, there'll be plenty of water – too late for Shenalle, though.*

A vudak with a grizzled hair crest passed him and raised his palm to acknowledge him. Fevend was one of the worst-affected older men in the clan; his tremble was continuous.

Faril returned the greeting. Some older vudaki were excused from mining; their fitness and bodily functions were compromised. Younger adults mined the ores. The adults had taken the brunt of the water shortage on this planet, since their zosa organs were mature and better able to cope than the children's. And Garchon had had some success with chelation therapy to reduce the toxic contamination in their bodies.

He'd started Shenalle on it once he knew it was safe for her; but it was too late. As the only child born on Zero, she'd never stood a chance of growing up. *I know I'll lose her.* Faril had seen the trembling in Shenalle, but worse, due to her age and small size. *She's grown up with minimal access to water.* At five, she was half the height she should have been. It made no difference to Ensee and him. They still loved her.

Faril met Ensee at the sick bay. He gripped her hand in his and said nothing as they entered. *It was Omol's decision to lead us down here, but in the circumstances I'd have made the same one. Garchon tried his best, but the problem with the youngest children is to find the right level of effective therapy for their body weight. Especially Shenalle. And the whole clan, irrespective of age, suffers from constant thirst.*

Shenalle's medmachine overwhelmed her tiny frame. As she saw Faril, she smiled. "Daddy!" She tried to push herself up into a sitting position but was strapped in.

And then it happened. Her whole body shook, her eyes rolled back in her head, and she became rigid. Her body still shook in pulses. The medmachine emitted a storm of beeps, then fell silent for several thousandths.

Garchon hurried over and gave Shenalle a shot. After a thousandth or two, her body relaxed. The machine beeped again, followed by silence.

Faril's gaze locked with Ensee's.

The machine beeped again. Silence. Another beep, then a silence. The medmachine settled back into a rhythm of beeps and silences. But Shenalle didn't stir.

Garchon consulted the readouts on the medmachine. At last he said, "Faril, Ensee, I'm so sorry. She's fallen into a coma."

The Voth caused all *of this,* Faril thought.

*

Reception Centre, Texas, 10th March, 2102.

Robert pulled Halka against him. "Have you decided what you're going to do?"

Halka sighed. "I feel torn in two, Robert. I want to go with Ayar – I need to find out about *my* parents, too – but I don't want to leave you."

Robert digested this for a moment. "I don't want you to leave me, either," he said, "but if I go with you I'll eventually run out of the drugs. Then I'll become ill again, and die."

"It depends how long we're gone for," she reminded him.

"The trouble is, we don't *know* how long it'll take."

"And once you've found them, what then? You might feel you want to go off with them."

"I know. It's my destiny." Halka sighed. "I really feel torn. Yet I have to make a decision." She thought hard for a moment. "I suppose Dr Chapaire could program the formula for the drugs into the synth machines – it might work."

"Would that provide me with an unlimited supply of the drugs?"

"As long as there's material in the machines for them to transform, and you had access to them." She stroked his face with a finger. "We Zarduthi are very healthy, under normal circumstances – though we pick up injuries in battle sometimes – so I can't tell you if that would work."

"Let's talk to Eddie and Dr Chapaire. If there's a way she could do that, then of course I'll come with you." He thought for a moment, then added, "I think what Ayar said about all of you being changed in some way by your experiences here on Earth was quite profound."

"It was, wasn't it? And I suspect that we've changed the humans we've come into contact with, as well."

*

Zero, ship's time/date: 414.104.6.53.201 AD, (9th April, 2102).

Everyone had gathered outside for the funeral of Shenalle. She had never regained consciousness and her most violent seizure ever had had claimed her life. Soon she would be vaporised, returned to the dust of this planet as if she'd never existed.

Omol's heart surged like a river in flood. It burst with conflicting emotions that swirled first in this direction, then that. He was sad for his friend's loss, and felt guilty that his decision to come here had caused it, however indirectly. And he was glad he hadn't let Ghaneem have a child, which might also have died suffering so horribly. He'd yet to shed his burden of guilt over her death. Omol felt he could hardly breathe for the renewed pain of loss. He'd be pleased to leave Zero behind forever.

Faril and his partner Ensee raised their disruptors, aimed at their child's underdeveloped body, and fired…

The sands that pillowed the tiny body faded, in thermal vision mode, through a rainbow of strident colours that warred with their usual pastel tints, until the youngest Zarduthi became just a memory, and the hiss of disruptor fire ceased. *Shenalle wasn't old enough to be clan-claimed, although everyone acknowledges her life by being here,* Omol thought.

He'd steeled himself and called a meeting to address everyone after the funeral, to honour the child and acknowledge her existence. It only took a few thousandths to call everyone to order. The clan moved closer as one and seated themselves on the sand.

"Clan-kin, I need your co-operation to try to ensure our survival. Faril and Ensee have lost Shenalle due to the mobile heavy elements in the water." Omol looked around the seated warriors. "We must all avoid drinking the contaminated water, even though we only abstract water from the boreholes with the lowest contamination levels, but we *can* use it to wash ourselves or our clothes and bedding. Chelation treatment will continue for everyone affected."

"I ask your patience for a few more days," Omol said. "The same ores responsible for the loss of Shenalle and the illness of other children and adults will hopefully also be our way off-planet. The more powerful transmitter satellite we've created broadcasts on all the commgrid wavelengths, in all directions, and also on a shifting directional transmitter. It's taken longer to mine the extra ores but we have a better chance of rescue now. The condensation kit team have completed the first phase of their job and the project is now in the maintenance phase. The last few kits are now onstream.

"It could *still* be years before we're rescued. But we can't give up hope."

*

Reception Centre, 4th August, 2102.

Josie Carter opened the door to the office. She put her briefcase down on the desk, went over to the coffee machine and helped herself to a cup. "Edith?"

"Hallo, Josie." Edith stopped her dictation to the computer.

"Coffee?"

Dr Chapaire shook her head and went back to her work.

Josie couldn't help feeling excluded. Her work on this project approached its end. *I'll have to find myself another job soon.*

The door swung open behind her as she wandered back to her desk. Without looking round she knew it was Hardy. She'd seen his car outside when she arrived.

"I've just come to get some of your excellent coffee, Dr Chapaire," he said. "Hope that's OK. I managed to make contact with Jacques, and get him installed in Robert's villa."

"Excellent." She raised a finger to point to the machine in acknowledgement and carried on with her dictation.

He helped himself as Josie sat down and stirred her coffee.

"Hi Josie," Hardy said. He glanced at Edith, and added, "Why don't you come next door to drink that? It doesn't look as if you'll get any conversation during your coffee break otherwise."

"I am sorry, Josie, Monsieur Brencher, but I am trying to find a way to program the formula for the drug that keeps Robert well into the synth machines," Edith explained. "If I can, it will be a cheaper and more efficient way to produce the drug, in the same way that it revolutionised food production in famine areas."

"Oh, great idea!" Josie said. She suspected there was a reason for that but said nothing more as she turned back to Hardy. "Thank you, I *will* come to your office."

He led the way. She'd never been in his office before, and was curious to see it. She looked around. The decor resembled the office down the corridor, but without the occasional friendly gurgles from the coffee machine to punctuate the silence.

"Are you all right?" he asked, when they'd seated themselves on a couch.

"I feel somewhat out on a limb, to be honest."

"How do you mean?"

Josie gestured at nothing in particular. "Well, my social life is non-existent and my job here is winding down. I can't help envying Edith for her total involvement and commitment to the children, but now the only under-sixteens are Mil, Zanu Vakutar, and the two girls, Memech Guma and Selush Rukas."

"So if I invited you to dinner tonight, you'd be free?" His expression reminded her of a puppy panting with enthusiasm.

Josie laughed. "That sounds rather opportunist, Hardy. I don't think so."

"It wasn't *meant* to sound like that! Josie, I've wanted to tell you how sorry I am for what happened between us. Please forgive me."

Josie stared at him. "You've taken your time in coming up with an apology!" Anger replaced the sense of depression she'd had all day.

"Somehow the time's never been right. And I haven't been able to speak to you in private before."

"Well that's too bad, because it's rather late in the day to apologise now. It doesn't matter, anyway – let's just forget the whole business and try to work together normally."

"It matters to *me*," he said. "I wouldn't have hurt you for all the tea in China and all the coffee in Brazil put together! I wish I could turn back the clock and do it differently." He rubbed at his scar.

He does that when he's agitated. Abruptly his sincerity penetrated her anger. Josie exhaled slowly. "Hardy, what's done is done," she said. "But I accept your apology, if not the dinner invitation."

His mouth tightened. "I guess I should be grateful that you even came in here, or I might never even have had the chance to apologise to you." He drew in a breath. "It was important to me to do my job well. I've tried to be loyal to the World Presidency, JSEP, and above all to Earth's interests." He met her eyes. "That sounds like an awful excuse for what I did, but I swear to God it's the truth."

"I don't doubt it," Josie said, "and you were under a lot of pressure from President Langrishe to deliver Kaj and Halka back in one piece in France. But you shouldn't just sublimate yourself to your work all the time." She allowed a gentler note to enter her voice. "There are other things in life that are just as important." *And I'm a fine one to talk!*

Hardy nodded, but wouldn't look at her again.

She got up and went back into the office where Edith still worked on her program.

She opened her briefcase. Her notebook nestled between her ID and some personal documents. She stared at it for several moments, unable to bring herself to touch it.

"Well?" Edith asked. There was a dry note to her voice.

"He – Edith, he apologised to me. I think he's truly sorry that he hurt me." She heard the surprise in her own voice as if from a great distance.

"I expect he is," Edith murmured. "Wouldn't it be nice if

he could take up with you where he left off?"

"Well, don't worry, there's no danger of that ever happening! I've learned my lesson with him. With all men, actually." She sighed. "I'll never trust any of them again."

"Very sensible," Edith said. "I gave up on them a long time ago."

The phone rang. Edith answered it. "It's for you," she said. "Ayar."

Josie studied the holoimage of his face. He'd changed so much from the youth she'd met eight years ago. Lines of bitterness had settled around his eyes and twisted his mouth. *His mother's fate affected him a lot.* A rush of sympathy made her ask, "What can I do for you, Ayar?"

"I want to invite you and Dr Chapaire to my graduation ceremony, now that I've finished both my astronaut and pilot training."

Both accepted enthusiastically.

"Hardy, too, if he's there. I called him at home, but there was no reply so I left a message."

"Yes, he's here. We'll tell him."

Then Ayar added, "And I wondered if you could visit Chaneg Dar for me, Josie. I don't want to use the phone – it's not personal enough."

That hinted at what he wanted her to talk to Chan about, and that the phone wasn't private enough, rather than personal. "I'd be delighted to, since I've only got four under-sixteens on my books now. It'll keep me out of mischief. But why not go see her yourself?"

"I'm being assigned after graduation, so I have to stick around. Chaneg's the only one I haven't been in contact with recently, and I think she might be able to help me with something I've been working on in my spare time."

Josie knew for certain now what he was referring to. His

invitation to Hardy might have been a way to check if he was there and listening. But Ayar had shown much interest in Chan's progress towards becoming a *sensei*. "When do you need me to visit her?" she asked.

"As soon as possible. The ceremony is in three days' time. I'd love her to come."

"I'll arrange a flight for Edith and myself now."

There were footsteps in the corridor. Josie looked up. Through the vision panel in the door she glimpsed Hardy as he hurried by, mouth set and eyes averted. "I've just seen Hardy, let me go talk to him."

"All right."

She got up and followed his rapid paces down the corridor. "Hardy!"

He turned.

"Ayar's on the phone with an invite for you – to his graduation."

"I'll call him back. I can't talk now." His voice was terse.

"Has something happened?"

He nodded and strode towards the door without looking at her. "I'll call him at the Academy."

*

Tokyo, Japan, 5th August, 2102.

"I'm sorry, Josie, but I'd rather not meet – if you don't mind."

"Are you sure?"

"I'm sure. I have no wish to compromise my hard-won peace of mind."

"That's a pity," Josie said. "Ayar hoped we could meet so I could tell you about his idea."

"Why can't he come and see me himself?"

"He graduates from JSEP Academy in a couple of days

and has to stay where he is until he's assigned. Then he could be working anywhere, even offworld." Josie paused. "I have to say that I think it's incredibly important that you all stay in touch now that you can."

Chan sighed. "I know, but it's very disturbing when I even *think* about what happened to us. The best way I've found to cope day-to-day is to put it to the back of my mind. Besides, I have competition work, and I need a clear head for that. If my concentration goes I could lose my next contest."

"Fair enough," Josie said. "But then – you wouldn't consider an opportunity to find out what happened to your parents?"

"I know what happened to my mother," Chan said. "It's my father – and he probably doesn't know…" Her voice trailed off as she realised what Josie implied. "Perhaps."

"Can we meet, then?"

Chan hesitated for about two thousandths. *If there's any chance my father is alive I ought to take it, if only to tell him about Tambur.* "All right." *It'll be good to see Josie.*

"Good, I'm at the Plaza Hotel, here in Tokyo. Meet me here in an hour in the restaurant. And bring a good appetite – dinner's on me."

Chan couldn't help a grin at that. She showered and put on a short-sleeved stretch jumpsuit in a floral print. Her thoughts turned to Josie, whom she still regarded as her only ally against Mrs K. The worst part of it was, Chan got on well with the rest of her foster-family.

She closed the door of her *apaato* and locked it. Living with the Kobayashis hadn't worked out. As soon as she was old enough to leave, she had, without regrets. She still saw Ojin and Meiji at their judo and karate classes; they were as much her friends as ever, as was Kaito Kobayashi, who had always treated her with kindness and respect; but she couldn't bring herself to visit Mrs K.

It was five to eight when she arrived at the hotel. Chan allowed the waiter to seat her at a window table opposite Josie. *So Ayar's graduating from astronaut training*... "I've graduated, too," she volunteered as soon as the greetings were over. "I'm a qualified instructor in the martial arts now, a *sensei*."

"Congratulations, when did that happen?" Josie smiled. She looked genuinely pleased.

"A couple of months ago. Mr. Noguchi has given me a job and I love working for him. It means I can continue my competition work."

"Have you competed much recently?"

"A couple of times. Nobody's beaten me yet." Chan smiled. "That sounds big-headed, but –"

"I know you well enough to know it's the truth," Josie said. "You should feel proud of yourself."

"It isn't how one should feel if one were Japanese."

"But you're not. I'm certain your father would be proud of you if he knew. Which brings me to the reason for this meeting. Ayar has need of a skilled instructor in the martial arts. One with a little experience of living on a clanship."

"He's going to try to find our parents, then?"

Josie nodded. "He and Eddie Harkness are sure they can retrace the *Bekel*'s course. Ayar's desperate to find his father, and they're certain the Voth will come *here* next." She smiled. "I think he plans to head them off at the pass."

Chan frowned. "What does that mean?" She hadn't heard the expression before.

Josie explained. "They think he'll be assigned to the *Bekel* to continue his work with Eddie. If he is, there'll be an opportunity at some point in the future. He thought you might take a sabbatical and join him."

"I suspect Mr. Noguchi would give me leave of absence. I

certainly wouldn't pass up the opportunity." She sighed. "I know I was reluctant earlier, but I don't want to have my hopes raised and then dashed. When will he know where he's been assigned?"

"After the graduation ceremony. He'll call you." It was Josie's turn to hesitate. "Can you come to that tomorrow?"

Chan shook her head. "My competition's tomorrow."

"Fair enough – good luck! As soon as we know anything's on, I'll no doubt have need of your services as an instructor as well."

"*You're* going?"

"Strictly as a social worker, you understand – I don't "do" fighting, but I might need to defend myself."

"Well, well, well..." Chan met Josie's eyes and smiled. "Shulai-mer, Josie-ghar!"

"I thought shulai meant 'hello'."

"It does, but the -mer suffix makes it into 'welcome'."

"I didn't know that, but thank you. Will I have to learn Zarduthi?"

"I wouldn't have thought so. We all speak English as well as our foster-home languages, and besides, you can always have a translator fitted."

The waiter had hovered for some time. He approached their table. "Are you ready to order?"

*

JSEP Academy Parade Ground, Houston, 6th August, 2102.

Josie parked where the car park marshal directed her, and she and Edith got out, ready to meet up with Eddie and his family for the parade. Hardy had a meeting with President Sanchez just before the passing out ceremony, and wouldn't be able to meet up with them in time, so he would attend separately.

The two women walked over to meet Eddie, Juli, Kaj and Lucy. Seating was laid out in rising straight rows reminiscent of theatre seating. They'd been allocated seats together. Lucy was very good and watched with attention.

Josie identified Ayar and the Zarduthi children who would pass out this year by their height and slim, wiry build. She watched them join in with their contemporaries. At the end of the parade, some of the graduates were called up to receive awards.

"Ayar Dekkutz, for services rendered to Earth technology!"

Ayar jerked as if shot. *He didn't expect that.* Nevertheless he marched up to the podium and received something pinned on his uniform, and what looked like a certificate. Then he shook hands and saluted the official at the podium, turned on his heel and marched back to his place.

When everyone had been acknowledged for their achievements and awards, the students flung their caps into the air in the traditional ceremony. Ayar joined in with gusto.

And as they filed out of the parade ground and back to their quarters, every new graduate received what Josie later discovered was an envelope that contained their orders and postings.

As civilian employees of JSEP, Josie and Edith hadn't taken part in these ceremonies, but they enjoyed them none-the-less. After that, the officials left the parade ground.

*

The JSEP cadets' mess, two hours later.

"What's the matter, Ayar?"

The destination on the order slip blurred before Ayar's eyes. He brought it closer and read it again. "Mars colony. I've been assigned to the Mars colony run." He stared at Eddie. "You realise what this means?"

"When do you leave?"

"In three days' time. I'm on furlough until then."

"Well," Eddie said, "no time like the present."

"You mean – go ahead *now*?"

"Of course. You want to find your dad, don't you?"

"You know I do."

"Ayar, I could be posted elsewhere as well. The way I see it, we've got three days. There might not be another chance."

"Can we get everyone else here in that time? If we leave anyone behind, they could suffer for what *we* do."

"You could always take a hostage against that eventuality."

"Like who?"

Eddie shrugged. "Hardy Brencher is a name that suggests itself. In fact, I wouldn't be at all surprised if he's behind that posting." He pointed to the order slip.

"Hardy's been good to me. He saved my life."

"True, but you said yourself you can't be sure how far to trust him. So you didn't confide in him about our little venture."

"I don't want him to be in trouble if we get caught." Ayar spread his hands to indicate that part of the discussion was closed. He'd begun to recover from the shock of his assignment. "I won't involve him."

"Fair enough."

"How many can we count on if we go now?"

"You, me, Josie and Dr Chapaire, Kaj, Davan and her husband Jafar, perhaps Mil, Chan if Josie managed to persuade her, Halka and Robert. Anyone else Josie can contact in the time. How many do you need to run the ship?" Eddie countered.

"It isn't just that – it's how many we need for an efficient fighting force as well."

"You think it'll come to that?"

"I'm certain." It occurred to Ayar that Hardy's skills would be useful, especially as there were so few of them, but he dismissed the thought. “How about your Juli?”

“She isn’t ‘my’ Juli any more,” Eddie said. “Anyway, she has Lucy to look after, and I’m don’t want either of them in a war zone.” He thrust out his lower lip in a half-rueful, half-brooding smile. “And I don’t think it would be a good idea for her to be in trouble for kidnapping Zarduthi children again!”

“Probably not.” Ayar gave Eddie a sidewise glance. “But it’s all right for you?”

“I have very little left to lose now.”

“And perhaps something to gain, if only the doubtful distinction of being the only human engineer on a Zarduthi clanship! Come on, let’s go talk to Josie. She’s our best hope to fill the ship up a bit.”

CHAPTER 26 – No Time like the Present

Bekel docking bay, Galatea Station, 9th August, 2102.

HARDY BRENCHER SLIPPED AMONG THE SHADOWS in the docking bay. Ahead of him, Davan Gharm – now Davan Ashraf – and her husband Jafar moved with almost equal stealth as they approached the walkway.

He'd watched the Zarduthi children enter their clanship, one by one, from his vantage point in the bay office over the last two days. They weren't the only ones to enter, and so far no-one had come out, except Eddie Harkness's engineering crew, well before the children had arrived. With their work finished and the ship tidied up, they had no reason to be onboard. Most would be assigned elsewhere on their return from furlough; their experience was valuable, since JSEP would now build a fleet of more than the current three ships designed on Zarduthi lines.

The children had no reason to be onboard either – unless they were up to something…

Hardy had suspected Ayar would try to take the ship back at some point. When he'd learned of Ayar's posting, before the graduation ceremony, he'd been certain he'd move now.

He'd monitored Ayar's calls ever since he'd vowed to destroy the Voth species when he discovered how his mother had died. Ayar had never mentioned it to him, but the volume of calls had increased since then. So had Josie's and Edith's, so Hardy assumed they were in on the plan, confirmed as he'd watched *them* enter the ship as well. Their jobs would end soon, so it made sense that they might leave with the children.

Davan and Jafar had disappeared. *Time to move.* Hardy swallowed his fear, which lay like nausea in his throat, at the thought of the walkway. *They'll know someone's boarded when the airlock operates, of course, but I can't help that. At least I can try to persuade Ayar not to go ahead – though the ship's rightfully his if anyone's.*

He stepped onto the walkway. He remembered the way it had bucked under him when he'd pinned down the Neoluddite terrorists. Fortunately it was still this evening and there were no stun bolts to reckon with. He made rapid progress along it – though his palms were slick with sweat inside his gloves, and the fear had now transformed into real nausea – and pressed the switch for the airlock door to open. He was impatient to be done with the procedure, so that he could do what he was here for and get off the ship again, but air pressure equalisation couldn't be hurried.

As he left the airlock, he flicked back the leaves of his visor, just as the corridor lighting changed colour. Ayar had explained this warning system to him, so he knew what the orange light flashes meant. *Oh shit! I don't want to be onboard when the ship leaves dock.*

He clanked down the corridor towards the Control Room, certain that that was where he'd find Ayar; the Magnetix sandals made what sounded to him like a thunderous clash on the metal floor. The sensation of movement, when it came, was very gentle, but that didn't alter his reaction. The nausea which had threatened on the walkway burst forth. Globules floated in the air as he continued to retch.

The Control Room door swung open, and a space-suited figure walked towards him. He recognised Josie's chestnut brown hair out of the corner of one eye as tears poured down his face. Embarrassment made him turn away, but she still came closer.

"What are you doing here, Hardy?"

"I might ask the same of you," he gasped between heaves. *Surely this can't go on?*

"Let me help you."

"Best help's to go back," he mumbled, and felt for a tissue. He encountered only pocketless spacesuit.

"We can't. You'll have to come *with* us now." She didn't look pleased.

"We saw the airlock operate, so we knew someone had come aboard. I guess it gives us an extra person." *Ayar's voice.* "You'd better see Dr Chapaire. The ship's cleaning devices will clear up once we're under way." Ayar put an arm under Hardy's elbow and supported him into the Control Room. "What made you come aboard?"

"I intended to persuade you not to take the ship. I'd have kept quiet about this, but it's too late now."

"We're not going back. Sit there." Ayar indicated an unmanned control column console.

Hardy collapsed onto the seat and wiped his eyes. "I've never been so badly affected," he croaked, as the seating tried to reconfigure itself around him.

Dr Chapaire came into view. "Poor Monsieur Brencher," she said. "But you know, many astronauts are affected by space sickness."

"Really?"

"Yes, it is common. It is a form of travel sickness, related to vertigo."

"I have vertigo."

"Oh, poor you. It will be worse then." Hardy suspected her sympathy was less than genuine. "But I can give you something which will take away the nausea." She extracted a packet from her bag and passed it to him. "Now, I want you to take these pills, two now, then one every six hours for the rest of the journey. Let me know when you need some more."

"Do Zarduthi get space sick?" Hardy asked.

"Of course not," Ayar retorted. "Perhaps humans aren't

well-adapted for space travel!"

"Possibly not, since the ear structure is different in the Zarduthi," Dr Chapaire agreed. "I do not expect Monsieur Brencher to be the only sufferer."

"We'd better get you to a cabin so that you can clean up and lie down." Ayar motioned to Chaneg Dar. Hardy made to follow her, then saw Davan embrace her brother. Her husband stood by quietly. When they drew apart, Davan said to Mil, "Do you remember Jafar from the wedding?"

"Of course I do!" Mil extended his hand. "How are you, Jafar?"

"I'm good," Jafar said, as they shook hands.

"You're not as tall as I expected you'd get!" Davan told Mil. For her husband's benefit she'd reverted to English. "Though I guess you are only thirteen – there's still time!"

The atmosphere in the Control Room was warm and joyful. There was the sense of a reunion. Everyone seemed happy. Even Ayar's eyes sparkled.

"How many of you are here?" Hardy asked Ayar.

"Zarduthi? All thirty-three of us. Josie's a star. She managed to get every one of us here on time. Plus six humans. Seven including you."

"She did well." Hardy sought to make eye contact with her.

She watched him and scowled. She averted her eyes the instant after their gaze met.

He followed Chan out of the Control Room.

*

Kazid *Shuttle 4, Zero, same day. Ship's time/date: 415.251.5.98.543 AD.*

Omol strode towards the tower where the shuttle lay. Sand kicked up in puffs that the wind dissipated behind him. Above, between the sinuous tendrils of the aurorae, stars twinkled as their light passed through the atmosphere.

Tangar called something to him, but the wind flung his words away.

Omol finally processed them as, "Hurry, Omol! Afdar wants to talk to you personally."

He quickened his pace. He was anxious to speak to Afdar Maavid too. In a few thousandths he reached the tower and clambered up the rungs set in it to the shuttle, where Tangar awaited him. He took his arm and pulled him inside the chamber. Omol seated himself beside the simtank. In its projection area was the holo of another clanship's Control Room. "It's good to see you, Afdar," he said.

Afdar acknowledged that with an inclination of his head. He was middle-aged, with broader shoulders than the average Zarduthi, and faint scars on his chin. Several gold crowns glinted when he spoke – the result of an accident which had smashed his jaw. Omol knew him well and respected him; he ran a tight ship. "Tangar said you've been stranded on a desert planet for the last eleven years."

"Our ship was severely damaged by Voth fire. We left when they boarded it, and destroyed it and them together. We made it here in the shuttles – this planet was all we had fuel for. We've eked out an existence so far, but we lost one of the shuttles on landing and we've had problems with limited, polluted water supplies and have lost a child and several adults. We need to get off-planet before we lose anyone else."

"We're taking an exact bearing now, so keep talking! We should be there in a few days." Afdar paused and met Omol's eyes. "How many of you are there?"

"One hundred and ninety-one people, including forty-six juveniles."

"You do realise that while we can manage for a short

while, we won't be able to permanently absorb everyone from your clan on this ship?"

Omol inclined his head again. "Hopefully you won't have to keep all of us for long," he said. "Have you heard from Eren Gharm's people, over on Declain? We provided the *Bekel* with a distraction so the shirolli could get away, but then we were attacked."

"As far as we know they disappeared without trace eleven years ago. But we've been fighting Voth expansionism in the Haveertel system and couldn't to do anything about it until now."

That aroused Omol's interest. "Did you win?"

"Of course, but we've sustained losses. We had help from two other clanships, which will follow us to Declain – I should think we'll reassign some of your people amongst those clans when we rendezvous there."

"I understand. Have you got that bearing on us now?"

"I believe so." Afdar stood to pace up and down before his control column. "We'll contact you again in two days' time."

Omol repeated his inclination of the head and cleared the simtank of all images. He embraced Tangar. "Well done!"

Tangar let a sigh escape him as he returned Omol's embrace. "It looks like we're back on the route to Declain. It took a while but we arrived."

"Yes." Omol felt emotional pressure build up inside him. While he was glad they'd be rescued – he was desperate to get off Zero – the approaching break-up and redistribution of the clan amongst other ships felt like a mortal wound. "Though how Eren's clan could survive all this time beats me."

"*We* did."

"We weren't fighting the Voth on our own." Omol stumbled out of the shuttle and across the floor to the exit, and clambered back down the inset rungs to ground level again.

The brisk wind stole the air from his mouth, and sand scoured his face. But this time he barely noticed it. He needed time to come to terms with the reality of their future – now their rescue was confirmed.

*

Control Room, the Bekel*, one hundredth (approximately five minutes) later.*

"Galatea Station are hailing us, Ayar," Mil said.

"Display."

The simtank filled up with the view of a man Ayar had never seen before. "Heave to, *Bekel*. Dekkutz, we know you're in there. Return to base at once."

"Who's that?"

"Michael Melville," Eddie supplied. "Station Commander." His tone implied disapproval.

Ayar waited for him to speak. *With every second we move further away from Galatea.*

The message repeated.

"The *Bekel* has no base," Ayar replied. "Galatea Station was a temporary dock. We have engaged the ion drive and will not return to Earth."

Melville tried to adopt a fatherly tone. "What do you hope to achieve, Ayar?"

"We're going to find our parents, and make war on the Voth before they come to Earth to destroy you."

Melville's tone hardened. "You do realise that you're now officially deserters and subject to the processes of court-martial from JSEP?"

"Yes – with one exception, Mr. Hardy Brencher, who came onboard to try to stop us. We were not aware of his presence when we left. I would like it held on record that he did not intend to leave with us, and is incapacitated with space-sickness." Ayar cast a glance at Eddie. "We are not holding him hostage, but it isn't possible to return him to Galatea. However, I pledge he will not be harmed in any way by anyone onboard. Goodbye."

Mil saw Ayar's sign and hit the button. As the image in the tank shivered and faded, Ayar waved to it, just the way the humans did. It disappeared a split-thousandth later.

If he ever returned to Earth, he'd be in trouble for desertion. He'd disobeyed orders *and* cheeked a senior officer. Earth's space program was run on strict military lines. Ayar knew his regulations as well as any other JSEP employee. A court-martial was the legal outcome. The reality was death by firing squad, unless reprieved.

There was no going back.

And what does the future out in space hold? Ayar shivered. Surely nobody could help some fear, in the face of what he must stand fast against and overcome – for the sakes of both his clan and the humans he'd pledged to serve.

He squared his shoulders. "Set a course for the Declaini system, Davan."

*

Not the end!
If you've enjoyed this story, pick it up again in
The Zarduth Imperative: Clanship,
due to arrive via hyperspace communications
in six months' time.

The Zarduth Imperative: Discovery and *Clanship* are also available as e-books from Amazon Kindle and all good e-book suppliers.

To access the universe of *The Zarduth Imperative: Discovery and Clanship*, including starmaps, a timeline, and other forthcoming publications by this author, visit www.Zarduth.com.